LIFE BEFORE MAN

LIFE BEFORE MAN is "full of such pleasures, cleverly plotted and slyly ironic, it is Atwood at her best."

—*The Atlantic Monthly*

"Its characters are rooted in such profound emotional truth that they will haunt your imagination like people in real life who have touched some deep chord in you."

—*Newsday*

"Crisp, carefully ironic, contemporary . . . emotionally powerful, intelligent, and very adult."

—*Ms.* Magazine

LIFE BEFORE MAN is "easily her best novel to date. . . . She may think her people are on the way to extinction. But she makes me both hope and believe that they will survive."

—*The New York Times*

"The momentum and verve of LIFE BEFORE MAN are in the interwoven manner of its telling, and in the author's deadly accurate satire and mastery of understatement. Moving flawlessly from wit to pathos and back, Atwood constructs a superb living exhibit in which the artifacts are unique (but representative) lives in process. There is ample treasure in this novel."

—*The Chicago Tribune*

LIFE BEFORE MAN

Margaret Atwood

FAWCETT POPULAR LIBRARY • NEW YORK

LIFE BEFORE MAN

This book contains the complete text of the original hard-
cover edition.

Published by Fawcett Popular Library, a unit of CBS Publica-
tions, the Consumer Publishing Division of CBS Inc., by arrangement with Simon and Schuster, a Division of Gulf &
Western Corporation

ISBN: 0-445-04636-8

Printed in the United States of America

First Fawcett Popular Library printing: February 1981

10   9   8   7   6   5   4   3   2   1

For G.

Note: *Lesje* is pronounced "Lashia."

Acknowledgments

I would like to thank the following people who supplied comment, information, support, or other kinds of help: Carl Atwood, Lenore Mendelson Atwood, Ruth Atwood, Peter Boehm, Liz Calder, J. A. Donnan, Kate Godfrey Gibson, Jennifer Glossop, Beverley Hunter, Matla Kavin, Marie Kwas, Jay Macpherson, Marie Thompson, Fred J. Roberts, Rick Salutin, J. B. Salsberg, Savella Stchishin, Zenia Stchishin, Nan Talese, Mrs. Walpert, Jean Wachna, Mrs. Werblinsky.

I would also like to thank Donya Peroff, my tireless researcher for many years; Phoebe Larmore, my agent; and the many staff members of the Royal Ontario Museum and the Planetarium who gave me their time, especially Joanne Lindsay of Vertebrate Paleontology, who guided me through the Upper Cretaceous with a steady hand.

Instead of a part of the organism itself, the fossil may be some kind of record of its presence, such as a fossilized track or burrow . . . . These fossils give us our only chance to see the extinct animals in action and to study their behavior, though definite identification is only possible where the animal has dropped dead in its tracks and become fossilized on the spot.

—Björn Kurtén, *The Age of the Dinosaurs*

Look, I'm smiling at you, I'm smiling in you, I'm smiling through you. How can I be dead if I breathe in every quiver of your hand?

—Abram Tertz (Andrei Sinyavsky), *The Icicle*

Part One

ELIZABETH

I don't know how I should live. I don't know how anyone should live. All I know is how I do live. I live like a peeled snail. And that's no way to make money.

I want that shell back, it took me long enough to make. You've got it with you, wherever you are. You were good at removing. I want a shell like a sequined dress, made of silver nickels and dimes and dollars overlapping like the scales of an armadillo. Armored dildo. Impermeable; like a French raincoat.

I wish I didn't have to think about you. You wanted to impress me; well, I'm not impressed, I'm disgusted. That was a disgusting thing to do, childish and stupid. A tantrum, smashing a doll, but what you smashed was your own head, your own body. You wanted to make damn good and sure I'd never be able to turn over in bed again without feeling that body beside me, not there but tangible, like a leg that's been cut off. Gone but the place still hurts. You wanted me to cry, mourn, sit in a rocker with a black-edged handkerchief, bleeding from the eyes. But I'm not crying, I'm angry. I'm so angry I could kill you. If you hadn't already done that for yourself.

Elizabeth is lying on her back, clothes on and unrumpled, shoes placed side by side on the bedside rug, a braided oval bought at Nick Knack's four years ago when she was still interested in home furnishings, guaranteed genuine old lady twisted rags. Arms at her sides, feet together, eyes open. She can see part of the ceiling, that's all. A small crack runs across her field of vision, a smaller crack branching out from it. Nothing will happen, nothing will open, the crack will not widen and split and nothing will come through it. All it means is that the ceiling needs to be repainted, not this year but the

3

next. Elizabeth tries to concentrate on the words "next year," finds she can't.

To the left there is a blur of light; if she turns her head she will see the window, hung with spider plants, the Chinese split-bamboo blind half rolled up. She called the office after lunch and told them she would not be in. She's been doing that too often; she needs her job.

She is not in. She's somewhere between her body, which is lying sedately on the bed, on top of the Indian print spread, tigers and flowers, wearing a black turtleneck pullover, a straight black skirt, a mauve slip, a beige brassiere with a front closing, and a pair of pantyhose, the kind that come in plastic eggs, and the ceiling with its hairline cracks. She can see herself there, a thickening of the air, like albumin. What comes out when you boil an egg and the shell cracks. She knows about the vacuum on the other side of the ceiling, which is not the same as the third floor where the tenants live. Distantly, like tiny thunder, their child is rolling marbles across the floor. Into the black vacuum the air is being sucked with a soft, barely audible whistle. She could be pulled up and into it like smoke.

She can't move her fingers. She thinks about her hands, lying at her sides, rubber gloves: she thinks about forcing the bones and flesh down into those shapes of hands, one finger at a time, like dough.

Through the door, which she's left open an inch out of habit, always on call like the emergency department of a hospital, listening even now for crashes, sounds of breakage, screams, comes the smell of scorching pumpkin. Her children have lighted their jack-o'-lanterns, even though there are still two days before Halloween. And it isn't even dark yet, though the light at the side of her head is fading. They love so much to dress up, to put on masks and costumes and run through the streets, through the dead leaves, to knock on the doors of strangers, holding out their paper bags. What hope. It used to touch her, that excitement, that fierce joy, the planning that would go on for weeks behind the closed door of their room. It used to twist something in her, some key. This year they are remote from her. The soundless glass panel of the hospital nursery where she would stand in her housecoat for each of them in turn, watching the pink mouths open and close, the faces contort.

She can see them, they can see her. They know something

is wrong. Their politeness, their evasion, is chilling because it's so perfectly done.

They've been watching me. They've been watching us for years. Why wouldn't they know how to do it? They act as though everything is normal, and maybe for them it is normal. Soon they will want dinner and I will make it. I will lower myself down from this bed and make the dinner, and tomorrow I will see them off to school and then I will go to the office. That is the proper order.

Elizabeth used to cook, very well too. It was at the same time as her interest in rugs. She still cooks, she peels some things and heats others. Some things harden, others become softer; white turns to brown. It goes on. But when she thinks about food she doesn't see the bright colors, red, green, orange, featured in the *Gourmet Cookbook*. Instead she sees the food as illustrations from those magazine articles that show how much fat there is in your breakfast. Dead white eggs, white strips of bacon, white butter. Chickens, roasts and steaks modeled from bland lard. That's what all food tastes like to her now. Nevertheless she eats, she overeats, weighting herself down.

There's a small knock, a step. Elizabeth moves her eyes down. In the oak-framed oval mirror above the dressing table she can see the door opening, the darkness of the hall behind, Nate's face bobbing like a pale balloon. He comes into the room, breaking the invisible thread she habitually stretches across the threshold to keep him out, and she is able to turn her head. She smiles at him.

"How are you, love?" he says. "I've brought you some tea."

NATE

He doesn't know what "love" means between them any more, though they always say it. For the sake of the children. He can't remember when he started knocking at her door, or when he stopped considering it his door. When they moved the children into one room together and he took the vacant bed. The vacant bed, she called it then. Now she calls it the extra bed.

He sets the cup of tea down on the night table, beside the clock radio that wakes her every morning with cheerful breakfast news. There's an ashtray, no butts; why should there be? She doesn't smoke. Though Chris did.

When Nate slept in this room there were ashes, matches, ringed glasses, pennies from his pockets. They used to save them in a peanut butter jar and buy small gifts with them for each other. Mad money, she called it. Now he still empties the pennies out of his pockets every night; they accumulate like mouse droppings on top of the bureau in his room, his own room. Your own room, she calls it, as if to keep him in there.

She looks up at him, her face leached of color, eyes dark-circled, smile wan. She doesn't have to try; she always tries.

"Thanks, love," she says. "I'll get up in a minute."

"I'll make dinner tonight, if you like," Nate says, wanting to be helpful, and Elizabeth agrees listlessly. Her listlessness, her lack of encouragement, infuriates him, but he says nothing, turns and closes the door softly behind him. He made the gesture and she acts as if it means nothing.

Nate goes to the kitchen, opens the refrigerator and pokes through it. It's like rummaging through a drawer of jumbled clothes. Leftovers in jars, bean sprouts gone bad, spinach in a plastic bag starting to decay, giving off that smell of decomposing lawn. No use expecting Elizabeth to clean it. She used to clean it. She will clean other things these days, but not the refrigerator. He'll tidy it up himself, tomorrow or the next day, when he gets around to it.

Meanwhile he'll have to improvise dinner. It's no large trial, he's often helped with the cooking, but in former times—he thinks of it as the olden days, like a bygone romantic era, like some Disneyland movie about knighthood—there were always supplies. He does most of the grocery shopping himself now, carting a bag or two home in the basket of his bicycle, but he forgets things and gaps are left in the day: no eggs, no toilet paper. Then he has to send the kids to the corner store, where everything is more expensive. Before, before he sold the car, it wasn't such a problem. He took Elizabeth once a week, on Saturdays, and helped her put the cans and frozen packages away when they got home.

Nate picks the dripping spinach out of the vegetable crisper and carries it to the garbage can; it oozes green liquid. He counts the eggs: not enough for omelettes. He'll have to make macaroni and cheese again, which is all right since the kids love it. Elizabeth will not love it but she will eat it, she'll wolf it down absently as if it's the last thing on her mind, smiling like a slowly grilling martyr, staring past him at the wall.

Nate stirs and grates, stirs and grates. An ash drops from his cigarette, missing the pot. It isn't his fault Chris blew his head off with a shotgun. A shotgun: this sums up the kind of extravagance, hysteria, he's always found distasteful in Chris. He himself would have used a pistol. If he were going to do it at all. What gets him is the look she gave him when the call came through: *At least he had the guts. At least he was serious.* She's never said it of course, but he's sure she compares them, judges him unfavorably because he's still alive. Chickenshit, to be still alive. No balls.

Yet at the same time, still without saying it, he knows she blames him, for the whole thing. If you had only been this or that, done this or that—he doesn't know what—it wouldn't have happened. I wouldn't have been driven, forced, compelled . . . that's her view, that he failed her, and this undefined failure of his turned her into a quivering mass of helpless flesh, ready to attach itself like a suction cup to the first crazy man who ambled along and said, You have nice tits. Or whatever it was Chris did say to get her to open the Love Latch on her brassiere. Probably more like, You have nice ramifications. Chess-players are like that. Nate knows: he used to be one himself. Nate can never figure out why women find chess-playing sexy. Some women.

So for a week now, ever since that night, she's spent the afternoons in there lying on the bed that used to be his, half his, and he's been bringing her cups of tea, one each afternoon. She accepts them with that dying swan look of hers, the look he can't stand and can't resist. It's your fault, darling, but you may bring me cups of tea. Scant atonement. And an aspirin out of the bathroom and a glass of water. Thank you. Now go away somewhere and feel guilty. He's a sucker for it. *Like a good boy*.

And he was the one, not her, not Elizabeth, who had to go and identify the body. As her stricken eyes said, she could hardly be expected to. So dutifully he had gone. Standing in that apartment where he'd been only twice but where she had been at least once every week for the past two years, fighting nausea, nerving himself to look, he'd felt that she was there in the room with them, a curve in space, a watcher. More so than Chris. No head left at all, to speak of. The headless horseman. But recognizable. Chris's expression had never really been in that heavy flat face of his; not like most people's. It had been in his body. The head had been a trouble-maker, which was probably why Chris had chosen to shoot at it instead of at some other part of himself. He wouldn't have wanted to mutilate his body.

A floor, a table, a chess set by the bed, a bed with what they called the trunk and limbs lying on it; Nate's other body, joined to him by that tenuous connection, that hole in space controlled by Elizabeth. Chris had put on a suit and tie, and a white shirt. Nate, thinking of that ceremony—the thick hands knotting the tie, straightening it in the mirror, God, his shoes were shined even—wanted to cry. He put his hands in his jacket pockets; his fingers closed on pennies, the house key.

"Any reason why he left your number of the table?" the second policeman said.

"No," Nate said. "We were friends of his, I guess."

"Both of you?" the first policeman said.

"Yes," said Nate.

Janet comes into the kitchen as he's sliding the casserole dish into the oven.

"What's for dinner?" she asks, adding "Dad," as if to remind him who he is.

Nate finds this question suddenly so mournful that for a moment he can't answer. It's a question from former times, the olden days. His eyes blur. He wants to drop the casserole on the floor and pick her up, hug her, but instead he closes the oven door gently.

"Macaroni and cheese," he says.

"Yum," she says, her voice remote, guarded, giving a careful imitation of pleasure. "With tomato sauce?"

"No," he says, "there wasn't any."

Janet runs her thumb across the kitchen table, squeaking it on the wood. She does this twice. "Is Mum resting?" she says.

"Yes," Nate says. Then, fatuously, "I took her a cup of tea." He puts one hand behind him, against the kitchen counter. They both know what to avoid.

"Well," Janet says in the voice of a small adult, "I'll be seeing you soon." She turns and goes back through the kitchen door.

Nate wants to do something, perform something, smash his hand through the kitchen window. But on the other side of the glass there's a screen. That would neutralize him. Whatever he does now will be absurd. What is mashing a window compared with blowing off your head? *Cornered.* If she'd planned it, she couldn't have done it better.

Friday, October 29, 1976

LESJE

Lesje is wandering in prehistory. Under a sun more orange than her own has ever been, in the middle of a swampy plain lush with thick-stalked plants and oversized ferns, a group of bony-plated stegosaurs is grazing. Around the edges of this group, protected by its presence but unrelated to it, are a few taller, more delicate camptosaurs. Cautious, nervous, they lift their small heads from time to time, raising themselves on their hind legs to sniff at the air. If there is danger they will give the alarm first. Closer to her, a flock of medium-sized pterosaurs glides from one giant tree-fern to another. Lesje crouches in the topmost frond-cluster of one of these trees, watching through binoculars, blissful, uninvolved. None of the dinosaurs takes the slightest interest in her. If they do happen to see or smell her, they will not notice her. She is something so totally alien to them that they will not be able to focus on her. When the aborigines sighted Captain Cook's ships, they ignored them because they knew such things could not exist. It's the next best thing to being invisible.

Lesje knows, when she thinks about it, that this is probably not everyone's idea of a restful fantasy. Nevertheless it's hers; especially since in it she allows herself to violate shamelessly whatever official version of paleontological reality she chooses. In general she is clear-eyed, objective, and doctrinaire enough during business hours, which is all the more reason, she feels, for her extravagance here in the Jurassic swamps. She mixes eras, adds colors: why not a metallic blue stegosaurus with red and yellow dots instead of the dull greys and browns postulated by the experts? Of which she, in a minor way, is one. Across the flanks of the camptosaurs pastel flushes of color come and go, reddish pink, purple, light pink, reflecting emotions like the contracting and expanding chromatophores in the skins of octopuses. Only when the camptosaurs are dead do they turn grey.

After all it's not so fanciful; she's familiar with the coloration of some of the more exotic modern lizards, not to mention mammalian variations such as the rumps of mandrills. Those bizarre tendencies must have developed from somewhere.

Lesje knows she's regressing. She's been doing that a lot lately. This is a daydream left over from her childhood and early adolescence, shelved some time ago in favor of other speculations. Men replaced dinosaurs, true, in her head as in geological time; but thinking about men has become too unrewarding. Anyway, that part of her life is settled for the time being. Settled, as in: the fault settled. Right now *men* means William. William regards them both as settled. He sees no reason why anything should ever change. Neither does Lesje, when she considers it. Except that she can no longer daydream about William, even when she tries; nor can she remember what the daydreams were like when she did have them. A daydream about William is somehow a contradiction in terms. She doesn't attach much importance to this fact.

In prehistory there are no men, no other human beings, unless it's the occasional lone watcher like herself, tourist or refugee, hunched in his private fern with his binoculars, minding his own business.

The phone rings and Lesje jumps. Her eyes spring open, the hand holding her coffee mug flies into the air, fending off. She's one of those people unduly startled by sudden noises, she tells her friends. She sees herself as a timorous person, a herbivore. She jumps when people come up behind her and when the subway guard blows his whistle, even when she knows the people are there or the whistle will be blown. Some of her friends find this endearing but she's aware that others find it merely irritating.

But she doesn't like being irritating, so she tries to control herself even when nobody else is with her. She puts her coffee mug down on the table—she'll wipe the spill up later—and goes to answer the phone. She doesn't know who she expects it to be, who she wants it to be. She realizes that these are two different things.

By the time she picks up the phone the line is already open. The hum on the phone is the city's hum, reverberating outside the plate glass, amplified by the cement cliffs that face her and in which she herself lives. A cliff dweller, cliff hanger. The fourteenth level.

Lesje holds the phone for a minute, listening to the hum as if to a voice. Then she puts it down. Not William in any case. He's never phoned her without having something to say, some pragmatic message. I'm coming over. Meet me at. I can't make it at. Let's go to. And later, when they'd moved in together, I'll be back at. And lately, I won't be back until. Lesje considers it a sign of the maturity of the relationship that his absences do not disturb her. She knows he's working on an important project. Sewage disposal. She respects his work. They've always promised to give each other a lot of room.

This is the third time. Twice last week and now. This morning she mentioned it, just as a piece of conversation, to the girls at work, women at work, flashing her teeth in a quick smile to show she wasn't worried about it, then covering her mouth immediately with her hand. She thinks of her teeth as too large for her face: they make her look skeletal, hungry.

Elizabeth Schoenhof was there, in the cafeteria where they always went at ten-thirty if they weren't working too hard. She's from Special Projects. Lesje sees a fair amount of her because fossils are one of the more popular museum features and Elizabeth likes to work them in. This time she'd come over to their table to say she needed a little of Lesje's material for a display-case series. She wanted to juxtapose some of the small items from Canadiana with natural objects from the same geographical regions. *Artifact and Environment*, she was calling it. She could use some stuffed animals to go with the pioneer axes and traps, and a few fossil bones for atmosphere.

"This is an old country," she said. "We want people to see that."

Lesje is against this eclectic sort of promotion, though she sees the need for it. The general public. Still, it trivializes, and Lesje registered an inner objection when Elizabeth asked, in that competent maternal manner of hers, whether Lesje couldn't find her some really interesting fossils. Weren't all fossils interesting? Lesje said politely that she would see what she could do.

Elizabeth, adept at cataloguing the reactions of others, for which Lesje holds her in some awe—she herself, she feels, cannot do this—explained carefully that she meant visually interesting. She really would appreciate it, she said.

Lesje, always responsive to appreciation, warmed. If Elizabeth wanted some outsize phalanges and a cranium or two she was welcome to them. Besides, Elizabeth looked terrible, white as a sheet, though everyone said she was coping marvelously. Lesje can't imagine herself in that situation, so she can't predict how she herself would cope. Of course everyone knew, it had been in the papers, and Elizabeth had not made much of an effort to hide the facts while it was going on.

They all scrupulously avoided mentioning Chris or anything relating to him in front of Elizabeth. Lesje caught herself blinking when Elizabeth said she wanted to use a flintlock in the display. She herself wouldn't have chosen guns. But perhaps these blind spots were necessary, were part of coping marvelously. Without them, how could you do it?

To change the subject she said brightly, "Guess what? I've been getting anonymous phone calls."

"Obscene?" Marianne asked.

Lesje said no. "Whoever it is just lets the phone ring and then when I answer he hangs up."

"Wrong number, probably," Marianne said, her interest flagging.

"How do you know it's a he?" Trish asked.

Elizabeth said, "Excuse me." She stood up, paused for a moment, then turned and walked steadily as a somnambulist across the floor towards the door.

"It's awful," Trish said. "She must feel terrible."

"Did I say something wrong?" Lesje asked. She hadn't meant to.

"Didn't you know?" Marianne said. "He used to phone her like that. At least once a night, for the last month. After he quit here. She told Philip Burroughs, oh, quite a while before it happened. You'd think she would've known it was building up to something."

Lesje blushed and brought her hand up to the side of her face. There were always things she didn't know. Now Elizabeth would think she'd done that on purpose and would dislike her. She couldn't figure out how that particular piece of gossip had slipped by her. They'd probably talked about it right here at this table and she hadn't been paying attention.

Lesje goes back to the living room, sits down in the chair beside her spilled coffee, and lights a cigarette. When she smokes she doesn't inhale. Instead she holds her right hand in front of her mouth with the cigarette between the first two fingers, thumb along the jawbone. That way she can talk and laugh in safety, blinking through the smoke that rises into her eyes. Her eyes are her good point. She can see why they wore veils, half-veils, in those Middle Eastern countries. It had nothing to do with modesty. Sometimes when she's alone she holds one of her flowered pillowcases across the lower half of her face, over the bridge of her nose, that nose just a little too long, a little too curved for this country. Her eyes, dark, almost black, look back at her in the bathroom mirror, enigmatic above the blue and purple flowers.

Saturday, October 30, 1976

ELIZABETH

Elizabeth sits on the grey sofa in the underwater light of her living room, hands folded in her lap sedately, as if waiting for a plane. The light here is never direct, since the room faces north; she finds this peaceful. The sofa is not really grey, not only grey; it has a soft mauve underfigure, a design like veining; a batik. She chose it because it didn't hurt her eyes.

On the mushroom-colored rug, near her left foot, there's a scrap of orange crêpe paper, a spillover from something the children are doing in their room. A scrap of flame, jarring. But she lets it lie. Ordinarily she would bend, pick it up, crumple it. She doesn't like anyone disturbing this room, the children or Nate with his trails of sawdust and spots of linseed oil. They can make as much mess as they like in their own rooms, where she doesn't have to cope with it. She once thought of having plants in this room as well as in her bedroom but decided against it. She doesn't want anything else she will have to take care of.

She closes her eyes. Chris is in the room with her, a weight, heavy, breathless, like the air before a thunderstorm. Sultry. Sultan. Sullen. But it isn't because he's dead, he was always like that. Backing her against the door, his arms clamping around her, shoulders massive when she tried to push him off, face heavily down on hers, force of gravity. Leaning on her. I won't let you go yet. She hates it when anyone has power over her. Nate doesn't have that kind of power, he never had. She married him easily, like trying on a shoe.

She's in the room on Parliament Street, drinking wine, the slopped glasses making mulberry rings on the linoleum of his rented table, she can see the design on the oilcloth, tasteless wreaths of flowers, lime-green on yellow, as if it's been burned

into her eyes. They always whisper in that room, though
there's no need to. Nate is several miles away from them and
he knows where she is anyway, she leaves the number in case
of an emergency. Their whispers and his eyes with their flat
hot surfaces, a glint like nailheads. Copperheads. Pennies on
the eyes. Gripping her hand across the table as though, if he
lets go, she will slide down past the edge of the table, the edge
of some cliff or quicksand, and be lost forever. Or he will.

Listening, her eyes on the wrinkled surface of the table, the
squat candle he bought from some street peddler, the deliberately tacky plastic flowers and the owl he'd stolen from work,
not even mounted, eyeless, his macabre joke. The wreaths
turning slowly on the surface of the table as on an oily sea,
floating out; somewhere they did that as a blessing. Then rising, the violence in his hands held back, everything held back,
falling, salt body stretching along her, dense as earth, on that
bed she would never stay to sleep in, the sheets always a little
damp, smoky, holding back until nothing could be held back.
She has never seen that room by daylight. She refuses to imagine what it looks like now. The mattress bare. Someone would
have come, cleaned the floor.

She opens her eyes. She must focus on something simple and
clear. There are three bowls on the sideboard, pinkish mauve,
porcelain, Kayo's, he's one of the best. She's confident in her
taste, she knows enough to have earned that confidence. The
sideboard is pine, she bought it before pine became fasionable,
had it stripped down before having things stripped down became fashionable. She couldn't afford it now. It's a good
piece, the bowls are good pieces. She wouldn't have anything
in this room that was not a good piece. She lets her eyes slide
over the bowls, over the subtle colors, their slightly asymmet-
rical curves, wonderful to have that sense, where to be off balance. There's nothing in them. What could you possibly put
into such bowls? Not flowers or letters. They were meant to
hold something else, they were meant for offerings. Right now
they hold their own space, their own beautifully shaped absence.

There was your room and there was everything else outside,
and that barrier between the two. You carried that room
around with you like a smell, it was a smell like formaldehyde
and the insides of old cupboards, mousy, secretive, like musk,
dusky and rich. Whenever I was with you I was in that room,

even when we were outside, even when we were here. I'm in it now, only now you've locked the door, brown door with scaling paint, varnish, the brass-colored lock and the chain, two bullet holes through the wood where, you told me, they'd been shooting in the hallway the week before. It wasn't a safe neighborhood. I always took taxis, asked the driver to wait until I'd pressed the buzzer and was safe in the foyer with its gap-toothed mosaic floor. Safe, always a joke. The door's locked, not for the first time; you don't want me ever to get out. You always knew I wanted to get out. But at the same time we were conspirators, we knew things about each other no one else will ever know. In some ways I trust you more than I've ever trusted anyone.

I have to go now, she says. He's twisting a length of her hair, twisting and untwisting it. He runs his index finger between her lips, left-handed, across her teeth; she can taste wine and her own sweat, taste of herself, blood from a bitten lip, she no longer knows whose.

Why, he says.

I just have to. She doesn't want to say *the children* because it will make him angry. But she doesn't want them to wake up and not know where she is.

He doesn't answer; he keeps twisting and untwisting her hair, his own hair brushing her neck like feathers, his fingers sliding now over her chin and throat, as if he's deaf, as if he can no longer hear her.

Saturday, October 30, 1976

LESJE

Lesje is walking beside William, hand in cool hand. There are no dinosaurs here; only similar walkers, on the prowl like themselves, an apparently aimless prowl through the lighted grid of the central city. In passing, Lesje glances into the windows of dress shops, department stores, appraising the cadaverous mannequins who stand with their pelvises thrust forward, hands angular on hips, legs apart, one knee bent. If these bodies were in motion they would be gyrating, jerking, a stripper's orgasmic finale. Since they are frozen plaster and wire, however, they are in good taste.

Lesje has been spending quite a lot of time lately in these same shops, on her way home from work. She flips through the racks, looking for something that might become her, something she might become. She almost never buys anything. The dresses she tries on are long, flowing, embroidered, very different from the denims and subdued classics she habitually wears. Some with full skirts; the peasant look. How her grandmother would laugh. That little sound, like a door creaking, that used to come from behind her tiny walnut-colored hands.

She's thought about getting her ears pierced. Sometimes, after checking through the dresses, she goes to the perfume counter and tries the testers on her wrists. William says he isn't interested in clothes. His one stipulation is that she must not cut her hair. This is all right, since she doesn't want to cut it. She's not betraying anything.

William asks her if she'd like something to drink. She says she wouldn't mind a coffee. They didn't come out to drink; they'd intended to go to a movie. But they spent too much time poring over the entertainment pages of the *Star,* trying to decide. Each wanted the other to take the responsibility.

18

Lesje wanted to see a re-run of *King Kong* at the university film series. William finally confessed that he'd always wanted to see *Jaws*. Lesje didn't mind, she could see how well they'd done the shark, which was after all one of the more primitive life forms still extant. She asked William if he knew that sharks had floating stomachs and if you suspended one by its tail it would become paralyzed. William didn't know this. By the time they got to *Jaws* it was sold out and *King Kong* had started half an hour earlier. So they're walking instead.

Now they're sitting at a little white table on the second level of the Colonnade. William is having a Galliano, Lesje a Viennese coffee. Gravely she licks whipped cream from her spoon, while William, having forgiven her for causing him to miss *Jaws*, is explaining his latest problem, which has to do with whether more energy is lost in the long run by using the heat from incinerated garbage to run steam generators than by just letting the stuff go up in smoke. William is a specialist in environmental engineering, though the small raucous voice that occasionally makes itself heard behind Lesje's studiously attentive face refers to it as sewage disposal. However, Lesje admires William's job and agrees with him that it's more important to the survival of the human race than hers is. Which is true, they're all in danger of drowning in their own shit. William will save them. You can see it just by looking at him, his confidence, his enthusiasm. He orders another Galliano and expounds on his plans for generating methane gas from decomposing excrement. Lesje murmurs applause. Among other things, it would solve the oil crisis.

(The real question is: Does she care whether the human race survives or not? She doesn't know. The dinosaurs didn't survive and it wasn't the end of the world. In her bleaker moments, of which, she realizes, this is one, she feels the human race has it coming. Nature will think up something else. Or not, as the case may be.)

William is talking about dung beetles. He's a good man; why is she so unappreciative? Dung beetles were once of interest to her. The way in which Australia solved its pasturage problem—layers of dried sheep raisins and cow pads keeping the grass from growing—by a massive importation of giant African dung beetles, was once a beacon of hope. Like William, she saw it as elegant ecological problem-solving. But she's heard it before, and before. Finally it's William's optimism, his belief that every catastrophe is merely a problem looking for a brilliant solution, that gets to her. She thinks of William's brain as pink-cheeked, hairless. William Wasp, she used to call him, fondly enough, before she realized that he found it a racial slur.

"I don't call you Lesje Latvian," he'd said, aggrieved.

"Lithuanian," she said. "Litvak." William had trouble with the Baltic states. "I wouldn't mind if you did." But she was lying. "Can I call you William Canadian?"

Billy Boy, charming Billy. Where have you been all the day. Shortly after this they had an argument about the Second World War. It's William's opinion that the British and, of course, the Canadians, including his father, who was a captain in the Navy, making William the world's authority, entered the war from superior moral principals, to save the Jews from being reduced to gas molecules and vest buttons. Lesje disputed this view. Saving a few Jews was a sideline, she said. Really it was grab and counter-grab. Hitler could have frizzled Jews to his heart's content if he hadn't snatched Poland and invaded the Netherlands. William found this point of view ungrateful. Lesje then produced the corpse of her Aunt Rachel, who hadn't been saved, whose anonymous gold teeth had plumped some Swiss bank account. What reply to this indignant ghost? William, routed, went into the bathroom to shave. Lesje felt a little cheap.

(Then there was her other grandmother, her mother's mother, who'd said: We welcomed Hitler at first. We thought he would be better than the Russians. You see what's happened now. Which was ironic, since her husband had been practically a Communist, back in the Ukraine. That's why they had to leave: the politics. He wouldn't go to church even, he wouldn't put a foot in a church. I spit on the church, he'd say. Long after his death Lesje's grandmother was still weeping about it.)

She's noticed recently that she's no longer waiting for William to propose to her. Once she thought it would follow as a matter of course. You lived with someone first, to try it out. Then you got married. That's what her friends from university were doing. But William, she now see, finds her impossibly exotic. True, he loves her, in a way. He bites her on the neck when they make love. Lesje doesn't think he'd let himself go like that with a woman of, as she once caught him putting it, his own kind. They would make love like two salmon, remotely, William fertilizing the cool silvery eggs from a suitable distance. He'd think of his children as *issue*. His issue, uncontaminated.

This is the crux: William does not want to have a child by her. With her. Though she's hinted; though she could spring one on him unannounced. Gues what, William, I have a bun in the oven. Your bun. Well, he'd say, take it out.

Oh, very unfair to William. He admires her mind. He encourages her to use technical language in front of his friends. It gives him a hard-on when she says Pleistocene. He tells her she has beautiful hair. He gazes into her sloe eyes. He's proud of her as a trophy and as a testimony to his own wide-mindedness. But what would his family in London, Ontario, think?

Lesje pictures this family as numerous and pinkish blond. The members of it spend most of their time playing golf, between strenuous rounds of tennis. When they aren't doing this they gather on terraces—she sees them doing this even in the winter—and drink cocktails. They are polite to strangers but make remarks behind their backs, such as, "Fellow doesn't know who his own grandfather is." Lesje is confident about her grandfathers; it's the great-grandfathers that are the problem.

She knows William's family isn't really like this. But, like her parents, she grants extra rungs on the ladder to anyone with an authentic British name who doesn't noticeably live on a park bench. She knows she shouldn't do this. William's family probably doesn't have much more money than her own family does. They only have more pretensions.

Once she'd been afraid to meet them, fearing their verdict. Now she'd love to. She'd paint her teeth gold and come in jingling a tambourine and stamping her feet, her head covered with fringed shawls. Living up to their horrified expectations. Her grandmother clapping diminutive mole-paw hands together, creaking with laughter, cheering her on. Blood will tell. "We was talking to God when they was talking to pigs." As if age, in people as in cheese, was a plus.

"There were no dung beetles in the Neo-Devonian," Lesje says.

William is brought up short. "I don't follow you," he says.

"I was just wondering," she says. "About the parallel evolution of dung beetles and shit. For instance: which came first, man or venereal disease? I suppose hosts always have to precede their parasites, but is that really true? Maybe man was invented by viruses, to give them a convenient place to live."

William decides she's joking. He laughs. "You're putting me on," he says. He thinks she has an offbeat sense of humor.

An albertosaurus, or—the name Lesje prefers—a gorgo-saurus, pushes through the north wall of the Colonnade and stands there uncertainly, sniffing the unfamiliar smell of human flesh, balancing on its powerful hind legs, its dwarfed front legs with their razor claws held in close to its chest. In a minute William Wasp and Lesje Litvak will be two lumps of gristle. The Gorgosaurus wants, wants. It's a stomach on legs, it would swallow the world if it could. Lesje, who has brought it here, regards it with friendly objectivity.

Here's a problem for you, William, Lesje thinks. Solve this.

Nate

He hasn't worn a raincoat. The light drizzle beads his heavy
sweater, his beard, collects on his forehead, begins to trickle.
Since he has no raincoat, since he's wet and shivering, how
can she refuse to let him in?

He parks his bike in the driveway, chaining it to the lilac
bush snapping the lock. As usual; but it isn't as usual. He
hasn't seen her for a month. Four weeks. Tears from her,
hangdog shrugs from him, and a lot of afternoon soap stuff
from both of them, including *It's better this way*. She's
phoned him a couple of times since, wanting him to come
over, but he's avoided it. He doesn't like doing the same thing
over again, he doesn't like predicability. This time, however,
he phoned her.

She lives in an A, 32A, a flat in one of the big older houses
east of Sherbourne. Main number at the front, the A entrance
around at the side. When he rings she opens the door immediately. She's been waiting for him. No fresh-washed hair and
velvet dressing gown though; just a pair of slacks and a
slightly grubby light-green sweater. She has a glass, half-
empty. A lemon peel floats in it, an ice cube. Fortification.

"Well," she says. "Happy Anniversary."

"Of what?" he says.

"Saturday was always our day." She's on the edge of being
drunk, she's bitter. He can't blame her. Nate finds it hard to
blame anyone for anything. He's been able to understand her
bitterness, most of the time. He just hasn't been able to do
much about it.

"Not that she ever stuck to it," Martha goes on. "Emergency this, emergency that. So sorry to interrupt, but one of
the children's heads just fell off." Martha laughs.

Nate wants to take her by the shoulders and give her a

good shake, throw her against the wall. But of course he can't. Instead he stands, dripping onto her hall floor, looking at her dumbly. He feels his body sagging on his spine, the flesh drooping like warm taffy on a sucker stick. Butterscotch. Don't run with the stick in your mouth, he'd tell the kids, already seeing them fall, seeing the pointed stick skewering up through the roof of the mouth. Running, kneeling, lifting, a howl, his own voice. Oh my god.

"Could you keep the children out of it?" he says.

"Why?" Martha says. "They were in it, weren't they?" She turns from him and walks down the hall into her living room.

I should leave now, Nate thinks. But he follows her, slipping his wet shoes off first, feet padding along the old rug. The old rut.

Only one light on. She's arranged it, the lighting. She sits across the room from the light, in shadow, on the sofa. Plush-covered sofa where he first kissed her, unpinned her hair, stroking it down over her wide shoulders. Broad, capable hands. He'd thought he would be safe in those hands, between those knees.

"That was always her excuse," Martha says. She's wearing crocheted wool slippers. Elizabeth would never wear crocheted wool slippers.

"She never disliked you," Nate says. They've done this before.

"No," Martha says. "Why dislike the housemaid? I did the dirty work for her. She should've paid me."

Nate feels, not for the first time, that he has told this woman too many things. She's misinterpreting, she's using his own confidences against him. "That's unfair," he says. "She respects you. She never tried to interfere with anything. Why should she?" He doesn't reply to the crack about the dirty work. Is that how you felt about it? he wants to ask, but he's afraid of the answer. *Get your ashes hauled.* Casual talk at high-school lockers. He can smell himself, the wet socks, turpentine on his pants. She used to tease him, scrubbing his back as they sat in her claw-footed tub. *Your wife doesn't take care of you.* In more ways than one.

"Yeah," says Martha. "Why should she? She always wanted to have her cake and eat it too. That's you, Nate. Elizabeth's cake. You're a piece of cake."

Nate remembers that when he first saw her, behind her desk at Adams, Prewitt and Stein, she was furtively chewing gum, a habit she renounced when he hinted he didn't like it.

"I understand why you're angry," he says. This is one of Elizabeth's tactics, understanding, and he feels sneaky using it. He knows he doesn't really understand. Elizabeth doesn't either, when she says that to him. But it always deflates him.

"I don't give a piss whether you do or not," Martha says belligerently. No sops of understanding for her. She's looking at him directly, though her eyes are in shadow.

"I didn't come over to talk about this," Nate says, not sure what exactly they've been talking about. He's never sure in conversations like this. The clear thing is that she feels he's wrong. He's wronged her. He's done her wrong. But he tried to be straightforward about it from the beginning, he didn't lie. Someone should give him credit for that.

"So why did you come?" Martha says. "Running away from mother? Wanted some other nice lady to give you a cookie and a tumble in the sack?"

Nate finds this brutal. He doesn't answer. This is, he realizes, what he had wanted, though he doesn't want it at the moment.

Martha wipes the back of her hand across her mouth and nose. She's dimmed the lights, Nate guesses now, not for romantic effect but because she expected to cry and didn't want him to be able to see too well. "You can't turn it off and on that easily," she says.

"I thought we could talk," Nate says.

"I'm listening," Martha says. "I'm real good at it." Nate doesn't think this is necessarily true. She's good at it when he talks about her, granted. All ears. *You have the best thighs in the world.* She does have nice thighs, but the best in the world? How would he know?

"I guess you've heard what happened," he says at last. Unable to say why Chris's death should make him want comfort. By popular wisdom he should be overjoyed, his horns gone, the stain on his honor wiped out by blood.

"You mean about Elizabeth," Martha says. "Everyone in this town always knows what happens to everybody else. They all came and told me, you can bet on it. They love it. They love to watch me when they drop your name. Both of your names. Elizabeth's lover dynamited his head. Some of them say Elizabeth's *man.* So what? What'm I supposed to say? Tough tits? Serves her right? She finally got him?"

Nate has never known her to be so hard, even during their most violent arguments. What he liked about her at first was her vagueness, her lack of focus, an absence of edges that gave her a nebulous shimmer. Now it's as if she's been dropped on the sidewalk from a great height and has frozen there, all splayed angles and splinters.

"She hadn't seen him for a while," he says, taking Elizabeth's side as Martha ritually forces him to. "He wanted her to leave the children. She couldn't do that."

"Of course not," Martha says. She stares down at her empty glass, lets it fall to the rug between her feet. "Supermom could never leave the children." She starts to cry, making no effort now to hide her face. "Move in with me," she says. "Live with me. I just want us to have a chance."

Nate thinks, Maybe we already had one. They don't now. He begins to ease himself forward, out of the chair. She'll be on him in a minute, arms winding like seaweed around his neck, wet face on his chest, pelvis shoved against his groin while he stands there withered.

"How do you think it feels?" she says. "Like a backstairs romance with the kitchen help, only everyone knows, and you go back at night to your goddamned wife and your goddamned kids and I read murder mysteries till four in the morning just to keep myself sane."

Nate meditates on the kitchen help. Her choice of metaphor puzzles him. Who has back stairs any more? He remembers one evening, the two of them wrapped in a sheet, on the bed together drinking gin, watching *Upstairs, Downstairs* and laughing. The maid pregnant by the son and heir, being lectured by the ice-faced mother. That was early on, when they were having a good time. It wasn't a Saturday; it was before Elizabeth said, Let's be reasonable about this. We have to know we can depend on each other at certain times. She took Thursdays, he took Saturdays because it was the weekend and Martha wouldn't have to get up early the next morning. And that other evening, when Martha said, I think I'm pregnant. His first thought: Elizabeth won't put up with that.

If I console her, she'll say I'm a hypocrite, he thinks. If I don't, I'm a prick. Out now while there's time. This was a bad mistake. Pick up my shoes in the front hall, shouldn't have locked the bike. "Maybe we can have lunch sometime," he says at the living-room door.

"Lunch?" Her voice follows him down the hall. "Lunch?" A retreating wail.

He pedals his bicycle through the rain, aiming deliberately for puddles, soaking his legs. Fool. There's something missing in him that other people have. He can never foresee the future, that's it, even when it's clear. It's a kind of deformity, like being tall. Other people walk through doorways, he hits his head. Once or twice and a rat would learn to stoop. How many times, how long will it take?

After half an hour he stops at the corner of Dupont and Spadina, where he knows there's a phone booth. He leans his bike against the side of the booth, goes in. Glass cubicle, light on, total exposure. Feeble-minded creep goes into booth, removes clothes, stands there waiting for Superman to take over his body while people stare from passing cars and some old lady calls the police.

He takes a dime from his pocket, holds it. His token, his talisman, his one hope of salvation. At the other end of the line a thin woman waits, her pale face framed by dark hair, her hand lifted, fingers upraised in blessing.

No answer.

Sunday, October 31, 1976

Elizabeth

Elizabeth sits in her kitchen, waiting to be surprised. She's always surprised at this time of the year; she's also surprised on her birthday, at Christmas and on Mother's Day, which the children insist on celebrating even though she tells them it's commercial and they don't have to. She's good at being surprised. She's glad she's put in a lot of practice: she'll be able to walk through it tonight with no slips, the exclamation, the pleased smile, the laugh. Her remoteness from them, the distance she has to travel even to hear what they're saying. She wants to be able to touch them, hold them, but she can't. Good-night kisses on her cheek, cold dewdrops; their mouths perfect pink flowers.

The smell of scorching pumpkin drifts down the hall: their two jack-o'-lanterns, displayed side by side in the living-room window, finally, the legitimate way on the legitimate night. Already admired sufficiently by her. Scooped out on spread newspapers in the kitchen, handfuls of white seeds in their network of viscous threads, some grotesque and radical form of brain surgery; two little girls crouching over the orange heads with spoons and paring knives. Little mad scientists. They were so intense about it, especially Nancy. She wanted hers to have horns. Finally Nate suggested carrots, and Nancy's pumpkin now has lopsided horns in addition to its scowl. Janet's is more sedate: a curved smile, half-moon eyes upturned. Serenity if you look at it from a certain angle, idiocy from another. Nancy's has a fearsome energy, a demonic glee.

They will burn this way all evening and then the festival will be over. Janet, reasonable child, will consign her pumpkin to the garbage, clearing the decks, ready for the next thing. Nancy, if last year is any indication, will protect hers,

28

keeping it on her dresser until it sags and rots, unwilling to throw it away.

They've made her turn out the light and sit in darkness, with only one candle; she wasn't able to explain to them why she doesn't want to do this. The light flickers on the walls, on the dirty dishes waiting to be scraped and put into the dishwasher, on the sign she herself tacked to the kitchen cupboard over a year ago:

CLEAN UP YOUR OWN MESS!

Sensible advice. It's still sensible advice, but the kitchen itself has changed. It's no longer familiar, it's no longer the kind of place in which sensible advice can be followed. Or at least not by her. On the refrigerator there's a painting, curling at the edges, Nancy's from last year; a girl smiles a red smile, the sun shines, bestowing spokes of yellow; the sky is blue, all is as it should be. A foreign country.

A dark shape jumps at her from the doorway. "Boo, Mum."

"Oh darling," Elizabeth says. "Let me see."

"Am I really scary, Mum?" Nancy says, clawing her fingers menacingly.

"You're very scary, love," Elizabeth says. "Isn't that wonderful."

Nancy has made yet another variation of her favorite costume. She calls it a monster, every year. This time she's pinned orange paper scales to her black leotard; she's modified Janet's old cat's head mask by adding silver tinfoil horns and four red fangs, two upper, two lower. Her eyes gleam through the cat eyes. Her tail, Janet's former cat's tail, now has three red cardboard prongs. Elizabeth feels something other than rubber boots might have been more suitable, but knows it's fatal to criticize. Nancy is so excited she might start to cry.

"You didn't scream," Nancy says reproachfully, and Elizabeth realizes she's forgotten this. An error, a failure.

"That's because you took my breath away," she says. "I was too frightened to scream."

Nancy is satisfied with this. "They'll all be really scared," she says. "They won't know who I am. Your turn," she says into the hall, and Janet makes a prim entrance. Last year she was a ghost, the year before that she was a cat, both standard.

She tends to play it safe; to be too original is to be laughed at, as Nancy sometimes is.

This year she wears no mask. Instead she's made her face up, red lips, arched black brows, rouged cheeks. It isn't Elizabeth's makeup, since Elizabeth doesn't as a rule use any. Certainly not red lipstick. She has on a shawl made from a gaudy flowered tablecloth someone gave them—Nate's mother?— and which Elizabeth promptly donated to the playbox. And underneath it a dress of Elizabeth's, hitched and rolled around the waist to shorten it, belted with a red bandana. She looks surprising old, like a woman shrunken by age to the size of a ten-year-old; or like a thirty-year-old dwarf. A disconcertingly whorish effect.

"Wonderful, darling," Elizabeth says.

"I'm supposed to be a gypsy," Janet says, knowing with her usual tact that Elizabeth can't be totally depended on to figure this out and wanting to save her the embarrassment of asking. When she was younger she explained her drawings this way. Nancy, on the other hand, was hurt if you didn't know.

"Do you tell fortunes?" Elizabeth asks.

Janet smiles shyly with her bright red lips. "Yes," she says; then, "Not really."

"Where did you get my dress?" Elizabeth asks carefully. They're supposed to ask before borrowing things, but she doesn't want to spoil the evening by making an issue of it.

"Dad said I could," Janet says politely. "He said you weren't wearing it any more."

It's a blue dress, dark blue; the last time she wore it was with Chris. His hands were the last hands to undo the hook at the back, since, when she put the dress on to go home, she didn't bother to do the hook back up again. It's upsetting to see her daughter wearing it, wearing that invitation, that sexual flag. Nate has no right to make a decision like this about something of hers. But it's true, she isn't wearing it any more.

"I wanted you to be surprised," Janet adds, sensing her dismay.

"That's all right, darling," Elizabeth says: the eternal magic words. It's somehow more important to them to surprise her than to surprise Nate. Occasionally they even consult him. "Has your dad seen you yet?" she asks.

"Yes," Janet says.

"He pinned on my tail," Nancy says, hopping on one foot. "He's going out."

Elizabeth goes to the front door to see them off, standing in the lighted oblong as they negotiate the porch steps, carefully because of Nancy's mask and tail. They're carrying shopping bags, the biggest ones they could find. She's been over the instructions: Only this block. Stay with Sarah because she's older. No crossing in the middle of the street, only at corners. Don't bother people if they don't want to answer the door. Some of the people around here may not understand, their customs are different. Home by nine.

Voices other than theirs are already calling: *Shell out. Shell out. The witches are out.* It's a revel, one of the many from which she once felt and still feels excluded. They weren't allowed to have pumpkins and they weren't allowed to dress up and shout in the streets like the others. They had to go to bed early and lie in the darkness, listening to the distant laughter. Her Auntie Muriel hadn't wanted them running up dentists' bills by eating a lot of candy.

Sunday, October 31, 1976

NATE

First, Nate washes his hands carefully with the oatmeal soap Elizabeth favors these days. There's something harsh about it, Scottish, penitential. Once she'd indulged herself in sandalwood, cinnamon, musk, Arabian fragrances, pastel and lavish at the same time. That was when she was buying lotions with exotic names and the occasional bottle of perfume. She hadn't rubbed these lotions on him and it wasn't for his benefit she dabbed herself behind the ears, though he could dimly remember a time when she might have. He could remember it vividly, he knows, if he wanted to, but he doesn't want to think about it, those odors, that fragrant moth dance performed for him alone. Why tease those nerves? Everything is gone, the bottles are empty, things get used up.

So now it's oatmeal soap, with its hints of chapped skin and chilblains. And, for the hands, nothing fancier than glycerine and rosewater.

Nate applies some of this to his own hands. He doesn't usually dip into Elizabeth's cosmetics; only when, as now, his hands feel clumsy and raw, abraded by the Varsol he uses to get the paint and polyurethane off them. There's always a brown line left though, a half-moon around the base of each nail; and he can never quite rid himself of the paint smell. He welcomed this smell once. It said, *You exist.* Far from the abstractions of paper, torts and writs, the convolutions of a language deliberately dried so that it was empty of any sensuous values. That was in the days when physical objects were thought to have a magic, a mysterious aura superior to the fading power of, say, politics or law. He'd quit in his third year of practice. Take an ethical stance. Grow. Change. Realize your potential.

Elizabeth had approved of this move because it was the sort of thing that would infuriate her aunt. She'd even said they could live on her salary till he got started. Her indulgence proved that she wasn't at all like Auntie Muriel. But as time went on and he did little more than break even, she'd been less and less approving. Supportive, as they said. This house, too small really, the tenants on the third floor, the workshop in the basement, were supposed to be temporary, she'd reminded him. Then stopped reminding.

It's partly her fault. Half of her wants a sensitive, impoverished artist, the other half demands a forceful, aggressive lawyer. It was the lawyer she married, then found too conventional. What is he supposed to do?

Occasionally, though by no means all the time, Nate thinks of himself as a lump of putty, helplessly molded by the relentless demands and flinty disapprovals of the women he can't help being involved with. Dutifully, he tries to make them happy. He fails not because of any intrinsic weakness or lack of will, but because their own desires are hopelessly divided. And there's more than one of them, these women. They abound, they swarm.

"Toys?" his mother said. "Is that useful?" Meaning: all over the world people are being tortured and imprisoned and shot, and you make toys. She'd wanted him to be a radical lawyer, defending the unjustly accused. How to tell her that, apart from the sterile monetary transactions, contracts, real estate, most of the people he'd had to deal with at Adams, Prewitt and Stein had in fact been accused justly? She would have said it was only training, an apprenticeship he had to undergo to make him ready for the big crusade.

The Amnesty International newsletter still arrives every month, his mother's copy, marked with asterisks to show him where to send his courteously worded letters of protest. Children tortured in front of their mothers. Sons disappearing, to surface months later, fingernails missing, skins covered with burns and abrasions, skulls crushed, tossed on roadsides. Old men in damp cells dying of kidney problems. Scientists drugged in Soviet lunatic asylums. South African blacks shot or kicked to death while "escaping." His mother has a map of the world taped to her kitchen wall, where she can contemplate it while drying the plates. She sticks little stars on it, red ones, the kind the teacher used to dole out for second-best in print-

ing. These innocent grade-school stars mark each new re-
ported case of torture or mass murder; the world is now a
haze of stars, constellation upon constellation.

Nevertheless his mother crusades, dauntless astronomer,
charting new atrocities, sending out her communications, politely written and neatly typed, unaware of the futility of what
she is doing. As far as Nate is concerned she may as well be
sending these letters to Mars. She'd brought him up to believe
that God is the good in people. Way to fight, God. Nate finds
these newsletters of hers so overwhelmingly painful that he's
no longer able to read them. As soon as they arrive, he slips
them into the wastepaper basket, then goes to the cellar to
pound and chisel. He consoles himself by thinking that his
toys are the toys the tortured children would play with if they
could. Every child should have toys. To remove all toys because some do not have them is not the answer. Without his
toys, surely there would be nothing to fight for. So he will let
his mother, worthy woman that she is, compose the letters; he
will make the toys.

Tonight he's been finishing rocking horses; five of them,
he finds it easier to do them in lots of five. He sanded them yesterday. Today he's been painting eyes. Round eyes, expressionless, the eyes of creatures made to be ridden for the pleasure
of others. The black eyeliner of the girls on the Strip. This
isn't how he intended the horses to look: he intended joy. But
more and more, recently, the toys he makes have this blank
look, as if they can't see him.

He no longer tells people he makes handmade wooden toys
in his basement. He says he's in the toy business. This isn't
because cottage industry has ceased to be viewed as charismatic or even cute. He never thought of it as charismatic or
cute; he thought of it as something he might be able to do
well. To do one thing well: this was what he wanted. Now he
does it well enough. He has a monthly balance sheet. After
supplies and the gouge the stores take are deducted, he has
money left to pay half the mortgage interest and to buy gro-
ceries, cigarettes, enough liquor to coast on. Elizabeth isn't
supporting him. She just acts as though she is.

Nate begins to shave. He lathers his throat, meaning only
to trim around the edges of his beard, free his neck and the
underside of his jaw of bristles; but he finds the razor moving
upwards, circling the edges of his beard like a lawnmower
circling a lawn. He's shaved his beard half off before he
knows that it's his intention to destroy it. From behind the

coarse dark hair his face emerges, the face he hasn't seen in five years, pallid, blood-speckled, dismayed at this exposure. His hands have decided it's time for him to be someone else.

He rinses his face. He doesn't have any after-shave—it's so long since he's used it—so he rubs some of Elizabeth's glycerine and rosewater over his new-mown skin. The face that looks back at him from the bathroom mirror is more vulnerable, but also younger and grimmer, the jaw clearly visible now, its furry wisdom gone. A man stroking his beard is one thing, a man stroking his jaw is another.

Before leaving the house he goes into his own room and scrabbles through the piles of coins on his bureau, looking for dimes. Then he changes his socks. He doesn't expect to be taking his socks off this evening; it's highly unlikely that he will. However. His feet are white and rootlike, the toenails greyish yellow from the cellar life they're forced to lead. He sees his feet for an instant, browned and running, on sand, on sun-warmed rock. Far from here.

LESJE

Lesje and William are having a game of cribbage. They sit at a card table, the same card table on which they eat meals when they eat together, beside their picture window, which has a breathtaking view of the picture window in the apartment building opposite theirs. This window is lighted, since it's dark, and two people are sitting behind it, eating what Lesje takes to be spaghetti. On the streets below, Lesje assumes, it's all happening. That was why she wanted to live here, at the crux, in the heart: because it would all be happening. "It" and "all" are words that have, however, retained their abstractness. She hasn't yet found either of them.

Lesje has stuck a paper jack-o'-lantern, purchased at Woolworth's, to the inside of their own picture window. Last year she bought some candy, hoping to be visited by a parade of little children in costumes; but no children, it appears, can penetrate to the fourteenth floor of this apartment building. The people who live here, whom she sees only in the elevators, appear to be young and either single or childless.

Lesje would like to be out roaming the streets herself, watching. But William has suggested cribbage, which relaxes his mind.

"Fifteen two, fifteen four, fifteen six and a pair is eight," says William. He moves his plastic toothpick. Lesje has a mere fifteen two in the crib, a pair of aces she put there herself. She shuffles and cuts, William deals. He picks up his cards and his lips purse. He's frowning, deciding what to set aside for himself.

Lesje's hand is so bad there's not much choice. She permits herself a walk by moonlight, along a path trampled by the giant but herbivorous iguanodons; she can see the three-toed prints of their hind feet in the mud. She follows their trail until the trees thin and there, in the distance, is the lake, silvery, its surface broken here and there by a serpentine head, the curve of a plunging back. That she should be so privileged. How will she ever convince the others of what she has seen?

(The lake, of course, is Lake Gladys, marked clearly on the chart on page 202 of *The Lost World* by Sir Arthur Conan Doyle. Lesje read this book at the age of ten. It was filed in the school library under Geology, and she'd been doing a project on rocks. Rocks had been her big thing before dinosaurs. Her friends at school read Trixie Belden, Nancy Drew, Cherry Ames the stewardess. Lesje hadn't cared much for those stories. She didn't as a rule like stories that weren't factual. But *The Lost World* was different. They'd found a plateau in South America on which the life forms of the Upper Jurassic had continued to survive, along with other, more modern forms. She can't remember which came first, her passion for fossils or this book; she thinks it was the book. No matter that all those on the expedition had been men. She'd fallen in love, not with Professor Challenger, the loudmouthed assertive one, or even the young reporter or the sharpshooting English lord. It was the other one, the dry, skeptical one, the thin one; Professor Summerlee. How many times has she stood at the edge of this lake, his thin hand in hers, while together they've witnessed a plesiosaur and he's been overcome, converted at last?

She still has this book. She didn't exactly steal it, she just forgot several times to renew it and then was so embarrassed by the librarian's sarcasm that she lied. Lost, she said. *The Lost World* is lost.)

The lake glimmers in the moonlight. Far out, on a sandbar, a mysterious white shape flickers.

William has moved his toothpick again. She hasn't been paying attention, he's at least twenty points ahead of her. "Your go," he says. Satisfaction rosies his cheeks.

"Fifteen two," she says.

"It's your next crib," William says, consoling her, as he can well afford to.

The phone rings. Lesje jumps, dropping the jack of diamonds. "Could you get it, William?" she says. She suspects it's the wrong-number man; she's not in the mood for a monotone serenade.

"It's for you," William says, puzzled.

When she comes back, he says, "Who was it?"

"Elizabeth's husband," Lesje says.

"Who?"

"Exactly," says Lesje. "Elizabeth's husband Who. You've met him; at the Christmas party last year. You remember Elizabeth, sort of statuesque-looking; she's the one who . . ."

"Oh, right," says William. The sight of his own blood makes him queasy, so he didn't much appreciate hearing the story of Chris, though Lesje had to tell it to him, she'd been upset. "What did he want?"

"I'm not sure," says Lesje.

Sunday, October 31, 1976

NATE

Nate is running. His bicycle is behind him somewhere in the darkness, parked against a bench. The air is cool, strange against his new-scraped face.

He runs for pleasure, taking it easy, jogging over dying grass grey in the street lights, through fallen leaves whose colors he can barely see but guesses: orange, yellow, brown. They collect the leaves in green garbage bags and truck them away now, but once they raked them into piles and burned them in the streets, the smoke rising wispy and sweetish from the centers of the mounds. He used to run with the others along the street, making sounds like a dive bomber, and then jump, clearing the mounds of leaves like hurdles. Forbidden, but if you missed it didn't matter, the leaves were only smoldering. Men shaking rakes, telling them to bugger off.

Who did he run with, twenty or was it twenty-five years ago? Someone called Bobby, Tom something. They're gone now, faceless; he gives them the nostalgia due to those who have died young. Casualties, though of nothing but his own memory. It's himself, his lace-up breeks with leather knee patches, those goddamn wool socks always falling down, mittens ice-beaded and soggy from bombarding the enemy, nose dripping over his upper lip, himself running he mourns.

And after that, no longer for pure fun, sprinting at high school and third man on the relay team, around the track with the stick he would pretend was dynamite, he had to pass it on before it exploded. He was too skinny for football then but he could run. They never won anything, though once they came second. *Mr. Clean,* they called him in the yearbook. His mother thought it was a compliment.

When he was at law school he used to come here to the same place, Queen's Park, an oval like a track. *Queens' park.*

He remembers the jokes, the couples he really did see, in trenchcoats, windbreakers, the casual intersections that aroused in him only a mild curiosity, a mild embarrassment. It was around that time his back started acting up and he stopped running; shortly after he met Elizabeth. An evolutionary mistake, the doctor said, meaning his height; men should have stopped at five feet. Now they were unbalanced. He told Nate that his right leg was infinitesimally shorter than his left, not uncommon in tall men, and he should wear a built-up heel. A piece of information about which Nate has done nothing. He refuses to join the ranks of the tin woodmen, those with false teeth, glass eyes, rubber breasts, orthopedic shoes. Not yet, not yet. Not before he has to.

He runs clockwise, against the traffic, the cars meeting and passing him owl-eyed, dark and sleek. Behind him are the Parliament Buildings, squat pinkish heart of a squat province. In the interior, red plush and plump as a cushion, seedy lucrative deals are no doubt being made, decisions about who will build what where, what will be torn down, who will profit. He recalls with more than discomfort, sheer disbelief, that he once thought he would go into politics. Municipal probably. *Pompous nit.* Stop the developers, save the people; from what, for what? He was once among those who felt the universe should be just and merciful and were prepared to help it achieve this state. That was his mother's doing. He recalls his convoluted pain, his sense of betrayal when he realized finally how impossible this was. Nineteen-seventy, civil rights abolished, a war with no invaders and no enemy and the newspapers applauding. It wasn't arbitrary arrests, the intimidation, the wrecking of lives that had appalled him; that was no surprise. He'd always known such things happened elsewhere, and despite the prevailing smugness he'd never doubted they could happen here. It was the newspapers applauding. Editorials, letters to the editor. The voice of the people. If that was all they had to say he'd be damned if he'd be their megaphone.

His idealism and his disillusionment now bore him about equally. His youth bores him. He used to wear a suit and listen to conversations between older men about those in power, hoping to learn something. Remembering this, he cringes; it's like the string of love beads he wore once, briefly, when that fashion was on the wane.

Ahead of him, across the street to the left, is the Museum, illuminated now by garish orange floodlights. He used to lurk there by the doorway at closing time, hoping to catch Elizabeth on her way out. At first she'd been remote and a little condescending, as if he was some sort of perverted halfwit she was being kind to. It knocked him out; that, and the impression she gave of knowing exactly what she was doing. Lapping Queen's Park on Saturday mornings he would think of her inside the grey buildings, sitting like a Madonna in a shrine, shedding a quiet light. Though actually she never worked on Saturdays. He would think of himself running towards her as she receded in front of him, holding a lamp in her hand like Florence Nightingale. He's glad he never told her about this ludicrous vision. She would have laughed even then, behind his back, and brought it up later to taunt him. Chocolate box, she would have said. The lady with the lamp. Jesus Christ. The lady with the axe, more like it. Now it's a different figure he runs towards.

He passes the War Memorial at the apex of the park, a granite plinth featureless and without ornament, except for the Gothic wen at the top. No naked women carrying flowers, no angels, not even any skeletons. Just a signpost, a marker. SOUTH AFRICA, it says on the other side; he used to see that in the mornings, driving to work, before he sold the car. Before he quit. Which war? He's never thought much about it. The only real war took place in Europe, Churchill saying they would fight on the beaches, a hot trade in chewing gum and women's stockings, his father vanishing in a thunderclap somewhere over France. With gentle shame he recalls how he cashed in on that. *Cut it out, you guys, his dad was killed in the war.* One of the few uses for patriotism he still considers valid; and about the only use for the death of his father, whom he cannot at all remember.

He's running south, Victoria College and St. Mike's on his left. He's almost around. He slows; he can feel the effort now, in his calves, his chest, the blood thudding in his head. He hasn't breathed deeply like this for a long time. Too bad about the exhaust fumes. He should stop smoking, he should run like this every day. He should get up at six every morning, run for half an hour, cut down to a pack a day. A regular program and watch the eggs and butter. He's not forty yet, not nearly; possibly he isn't even thirty-five. He's thirty-four, or was that last year? He's always had trouble remembering the exact year of his birth. So has his mother. It's as if they both entered into a conspiracy some time ago to pretend he wasn't actually born, not like everyone else. Nathanael: Gift of God. His shameless mother takes care to point out this meaning. She pointed it out to Elizabeth soon after their marriage. Thanks a lot, God, Elizabeth said later, genially then. And later less genially.

He starts running harder again, sprinting towards the shadows where he's left his bicycle. Once around. He used to be able to do this twice, he worked up to three times almost. He could do that again. On sunny days he would run watching his shadow, on the right till the Memorial, on the left coming back; a habit that started when he was on the relay team. Beat your shadow, said the coach, a Scot who taught Grade Nine English when he wasn't teaching P.T. *The Thirty-nine Steps* by John Buchan. His shadow pacing him; even when there were clouds he could feel it still there. It's here with him now, odd in the street lights so much dimmer than the sun, stretching ahead of him as he passes each light, shrinking, headless, then multiplying and leaping ahead of him again.

He never used to run at night; he doesn't like it much. He should stop this and go home. The children will be back soon, perhaps are already back, waiting to show him their paper bags. But he keeps running, as if he must run; as if there's something he's running towards.

ELIZABETH

Elizabeth sits on her mild sofa, facing the bowls. Two disembodied heads burn behind her. The bowls are on the pine sideboard. Not her own bowls, she wouldn't let them use hers, but three bowls from the kitchen, a Pyrex casserole, a white china mixing bowl, and another mixing bowl, stainless steel.

In two of the bowls are the packages the children wrapped in the afternoon, little bundles in wrinkled orange and black paper napkins, a witch and cat motif. Tied at the top with string. They wanted ribbon but there wasn't any. In each package are some candy kisses, a miniature box of Smarties, a box of raisins. They wanted her to make gingerbread cookies with jack-o'-lantern faces on them, the way she usually did, but she said she didn't have time this year. A lame excuse. They know how much time she spends lying in there on her bed.

The third bowl, the steel one, is full of pennies, for the UNICEF boxes the children carry around with them these days. Save the children. Adults, as usual, forcing the children to do the saving, knowing how incapable of it they are themselves.

Soon the doorbell will ring and she'll open the door. It will be a fairy or a Batman or a devil or an animal, her neighbors' children, her children's friends, in the shapes of their own desires or their parents' fears. She will smile at them and admire them and give them something from the bowls, and they will go away. She will close the door and sit down again and wait for the next ring. Meanwhile her own children are doing the same thing at the houses of her neighbors, up and down the front paths, across the lawns, grass for the newcomers like herself, withered tomato plants and faded cosmos flowers for the Italians and Portuguese whose district has so recently been perceived as quaint.

Her children are walking, running, lured by the orange lights in front windows. Later that night she will go through their loot while they sleep, looking for evidence of razor blades in apples, poisoned candy. Although their joy cannot touch her, fear for them still can. She does not trust the world's intentions towards them. Nate used to laugh at her concerns, what he called her obsessions: sharp table corners when they were learning to walk, open wall plugs, lamp cords, ponds, streams and puddles (you can drown in two inches of water), moving vehicles, iron swings, porch railings, stairs; and more recently, strange men, cars that slow down, ravines. They had to learn, he'd say. As long as nothing serious happens she looks foolish. But if anything ever does, it will be no consolation to have been right.

It should be Nate sitting on this sofa, waiting for the doorbell to ring. It should be him this time, opening the door not knowing who it will be, handing out the candy. Elizabeth has always done it before but Nate should know she isn't up to it this year. If he used his head he would know.

But he's out; and he hasn't, this time, told her where he is going.

Chris came to the door once, not telling her, rang the bell. Standing on the porch, the overhead light turning his face to moon craters.

What are you doing here? She'd been angry: he shouldn't have done that, it was an invasion, the children's room was right overhead. Pulled her outside onto the porch, brought his face down to hers wordlessly, in the spotlight. Go away. I'll call you later but please go away. You know I can't do this. A whisper, a kiss, blackmail payment, hoping they wouldn't hear.

She wants to turn out the lights, extinguish the pumpkins, bolt the door. She can pretend she isn't home. But how will she explain the full bowls of candy, or, even if she throws the packages away, the questions of their friends? *We went to your house but there was no one home.* Nothing can be done.

The doorbell rings, rings again. Elizabeth fills her hands, negotiates the door. Easier to have put the bowls at the bottom of the stairs; she'll do that. It's a Chinaman, a Frankenstein monster and a child in a rat suit. She pretends not to recognize them. She hands each a bundle and drops coins into their slotted tins. They twitter happily among themselves, thank her, and patter across the porch, not knowing, really, what night this is or what, with their small decorated bodies, they truly represent. All Souls. Not just friendly souls but all souls. They are souls, come back, crying at the door, hungry, mourning their lost lives. You give them food, money, anything to substitute for your love and blood, hoping it will be enough, waiting for them to go away.

Part Two

ELIZABETH

Elizabeth walks west, along the north side of the street, in the cold grey air that is an extension of the unbroken fish-grey sky. She doesn't glance into the store windows; she knows what she looks like and she doesn't indulge in fantasies of looking any other way. She doesn't need her own reflection or the reflections of other people's ideas of her or of themselves. Peach-yellow, applesauce-pink, raspberry, plum, hides, hooves, plumes, lips, claws, they are of no use to her. She wears a black coat. She's hard, a dense core, that dark point around which other colors swirl. She keeps her eyes straight, her shoulders level, her steps even. She marches.

On some of the lapels, breasts, approaching her there are still those reminders, red cloth petals of blood spattered out from the black felt hole in the chest, pinned at the center. Remembrance Day. A little pin in the heart. What is it they peddle for the mentally disturbed? Seeds of Hope. In school they used to pause while someone read a verse from the Bible and they sang a hymn. Heads bowed, trying to look solemn, not knowing why they should. In the distance, or was it on the radio, guns.

> If we break faith with us who die
> We shall not sleep, though poppies grow
> In Flanders fields.

A Canadian wrote that. *We are the Dead.* A morbid nation. In school they had to memorize it two years in a row, back when memorizing was still in fashion. She'd been chosen to recite it, once. She was good at memorizing; they called it being good at poetry. She was good at poetry, before she left school.

Elizabeth has bought a poppy but she hasn't worn it. It's in her pocket now, her thumb against the pin.

She can remember when this walk, any walk through this part of the city, would have excited her. Those windows with their promises that are, finally, sexual, replacing earlier windows and earlier promises that offered merely safety. Tweeds. When did that happen, the switch to danger? Sometime in the past ten years the solid wool suits and Liberty scarves moved out in favor of exotica: Indian imports with slit skirts, satin underwear, silver talismans to dangle between the breasts like minnows on a hook. Bite here. And then the furniture, the *milieu*, the accessories. Lamps with colored shades, incense, whole shops devoted to soap or thick bath towels, candles, lotions. Enticements. And she was enticed. It once made her skin burn merely to walk along these streets, the windows offering themselves, not demanding anything, certainly not money. Just a word, Yes.

The goods are much the same now, although the prices have gone up and there are more stores, but that caressing scent is gone. These days it's all merchandise. You pay, you get, you get no more than you see. A lamp, a bottle. If she had a choice she would take the former, the other, but there's a small deadening voice in her now that cancels choice, that says merely: False.

She stops in front of a newspaper box, bending to look in through the square glass window. She should buy a paper, to have something to read in the waiting room. She doesn't want to be left with nothing she can concentrate on, and at the moment she can't bear the kinds of magazines they keep in such places. Full-color magazines, brighter than life, about health and motherhood and washing your hair in mayonnaise. She needs something in black and white. Bodies falling from tenth-floor balconies, explosions. Real life. But she doesn't want to read a paper either. They're full of the Québec election, which will happen in three days and in which she is not the least interested. She's no more interested in elections than she is in football games. Contests between men, both of them, in which she's expected to be at best a cheerleader. The candidates, collections of grey dots, opposing each other on the front pages, snorting silent though not wordless challenges. She doesn't care who wins, though Nate does; though Chris would have. There was always that unvoiced accusation, directed at her, as if who she was, the way she spoke, was a twist on his own arm, an intrusion. The language question, everyone said.

There's something wrong with my ears. I think I'm going deaf. From time to time, not all the time, I hear a high sound, like a hum, a ringing. And I know I've been having difficulty hearing what other people say to me. I'm always saying, Pardon?

No, I haven't had a cold. No.

She rehearses the speech, then repeats it to the doctor and answers the doctor's questions, hands in her lap, feet side by side in their black shoes, purse beside her feet. A matron. The doctor is a round, sensible-looking woman in a white smock, with a light attached to her forehead. She questions Elizabeth kindly, making notes in the Egyptian hieroglyphs of doctors. Then, after they go through a door and Elizabeth sits down in a black leatherette chair, she looks into Elizabeth's mouth and then her ears, one after the other, using a light on the end of a probe. She asks her to hold her nose and blow, to see if there are any popping sounds.

"No obstructions," the doctor says cheerfully.

She fits a set of headphones onto Elizabeth's head. Elizabeth stares at the wall, on which hangs a picture done in painted plaster: a tree, a fairy-faced child gazing up at the branches, and a poem in scrolled script:

> I think that I shall never see
> A poem lovely as a Tree.
> A Tree whose hungry mouth is pressed
> Against the Earth's sweet flowing breast. . . .

Elizabeth reads this far, then stops. Even the idealized tree in the plaster oblong looks like a kind of squid, its roots intertwined like tentacles, sticking itself onto that rounded bulge of earth, sucking, voracious. Nancy started biting her in the sixth month, with the first tooth.

The doctor twiddles buttons on the machine attached by wires to Elizabeth's headphone, producing first high science-fiction sounds, then low vibrations, rumors.

"I can hear it," Elizabeth says each time the sound changes. She can tell what kinds of things this woman would have in her living room: chintz slipcovers, lamps with bases made of porcelain nymphs. Ceramic poodles on her mantelpiece, like Nate's mother. An ashtray with ladybird beetles on the rim, in natural colors. This whole room is a time warp.

The doctor removes Elizabeth's headphones and asks her to go back to the outer office. They both sit down. The doctor smiles benignly, indulgently, as if she's about to tell Elizabeth she has cancer of the ears.

"There's absolutely nothing wrong with your hearing," she says. "Your ears are clear and your range is normal. Perhaps you may have a very slight residual infection that causes plugging from time to time. When that happens, just hold your nose and blow, as you'd do in an airplane. The pressure will clear your ears."

("I think I'm going deaf," Elizabeth said.

"Maybe," said Nate, "there are just some things you don't want to hear.")

Elizabeth thinks the receptionist looks at her strangely when she says she won't be needing another appointment. "Nothing wrong with me," she says, explaining. She goes down in the elevator and walks through the archaic brass and marble lobby, still marching. By the time she reaches the outer door the humming has begun again, high-pitched, constant, like a mosquito or a child's tuneless song, or a power line in winter. Electricity somewhere. She remembers a story she read once, in *Reader's Digest*, while sitting in the dentist's waiting room, about an old woman who started hearing angel voices in her head and thought she was going mad. After a long time and several investigations they discovered she was picking up a local radio station through the metal in her bridgework. *Reader's Digest* repeated this story as a joke.

It's almost five, darkening; the sidewalk and road are slick with drizzle. Traffic packs the lanes. Elizabeth steps across the gutter and begins to walk diagonally across the street, in front of one stationary car, behind another. A green delivery truck jams to a stop in the moving lane, three feet from her. The driver leans on his horn, shouting.

"You idiot, you wanna get yourself killed?"

Elizabeth continues across the road, ignoring him, her pace steady, marching. Does she want to get herself killed. The hum in her right ear shuts off like a cut connection.

There's nothing wrong with her ears. The sound is coming from somewhere else. Angel voices.

Monday, November 15, 1976

LESJE

Lesje is having lunch with Elizabeth's husband, the husband belonging to Elizabeth. Possessive, or, in Latin, genitive. This man doesn't seem like Elizabeth's husband, or anyone else's for that matter. But especially not Elizabeth's. Elizabeth, for instance, would never have chosen the Varsity Restaurant. Either he has no money, which is possible considering the frayings and ravelings everywhere on his surface, patchy, like rock lichen; or he doesn't think she'll base her opinion of him on his choice of restaurants. It's a restaurant left over when others like it became classy, preserving its fifties furnishings, its grubby menus, its air of cheesy resignation.

Ordinarily Lesje would never eat here, partly because she associates the Varsity Restaurant with being a student and she's no longer that young. She isn't sure why she's having lunch with Elizabeth's husband at all, except that something in the way he asked her—the invitation had been a kind of outburst—made it impossible for her to say no.

The anger and desperation of others have always been her weak points. She's an appeaser and she knows it. Even in the women's group she went to in graduate school, mostly because her roommate shamed her into it, she'd been cautious, afraid of saying the wrong thing; of being accused. She'd listened with mounting horror to the recitals of the others, their revelations about their grievances, their sex lives, the callousness of their lovers, even their marriages, for some of them were married. The horror wasn't caused by the content but by Lesje's realization that they were expecting her to do the same thing. She knew she couldn't, she didn't know the language. It would be no good to say that she was just a scientist, she wasn't political. According to them, everything was political.

53

Already they were looking at her with calculation: her murmurs of assent had not been enough. Soon they would confront her. Panic-stricken, she searched her past for suitable offerings, but the only thing she could think of was so minor, so trivial, that she knew it would never be accepted. It was this: On the gold dome of the Museum's lobby, up at the top, it said: THAT ALL MEN MAY KNOW HIS WORK. It was only a quotation from the Bible, she'd checked on that, but it might keep them busy; they were very big on the piggishness of God. On the other hand, they might reject it completely. Come on, Lesje. Something *personal*.

She'd told her roommate, who was a social historian with tinted granny glasses, that she didn't really have time for the group, as her palynology course was heavier than she'd thought. Neither of them believed this, and shortly afterwards Lesje moved into a single apartment. She couldn't stand the constant attempts to engage her in meaningful dialogue while she was eating her corn flakes or drying her hair. At that time nuances had bothered her; she was much happier among concrete things. Now she feels it might have been useful to have listened more carefully.

Nate hasn't yet frightened her by asking her to tell him about herself, though he's been talking since they sat down. She ordered the cheapest thing on the menu, a grilled cheese sandwich and a glass of milk. She listens, eating in small bites, concealing her teeth. Nate has given no hint yet as to why he called her. At the time she thought it might be because she'd known Chris, she knew Elizabeth, and he needed to talk about it. She could understand that. But so far he hasn't mentioned either of them.

Lesje can't see how he can get through a conversation, even five minutes of one, without mentioning an event that to her would have loomed very large in the foreground. If it were her life, which is isn't. Until this lunch, this grilled cheese sandwich and—what is he eating?—a hot turkey sandwich on white bread, she thought about Nate, if at all, simply as the least interesting figure in that tragic triangle.

Elizabeth, who stalks about the Museum these days white-skinned, eyes black-shadowed, a little too plump to carry it off entirely but otherwise like some bereft queen out of a Shakespearean play, is of course the most interesting. Chris is interesting because he is dead. Lesje knew him, but not very well. Some people at work found him remote, others too intense. He was rumored to have a ferocious temper, but Lesje never saw it. She worked on only one project with him: Smaller Mammals of the Mesozoic. It's finished now, installed in its glass case with push buttons wired for the voices. Lesje did the specifications and Chris built the models, using the musk-rat fur and rabbit and woodchuck, doctored, to cover the wooden forms. She used to visit him in that shadowy work-room, at one end of the corridor where they kept the stuffed owls and the other large birds. Specimens, two of each kind, in little pull-out metal drawers, like an animal morgue. She would bring coffee for both of them and drink hers while he worked, putting the shapes together with wood and Styro-foam. They guessed together about certain details: eyes, col-ors. It was odd, watching such a massive man concentrate himself on meticulous details. Chris wasn't unusually tall; he wasn't even overly muscular. But he gave an impression of mass, as though he would weigh more than anyone else the same size, as if his cells were closer together, squeezed inward by some irresistible gravitational force. Lesje never thought about whether she liked him or not. You don't like or dislike a boulder.

Now he's dead and therefore immediately more remote, more mysterious. His death baffles her: she can't imagine ever doing anything like that herself, and she can't imagine anyone she knows doing it. Chris seemed like the last person who would. To her at any rate. Though people aren't her field, so she's no judge.

But Nate; she hasn't thought much about Nate. He doesn't look like a betrayed husband. Right now he's talking about the election in Québec, which is taking place at this very mo-ment. He bites into a piece of turkey, chews; gravy traces his chin. The Separatists, he feels, ought to win, because the other government is so corrupt. Also because of the notorious behavior of the Federal Government in 1970. Lesje vaguely re-members that some people were arrested, after the kidnap-pings. She was working very hard on her Invertebrates course at the time; fourth year, and every mark counted.

Does he think it would be a good thing in the long run? Lesje asks. That isn't the point, Nate says. The point is a moral one.

If William had said this Lesje would have found it pomp-ous. She doesn't find it pompous now. Nate's long face (surely he used to have a beard; she recalls a beard, at parties and when he'd come with his children to pick Elizabeth up after work; but the face is hairless, pale), his body hanging from his shoulders like a suit from a hanger, nonchalant, impresses her. He's older, he must know things, things she could only guess at; he must have accumulated wisdom. His body would be wrinkled, his face has bones. Unlike William's. William has put on weight since they've been living together; his bones are retreating back into his head, behind the soft barricades of his cheeks.

William is against the Parti Québécois because of their wish to flood James Bay and sell the electrical power.

"But the other side is doing that, too," Lesje said.

"If I lived there I wouldn't vote for either of them," William said purely.

Lesje herself doesn't know how she would vote. She thinks she would probably move, instead. Nationalism of any kind makes her uneasy. In her parents' house it was a forbidden subject. How could it be otherwise, with the grandmothers both lurking, questioning her separately, waiting to pounce? They'd never met. Both had refused to go to her parents' wedding, which had been a civil ceremony. But the grandmothers had focused their rage not on their offending children but on each other. As for her, they'd both loved her, she supposes; and both had mourned over her as if she were in some way dead. It was her damaged gene pool. Impure, impure. Each thought she should scrap half her chromosomes, repair herself, by some miracle. Her Ukrainian grandmother, standing in the kitchen behind Lesje while she sat in a chrome and plastic chair reading *The Young People's Book of Stalactites and Stalagmites*, brushing her hair, talking to her mother in a language she didn't understand. Brushing and weeping silently.

"Mum, what's she saying?"

"She says your hair is very black."

The Ukrainian grandmother bending to hug her, consoling her for a pain Lesje didn't yet know she had. She'd been given an egg once by the Ukrainian grandmother, one of the untouchable decorated eggs kept on the mantelpiece along with the family photos in silver-plated frames. The Jewish grandmother, finding it, had smashed the egg with her tiny boots, stamping up and down, a mouse's rage.

They're both old women, her mother said. They've had hard lives. You can't change anyone over fifty. Lesje wept over her handful of bright egg fragments while her little grandmother, repentant, stroked her with her brown paws.

She bought Lesje another egg, somewhere; which must have cost her more than the money.

Both grandmothers spoke as if they personally had been through the war, had been gassed, raped, run through with bayonets, shot, starved, bombed and cremated, and had by a miracle survived; which wasn't true. The only one who had actually been there was Aunt Rachel, her father's sister, older by twenty years, already married and settled by the time the family left. Aunt Rachel was a photograph on her grandmother's mantelpiece, a plump dumpy-looking woman. She'd been comfortably off, and that was all the picture revealed: comfort. No foreknowledge; that was added much later, by Lesje, guiltily looking. Her father and mother did not discuss Aunt Rachel. What was there to discuss? No one knew what had happened to her. Lesje, although she has tried, cannot imagine her.

Lesje does not say any of this to Nate, who's explaining to her why the French feel the way they feel. Lesje doesn't really care why. She just wants to stay out of the way.

Nate has almost finished his turkey sandwich; he hasn't eaten any of his fries. He's gazing at the table to the left of Lesje's water glass, picking apart one of the Varsity Restaurant's white rolls. His place is scattered with crumbs. Things have to be viewed in a historical context, he says. He abandons the roll and lights a cigarette. Lesje doesn't like to ask for one—hers are gone, and it's the wrong time to get up for more—but after a minute he offers her one and even lights it for her, staring at her nose, she feels, which makes her nervous.

She wants to ask: Why am I here? You didn't really invite me to lunch in this third-rate restaurant to settle the future of the nation, did you? But he's already signaling for the bill. As they wait for it, he tells her he has two daughters. He says their names and ages, then repeats them, as though reminding himself or making sure she's got it straight. He'd like to bring them to the Museum some Saturday, he says. They're very interested in dinosaurs. Could she perhaps show them around?

Lesje doesn't usual work on Saturdays, but how can she say no? Depriving his children of dinosaurs. She ought to be glad for the chance to spread the word, make converts, but she isn't: dinosaurs aren't a religion for her, only a preserve. Also she's oddly disappointed. There should have been more to it, after all that stuttering on the telephone, this assignation at a restaurant which, she suddenly realizes, Elizabeth can be depended on never to enter. Lesje says politely that she'd be more than delighted to walk Nate's children through the exhibits and answer any questions they might have. She starts to put on her coat.

Nate pays for the lunch, even though Lesje offers to pick up her half. She would rather pay for the whole lunch. He looks so broke. More importantly, it's still not at all clear to her what will be expected of her for this gift of a grilled cheese sandwich and a glass of milk; what she is being asked to do or give in return.

Monday, November 15, 1976

NATE

Nate sits in the Selby Hotel, drinking draft beer and watching television. TRANSIENT, PERMANENT, the sign in the entrance-way reads, in big type, as if the two things are the same. Once it was an old man's bar, a bar for poor old men. He drinks at the Selby out of habit: Martha's place is only three blocks away, and he'd fallen into the pattern of dropping in for a few beers either before seeing her or, if it was still early enough, after leaving. He hasn't yet chosen a new bar.

He'll have to soon: the Selby, which when he started to drink there was full of anonymous faces, is beginning to clog with people he knows. They aren't friends exactly and he knows them only because they all drink here. Still, he's become a regular, and many of the old regulars are gone. Workers from Cabbagetown, frayed, silent for the most part, mutterers of dependably gloomy rote phrases. Now the place is being taken over by the same people who are taking over the mews flats and back alleys of Cabbagetown. Photographers, men who say they're writing a book. They talk too much, are too cheerful, invite him to sit at their tables when he doesn't want to. He has some standing among them, a woodcarver, worker with his hands, artisan, the man with the knife. He prefers bars where he's the first of his kind.

The bar he'll look for will be sober, quiet, devoid of pinball machines and jukeboxes and pimply eighteen-year-olds who drink too much and throw up in the can. He wants a bar half full of men in zip-front jackets and open-necked shirts with the T-shirt collar showing, slow and steady drinkers; serious television-watchers like himself. He likes to tune in on the national news and then get the sports scores.

He can hardly do this in his own house, as Elizabeth has long since exiled his ancient portable black and white set from the living room, where she said it was out of place, then from the kitchen. She said she couldn't stand to have it blaring while she cooked and he could decide whether he wanted to watch television or eat, because if it was television she would go out for dinner and let him fend for himself. That was in the olden days, before Nate of necessity began to cook. He tried sneaking the set into the bedroom—he had visions of lying in bed watching the late movie, a Scotch and water in one hand, Elizabeth curled cosily beside him—but that didn't last a night.

The set ended up in Janet's room, where the children watch Saturday morning cartoons on it. When he moved into his own room he didn't have the heart to take it away from them again. Sometimes he watches it with them or sits in their room by himself during afternoon football games. But they're always asleep by the time the eleven o'clock news comes on. He could always watch it at his mother's, she never misses a night, but it's too far to go and she doesn't keep beer in the house. She wouldn't be too excited about this kind of thing anyway. Earthquakes, famines, that's different. Every time there's a famine on the news, Nate can predict his mother will be on the phone the next day, trying to bully him into adopting an orphan or selling Pieces for Peace to his toy retailers. Bits of colored wool made into gnomes, folded paper birds. "Christmas tree decorations aren't going to save the world," he tells her. Then she says she hopes the children are taking their cod liver oil pills every morning. She suspects Elizabeth of vitamin deficiencies.

Elizabeth, on the other hand, has no interest in watching any sort of news whatsoever. She hardly even reads the papers. Nate has never known anyone with as little interest in the news as Elizabeth.

Tonight, for instance, she went to bed at seven; she didn't even bother to stay up for the election results. Nate, watching everything fall apart up there on the screen, can't understand her indifference. This is an event of national and perhaps even international importance, and she's sleeping through it! The special crew of commentators can hardly contain themselves, one way or another. The Québeckers on the panel are trying hard to keep from grinning; they're supposed to be objective, but their faces twitch every time the computer flashes a new victory for the Parti Québécois. The English on the other hand are about to wet themselves. René Lévesque can hardly believe it; he looks as if someone has simultaneously kissed him and kneed him in the groin.

The cameras cut back and forth between the thin-lipped commentators and the crowds at P.Q. headquarters, where a wild celebration is going on. Dancing in the streets, jubilant outbursts of song. He tries to remember a similar kind of celebration on his side of the border, but the only thing he can think of is the first Russian-Canadian hockey series, when Paul Henderson scored the winning goal. Men hugged each other and the drunker ones cried. But this is no hockey game. Watching the discomfiture of the defeated Liberals, the stiff upper lips of the English newsmen, Nate grins. *Serves them fucking well right*. This is his own personal vengeance on all the writers of letters to the editors across the country. Repression begets revolution, he thinks, all you stockbrokers. *So eat shit*. Merely a quote from the Prime Minister, he'd say to the old ladies, if that was him up there on the screen.

Nevertheless, glancing around at the other drinkers, he's uneasy. His pleasure, he knows, is merely theoretical and quite possibly snobbish. No one here with him is much interested in theory. Not many of the book-writers out tonight, mostly zip-front jackets, and they aren't taking it well; they're grumpy and even downright surly, as if they're watching their nextdoor neighbors throwing a loud party to which they haven't been invited. "Fucking frogs," one of them mutters. "Shoulda kicked them out of the country a long time ago."

Someone else says it will mean the end of the economy: Who'll take the chance of investing? "What economy," his friend quips. "Anything's better than stagflation." A theme the commentators pick up, second-guessing the future between the songs and kisses.

Nate feels a surge of exhilaration shoot through him, up from the belly, almost sexual, out to the fingers where they hook around his glass. None of them knows, none of the bastards knows. The earth is shifting under their feet and they can't even feel it, anything can happen!

But instead of the wizened monkey-face of René Lévesque, who is thanking his supporters in the Paul Sauvé Arena up there on the screen, he sees Lesje, her eyes, her thin hands, floating across from him at the lunch table, veiled in smoke. He can't remember anything she said; did she even say anything? He doesn't care, he doesn't care if she never says anything at all. He just wants to look at her, into her, into those dark eyes which are possibly brown, he can't remember that either. He remembers the shadow in them, like the cool shadow under a tree. Why did he wait so long, jittering in phone booths, spastic, unable to speak? At lunch he picked rolls apart and talked politics when what he should have done, he should have taken her in his arms, right there in the Varsity Restaurant. Then they would have been transported, they would have been somewhere else. How could he know where, since it would be somewhere he's never been before? Some place utterly unlike the country inside Elizabeth's blue dressing gown, or the planet of Martha, predictable, heavy and damp. Holding Lesje would be like holding some strange plant, smooth, thin, with sudden orange flowers. *Exotics*, the florists called them. The light would be odd, the ground underfoot littered with bones. Over which she would have power. She would stand before him, the bearer of healing wisdom, swathed in veils. He would fall to his knees, dissolve.

Nate, pushing back this image, places it in time: a Saturday matinée of *She,* seen when he was an impressionable twelve and masturbating nightly. His mother used to nag him about those matinées; I'm sure they're bad for you, she said. All that cowboys and shooting. A woman draped in cheesecloth, terrible actress, he'd shot paper clips and spitballs at her and jeered with the rest, he'd mooned over her for weeks. Nevertheless he wants to leap onto his bicycle and pedal like a maniac over to Lesje's apartment building, walk like Spiderman up the wall, swoop through the window. *Don't say anything*, he'd tell her. *Come with me*.

True, she's living with some man or other. Nate can remember him dimly, holding Lesje's elbow at last year's Museum Christmas party, a negligible pink smudge. He forgets about him almost immediately and returns to Lesje, his hand lighting her cigarette. Another inch and he'd have touched her. But it's too soon to touch her. He knows she gets up in the morning, eats breakfast, goes to work where she does incomprehensible things, disappears at intervals into the ladies' room, but he doesn't want to contemplate these details. He knows nothing about her actual life and he doesn't want to know anything. Not too much, not yet.

ELIZABETH

They walk up the steps, bypassing the popcorn man with his candy apples and balloons and his noisemakers and plastic windmills, violent blue and red, a sound like dried birds still flapping. A family. When they come out again they will have to buy something for the children, because that is what families do.

Elizabeth said she would come with them because Nate was right, it's bad for the children that they never do anything as a family any more. The children were not fooled. They weren't overjoyed, merely surprised and a little apprehensive. "But you never come when Daddy takes us," Nancy said.

Now, in the vaulted rotunda with the Saturday river of children funneling through the turnstiles, she doesn't think she can take the pressure. This is where she works. It's also where Chris worked. It's all right for her to be here on weekdays, she has a good reason and a lot of memos to occupy her mind; but what is the point now? Why use her own free time to walk among empty suits and metal shells and bones discarded by their owners? Any more than she has to.

She'd taken care not to speak to him or even see him if possible during office hours. It wasn't that she cared who knew, though she didn't flaunt it, she didn't need to; in the Museum, by a process of discreet seepage, everybody ultimately knew everything. But she was paid to do a job, so many hours a day, and she took that seriously. She hadn't spent those hours on Chris.

Not since the first time, when they made love with most of their clothes on, lying on the floor of his workroom among scraps of fur, shavings of wood, beside the partly finished replica of an African ground squirrel. The glass eyes had not yet been inserted, the ragged sockets watched them. The whole

Museum still smells of that day: preservative, sawdust, and
the smell of Chris's hair, a molten smell, singed and rich.
Burned gold. His cold zipper which pressed into the flesh of her
inner thigh, the teeth rasping. She thought: I will never
again settle for anything less than this. As if it was a bargain,
which perhaps it was, though she'd never been able to see the
invisible bargainer on the other side.

The children are in the gift shop, looking at the dolls, cloth
lions from Singapore, clay babies from Mexico. Nate is fumbling with his wallet. It was his idea so he will pay, but she
knows, knew when they left the house, that he wouldn't have
enough money.

"Can you lend me five?" he says to her. "I'll pay you back
Monday."

She hands him the money, which she had ready in her
hand. It's always five. Sometimes he pays her back; when he
doesn't it's because he forgets. She no longer reminds him, as
she did in the days when she thought everything should be
fair.

"I won't go in," she says. "I'll meet you on the steps at
four-thirty. We can take the girls to Murray's for a sundae or
something."

He seems relieved. "Right," he says.

"Tell the children to enjoy themselves."

She walks south towards the park, meaning to cross the
road and stroll under the trees, perhaps sit on one of the
benches and breathe in the smell of fallen leaves. The last
smell of leaves she'll get before the snow. She stands on the
curb, waiting for a chance to cross. A few tattered wreaths
still on the cenotaph. SOUTH AFRICA, it says.

She turns and walks back towards the Museum. She'll go to
the Planetarium; that will kill the time. Even though she helps
with the posters and displays, she's never been in there. She
works during the weekday matinées and she wouldn't ordinarily go to something like that in the evening, on her own time.
But today she wants to go somewhere she's never been.

The lobby is brick-lined. There's a motto on the curved
wall:

THE HEAVENS ARE CALLING YOU AND WHEEL AROUND YOU
DISPLAYING TO YOU THEIR ETERNAL BEAUTIES
AND STILL YOUR EYE IS LOOKING ON THE GROUND

                                        —DANTE

And below that; INFORMATION. ADVANCE TICKET SALES.

Elizabeth finds it reassuring that even eternal beauties cost money. The show is at three. She goes to the window to buy a ticket, though she supposes she could get in on her pass card.

"Cosmic Disasters, or the Laserium?" the girl says.

"Pardon?" Elizabeth says. Then she realizes that "Cosmic Disasters" must be the name of the current show. *Laserium*, however, suggests nothing to her but a leper colony.

"The Laserium isn't until four-fifteen," the girl says.

"Cosmic Disasters, then," Elizabeth says. The Laserium, whatever that is, would be too late.

She stands around in the lobby examining the covers of the books in the bookshop window, *The Stars Belong to Everyone. The Universe. Black Holes.* She's never felt much friendliness towards the stars.

The auditorium is a dome; it's like being inside a breast. Elizabeth knows it's supposed to represent the sky; nevertheless she feels a little stifled. She leans back in the plush seat, gazing at the ceiling, which is blank but glows with a faint light. The children around her wriggle and twitter until the lights dim. Then they hush.

It's sunset. All around is the Toronto skyline, its outlines and signs: the Park Plaza squat now compared to the Hyatt Regency beside it; BRITANNICA to the east; Sutton Place, the weather building, the CN Tower. This is earth.

A voice tells them that they're seeing the skyline as it would look if they were standing on top of the Planetarium. "Hey, that's neat," the boy next to her says. He radiates bubble gum. Elizabeth feels him beside her, a warm reassuring presence. Rubber sneaker soles.

The light on the western horizon fades and the stars begin to shine. The voice names the constellations: the Bears, the Dippers, Cassiopeia's Chair, Orion, the Pleiades. The voice says that the ancients used to believe people could become stars or constellations when they died, which was a poetic thought but of course not true. The stars are in fact much more wonderful and surprising than the ancients imagined. They are flaming balls of gas. The voice goes into a rhapsody of numbers and distances, during which Elizabeth tunes out.

The North Star: a small white arrow points to it. The voice speeds up time and the stars wheel around the pole. To see that you would have to stand for nights with your eyes glued open. The ancients thought that the stars really moved that way, but of course it's the earth that rotates.

The ancients had other beliefs as well. Ominous music. To-day's show is about unusual stellar events, the voice says. The stars rotate backwards in time, to the year 1066. Picture of the Bayeux Tapestry, with William the Conqueror looking gleeful. The ancients believed that comets meant disruptions, war, pestilences, plagues, the birth of a great hero, the fall of a throne or the end of the world. The voice gives a dismissive laugh. Everyone knows better now.

Halley's Comet appears in the sky, faint at first, then bright-er and brighter, its tail streaming out like blown cloud. The voice gives some information on the composition of this tail. The word "comet" comes from *cometes*, hairy. The ancients thought of comets as hairy stars.

Halley's Comet fades, then vanishes. It will return, the voice says, in 1985.

Stars begin to fall, a few at a time, then more and more. They aren't really stars, the voice explains, merely meteorites. Meteorites come in showers. They are probably debris left over from exploded stars. As the stars fall, slides of paint-ings—crowd scenes, Dances of Death, burning buildings—flash on the dome and the voice recites a few verses from Shakespeare. Then the voice produces some Northern Lights and begins to discuss their causes. Some people claim to have heard them, a high rustling noise, but this has never been recorded. Elizabeth feels a thin whisper close to her ear.

She's cold. She knows it's warm in the room and she can smell the children, coats, popcorn oil; but the Northern Lights are making her cold. She wants to get up and leave the audito-rium. She looks around for the door, but she can't see it. She doesn't like the idea of groping around in the dark.

Now the voice is going to reveal something extraordinary. They've all heard about the Star of Bethlehem, haven't they? Yes. Well, maybe there really was a Star of Bethlehem. Above, the stars rotate back through centuries, two thousand years. See that?

The children breathe, *Oh*. A star is growing, bigger, bright-er, till its light fills half the sky. Then, diminuendo. Like a firework, it's gone.

"That was a supernova," the voice says. "A dying star." When a star came to the end of its life, it might explode, burning up all its remaining energy in one spectacular burst. Someday our own sun would do that. But not for billions of years.

Then the remaining matter, lacking the energy to balance

its own gravitational field, would collapse into itself, forming a neutron star. Or a black hole. The voice and its pointer locate a space in the sky where there is nothing. No one can see a black hole, says the voice; but because of their effects on objects around them they are known to exist. No light, for instance, shines through them. Nobody quite understands black holes yet, but they are thought to be stars collapsed to a density so great that no light can escape from them. They suck energy in instead of giving it out. If you fell into a black hole, you would disappear forever; though to anyone watching, you would appear to have been frozen for eternity on the black hole's event horizon.

The piece of blackness expands, perfectly round, lightless, until it fills the center of the dome. A man in a silver suit falls towards it, reaches it, stops.

The man hangs spread-eagled against the blackness while the voice explains that he has actually disappeared. He's an optical illusion. That would be a real cosmic disaster, the voice says. What if the earth, without knowing it, were approaching a black hole? The silver man vanishes and the stars twinkle again, while the voice explains that such a thing is not really very likely.

Elizabeth, shivering, stares up at the sky, which isn't really a sky but a complicated machine with tiny lights projected by slides and push-buttons. People do not become stars of any kind when they die. Comets do not really cause plagues. Really there is nobody in the sky. Really there is no round sphere of darkness, no black sun, no frozen silver man.

Saturday, November 20, 1976

LESJE

Lesje feels awkward, as if the bones of her elbows and knees aren't really touching but are attached to one another with string. Gangling. Surely her teeth are larger than usual, her chest is flatter. She pulls her shoulders back. Nate's children aren't exactly unfriendly, but there's a withholding, a narrow-eyed evaluation. The new teacher. Prove to us that we should be here. Prove you're worth our attention. Who are you anyway and what are you getting us into? Nate said when he asked her to do this that they were very interested in dinosaurs, but at the moment she doesn't believe it.

The three of them are looking through glass at the effigy of the paleontologist, kneeling in his cubicle among simulated rocks. He has a hat on and he's chalky white, with clean-cut First World War air-ace features and well-trimmed hair. Silent Sam, they've nicknamed him. Quite unlike Professor Morgan, whiskered and unkempt leader of the only dig Lesje has been privileged to attend, as flunky and chief varnisher. He kept his pipe tobacco in his right pocket and emptied the old pipes into his left one. Several times he caught fire and they had to put him out. *Balderdash. Man doesn't know what he's talking about.* He thought Lesje was one of the biggest jokes he'd heard. *So you want to be a paleontologist. Better off learning to cook. Worst coffee I ever tasted.* Lesje cringing—because she respected his opinion, had read every one of his papers she could get her hands on, and his book on carnivorous dinosaurs of the Canadian plains—appeasing him with more and better cups of coffee, or tea, or Scotch, running her ass off like some dumb airline stewardess, trying to find ways to please him, until she discovered there weren't any. Luckily her current boss, Dr. Van Vleet, isn't anything like that, though he must be even older. On the other hand Lesje can't imagine him digging anything up. He specializes in the classification of teeth.

But the man in the glass case is a model. He's holding a fossil; presumably he's undergoing the ecstasy of scientific discovery, but his face isn't giving any of that away.

"What's he doing?" Nancy wants to know. Lesje suspects she doesn't really want to know, but it's part of this charade that the children must ask polite questions and Lesje must turn herself inside out trying to answer them.

"He's plaster-coating a bone," Lesje says. "He has to do it very carefully because it isn't real bone, it's a fossil. The softer parts of the bone decayed away and the shape of the bone has been filled up with minerals so it's kind of like stone. It's very brittle."

"I know," Janet says. "Daddy told us."

"Is that your job?" Nancy says.

"Well, part of it," Lesje says.

"That's a funny job," Nancy says.

"Well, I do other things too," Lesje says, wondering why she's defending herself to a nine-year-old. Or is she eight? "Actually I've never done that much actual digging. I did a lot of bone preservation. Some of the fossils have to be preserved right away or they'll fall apart. We coat them with Gelva. That's a kind of resin."

The children stare through the glass at the rigid paleontologist, who the more you look resembles a corpse, Lesje thinks, with his pallor and fixed eyes. Janet's face is clamped as though she's caught an off smell, Nancy is curious but uninvolved. How can Lesje explain to them why she does this, why she loves doing this? The day they found the albertosaurus, a thigh, a vertebra. Morgan: "What have we here?" Disappointed because it was a well-known species. But Lesje: *Live again!* she'd wanted to cry, like some Old Testament prophet, like God, throwing up her arms, willing thunderbolts; and the strange flesh would grow again, cover the bones, the badlands would moisten and flower.

But that can't happen, so the next best thing is these displays, with the admittedly plastic vegetation among which the bones, articulated and rearticulated after furious argument over which way the creatures had actually walked, rear their gigantic heads and cavernous eye-sockets far above the craning necks of those who are, by the grace of their ancestors, still living.

In the Cretaceous twilight the children press buttons, watching the colored slides flip through their cycles while the Museum's automated voices drone. Lesje knows she's superfluous. Nate strolls up beside her, lounging, unconscious, and she wants to shake him. What is all this about, why has he put her through it? Made her sacrifice her free time (she could have been shopping! reading! copulating!) for this lack of an event? Is she being inspected, is it a test, has she failed? If he wants to make a pass at her—and she doesn't know what she would do if he did that, hasn't thought beyond that first pressure of his hand on some part of her body forbidden enough to be decisive—why doesn't he make it? (Not here and now, of course; not in front of the children. Who probably would not notice.)

But that doesn't seem to be the point.

Saturday, November 20, 1976

NATE

The three of them, ahead of him, indistinct in the cavernous dark. Monsters loom over them, reptilian, skeletal, wired into poses of menace as in some gargantuan tunnel of horrors. Nate feels his bones eroding, stone filling the cavities. Trapped. Run Nancy, run Janet, or time will overtake you, you too will be caught and frozen. But Nancy, secure in the belief that he can't see her, is calmly picking her nose.

Lesje's silhouette bends towards the children. Elongated: Our Lady of the Bones. " 'Extinct' means there aren't any more of them," she says. Nate hopes she won't find his children ignorant or stupid. He's sure he's explained to them several times what "extinct" means. And they've visited this gallery often, though Nancy prefers the Egyptian mummies and Janet likes the armor, the lords and ladies. Are they playing up to Lesje to help him out, asking questions to counterfeit interest, are they already that perceptive, that sly? Is he that obvious?

"Why not?" Janet says. "Why are they all extinct?"

"No one really knows," Lesje says. "The world changed, and the new conditions weren't suitable for them." She pauses. "We've found quite a few eggs with baby dinosaurs in them. Towards the end, they didn't even hatch."

"It got too cold, you turkey," Nancy says to Janet. "It was the Ice Age."

"Well, not exactly," Lesje begins, but thinks better of it.

She turns back towards him, hesitating, waiting.

Nancy runs, tugs at his arm to make him bend down. She wants to see the mummies now, she whispers. Janet, his squeamish one, will protest, there will be a compromise, time will flow on; soon everyone will be one day older.

How could he desert them? Could he endure those prearranged Saturday outings? To see them only once a week, for that would be the price, the pound of flesh. How've you been, kids. Great, Dad. Stilted. No bedtime stories, impromptu chases along the hallway, voices at the cellar door. Unfair. But it will be that or some other unfairness, Lesje, as yet untouched, intact, weeping in a bedroom doorway somewhere in the future. Bright paint flaking from her, pieces of thin curved glass, a broken ornament. As for him, slivers in his murderous hands, sitting in the bar at the Selby Hotel, pondering the ethical life. Would he be any better off than he is now? He would watch hockey games with the other drinkers, echoing their raucous cheers. The ethical life. He'd been taught it was the only desirable goal. Now that he no longer believes it's possible, why does he keep on trying to lead it?

Limping home from school, purple and cut because his mother had forbidden him to fight. *Even when they hit me first?* Even when they hit you first. But he'd thought of a way around her. *They were beating up a smaller boy.* Not good enough. *Three against one.* Still not good enough. *They called him a kike.* Ah, that did it. Fire flashed from her eyes. In the name of tolerance, kill. My beamish boy. Nate, hypocrite at six and two inches taller than any of his tormentors, fought with fierce joy, inventing new injustices to account for his triumphant black eyes. Deeds Not Creeds, as the Unitarians said.

He can rehearse all the reasons for not acting, in this or any other situation; yet he knows his own past well enough to fear that nevertheless he will unaccountably act. Despite his scruples, and more desperately, more senselessly because of them. Because of his selfishness, as someone will be sure to point out. Not Elizabeth though. She claims she doesn't care what he does, who his ladyfriends are, as she puts it, as long as the children are protected. As she also puts it. She means her children. Nate is sure she's secretly convinced she conceived them through parthenogenesis, having conveniently forgotten the night of the bath towel and the other night, the many other nights. Laziness and habit. As for him, he'd like to think his children had sprung fully formed from his forehead. Then they would be entirely his.

As it is, Nate knows who would get the children. Though they've never discussed separating. Even during the worst times, she's never told him to leave, he's never threatened it. But it hangs between them in every conversation; it's the secret weapon, the final solution, the one unspeakable thing. He suspects they both think about it almost all the time: considering, rejecting.

Better to stop now. Instead of sweeping Lesje up from the carpeted floor of the Vertebrate Evolution Gallery and running up the stairs with her to the seclusion of Mammals and Insects, he'll thank her and shake her hand, touching her anyway that once, the long thin fingers cool in his palm. Then he'll visit the mummies and after that the suits of armor, and he'll try to avoid seeing any of these artifacts as images of himself. Outside, he'll comfort himself with popcorn and a cigarette, substitutes for the double Scotch he will by that time really need. They will wait on the stone steps of the Museum, a family, leaning against the plaque at the right-hand side of the door, THE ARTS OF MAN THROUGH ALL THE YEARS, until Elizabeth materializes from whatever limbo she's wandered off to, her stocky figure in the black coat proceeding evenly up the steps to claim them at the appointed time.

Monday, November 29, 1976

ELIZABETH

Elizabeth lies propped in the bathtub. Once she took baths for pleasure; now she takes them for the same reason she eats. She's servicing her body, like servicing a car, keeping it well cleaned, its moving parts in trim, ready for the time when she may be able to use it again, inhabit it. For pleasure. She's eating too much, she knows that, but better too much than too little. Too little is the danger. She's lost the capacity to judge, since she's never really hungry. No doubt she's taking too many baths as well.

She's careful to have the water at less than body heat, as she has a fear of falling asleep in the tub. You can drown in two inches of water. They say if the water is the same temperature as your blood your heart might stop, but only if there's something wrong with it. As far as she knows there is nothing wrong with her heart.

She's brought work home from the office. She's bringing work home a lot, since she seems unable to concentrate on it there. She can't concentrate on it at home either, but at least there's no one who might walk in on her and find her staring at the wall. She's always done most of her own typing; she's a crack typist, why not, she did nothing but that for years, but also she doesn't like to delegate her work. She made her way up to her present position by having a good telephone manner and by always knowing the details of the job above her a little better than the person actually doing it, so she has a natural distrust of secretaries. Now, however, the paper is piling up. She'll have to seize hold soon.

She frowns, trying to focus on the book in front of her, held up in one dry hand.

But it is hard for us to grasp these changes. It is hard for us to put ourselves in the place of people living in the old

China (as millions still live in the Third World), toiling on small plots of land, losing almost all they produce to the feudal landlords, at the mercy of floods and famine— who after a long war oust the landlord.

Elizabeth closes her eyes. It's a catalogue, a traveling show. Peasant paintings. It's in England right now and they can have it in a couple of years, if they want it. She's supposed to be looking at the catalogue and giving feedback. She's supposed to write a memo saying whether she thinks the show would be worthwhile and interesting to the Canadian public.

But she can't, she can't care. She can't care about the Canadian public, much less about this catalogue written by some armchair Marxist in England. From his point of view she's a landlord. She wonders about her tenants, with their sallow faces and their abnormally quiet child, dressed always a little too neatly, a little too well. They're foreigners of some kind, but Elizabeth doesn't know what and it would be rude to ask. Something from Eastern Europe, she thinks, escaped. They are unobtrusive and they pay their rent, nervously, always a day ahead. Are they fighting a long war to oust her? There are no signs of it. These paintings are from a place so utterly alien to her that it might as well be on the moon.

She skips the introduction, turns to the pictures. *New Village, New Spirit. Continue to Advance. The New Look of Our Piggery.* It's blatant propaganda, and the pictures are ugly. With their crude bright colors and clearly drawn smiling figures they're like the Sunday-school handouts she loathed so much as a child. *Jesus loves me.* She never believed that for a second. Jesus was God and God loved Auntie Muriel; Auntie Muriel was absolutely certain of that. As far as Elizabeth was concerned God could not love both her and Auntie Muriel at the same time.

They never went to church before they moved to Auntie Muriel's. Which Auntie Muriel might have known. Elizabeth won a prize for memorizing scripture verses. Caroline, on the other hand, made a spectacle of herself. It was Easter; they had on their new blue hats, with the elastic that cut into Elizabeth's chin, and the matching coats. Size ten and size seven but identical: Auntie Muriel loved dressing them like twins. The pulpit was banked with daffodils but the minister was not talking about the Resurrection. He preferred Judgment. *And the sun became black as sackcloth of hair, and the moon be-*

*came as blood, and the stars of heaven fell into the earth, and
the heaven departed as a scroll when it is rolled together.*

Elizabeth pleated and unpleated her picture of Christ coming out of the hole in the rock, his face translucent, two blue
women kneeling before him. She folded his head back, then
pulled the top of the paper, making him pop up again like a
jack-in-the-box. The church smelled of perfume, too strong,
waves of dusting powder from Auntie Muriel beige and up-
right beside her. She wanted to take off her coat. *Look, look*,
said Caroline, standing up. She was pointing at the stained
glass window, the center one where Christ in purple knocked
at a door. She crouched, then tried to scramble across the pew
in front, dislodging Mrs. Symon's mink hat. Elizabeth sat still,
but Auntie Muriel reached across and jerked at the back of
Caroline's coat. The minister frowned from his grape-draped
pulpit and Caroline began to scream. Auntie Muriel took hold
of her arm, but she broke free and pushed past the line of
knees and ran down the aisle. They should have known, right
then and there. Something wrong. She said afterwards that the
purple was falling on her, but Auntie Muriel told everyone
she'd just had an upset stomach. Excitable, they said; little
girls often were. She should never have been brought to the
main service.

Auntie Muriel decided it was the minister's fault and spear-
headed the drive to get rid of him. They didn't have to listen
to that sort of thing. More like a Baptist. Years later he'd
been in the newspapers for doing an exorcism on a girl who
really had a brain tumor and died anyway. You see? said
Auntie Muriel. Crazy as a coot.

As for Caroline, when seven years later that scream took
final shape and she made it totally, calamitously clear what
she'd been trying to say, that was something else; that was a
judgment. Or a lack of willpower, depending on how Auntie
Muriel was feeling that day.

In the hospital, and afterwards in the institution, Caroline
would not talk or even move. She would not eat by herself
and she had to be diapered like a baby. She lay on her side
with her knees curled up to her chest, eyes closed, hands
fisted. Elizabeth sat beside her, breathing the sickly smell of
inert flesh. Damn you, Caroline, she whispered. I know you're
in there.

Three years after that, when Caroline was almost seven-
teen, an attendant was called away while she was in the bathtub. An emergency, they said. They were never supposed to

leave patients like Caroline alone in a bathtub; those were the rules. They weren't supposed to put patients like Caroline into bathtubs at all, but someone had decided it would help her to relax, uncurl her; that was what they said at the inquest. So it happened and Caroline slipped down. She drowned rather than making the one small gesture, the turn of the head, that would have saved her life.

Sometimes Elizabeth has wondered whether Caroline did it on purpose, whether all along, inside that sealed body, she'd been conscious and waiting for the chance. She has wondered why. Sometimes, though, she's merely wondered why she herself has never done the same thing. At these times Caroline is clear, logical, pure; marble in contrast to her own slowly percolating flesh, the gasps of her decaying lungs and spongy, many-fingered heart.

In the room someone is singing. Not singing but a hum; Elizabeth realizes she's been hearing it for some time. She opens her eyes to locate the sound; the pipes, it must be, vibration of distant water. The wallpaper is too bright, morning-glories, and she knows she should be careful. No openings. She hadn't found those people in the sixties who'd torn their cats apart and jumped out of high-rise windows because they thought they were birds in the least glamorous: she'd found them stupid. Anyone who had ever heard those voices before or seen what they could do would have known what they were saying.

"Shut up," Elizabeth says. Even this much acknowledgement is bad. She'll concentrate on the text. *Criticizing Lin Piao and Confucius before the remains of an ancient slave-owner's war chariots,* she reads. The charioteers were buried alive. She peers into the picture, trying to see them, but all she can make out are the skeletons of the horses. Indignant peasants clamor around the grave.

Her hand holds the book, her body stretches away from her through the water, surrounded by white porcelain. On the ledge, far away, so far she is sure she could never reach them, are the toys the children still insist on floating in their baths, though they should be too old: an orange duck, a red and white boat with a wind-up paddle wheel, a blue penguin. Her breasts, flattened by gravity, her belly. Hourglass figure. Nancy's *Little Riddle Book*:

> Two bodies have I
> Though both joined in one,

The stiller I stand
The quicker I run.

On the next page over was a riddle about a coffin. Hardly
suitable for children, she said that Christmas. Nate bought it,
in a little boxed set.

Her knees jut from the blue water like mountains; clouds of
bubble bath floating around them. *Bodykins*, imported. She
bought it for Chris, for both of them, in some sybaritic dream;
early, before she found out he didn't like having her look at
his body except from half and inch away. He didn't like having her stand back from him, he wanted her to feel him but
not see him. I'll get you where you live, he said, much later,
much too late. Where does she live?

Sand runs through her glass body, from her head down to
her feet. When it's all gone she'll be dead. Buried alive. Why
wait?

Tuesday, December 7, 1976

LESJE

Lesje is out for lunch with Marianne. They've just had a sandwich at Murray's, which is near and cheap; now they're walking over to Yorkville and Cumberland to look in the store windows. It's no longer the place to shop, says Marianne, whom Lesje regards as an authority on such things; too overpriced. Queen Street West is the place now. But Queen Street West is too far away.

Marianne habitually has lunch with Trish, who's off with the flu. They've asked her along on these expeditions before but usually she says no. She's behind in her work, she says, she'll grab a sandwich downstairs. Surely they don't have much to offer her in addition to the gossip they provide at morning coffee. Marianne openly admits—or is it a joke?—that she went into Biology to meet medical students and marry a doctor. Lesje doesn't approve of such frivolity.

Now, however, gossip is what she wants. She craves gossip, she wants to know anything Marianne can tell her about Elizabeth and especially about Elizabeth's husband Nate, who has not phoned, written or appeared since he shook hands with her beside the EXIT sign at the dinosaur gallery. She isn't interested in him, really, but she's baffled. She wants to know whether he often does such things, makes such odd approaches. However, she isn't sure how to obtain this information from Marianne without telling her what has happened so far; which she doesn't want to do. But why not? Nothing has happened.

They stop at the corner of Bay and Yorkville to look at a bunchy blue velvet suit with gold braid trim and a blouse underneath, cuff ruffles and a Peter Pan collar.

"Too goyish," Marianne says, which is her word for tacky taste. Despite her blue eyes and blond hair and her madrigal name, Marianne is Jewish; what Lesje thinks of as pure Jewish, in contrast to her own hybrid state. Marianne's attitude towards Lesje is complicated. Sometimes she seems to include her among the Jews; she'd hardly say *too goyish* in front of her if she thought of her as too goyish herself. Though, as one of Lesje's aunts explained to her, sweetly and maliciously, when she was nine, Lesje isn't really Jewish. She could be classified as truly Jewish only if it was her mother instead of her father. Apparently the gene is passed through the female, like hemophilia.

At other times, though, Marianne focuses on Lesje's Ukrainian name. It doesn't seem to bother her the way it would probably bother her parents; instead she finds it intriguing, though a little funny.

"Why should you worry? Ethnic is big these days. Change your last name and you'll get a Multiculturalism grant."

Lesje smiles at these jokes, but weakly. She's multicultural all right, but not in the way the grant-givers want. And her father's family has already changed its name at least once, though not to get a grant. They did it in the late thirties: who could tell, Hitler might invade, and even if he didn't there were enough anti-Semites in the country already. In those days, the aunts said, you didn't answer the door unless you knew who was knocking. Which is how Lesje has ended up with the unlikely name of Lesje Green; though she has to admit that Lesje Etlin wouldn't have been any more probable. For two years, when she was nine and ten, she told the teachers at school that her name was Alice. Lesje meant Alice, her mother said, and it was a perfectly good name, the name of a famous Ukrainian poet. Whose poems Lesje would never be able to read.

She changed it back, though, for the following reason. If she were to discover a country which had never been discovered before (and she fully intended to do this sometime), she would of course name it after herself. There already was a Greenland, which wasn't at all the sort of place she had in mind. Greenland was barren, icy, devoid of life, whereas the place Lesje intended to discover would be tropical, rich and crawling with wondrous life forms, all of them either archaic and thought extinct, or totally unknown even in fossil records. She made careful drawings of this land in her scrapbooks and labeled the flora and fauna.

But she couldn't call this place Aliceland; it wasn't right. One of her reservations about *The Lost World* concerned the names of the topographical features. Lake Gladys, for instance: *too goyish*. And the whole primitive plateau was called Maple White Land, after the artist whose sketches of a pterodactyl, found clutched in his delirious and dying hand, had first put Professor Challenger on the track. Lesje was sure—though it didn't say so in the book—that Maple White must have been a Canadian, of the pinkest and most frigid kind. With a name like that what else could he be?

Lesjeland, though. That sounded almost African. She could picture it on a map: seen that way, there was nothing ludicrous about it.

Once, after she was grown up, she'd gone to the Odessa Pavilion during the Caravan Festival. Usually she avoided Caravan. She distrusted the officially promoted goodwill, the costumes nobody wore any more. There were really no Poles like the ones in the Polish Pavilion, no Indians like the Indians, no yodeling Germans. She's not sure why she went, that time; perhaps she was hoping to find her roots. She'd eaten foods she remembered only vaguely from her grandmother's house and had never known the names for—*pirogi, medvynk*—and watched tall boys and auburn-braided girls in red boots leap about on a stage decorated with paper sunflowers, singing songs she couldn't sing, dancing dances she'd never been taught. According to the program, some of the dancers were named Doris and Joan and Bob, although others had names like hers: Natalia, Halyna, Vlad. At the end, with that element of self-mockery she recognized too in Marianne when she said *schwartze*, imitating her mother's views on cleaning ladies, they sang a song from Ukrainian summer camp:

> I'm not Russian, I'm not Polish,
> I am not Romanian,
> Kiss me once, kiss me twice,
> Kiss me, I'm Ukrainian.

Lesje admired the bright costumes, the agility, the music; but she was an outsider looking in. She felt as excluded as if she'd been surrounded by a crowd of her own cousins. On both sides. *Kiss me, I'm multicultural.*

She hadn't been sent to Ukrainian summer camp or to Jewish summer camp. She hadn't been allowed to go either to the golden church with its fairy-tale onion dome or to synagogue. Her parents would have been happy to send her to both, if it would keep the peace, but the grandmothers wouldn't allow it.

Sometimes she thinks she was produced, not by her parents in the usual way, but by some unheard-of copulation between these two old ladies who never met. They'd existed in an odd parody of marriage, hating each other more than either hated the Germans, yet obsessed with each other; they'd even died within a year of each other, like an old devoted couple. They'd infested her parents' house in relays, fought over her as if she'd been a dress at a bargain. If one baby-sat for her the other must be given a turn or there would be histrionics: weeping from her Grandmother Smylski, rage from her Grandmother Etlin (who'd kept her name, who'd refused to scurry for cover with the rest of them). Neither of them had ever learned English very well, though Grandmother Etlin had picked up some scatological curses from the neighborhood children who hung around her store, which she'd used in garbled versions when she wanted to get her own way. "Jesus asshole, dog poop, I hope you die!" she would scream, stamping her black boots on the front doorstep. She knew the front doorstep was the best place to do this: Lesje's parents would do almost anything to get her inside, away from the observation of the street. *English people.* These bland clones of their imagination did not have tiny black-booted grandmothers who screamed, "I hope your bum falls off!" on the front doorstep; or anything remotely equivalent. Lesje knows better, now.

The strange thing about her grandmothers was how much alike they were. Both of their houses were small and dark and smelled of furniture polish and mothballs. They were both widows, they both had sad-eyed single male boarders stashed away in upstairs rooms, they both had fancy china and front rooms crowded with silver-framed family photos, they both drank tea in a glass.

Beofre she was old enough to go to school she'd spent half the week with each of them, since her mother had to work. She would sit on the kitchen floor, cutting pictures out of magazines and folders from the small travel agency where her mother worked, arranging them in piles—men in one pile, women in another, dogs in another, houses in another—while the grandmothers drank their tea and talked to the aunts (her father's sister, her mother's brothers' wives), in languages she couldn't understand and which her parents never spoke at home.

This should have made her trilingual. Instead she was considered bad at English, plodding, a poor speller, lacking in imagination. In Grade Five she'd been asked to write about "My Summer Holiday," and she'd written about her rock collection, with technical details of each rock. She'd been given a D and a lecture by the teacher. "You were supposed to write about something personal, something from your own life," the teacher said. "Not out of the encyclopedia. You must have done *something* else during your summer holidays."

Lesje didn't understand. She hadn't done anything else during her summer holidays, not anything she could remember, and the rock collection was something personal from her own life. But she could not explain this. She couldn't explain why her discovery that rocks were different from each other and had special names was so important. The names were a language; not many other people might know it, but if you found one who did, you would be able to talk together. Only about rocks, but that would be something. She would walk up and down the stairs murmuring these names, wondering if she was pronouncing them right. "Schist," she would say, "magma, igneous, malachite, pyrite, lignite." The names of the dinosaurs, when she found out about them, were even more satisfactory, more polysyllabic, soothing, mellifluous. Though she could not spell *receive* or *embarrass* or *career*, she spelled *diplodocus* and *archaeopteryx* from the beginning without a hitch.

Her parents thought she was becoming too wrapped up in these things and tried to give her dancing lessons to make her more sociable. Too late, she was not sociable. They blamed, silently of course, her Grandmother Etlin, who'd first taken her to the Museum, not because she had any interest in the things inside it but because it was cheap and out of the rain. Because her Grandmother Smylski had Mondays, Tuesdays and Wednesdays, Grandmother Etlin insisted on having three days as well, all in a row, even though it meant violating the Sabbath; which didn't bother Grandmother Etlin all that much. She kept kosher out of habit but was not in other ways visibly reverent. After Lesje started school they'd kept this Saturday custom. Instead of synagogue Lesje attended the Museum, which at first did look to her a little like a church or a shrine, as if you were supposed to kneel. It was quiet and smelled mysterious, and was full of sacred objects: quartz, amethyst, basalt.

(When her grandmother died, Lesje felt she should be put into the Museum, in a glass case like the Egyptian mummies, with a label where you could read about her. An impossible idea; but this was the form her mourning took. She knew better than to say it though, at shiva, sitting in a corner of her aunt's huge pink and white living room while they all ate coffee cake. They'd finally let her into the synagogue, too, but it hadn't been mysterious at all. Neither the bright, clean-lined synagogue nor the pink living room seemed at all like her grandmother. A glass case in a shadowy corner, with her black boots standing at the bottom and her few pieces of gold jewelry and the amber beads spread out beside her.)

"Explain me," her grandmother would say, holding her hand tightly, for protection Lesje decided much later; and Lesje would read the labels to her. Her grandmother understood not at all, but nodded wisely, smiling; not because of the impressive rocks, as Lesje thought at the time, but because her granddaughter seemed able to negotiate with ease in this world she herself found so incomprehensible.

In the last year of her grandmother's life, when Lesje was twelve and they were both getting a little old for these mornings, they'd seen something at the Museum which upset her grandmother. She's long ago got used to the mummies in the Egyptian gallery and she no longer said *Gevalt* every time they went into the dinosaur gallery, which was not at that time dark and equipped with voices. But this was something different. They'd seen an Indian woman, wearing a beautiful red sari with a gold band at the hem. Over the top of the sari was a white lab coat, and with the woman were two little girls, obviously her daughters, wearing Scottish kilts. They all disappeared through a door marked STAFF ONLY. "Gevalt," her grandmother said, frowning, but not with fear.

Lesje stared after them, entranced. This, then, was her own nationality.

"You'd look good in that," Marianne says. She sometimes gives Lesje advice on how she ought to dress, which Lesje ignores since she doesn't feel capable of following it. Marianne, who has to watch what she eats, thinks Lesje should be stately. She could be stately, Marianne says, if she wouldn't lope. They're looking at a long-skirted plum wool dress, subdued, exhorbitantly expensive.

"I'd never wear it," Lesje says; meaning, William never takes me anywhere I could wear it.

"Now here," says Marianne, moving to the next window, "you have your basic Elizabeth Schoenhof little black dress."

"Too goyish?" Lesje says, thinking Marianne is being derisive, and oddly delighted.

"Oh, no," Marianne says. "Look at the *cut*. Elizabeth Schoenhof isn't goyish, she's haute Wasp."

Lesje, deflated, asks what the difference is.

"Haute Wasp," says Marianne, "is when you don't have to give a piss. Haute Wasp is when you have this tatty carpet that looks like hell but cost a million bucks, and only a few people know it. Remember when the Queen picked up a chicken bone with her fingers and it was in all the papers, and suddenly it was *done?* That's haute Wasp."

Lesje feels she'll never be able to master nuances like these. William with his wines: full-bodied, bouquet. It all tastes like wine to her. Maybe Nate Schoenhof is haute Wasp, though somehow she doesn't think so. He's too hesitant, he talks too much, he looks around the room at the wrong moments. He probably doesn't even know what haute Wasp means.

Maybe Elizabeth doesn't either. Maybe this is part of being haute Wasp: you don't have to know.

"What about Chris?" she says. Surely the fact of Chris does not fit in with Marianne's definition.

"Chris?" says Marianne. "Chris was the chauffeur."

Thursday, December 23, 1976

ELIZABETH

Yes, I know I've suffered an unusual shock. I'm quite aware of that, I can feel the waves. I realize it was an act directed ostensibly at me though not really at me, childhood imprintings being what they are, though I can't say I know of any in his case that would account for it. He had a bad childhood but who didn't? I also realize that my reactions are normal under the circumstances and that he intended me to feel guilty and that I am not really guilty. Of that. I'm not sure whether or not I do feel guilty. I feel angry, from time to time; otherwise I feel devoid. I feel as though I'm leaking electricity. I know I'm not responsible and that there's little I could have done and that he might have killed me or Nate or the children instead of himself. I knew that at the time, and no, I did not phone the police or the mental hygiene authorities. They wouldn't have believed me. I know all these things.

I know I have to keep on living and I have no intention of doing otherwise. You don't have to worry about that. If I were going to take a carving knife to my wrists or do a swan dive off the Bloor Street Viaduct I'd have done it before now. I'm a mother if not exactly a wife and I take that seriously. I would never leave an image like that behind for my children. I've had that done to me and I didn't like it.

No, I don't want to discuss my mother, my father, my Auntie Muriel or my sister. I know quite a lot about them as well. I've already been down this particular yellow brick road a couple of times, and what I found out mostly was that there's no Wizard of Oz. My mother, my father, my aunt and my sister did not go away. Chris won't go away either.

I am an adult and I do not think I am merely the sum of my past. I can make choices and I suffer the consequences, though they aren't always the ones I foresaw. That doesn't mean I have to like it.

No thank you. I don't want pills to help me through. I don't wish to have my mood changed. I could describe this mood to you in detail but I'm not sure that would be of any benefit either to you or to myself.

Elizabeth sits on the grey bench in the Ossington subway station, black leather hands folded in her lap, feet in their boots placed neatly. Her tone, she knows, is slightly belligerent and she isn't sure why. The first time she ran through this conversation, sitting in her office that morning, she was totally calm. Having thus concluded that the psychiatrist Nate has so kindly decided she ought to see has nothing either to give her or to tell her, she phoned and canceled the appointment.

She's using the time she's freed to go home early. She will wrap Christmas presents, hiding the packages under the bed before the children get home from school. Already she knows the crackle of paper, the brightness of the ribbons, will be almost more than she can bear, those stars, blue and red and white, burning her eyes as if there's no atmosphere. It's the hope, the false promise of hope she can't tolerate. Everything is worse at Christmas; it always has been. But she'll get through it, she can depend on Nate to help in that, if in little else.

Perhaps this is what they're heading for: companionship, a thin arm extended, leaned on, two old people carefully descending from the front porch, one icy stair at a time. She'll make sure he takes his stomach pills and will monitor his intake of booze, he'll ask her to turn up her hearing aid and will read her amusing anecdotes from the daily papers. Military coups, massacres, that sort of thing. On weeknights they'll watch American sitcoms on television. They'll have photograph albums and when the children come over on Sundays with their own children these albums will be dredged out and they will all look at the photos, beaming; and seeing the picture of herself as she is today, this very instant, sitting here in the Ossington subway station waiting for the northbound bus, with the dim light filtering through the film of ash and oil on the plate glass windows, she will sense again this chasm opening in herself. Then they will have a lunch of creamed salmon on toast, with eggs grated on top, a dish suited to their limited budget. Nate will play with the grandchildren and she will do the dishes by herself in the kitchenette, feeling Chris's breath as usual on the back of her neck.

Almost better to think of herself alone, in a small apartment, with her bowls and a few plants. No, that would be worse. If Nate were with her, at least there would be something moving. Keep moving, they said to those almost frozen, those who had taken too many pills, those in shock. U-Haul, an Adventure in Moving. I want to be moved. Move me. *We are the numb. Long years ago/ We did this or that. And now we sit.*

The evening before, she knocked at the door of Nate's room, holding a pair of socks he'd dropped in the living room, presumably because they were wet. When he opened the door, he had no shirt on. Suddenly she, who hadn't wanted him to touch her for over two years, who'd found his long sparse body mildly repellant, who had chosen instead the thick, matted, richly veined flesh of Chris, who had rearranged time and space so that this torso she was now confronted with need never confront her, closeted as it was in an area clearly marked off from hers—she wanted him to wind his arms around her, string on bone but warm bone, press her, comfort and rock her. She wanted to say: Can anything be saved? Meaning this wreck. But he'd stepped back and she'd merely held out the socks, wearily, mutely, as usual.

Once she was always able to tell if he was in the house, whether she could actually hear him or not. Now she no longer can. He's absent more often now, and when he is there his presence is like light from a star that moved on thousands of light-years before: a phantom. He no longer, for instance, brings her cups of tea. They still give each other Christmas presents, though. The children would be disturbed if this ritual were omitted. She's finally bought him something for this year. It's a silver cigarette case. She thinks perversely of the contrast: the silver case emerging from his frayed pocket under the raveling sweater. Once he'd given her nightgowns, always a size too large, as if he thought her breasts were bigger than they were. Now it's books. On some neutral subject he assumes will interest her: antiques, pressed glass, quilts.

"Ready for Christmas?"

There's a man sitting beside Elizabeth. He's been sitting there for several minutes; she saw him as a brownish blur to the left, registered the shift as he crossed and recrossed his legs. Movement like rustlings in a hedge, furtive, almost not there. She turns her head, slightly, briefly, to look at him. He's wearing a brown topcoat, a little too small for him—it must pinch under the arms—and a brown hat. His eyes shine at her, brown also and small like raisins. His hands, gloveless, dark hair on the knuckles, rest on the thick suitcase he holds across his lap.

She smiles. A long time ago she learned to smile easily, graciously, it takes no effort. "Not quite. No one ever is, are they?"

The man nudges closer to her, his buttocks inching along the bench. She feels a slight pressure at her side.

"You look as if you're waiting for someone," he says.

"No," she says, "I'm not waiting for anyone. Only the bus."

"I think we must be neighbors," he says. "I'm sure I've seen you on the street."

"I don't think so," Elizabeth says.

"I'm sure I have. I wouldn't forget." He lowers his voice. "A woman like you."

Elizabeth shifts away from the pressure against her thigh. Her other thigh is now against the arm of the bench. She can always stand up. But he begins immediately to talk about real estate values. This is harmless enough, and Elizabeth knows something about it. They both bought around the same time, it seems, both experienced the tortures of renovation, though he's done his living-room floor in cork tile, a choice Elizabeth herself would not have made. He tells a story about his contractor, the lies, the failures to show up, the deficient wiring. Elizabeth relaxes, leaning back against the bench. He's ordinary enough, but it's a relief to talk with someone practical, someone who can accomplish things. Simple competence, feet on the ground. *Bedrock.*

The man has children, he says, three of them, and a wife. They discuss the local school. He likes to read, he tells her, but only nonfiction. Books about history, famous crimes, the world wars. He asks her what she thinks about the results of the Québec election. "They'll never pull it off," he says. "Too much debt."

"Probably," says Elizabeth, whose attention is wandering now that there's no threat.

"We could have a drink sometime," he says abruptly.

Elizabeth sits up. "I don't think . . ." she says.

"You wouldn't regret it," he says, his eyes shining. He leans towards her confidentially. Sweet brandy on his breath. "I know," he says. "I know what you want. You might not think so to look at me, but I know."

"Right now I don't want anything," Elizabeth says, realizing at once that this was false. What she wants is to want something.

"All right," says the man. "If you change your mind, let me know." He hands her a little card, which she holds in her gloved hand without looking at it. "The office number," he says.

"I'll do that," Elizabeth says, laughing, turning it into a joke. She can taste the brandy in his mouth, blue flame flickering over her tongue. She looks at the card. There's a name, two numbers, nothing more.

"What do you do?" she asks, clutching at work, the objective world.

"Here," the man says, unsnapping the clasps of his suitcase. "Take your pick. Have a souvenir." He lifts the lid. The suitcase is full of women's bikini briefs, samples: red, black, white, pink, mauve, trimmed with lace, sheer, embroidered, some with—she can see—split crotches.

"I do a lot of traveling," the man says mournfully. "Pushing the line. Airports. They're big customers, airports." He lifts a pair of black briefs with the word STOP embroidered on a hexagonal scrap of red satin. "A very popular item," he says, his voice switching to a salesman's insinuating baritone. He sticks his finger through the split crotch, wiggles it.

Elizabeth stands up. "There's my bus," she says lightly. His hand, tented in black nylon, clothed like a puppet in some woman's empty groin, is absurdly and at last, at last, exciting to her.

For an instant only. The man fades almost at once, flattens, greys.

"Thank you for the conversation," she says, feeling she should thank him for something.

He withdraws his hand, looks up at her sadly. "Do you think I'd do this," he says, "if I didn't have to?"

Thursday, December 23, 1976

NATE

When Nate is in the middle of his bath, soaping his long shankbones, Elizabeth opens the door and comes in without knocking. She closes the lid of the toilet and sits down on it, hunching forward, elbows on her dark-skirted knees. She wants to show him something she's bought as a Christmas present for Nancy. It's a small theatrical makeup kit; she got it at Malabar's, making a special trip. It has a few sticks of grease paint, some fake blood, and a couple of moustaches and pairs of eyebrows to match. Nancy will love it, Elizabeth says, and Nate knows she will. Elizabeth can always think up good presents for the children. He himself has to ask them what they want.

Elizabeth sitting on the toilet at right angles to his left shoulderblade makes him nervous. He has to turn his head to see her, whereas she can see most of him—naked, exposed—without making any effort. He's aware of the soap curds, the grey particles, the flecks of his own skin that litter the water. He scrubs his arms vigorously with the loofah, rough on the skin like a tiger's tongue. The loofah is his; he buys them at a little store on Bathurst that sells nothing but natural sponges; not one of those bath boutiques, but a grimy store, unadorned, that has the feel of raw materials. A small importer. Nate likes walking into this store, picking out his new sponge from the mounds of them that lie in heaps on the tiny counter. Himself, in aqua water, a knife between his teeth, cutting the raw sponge loose from coral rocks, making it to the surface gasping for breath, heaving the sponge overarm into the moored boat. Eyeball-to-eyeball combat with a giant squid, one tentacle cut loose, then another. Nothing to think about but getting free. Clouds of ink obscuring the water, round welts on his legs. Plunging the knife right in between its eyes.

Elizabeth doesn't like his loofahs. She says that because he doesn't take the time to rinse and dry them between baths, they get moldy. This is true, they do get moldy. She doesn't understand that if each loofah were allowed to continue forever, he'd be deprived of the pleasure of going to the little store for a new one.

When she opened the door she let in a draft. Nate pulls the plug and clambers out of the tub, a towel clutched to his groin, feeling like a stick man.

Now that he's standing up in this room that is obviously too small for both of them, he expects her to leave. But she shifts her knees towards the wall and asks, "Where are you off to?"

"How do you know I'm off to anywhere?" he says.

She smiles. More like herself, her old self; the self that is, like his, getting old. "You're taking a bath." She leans her chin on her interlaced fingers, looks up at him. That nymph-on-a-lilypad pose. He wraps his abdomen, tucking the towel in.

"I'm going to a party," he says. "A Christmas party."

"At Martha's?"

"How did you know?" He hasn't wanted to tell her; not that he has anything to hide. It continues to amaze him, the way she's able to keep track of his activities without even seeming to be interested.

"She invited me."

"Oh," he says. He might have known Martha would consider it appropriate to invite Elizabeth. He folds his arms across his chest; ordinarily he would use her Arrid Extra Dry to roller his armpits, but he can't do that with her in the bathroom. He can feel his mouth sagging downwards.

"Don't look so devastated," she says. "I'm not going."

"That's all over, you know," he says, feeling he has no moral obligation to tell her, telling her anyway.

"I know," she says. "I've been hearing quite a lot about it. She phones me at the office."

This is something Nate has always resented: they talk to each other, about him, behind his back. It was Elizabeth who started it. She'd invited Martha to lunch early on; to explain, she'd said, to get things clear. Martha had complained to him first, but she'd gone. "Why not be friendly?" Elizabeth said. "It's not as though I'm the jealous wife. I hardly have the right to be." She laughed softly, that furred laugh that had at first entranced him. "We might as well behave like reasonable adults."

"What did you talk about?" Nate asked Martha afterwards.

"You," she said.

"What about me?"

"About who owns you," Martha said. "We figured it out that Elizabeth really owns you, but I get fucking privileges one night a week."

"I don't believe Elizabeth would say a thing like that," Nate said.

"No," Martha said. "You're right, she wouldn't. She's too goddamned discreet. Let's say she just *gave me to understand*. She might think it, but the only one who'd ever say it is me. Old garbage-mouth."

Nate wanted to tell Martha not to demean herself, but he knew she didn't really feel she was demeaning herself. She saw it as saying what she thought. She conceived of herself as down-to-earth and honest, and of Nate and Elizabeth as hypocrites who evaded the issues. But she only said what she thought to Nate; never to Elizabeth.

By this time Nate no longer wants to know what they say to each other during those office phone calls. He doesn't want to go to Martha's party either, but he feels he ought to. His presence is supposed to establish the fact that they can still be friends. This is what Martha said to him on the phone. He doesn't much want to be friends with her, but he thinks he should want to. He wants to be kind and as gentle as possible. He won't stay long, he'll just put in an appearance, make a gesture, cast his shadow on the wall.

"She sounded all right to me," Nate says, too defensively. "When she asked me."

"Don't fool yourself," Elizabeth says. It's one of her axioms that Nate is always fooling himself. She puts her hands behind her on the toilet seat and leans back, which throws her breasts up and out. Is this an invitation, can it be possible? Nate refuses to believe it. He turns his head quickly away, scowls at himself in the mirror.

"I'll be back around ten," he says.

"I expect you will," Elizabeth says. "You're not too popular in that quarter, you know."

You know. Always meaning that he doesn't. Both of them do that: the constant hints that there are things he doesn't know, important things he's missed and that they, with their finer perceptions, can pick up every time.

Elizabeth stands up, brushes past him, picks up his loofah from where he's left it lying in the bathtub, squeezes it out.

"Take care of yourself," she says. She walks out of the bathroom, carrying the box of false moustaches.

Martha has made a large bowl of eggnog. It sits on her dining room table along with the bottles of Scotch and rye, the mixes, the ice in a bucket. A red paper accordion bell is suspended over the table. Nate bumps it with his head as he straightens up with his glass of Scotch. If he wants eggs he'll boil them. He always likes to know exactly what he's drinking.

Martha is wearing a long dress, some synthetic material, red, to match the bell. The neckline is too wide; it makes her shoulders look even broader than they are. Nate hasn't seen that dress before. One of her bare arms is hooked through the arm of the man standing beside her. She looks up into his face, talking, smiling. Apart from greeting him she's ignored Nate so far. The new man is pale blond, shorter than Nate, with a businessman's prim little paunch already beginning under the vest of his three-piece suit.

Nate knows a few of the people, leftovers from his earlier life. A couple of the receptionists and legal secretaries, two or three of the men who joined the firm around the same time he did. Someone slaps his shoulder.

"Nate. How's it going?" Paul Callaghan, one-time rival, now patronizing. "Still whittling away?"

"Pretty good," Nate says.

"You're probably smarter than all of us," Paul says. "Taking it easy. No heart attacks at forty for you." He floats past Nate, already smiling at someone else.

Nate is talking with a girl in a white dress. He's never seen her before, though she claims to have met him at one of Martha's parties, two years ago, she says. She's telling Nate about her job. She makes plastic models of Holstein cows which are sold to breeders and dealers. The cows have to be made exactly to scale, perfect in every detail. She's hoping to go into painted portraits of individual cows, for which she could get more money. She asks Nate what his sign is.

Nate knows he should leave the party. He's done his duty.

But the girl seizes his hand and bends over his palm, squinting at his life line. He can see a short distance down the front of her dress. He watches this pinched landscape idly. He isn't very good at casual encounters.

Martha is there, right beside his ear. She wants to have a word with him, she says. She takes his other hand and he allows himself to be led from the living room, down the hall into the bedroom. Coats are piled on the bed.

"You're disgusting," Martha says. "You make me want to puke."

Nate blinks at her, bending his head towards her as if this will help him to understand. Martha punches him in the face, then begins kicking him in the shins. She's hampered by the long skirt of her dress, so she slugs him, aiming for the belly, hitting him in the rib cage. Nate catches her arms and holds her against him. Now she's crying. He could throw her onto the bed, roll her up in coats to hold her still, then try to find out what he's done.

"What did I do?" he says.

"Making up to her at my party, right in front of me. You always try to humiliate me," Martha says, her voice coming in spurts. "You know what? You succeed."

"I wasn't," Nate says. "We were talking about plastic cows."

"You just don't know how it feels to be left," Martha says. Nate loosens his grip. Martha steps back, snatches a Kleenex from the night table and blots her face. "Why don't you try feeling something for a change?"

The new man's head appears in the doorway, withdraws, reappears. "Am I interrupting something?" he says.

"Yes," Martha says rudely.

"I was just leaving," Nate says. He roots among the coats, fur and tweed, looking for his pea jacket.

"It's in the hall closet," Martha says. "I guess you know where that is."

Because of the snow, Nate hasn't brought his bicycle. It's five blocks to the subway station but he's glad, he wants to walk. His right eyebrow where Martha hit him is beginning to hurt. Is the skin cut? She was wearing a ring. What bothers him isn't the pain but the wise look Elizabeth will give him.

He's only gone half a block before he hears Martha behind him.

"Nate. Stop."

He turns. She's running, slipping towards him in her gold shoes, her long red dress, no coat. Smiling, gleeful, her eyes brilliant. "I just took all the pills in the bathroom cabinet," she says. "Sixty-two aspirin with codeine, twenty-four Valiums. I thought you might like to say good-bye."

"That was stupid, Martha," Nate says. "Did you really?"

"Wait and see," she says, laughing. "Wait till five in the morning when you get to inspect the body. Hell, you can cart me away to that cellar of yours. You can shellac me. I won't bother you with demands any more."

The man in the three-piece suit is picking his way down Martha's steps. "Martha," he calls, slightly peevish, as if calling a runaway cat.

"Martha says she took all the pills in the bathroom," Nate says to him.

"Well, she was just in there. Why would she do that?" the new man asks Nate.

"Stop discussing me as if I'm a *thing*," Martha says. She's swaying a little. Nate takes off his pea jacket and hands it to her. "Here," he says.

"I don't need that," Martha says. She begins to cry again.

"We'll have to take her down to the hospital," Nate says. He's familiar with the procedure, he's been through it with the kids. Mothballs, baby aspirins, Elizabeth's birth control pills.

"I'm not going," Martha sobs. "I want to die."

"We can take my car," the new man says. "It's in the driveway." Nate grips Martha under the arms. She goes limp. He begins to drag her towards the new man's car, which is new also, a dark blue Torino. One of her shoes comes off and the new man picks it up and carries it along behind them, like a trophy in some kind of sports parade or religious procession.

"Give me my goddamned shoe," Martha says when they're in the car. She buckles the shoe on, then checks her hair in the rear-view mirror. The new man is driving; Nate sits in the back with Martha, to keep her from, as the new man says, "doing anything." By the time they reach Emergency Admissions at the Toronto General she seems quite cheerful.

"You can't make me go in there," she says to Nate.

"You can walk in or be dragged in," he tells her. "Did you really take those pills?"

"Guess," she says. "You're so good at female psychology. You figure it out." But she walks in between them with no more protest.

She lets them tell the Admissions nurse all about the pills. Nate explains that they don't know whether she's really taken them or not.

"Did you check the bottles?" the nurse says. "Were they empty?"

They didn't think to look for bottles, Nate says. They were in too much of a hurry.

"Actually this is all a joke," Martha says. "They've been drinking. It's the Christmas spirit, they thought it would be fun to cart me down here and make me get my stomach pumped out."

The nurse hesitates, looking severely from Nate to the new man. "You can smell the liquor," Martha says. "They aren't like this except when they drink. See, they've been fighting."

The nurse squints at Nate's swelling eye. "Is this true?" she says.

"They used force," Martha says. "You can see the finger-marks on my arms. Do I seem to you like someone who's just swallowed a bottle of pills?" She stretches out her bare arms. "Would you like to see me walk a straight line?"

Tuesday, December 28, 1976

LESJE

Lesje joins the queue in front of the cashier at the liquor store. The time is past when they'd ask to see her birth certificate, but she still gets the same cold feeling. Whenever she has to present a document proving she is who she is, she's convinced they'll find something out of order or that it will have someone else's name stamped on it. The worst that ever happens is that they mispronounce her name, giving her the look that says, we thought you were one of us but now we can tell you aren't.

She's buying a bottle of wine to celebrate the return of William, which will take place this evening. William is in London, Ontario, celebrating Christmas with his family. Impossible, of course (Of course! She agrees!) for her to have gone with him. Last year this separation between them seemed like a conspiracy, both of them giggling over the puritanism, xenophobia and general dingy-mindedness of their respective families. This year it seems like a betrayal.

Not that she could have gone with him, even if invited. She was expected to go to her parents' house for Christmas dinner, and dutifully she'd gone, as she did every year. How can she deprive them of their only daughter, their only child, they who have deprived themselves of whole platoons of sisters, brothers, uncles, aunts, cousins and second cousins, all, it's understood, for her sake?

Her parents' house is neither far enough north to be impressive, like the aunts' houses, nor far enough south to be quaint, like the grandmothers'. Her mother's brothers did well in real estate, her father's sister married into a china shop. Her parents began the trek north but got stuck halfway up, on a nondescript street south of St. Clair. It was as if all their desire for transformation and change had gone into one act, their marriage to each other. They had none left over for two-car garages.

Her father doesn't possess that ferocious instinct for business, or is it survival, which is supposed to be Jewish; which had impelled her grandfather from door to door, buying cast-offs; and which once gave her grandmother six stitches in the head, defending her front-parlor variety store against a young man with an iron bar. *Turn your back, they steal you blind. Not the Chinese kids though. Them you don't have to watch.* Lesje's father rolled to his present modest eminence of color television and a secondhand Chev on used fur coats, on bubble gum and jawbreakers, two for a penny and the pennies carefully saved. And was he grateful? No. Married a *shiksa*, and of the worst kind too. (Like Lesje.)

He owned a dress business, true, but reluctantly: his mother almost forced him into it after his father died. *Little Nell Dresses,* it's now called; once it was called *Tinker Bell.* Her grandfather once had a partner who got these names out of books he'd read. The dresses are for small girls; Lesje grew up wearing them and resenting them. For her, luxury was not the piqué and lace collars of the Little Nell line, but the jeans and T-shirts the other girls wore.

Little Nell neither expands nor collapses. It doesn't even make the dresses; they're made in Montreal. It merely distributes them. It's just there, like her father; and like him the methods of its existence are unknown to her.

She sat at the table covered with her mother's good linen cloth, watching her father with a certain sadness as he swallowed down the turkey and cranberry sauce, the mashed potatoes, the mince pie dictated by a religious holiday he would never have observed in the natural course of events and which her mother would have observed fourteen days later. At Christmas they always ate Canadian food. A capitulation, that turkey; or perhaps one more piece of neutral ground for both of them. Every year they chewed their way through this dinner, proving something or other. Elsewhere, one set of cousins was recovering from Hanukkah, another set was getting ready to sing the songs and dance the dances they'd learned at Ukrainian summer camp. Lesje's mother, in the kitchen putting hard sauce on the slabs of mince pie, sniffled with quiet stoicism. This too happened every year.

She could never ask William to this meal or even to this house. Don't irritate your father, her mother said. I know young people are different now but he still thinks of you as his little girl. You think he doesn't know you're living with some-one? He knows. He just doesn't want to know.

"How's the bone business?" her father asked, the usual joke, his way of reconciling himself to her choice of job.

"Really great," she told him. He didn't see the attraction for a pretty girl, crawling around in the dirt, scratching for buried bones, like a dog. After first-year university, he'd asked her what she was going to be. A teacher, maybe?

"A paleontologist," she'd said.

A pause. "So what are you going to do for a living?"

Her Ukrainian grandmother had wanted her to be an air-line stewardess. Her Jewish grandmother had wanted her to be a lawyer and also to marry, another lawyer if possible. Her father wanted her to make the most of herself. Her mother wanted her to be happy.

Lesje is uncertain about her choice of wine, since William fancies himself a connoisseur. He tends to condescend. He once sent back a bottle in a restaurant, and Lesje thought, He's been waiting a long time for the chance to do that. She dug out from the garbage the bottle they shared the night before he left and copied down the name on the label. He chose that one. If he sneers, she'll tell him. But this thought fails to cheer her.

She sees Nate Schoenhof in front of her in the line. Her breath jumps; suddenly her curiosity is with her again. For a month and a half he's been invisible, she hasn't even seen him waiting for Elizabeth at the Museum. For a time she felt, not rejected exactly, but disappointed, as if she'd been watching a movie and the projector had broken down partway through. Now she feels as if she has things to ask him. She says his name, but he doesn't hear her, and she can't step out of the line to touch his sleeve. But the man behind him notices and pokes him for her. He turns, sees her.

He waits for her at the door. "I'll walk you back," he says.

They set off, carrying their bottles. It's dark now and the snow is still falling, clumps of wet flakes drifting windlessly down, the air moist, the sidewalk mushy underfoot. It isn't cold. Nate turns onto a side street and Lesje follows, even though she knows it's out of her way, this is east and she should be going south. Perhaps he's forgotten where she lives.

She asks him if he had a nice Christmas. Terrible, he says, how about hers?

"Pretty awful," she says. They laugh a little. It's hard for her to say how bad it was or why it was that bad. "I hate it," she says. "I always have."

"I didn't used to," he says. "When I was a kid I kept thinking something magic would happen; something I didn't expect."

"And did it?" she says.

"No," he says. He thinks for a minute. "Once I really wanted a machine gun. My mother absolutely refused. She said it was an immoral toy, why did I want to play at killing people, there was enough cruelty in the world and so on. But there it was on Christmas morning, under the tree."

"Wasn't that magic?"

"No," Nate says. "By then I didn't want it."

"Do your kids like it?" Lesje says.

Nate says he thinks so. They liked it better when they were too young to know what presents were, when they just crawled around in the paper.

Lesje notices that one of his eyes is puffy and dark, with what looks like a healing cut above it. She doesn't want to ask what's wrong with it—it seems too personal—but she does anyway.

He stops, looks at her mournfully. "Someone hit me," he says.

"I thought you were going to say you bumped into a door," Lesje says. "Were you in a fight?"

"Not as far as I was concerned," he says. "A woman hit me."

Lesje can't think of a good thing to say, so says nothing. Why would anyone want to hit such a man?

"It wasn't Elizabeth," Nate says. "She'd never hit anyone physically. It was someone else. I guess she had to."

He's letting her in, letting her listen in. She isn't sure she wants this. Nevertheless her hand moves up, drawn to his mysterious wound, touches his forehead. She sees her purple-and white-striped mitten silhouetted against his skin.

He stops, looks down at her, blinking, as if he can't believe what she's just done. Is he about to cry? No. He's making a gift of himself, handing himself over to her, mutely. Here I am. You may be able to do something with me. She realizes that this is what she's been expecting from him, ever since his first phone call.

"It isn't fair," he says.

Lesje doesn't know what he's talking about. She opens her arms. One of his arms goes around her; in the other he holds his paper bag. Her wine bottle falls to the sidewalk, the sound muffled by the snow. As they're walking away she remembers it and turns, expecting to see it cracked, the snow around it red; it's too late to go back for another. But it's intact, and suddenly she feels very lucky.

Part Three

Monday, January 3, 1977

ELIZABETH

It's the third of January. Elizabeth is sitting on the slippery
rose-colored chesterfield in her Auntie Muriel's parlor, which
is truly a parlor and not a living room. It's a parlor because of
the spider and the fly. It isn't a living room, because Auntie
Muriel cannot be said to live.

Auntie Muriel is both the spider and the fly, the sucker-out
of life juice and the empty husk. Once she was just the spider
and Uncle Teddy was the fly, but ever since Uncle Teddy's
death Auntie Muriel has taken over both roles. Elizabeth isn't
even all that sure Uncle Teddy is really dead. Auntie Muriel
probably has him in a trunk somewhere in the attic, webbed
in old écru lace tablecloths, paralyzed but still alive. She goes
up there for a little nip now and then. Auntie Muriel, so pal-
pably not an auntie. Nothing diminutive about Auntie Muriel.

Elizabeth knows her view of Auntie Muriel is exaggerated
and uncharitable. Such ogres don't exist. Nevertheless, there is
Auntie Muriel, sitting opposite her, large as life, the solid bulk
of her torso encased in two-way stretch elastic with plastic
boning, the jersey of her mild blue beautifully tailored dress
stretching across her soccer-player's thighs, her eyes, like two
pieces of gravel, cold and unreflecting, directed at Elizabeth,
taking in, Elizabeth knows, every disreputable detail of her
own appearance. Her hair (too long, too loose), her sweater
(should have been a dress), the absence of a lipstick-and-
powder crust over her face, all, all are wrong. Auntie Muriel
is gratified by this wrongness.

She's just a friendless old lady, Elizabeth thinks, trying out
this excuse. But why? Why is she friendless? Elizabeth is
aware of the way she ought to be thinking. She's read magazines and books, she knows the lines. Auntie Muriel was
thwarted in youth. She had a domineering father who stunted
her and wouldn't let her go to college because college was for

105

boys. She was forced to embroider (embroider! with those stumpy fingers!), a torture she later imposed on Elizabeth, who however turned out to be somewhat better at it and whose cutwork tea cloth with pink French knots still lies folded in a trunk in Elizabeth's closet, testament to her skill. Auntie Muriel had a strong personality and a good mind and she was not pretty, and patriarchal society punished her. These things are all true.

Nevertheless, Elizabeth can forgive Auntie Muriel only in theory. Given her own sufferings, why has Auntie Muriel chosen to transfer them, whenever possible, to others? Elizabeth can still see herself, at the age of twelve, writhing on her bed with her first menstrual cramps, nauseated with pain, Auntie Muriel standing over her holding the bottle of aspirin out of reach. *This is God's punishment.* She never said for what. In Elizabeth's view, no mere career would ever have satisfied Auntie Muriel's lust for slaughter. She should have been sent into the Army. Only in a tank, helmeted, gauntleted, her guns directed at something, anything at all, would she have been happy.

So why is Elizabeth here? More importantly: why has she brought the children? Exposed them to this malignancy. They sit beside her, subdued, wearing the white knee socks and Mary Janes they won't willingly put on for any other occasion, little mouths carefully shut, hair clipped back from their faces with tight barrettes, hands in their laps, goggling at Auntie Muriel as if she's a wonder, a mammoth or a mastodon, say, like the ones at the Museum, recently dug out of an iceberg.

In fact the children like to visit Auntie Muriel. They like her big house, the silence, the polished woodwork, the Persian carpets. They like the little crustless sandwiches Auntie Muriel sets out, even though they carefully take only one each; and the grand piano, though they aren't allowed to touch it. When Uncle Teddy was alive, he used to give them quarters. Not so Auntie Muriel. When Elizabeth's own mother had finally succeeded in frying herself to a crisp in that last tiny room on Shuter Street, setting fire to her mattress with a dropped cigarette and too drunk to know she was burning, Auntie Muriel drew up a list after the funeral. It contained all the items she'd ever lent, given or donated. *One light bulb, 60 watt, over the sink. One blue plastic shower curtain. One paisley Viyella housecoat. One Wedgwood sugar bowl.* Miserly gifts and chipped discards. Auntie Muriel wanted them back.

They smelled the smoke and broke the door down and got her out of there, but she already had third-degree burns on half her body. She lived for a week in hospital, lying on the mattress wet with drugs and the body's futile defenses, white cells leaking into the sheets. Who knows what she was remembering, whether she even knew who I was? She hadn't seen me for ten years, but she must have had some dim idea she'd once had daughters. She let me hold her hand, the left one that wasn't burned, and I thought: She looks like the moon, the half-moon. One side still shining.

Elizabeth has always considered Auntie Muriel responsible for this death. As for others, her sister's, for instance. Nevertheless, she is here. Partly because she's a snob, which she admits. She wants the children to see that she grew up in a house with a dinner gong and eight bedrooms, not in one like the diminutive row-house (though charming, and what a lot she's done with it) where they now live. Also, Auntie Muriel is their only close living relative. Elizabeth feels that this is because Auntie Muriel has either killed or driven away all the others, but never mind. She is their roots, their root, their twisted diseased old root. Other people, such as those in Buffalo, think that Toronto has changed, shaken off its blue-law ways, become chic and liberal, but Elizabeth knows it hasn't. At its core, where there should be a heart, there is only Auntie Muriel.

She has exiled Auntie Muriel from Christmas, having said no, finally, four years ago, to the dark table with six insertable leaves, the symmetrically arranged crystal dishes of pickle and cranberry sauce, the linen tablecloth, the silver napkin rings. Nate refused to come with her any more; that was why. He said he wanted to enjoy his children and his dinner and there was no point going to Auntie Muriel's if Elizabeth was going to collapse into bed with a headache as soon as they got home. Once, in 1971, she'd thrown up onto a snowbank on the way back: turkey, cranberry sauce, Auntie Muriel's selection of relishes, the works.

At first she'd resented Nate's refusal, interpreted it as a lack of support. But he'd been right, he is right. She should not be here.

Auntie Muriel is continuing her monologue, which is directed ostensibly at the children but actually at Elizabeth. They should never forget, she says, that their grandfather owned half of Galt. *Great-grandfather, Guelph,* Elizabeth thinks. Perhaps Auntie Muriel is going senile at last; or perhaps this family mythology is only a mythology after all, and, like any oral history, its details are undergoing mutation. Auntie Muriel does not correct herself, though. She has never been known to correct herself. She is now saying that Toronto is not what it was, and for that matter neither is the entire country. The Pakis are taking over the city and the French are taking over the government. A shopgirl (implied: foreign, dark-skinned, accented, or all three) was rude to her in Creeds just last Wednesday. And as for Creeds, it has gone completely downhill. They used to put fur coats in the windows and now they put belly dancers. She supposes that Elizabeth, with her attitudes (implied: degenerate), thinks this is all right, but she herself will never get used to it. She is old, she remembers better things.

Elizabeth doesn't know which is worse, this conversation or last year's, in which Auntie Muriel subjected the children to an account of the trials and tribulations she'd undergone in her attempt to gather the entire family together in one corner of the Mount Pleasant Cemetery. In the story, she'd made no distinction between the living and the dead, referring to her own plot as though she herself were already in it and to the others as if they were guests at a picnic she was throwing. Uncle Teddy was already in the right place, of course, but Elizabeth's mother and sister had to be moved from St. James and her grandfather from the old Necropolis. As for Elizabeth's father, there was no telling where he'd wandered off to.

Elizabeth could probably have interfered with these operations if she wanted to, but she didn't have the strength. She knew what Auntie Muriel was like when thwarted. If Auntie Muriel wanted to play chess with her dead relatives, let her. Luckily they were all in urns rather than coffins. They had no idea, Auntie Muriel said, how cheeky certain lawyers and cemetery supervisors could be. Of course these days a lot of them had foreign accents. She'd then described an intricate series of real estate dealings that seemed to concern the trading-off of one plot in exchange for another. Her ultimate plan was to acquire a large block of holdings and then exchange it for a mausoleum. Elizabeth refrained from asking whether or not Auntie Muriel had reserved a spot for her.

Going home in the taxi, Nancy says, "She's funny."

This view of Auntie Muriel has never occurred to Elizabeth before. Funny in what way, she wants to know.

"She says funny things."

And Elizabeth realizes that, for them, this is all Auntie Muriel is: a curiosity. They like going to see her for the same reason they like going to the Museum. She cannot touch them or harm them, they are out of her reach. She can touch and harm only Elizabeth. Because Auntie Muriel once had all power over her, she will always have some. Elizabeth is an adult in much of her life, but when she's with Auntie Muriel she is still part child. Part prisoner, part orphan, part cripple, part insane; Auntie Muriel the implacable wardress.

She goes to visit her, then, out of defiance. Look, I've grown up. I walk on two legs, unsteadily maybe, but you haven't got me into one of those urns of yours, not yet, I live my life despite you and I will continue to live it. And see, these are my children. Look how beautiful, how intelligent, how normal they are. You never had children. You can't touch them. I won't let you.

Saturday, January 15, 1977

LESJE

Lesje is doing something seedy. If someone, one of her friends, Marianne for instance, was doing the same thing and told her about it, she would think: seedy. Or even tacky. Very tacky, to be having an affair with a married man, a married man with two children. Married men with children are proverbially tacky, with their sad stories, their furtive lusts and petty evasions. Tackier still to be doing it in a hotel, of necessity a comparatively tacky hotel, since Nate is, as he says, a little broke. Lesje hasn't offered to pay the hotel bill herself. Once, long ago, her women's group might have sneered at this reluctance, but there is a limit.

Lesje doesn't feel tacky. She isn't sure whether Nate does or not. He's sitting in one of the chairs (there are two, both cheap Danish Modern with frayed corners, to match the blue frayed bedspread which is as yet undisturbed), telling her how terrible he feels that they have to be in this hotel instead of somewhere else. The somewhere his tone implies is not another, more acceptable hotel. It's a summer field, a deserted sun-warmed beach, a wooded knoll with breezes.

Lesje doesn't mind the hotel, even though the hum from the air conditioner is beginning to get to her. It's spewing out thick hot air which smells of upholstery and cigar butts, and they haven't been able to find the switch that turns it off. If this hotel had been a choice, she'd feel differently about it, but it's a necessity. The can't go to Lesje's apartment because of William, who was out when Lesje left but who may reappear at any moment, to find the note Lesje has thoughtfully propped on the card table: *Back at 6:00*. They can't go to Nate's, ever, unless Lesje takes time off work during the week. She works the same hours Elizabeth does, though Elizabeth probably has more flexibility. But today is Saturday and

Elizabeth is at home. Not to mention the children. Nate hasn't mentioned the children, but even so he's managed to convey to Lesje that although he respects her, admires her and desires her, to his children she represents an evil from which he must protect them.

Hence this afternoon hotel. They've come to it by subway, since neither of them owns a car. This fact also rules out necking on side streets, which is what they should be doing at this preliminary stage, in Lesje's opinion. They have in fact necked on side streets, but it's been uncomfortable: feet freezing in slush, passing cars splattering them with brown sludge, arms hugging the bolster shapes of each others' winter coats. But no groping in the front seat.

Lesje considers groping in the front seat almost an essential. The only other affairs she's had have been with William, champion groper, and before him a geologist in fourth-year university who even then, in 1970, had a crew cut. Neither of these affairs was exactly romantic; both had been based on mutual interests, of a sort. It was hard for Lesje to find men who were as monomaniacal about their subjects as she was about hers. They existed, but they tended to go out with Home Economics types. After a day of pondering surds and pingoes they wanted to put their feet up and eat grated carrot and marshmallow salads. They didn't want to talk about Megalosaurus tibias or whether the pterosaurs had three-chambered or four-chambered hearts, which was what she wanted to talk about. The geologist had been fine; they could compromise on rock strata. They went on hikes with their little picks and kits, and chipped samples off cliffs; then they ate jelly sandwiches and copulated in a friendly way behind clumps of goldenrod and thistles. She found this pleasurable but not extremely so. She still has a collection of rock chips left over from this relationship; looking at it does not fill her with bitterness. He was a nice boy but she wasn't in love with him. She is not exactly a paradigm of modish chic, she knows that, but she could never quite fall in love with a man who says "wow."

As for William, what they have in common is an interest in extinction. She confines it to dinosaurs, however. William applies it to everything. Except cockroaches; a cockroach has been found living in a nuclear reactor. The next age, according to William, will be the age of the insects. On most days he's quite cheerful about this.

Lesje isn't sure what she means by *in love*. Once she thought she was in love with William, since it upset her that he did not ask her to marry him. But recently she's begun to question this. At first she welcomed the relative simplicity, even the bareness, of their life together. They were both committed to their jobs, and they had, it seemed, easily met expectations and only minor areas of friction. But Nate has changed things, he has changed William. What was once a wholesome absence of complications is now an embarrassing lack of complexity. For instance, William would have lunged as soon as they were inside the door. Not so Nate.

They sit on either side of the large double bed which looms like fate in the center of the room, each with a cigarette, drinking out of the hotel glasses which contain Scotch from Nate's pocket flask mixed with tap water. Gazing across the bed as if it's a fathomless gulf, while Nate apologizes, Lesje listens, veiling her face with her hand, smoke making her squint. Nate doesn't want just an affair, he says. Lesje is touched by this; she doesn't think to ask what he does want. William has never been at such pains to explain himself.

Lesje feels that something momentous is about to take place. Her life is about to change: things will not be as they have been before. The walls of the hotel, patterned with greenish lozenges, are dissolving, she is moving through the open air, no longer snow-filled and tinged with exhaust fumes but clean and sunny; on the horizon there's the glimmer of water. Why then doesn't Nate stub out his cigarette, stand up, take her in his arms? Now that he has her in this tacky bedroom.

But instead he pours himself another drink and continues to explain. He wants everything to be clear at the beginning. He doesn't want Lesje to think she's breaking up a marriage. As she no doubt knows, Elizabeth has had other lovers, the most recent of whom was Chris. Elizabeth has never made any secret of that. She thinks of Nate as the father of her children but not as her husband. They haven't lived together, he means slept together, for several years, he isn't sure how many. They've stayed in the same house together because of the children. Neither of them can stand the thought of living apart from the children. So naturally Elizabeth will have no objection to his doing what Lesje wishes he would hurry up and do.

The mention of Elizabeth startles Lesje, who realizes that she hasn't been thinking about her at all. She ought to be thinking about her. You don't just stroll into another woman's life and take over her husband. Everyone in the women's group agreed, in theory at least, on the reprehensibility of such behavior, although they also agreed that married people should not be viewed as each other's property but as living, growing organisms. What it boiled down to was that man-stealing was out but personal growth was commendable. You had to have the right attitude and be honest with yourself. These convolutions had discouraged Lesje; she hadn't understood why so much time was being spent on them. But at that point she'd never been in such a situation, and now she is.

She certainly doesn't want to play Other Woman in some conventional, boring triangle. She doesn't feel like an other woman; she isn't wheedling or devious, she doesn't wear negligées or paint her toenails. William may think she's exotic, but she isn't really; she's straightforward, narrow and unadorned, a scientist; not a web-spinner, expert at the entrapment of husbands. But Nate no longer seems like Elizabeth's husband. His family is surely external to him; in himself he's single, a free agent. And Elizabeth is therefore not the wife of Nate, she isn't a wife at all. Instead she's a widow, Chris's widow if anyone's, moving unpaired and grieving down an autumn avenue, leaves from the over-arching trees falling on her faintly disheveled hair. Lesje consigns her to this mournfully romantic picture, frames her, and then forgets about her.

William is another matter. William will mind; he will definitely mind in one way or another. But Lesje doesn't intend to tell him about this, at least not yet. Nate has implied that although Elizabeth would give the seal of approval to what he's doing and may even be pleased for him, since in a way they are good friends, now is not the right time to tell her. Elizabeth has been making an adjustment, not as quick an adjustment as he'd like to see but definitely an adjustment. He wants her to finish doing that before he gives her something new that she has to adjust to. It has something to do with the children.

So if Nate is going to protect Elizabeth and the children from Lesje, Lesje is entitled to protect William from Nate. She feels tender towards William when she considers his need for protection. He's never needed it before. But now she reflects upon the unconscious nape of his neck, the vulnerability of the hollow at the angle of his collarbone, his jugular veins, so perilously close to the skin, his inability to tan instead of burn, the wax in his ears unseen by him, his childlike pomposity. She has no desire to hurt William.

Nate puts down his glass, grinds his cigarette into the hotel ashtray. He's come to the end of ethics. He negotiates the perimeter of the blue bed, walks to Lesje, kneels in front of her where she sits in her Danish Modern chair. He takes her hand away from her mouth, kisses her. She has never been touched with such gentleness. William's style has a lot of adolescent roughhouse, she now realizes, and the geologist was always in a hurry. Nate isn't in a hurry. They've been here two hours and she still has all her clothes on.

He picks her up, places her on the bed, lies down beside her. He kisses her again, tentatively, lingering. Then he asks what time it is. He himself has no watch. Lesje tells him it's five-thirty. He sits up. Lesje is beginning to feel slightly unattractive. Are her teeth too large, is that it?

"I have to phone home," he says. "I'm supposed to be taking the kids to dinner at my mother's."

He lifts the telephone from the table and dials. The cord trails across Lesje's chest. "Hello, love," he says, and Lesje knows it's Elizabeth. "Just checking in. I'll pick them up at six, okay?"

The words "home," "love," and "mother" have disturbed Lesje. A vacuum forms around her heart, spreads; it's as if she doesn't exist. When Nate puts down the phone, she begins to cry. He folds his arms around her, soothing her, smoothing her hair. "There's lots of time, love," he says. "Next time will be better."

Don't call me that, she wants to say. She sits on the bed, feet over the side, hands dangling from her wrists, while Nate gets their coats, puts his own on, holds hers out for her. She wants to be the one going to dinner with him. To his mother's. She doesn't want to stay here on the blue bed alone, or walk out into the street alone, or go back to her apartment where she will also be alone whether William is there or not. She wants to pull Nate back onto the bed with her. She doesn't believe there is lots of time. There is no time, surely she will never see him again. She doesn't understand why her heart is beating so painfully, gulping for oxygen in the blackness of this outer space. He's taking something away from her. If he loves her, why has she been exiled?

NATE

Jackass, Nate whispers. Ninny. Fraud. He's reading the editorial in *The Globe and Mail*, and he usually says such things while doing this, but right now he means himself. *Idiot.*

He sees himself hunched forward on the hotel room chair, raving about his scruples while Lesje sits across the room from him, unattainable, shining like a cresent moon. He doesn't know why he didn't want to, couldn't. He was afraid. He doesn't want to hurt her, that's it. But she was hurt anyway. Why did she cry?

His hands are still shaking. Luckily there's a drink left in his pocket flask. He slides it out from beneath his sweater, gulps quickly, then lights a cigarette to hide the smell. His mother, virtuous woman, does not drink. She doesn't smoke either, but Nate knows which is lower on her point system of moral crimes. Sometimes she buys beer for him but she draws the line at spirits. Poisoning the system.

The children are out in the tiny kitchen with her, sitting up on the counter, watching her mash the potatoes. She does this by hand; she doesn't have an electric mixer. She beats eggs by hand, whips cream by hand. One of his earliest memories of his mother is of her elbow, whirling around like a strange fleshy wind machine. Her television set is black and white and even more primitive than his. She wears aprons, printed ones with bibs.

From the cellar below him the pathos of his childhood rises to engulf him: down there are his baseball glove, the leather cracked, three pairs of outgrown running shoes, his skates, his goalie pads, carefully embalmed in trunks. Though she gives away almost everything else, his mother keeps these objects as if they're relics, as if he's already dead. In fairness Nate has to admit that if she hadn't, he might have kept them himself. The goalie pads, anyway.

He's read that goalies get ulcers; it figures. He wasn't heavy enough to play anything else, he didn't have the weight to check. He remembers the anxiety, everyone expecting him to hurl himself in front of a frozen rubber bullet traveling at the speed of light; the despair when he missed. But he loved it. It was pure: you won or you lost and it was obvious which. When he said this to Elizabeth she thought it was childish. Her own concepts of winning and losing are greyer and more snarled. Is this because she's female? But his children understand it, so far; Nancy, anyway.

He can see the children over the top of his *Globe and Mail*, their small heads framed by his mother's red-starred map of world-wide civil-rights violations. Beside it there's a new poster which reads: ONE FLASH AND YOU'RE ASH. His mother has added the abolition of nuclear energy to her long list of crusades. Oddly enough, it's not a trip she lays on the children. Nor does she tell them to eat up their dinners because of the starving children in Europe, or Asia, or India. (Himself, guiltily stuffing down bread crusts under his mother's blue benevolent gaze.) She doesn't ask if they are saving their allowances for the Bandage Campaign. She doesn't drag them through services at the Unitarian Church, with it's noncommittal interior and its idealistic hymns about the Brotherhood of Man and its icon of a small black boy beside a trash can where most churches have God. The last time they had dinner with his mother, Nate almost choked on his turnips when Nancy began to tell a Newfie joke. But his mother actually laughed. She lets the children tell all kinds of jokes to her: moron jokes, Moby Dick jokes, and many more of dubious taste. "What's blue and covered with cookies and flies? A dead Girl Guide."

Nate would have been told it wasn't nice to make fun of morons or whales or Girl Guides: all were worthy. Much less Newfies. Is it because Nancy and Janet are girls and therefore not expected to reach the level of high seriousness that was and still is expected of him? Or is it merely because his mother is now a grandmother and these are her grandchildren? In any case, she spoils them rotten. She even gives them candy. Although he loves her for it, Nate finds himself resenting it. He can hear his mother laughing now, above the sound of the potato masher. He wishes she'd laughed more with him.

She smiled though. She was raised a Quaker, and Quakers,

from what he'd seen of them, were smilers rather than laugh-
ers. Nate isn't sure why she switched to the Unitarians. He's
heard Unitarianism called a featherbed for falling Christians,
but his mother doesn't seem like a woman who has fallen anywhere. (Where is the featherbed for falling Unitarians? he
wonders. Such as himself.)

He tries not to discuss theology with his mother. She still
believes that goodness will win.

She's always used the war as an example, virtue triumphant, despite the fact that it killed his father. He can't remember whether it was before or after this death that she took
up part-time nursing at the veterans' hospital where she still
works, the legless and armless men that were young when she
started there aging along with her, becoming, she tells him,
more and more bitter, fading one by one, dying. She should
leave such a depressing job, get something more cheerful;
he's advised her to do that. But "Everyone else has forgotten
them," she says, looking at him reproachfully. "Why should
I?" For some reason her pious sacrifices infuriated him. Why
shouldn't you, you're human, Nate has wanted to reply. But
never has.

His father, no amputee but a simple dead man, smiles down
at him now from the mantelpiece, a young face framed by the
severe lines of a uniform. Violator of his mother's pacifist ide-
als, nevertheless a hero. It had taken Nate a long time to find
out exactly how his father had died. "He was a hero," was all
that his mother would say, leaving him with visions of rescues
on the beach, his father wiping out enemy machine-gun nests
single-handed or floating like a dark bat over some blacked-
out town, his parachute billowing like a cape behind him.

Finally, on his sixteenth birthday, he'd asked again and this
time—convinced perhaps that he was ready for the facts of
life—she'd told him. His father had died in England, of hepa-
titis, without ever reaching the real war.

"I thought you said he was a hero," he'd said, disgusted.

His mother's eyes grew round and bluer. "But Nathanael.
He *was*."

Still and all, he wishes he'd known sooner; he would have
felt less overshadowed. It's hard to compete with any dead
man, he knows, much less a hero.

"Dinner, Nate," his mother calls. She enters carrying the
potatoes, the girls follow with knives and forks, and they all
crowd around the diminutive oval table at one end of his
mother's living room. Nate has asked earlier if there was any-

thing he could do, but since he got married his mother has banished him to the living room during mealtime preparations. She won't even let him wash the dishes any more.

They're the same dishes, beige with orange nasturtiums, he used to wash so endlessly, grudgingly. They depress Elizabeth, which is one of the reasons she almost never participates in these visits. Elizabeth says his mother's things invariably look as if she ordered them out of a stamp catalogue, and there's some truth to this. Everything in his mother's house is serviceable and, he has to admit, rather ugly. Her table has a plastic finish, her chairs are wipable, her dishes garish, her glassware will bounce on the floor. She doesn't have the time for frills, she says, or the money either. Another thing that bothers her about the wooden toys he makes is the price. "Only rich people can afford them, Nate," she says accusingly.

They eat hamburger patties fried in leftover bacon fat, mashed potatoes, and canned beets with margarine, while Nate's mother asks the children about school and laughs gaily at their terribly jokes. Nate feels his stomach go cold; the canned beets sink, mix uneasily with his furtive Scotch. They are, all three of them, so unsuspecting, so innocent. It's as if he's looking at them through a lighted window: inside, peace and tranquil domesticity, this house, the tastes, the smells even, so familiar to him. Good, unassuming. And outside, darkness, thunder, the storm, himself a wolflike monster in tattered clothes, fingernails ragged, lurking red-eyed and envious, snout pressed to the glass. He alone knows the darkness of the human heart, the secrets of evil. *Kaboom.*

"Ninny," he whispered to himself.

"What did you say, dear?" his mother asks, turning her bright blue eyes full upon him. Older now, with crinkles behind spectacles, but the same eyes, shining, earnest, always on the verge of some emotion he cannot quite face: disappointment, joy. The perpetual spotlight in which he's always lived, alone on the stage, the star performer.

"I was talking to myself," he says.

"Oh," his mother laughs, "I do that all the time. You must have inherited it."

After dessert, which is canned peaches, the three of them wash the dishes and Nate is again exiled to the living room to do whatever it is that men are supposed to do after dinner. Nate wonders whether, if his father had lived, his mother would have gone in for Women's Liberation. As it is she doesn't have to. She does, of course, on the theoretical level, and she's fond of pointing out the almost innumerable ways in which women's basic human rights have been cropped, stunted, mutilated and destroyed by men. But if he had slippers she'd bring them for him.

He'll phone Lesje, see her again. He won't see her again. He's a horse's ass, he's made a mess of it, she won't want to see him again. He has to see her again. He's in love with her, with that cool thin body, the face turned in upon itself in statue-like contemplation. She sits behind a lighted window, draped in soft white, playing the spinet, her moving fingers luminous against the keys. Growling, he leaps through the glass.

Saturday, January 15, 1977

ELIZABETH

Elizabeth is sitting at the small desk in her bedroom (maple, *c.* 1875). It has a matching chair which she bought at the same auction. It's a wonder to her how the ladies of that time ever managed to get their great cabbagy padded buttocks onto the chairs made for that purpose. You were supposed to perch gracefully, skirts falling, fake ass billowing around your hidden real ass. No visible support. The apparition of a cloud.

In this desk Elizabeth keeps: her checkbook and canceled checks, her bills, her budget, her lists of things needing to be done around the house (one list for urgent, another for long-term), her personal letters, and the journal she started four years ago but has failed to keep up. This desk has not been opened since Chris's death.

She can now think: *Chris's death.* She almost never thinks *Chris's suicide.* This would imply that Chris's death was something he did to himself; she thinks of it, on the contrary, as something he did to her. He's not feeling the effects of it, whereas she still is. For instance, she has not opened the desk until now because in the upper left-hand pigeonhole, held together tidily by an elastic band, is the bundle of letters he was sending her in September and October; all on lined notebook paper in ballpoint pen, the handwriting becoming larger and more spidery until finally, on October 15, there had been just two words filling and entire page. She should not have kept these letters, she knows; she should throw them out now, immediately, without looking at them again. But she's always been a saver.

She avoids looking at the letters as she bends over her checkbook. Now that she's into it, she's even getting a certain amount of pleasure out of it. Order from chaos, all those unpaid bills cleared out of the way, entered into her book. Nate has paid a few things that had to be paid—the phone bill, the hydro—but everything else has been waiting for her, sometimes with two or three politely outraged letters, requesting and then demanding. She likes to have her accounts settled, to owe nothing to anyone. She likes to know she has money in the bank. She intends always to have enough money for an emergency.

Unlike her mother, who'd sat crying for two days in the flowered chair by the window after their father was suddenly not there any more. "What am I supposed to do?" she asked the air, as if there was somebody listening who had a standard of behavior all ready for her. Her sister Caroline crawling up to her mother's lap, crying too, sliding off repeatedly, crawling back up her mother's slippery-skirted legs like some demented beetle.

Elizabeth had not wept or crawled. When it became obvious that their mother was not going to get up out of the chair and fix them dinner, she'd counted the quarters she'd been saving, the ones Uncle Teddy had been slipping down the front of her dress on their infrequent visits to Auntie Muriel's big house. She'd gone through her mother's purse, throwing the lipstick tubes and crumpled hankies onto the floor, finding nothing but a wrinkled two-dollar bill and some pennies. Then she'd let herself out of the apartment, using the keys from her mother's purse to lock the door behind her. She'd gone to the little grocery store three blocks away and bought some bread and cheese and marched back carrying the brown paper bag, stamping her rubber boots hard on the stairs as she climbed up. This was no great feat, she'd done similar things often enough before. "Eat this," she'd said to her mother, furious with her and with her sister. "Eat this and stop crying!"

It hadn't worked. Her mother had sniveled on, and Elizabeth had sat in the kitchen, chewing on her bread and cheese, in a white rage. She wasn't angry with her father. She'd always suspected he couldn't be depended on. She was angry with her mother for not having known it.

It was Auntie Muriel who had taught her how to keep a bank account, how to balance a checkbook, what *interest* was. Although Auntie Muriel regarded most books as frivolous trash and even schoolwork as of marginal value, she'd spent a good deal of time on this part of Elizabeth's education. For which Elizabeth is grateful. Money counts, Auntie Muriel used to say—still says, when anyone will listen—and Elizabeth knows it's true. If only because Auntie Muriel enforced the lesson so strongly: she supported Elizabeth, paid for her well-made underwear and her blue tweed coats and her piano lessons, therefore she owned her.

Auntie Muriel's attitude towards Elizabeth was equivocal. Elizabeth's mother was no good, therefore Elizabeth herself was probably no good. But Elizabeth was Auntie Muriel's niece, so there must be something to her. Auntie Muriel worked at developing those parts of Elizabeth that most resembled Auntie Muriel and suppressing or punishing the other parts. Auntie Muriel admired backbone, and Elizabeth feels that, underneath everything, she herself now has the backbone of a rhinoceros.

Auntie Muriel is unambiguous about most things. Her few moments of hesitation have to do with the members of her own family. She isn't sure where they fit into the Great Chain of Being. She's quite certain of her own place, however. First comes God. Then comes Auntie Muriel and the Queen, with Auntie Muriel having a slight edge. Then come about five members of the Timothy Eaton Memorial Church, which Auntie Muriel attends. After this there is a large gap. Then white, non-Jewish Canadians, Englishmen, and white, non-Jewish Americans, in that order. Then there's another large gap, followed by all other human beings on a descending scale, graded according to skin color and religion. Then cockroaches, clothes moths, silverfish and germs, which are about the only forms of animal life with which Auntie Muriel has ever had any contact. Then all sexual organs, except those of flowers.

This is how Elizabeth puts it for the amusement of others when she's telling Auntie Muriel stories; notably to Philip Burroughs of Greek and Roman, whose aunt is Janie Burroughs, who travels in the same wee circle as Auntie Muriel. Unlike Nate, Philip can be depended on to know what she's talking about.

Auntie Muriel may be a droll story, but this doesn't affect her malignance. She's a purist as well as a puritan. There are no shades of grey for Auntie Muriel. Her only visible moral dilemma is that she thinks she ought to rank her family with the Timothy Eaton Church members, because of their relation to her; but she feels compelled to place them instead with the cockroaches and silverfish, because of their deplorable behavior.

Such as that of Elizabeth's mother, which even now Auntie Muriel never fails to allude to. Elizabeth has never been sure why her mother vanished. Helplessness, perhaps; an inability to imagine what else to do. Auntie Muriel's version is that Elizabeth's mother deserted the family out of innate depravity—ran off with the son of her own father's lawyer, which Auntie Muriel saw as a kind of incest and which luckily didn't last long. She, Auntie Muriel, had rescued the deserted children and had begun immediately stuffing them with all the advantages.

Elizabeth, even as a child, did not fully accept this story. Now she thinks it may have been the other way around, that Auntie Muriel stole her and her sister away from their apartment while their mother was out on one of her expeditions, "looking for work," she told them. Then, once Auntie Muriel had the children safely barricaded into her own house, she'd probably told their mother she was unfit and it could be proved in court if necessary. This is more Auntie Muriel's style: self-righteous banditry.

She can remember the actual event but it tells her nothing. Playing movie-star cutouts with Caroline; then Auntie Muriel suddenly there, saying, "Get your coats on, children." Elizabeth had asked where they were going. "To the doctor," said Auntie Muriel, which seemed plausible.

Caroline at the third-floor window. *That's Mother. Where?* Down below on the sidewalk, her face upturned in the streetlight, a sky-blue coat, Mayflies fluttering around her. Opening the window, smell of new leaves. Calling, *Mummy, Mummy*, both of them. Auntie Muriel's footsteps on the stairs, along the hall. *What are you yelling about? That's not your mother. Now close the window or the whole neighborhood will hear.* The woman turning, walking away, head sadly down. Caroline screaming through the closed window, Auntie Muriel prying her fingers from the ledge, the catch.

For months Elizabeth put herself to sleep with a scene from *The Wizard of Oz*. The book itself had been left behind, it was part of the old life before Auntie Muriel's, but she could remember it. It was the part where Dorothy throws a bucket of water over the Wicked Witch of the West and melts her. Auntie Muriel was the witch, of course. Elizabeth's mother was Glinda the Good. One day she would reappear and kneel down to kiss Elizabeth on the forehead.

She leans back, closes her eyes. Dry eyes. Chris wanted her to
quit her job, leave her home and her two children. For him.
Throw herself on his mercy. His tender mercy. She'd have to
be crazy, he'd have to be crazy to think she ever would. No
visible support. He should have left things the way they were.

She sits up, reaches quickly for the bundle of letters, reads
the one on the top. FUCK OFF. His last message. She'd been
angry when she first read that.

She tucks the check stubs and paid bills and the duplicate
rent receipts from the tenants upstairs into an envelope, marks
it: *1976*. That finishes off the year. Now she can start another
one. Time hasn't stood still while she's been away, as she now
thinks of it. She's barely managed to hold things together at
the office, but she has a lot to catch up on. The quilt exhibit,
for instance, must be scheduled and promoted. The girls
need new underwear and Nancy needs new snowboots: she's
been coming home for days with a wet foot. And there's
something wrong with Nate. Something is happening in his
life; he hasn't told her about it. Perhaps he has a new ladyfriend, now that Martha has been used up. He's always told
her before, though. She riffles back through the days, looking
for clues; at the base of her skull the old chill begins, the old
fear, of events, cataclysms preparing themselves without her,
gathering like tidal waves at the other side of the world. Behind
her back. Out of control.

She stands up, turns the key in her desk. She has backbone.
She has money in the bank, not enough but some. She does
not have to depend, she is not a dependant. She is self-
supporting.

Wednesday, January 19, 1977

LESJE

Organisms adapt to their environments. Of necessity, most of the time. They also adapt to their own needs, often with a certain whimsy, you could almost say perversity. Take, for instance, the modified third claw on the hind foot of one of Lesje's favorite dinosaurs, the medium-sized but swift and deadly deinonychus. This third claw does not, like the other two, touch the ground; therefore it was not used for walking or running. Ostrom, the noted authority and discoverer of deinonychus, speculated from its position and its shape (sickle-curved, razor-sharp) that it was used for the sole purpose of disemboweling. Deinonychus's front legs, proportionately longer than those of tyrannosaurus or grogosaurus, held the prey at a suitable distance; deinonychus then stood on one foot while using the third claw of the other foot to slash upon the stomach of the prey. A balancing act; also an eccentric way of coping with life, that is, the capturing and preparation of food. Nothing else even close to deinonychus has yet been unearthed. It is this eccentricity, this uniqueness, this acrobatic gaiety, that appeals to Lesje. A kind of dance.

She has watched this innocent though bloody dance many times from the immunity of her treetop, which today happens to be a conifer. There is nothing in sight at the moment, though; not so much as a pterosaur. William has frightened everything away. He wanders below her among the bulbous-trunked cycad trees, ill at ease. Something is wrong; this isn't what he's used to. The sun is strange and there are odd smells. He hasn't yet realized he's in a different time.

Not realizing is his adaptation. Lesje is his environment, and his environment has changed.

William also sits at a card table, eating the Betty Crocker Noodles Romanoff Lesje has just dished out for him. She herself doesn't feel like eating right now. He's bombarding her with gloom: pollutants are pouring into the air, over three hundred of them, more than have yet been identified. Sulfuric acid and mercury are falling, metallic mist, acid rain, into the pure lakes of Muskoka and points north. Queasy fish rise, roll over, exposing bellies soon to bloat. If ten times more control is not implemented at once (at once!) the Great Lakes will die. A fifth of the fresh water in the world. And for what? Pantyhose, he says accusingly, fork dripping noodles. Rubber bands, cars, plastic buttons. Lesje nods; she knows, but she's helpless. He's doing it on purpose.

At this very moment, William continues relentlessly, birds are eating worms, and stable, unbreakable PCB's are concentrating in their fatty tissues. Lesje herself has probably been incapacitated for safe child-bearing due to the large quantity of DDT she has already stored in her own fatty tissues. Not to mention the radiation bombardment on her ovaries, which will almost certainly cause her to give birth to a two-headed child or to a lump of flesh the size of a grapefruit, containing hair and a fully developed set of teeth (William cites examples), or to a child with its eyes on one side of its face, like a flounder.

Lesje, who does not want to hear much more of this right now, truthful though it may be, counterattacks with the supernova theory *re*: the extinction of the dinosaurs. Eggshells grown so thin the young could not hatch, due to a dramatic increase of cosmic radiation. (This theory is not in good repute at the Museum, which favors a more gradual hypothesis; nevertheless, it gives William something to think about. It could happen here. Who can tell when a star may explode?) Lesje asks William if he'd like a cup of instant coffee.

William, glumly, says yes. It's this glumness of his, the disappearance of his customary buoyancy, that constitutes the adaptation. Like a dog sniffing the air, he senses the difference in Lesje; he knows, but he doesn't know what he knows. Hence his depression. When Lesje brings in the coffee he says, "You forgot I take cream." His voice is plaintive. Plaintiveness isn't something Lesje associates with William.

Lesje sits down in her easy chair. She wants to ruminate, but if she goes into the bedroom William will take it as an invitation, he'll follow her and want to make love. Lesje doesn't wish to do this right now. (Problem: copulation of deinonychus. Role of the third claw, sickle-shaped, razor-sharp: how kept out of the way? Accidents?) Despite the fact that every cell in her body has grown heavier, is liquid, is massive, is glowing with watery energy, each nucleus throwing out its own light. Collectively she blinks like a firefly; she's a lantern, a musky signal. No wonder William hovers, priapic, anxious because she's twice locked the bathroom door while taking a shower and once told him she had a bad case of heartburn. Awkward William bumbles, June bug against the screen.

But how is it that Nate has failed to appear? He was supposed to phone on the seventeenth; he's two days late. She makes excuses to waft past the phone in case it rings, she stays in when she would otherwise go out, goes out when she can no longer stand it. She should have given him the phone number at work; but he could get her easily through the switchboard if he wanted to. Could it be that he's already phoned, that William has answered and, divining everything, has said something so vicious or threatening that Nate will never phone again? She doesn't dare ask. She doesn't dare phone Nate, either. If Elizabeth answers, he'll be displeased. If one of the children answers he'll also be displeased. If he himself answers he'll be displeased too because he'll know it could just as well have been one of the others.

Lesje takes refuge in work. Which was once the perfect escape.

Part of her job involves the education of the public on matters pertaining to vertebrate paleontology. Right now the Museum is developing a dinosaur media kit for schools, which will include film strips and taped commentary, as well as booklets, posters and guides to the Museum's exhibits. It's hoped that this kit will be as popular as the sale of the models of diplodocus and stegosaurus (grey plastic, made in Hong Kong) and of the dinosaur coloring book indicate it will. But how much to tell? What for instance, of the family lives of the dinosaurs? What about their methods of egg-laying and—delicate subject, but always of interest—fertilization? Should these be ignored? If not, will the various religious and moralistic parent-action groups now gaining strength object to this material and boycott the kits? Such questions would not normally have occurred to Lesje, but they have occurred to Dr. Van Vleet, who has asked her to look into them and to propose some solutions.

Lesje closes her eyes, sees before her the articulated skeletons of the Museum exhibits, wired into a grotesque semblance of life. Who could possibly object to a copulation that took place ninety million years ago? The love lives of stones, sex among the ossified. Yet she could see how such gargantuan passions, the earth actually moving, a single nostril filling the screen, sighs of lust like a full-blast factory whistle, might be upsetting to some. She remembers the Grade Four teacher who threw out the toad eggs she'd brought to school. She'd hoped to describe to the class how she'd seen them being laid, in a ditch, the huge female toad gripped by a male so small it looked like a different animal. The teacher listened to this recital *solo*, then said she didn't think the class really needed to know about things like that. As usual Lesje had accepted the adult verdict and watched mutely while the teacher carried her jar of precious toad eggs out of the room to flush them down the girls' toilet.

Why didn't they need to know about things like that? Lesje now wonders. What do they need to know about? Probably not much. Certainly not the questions that occur to her at times of free-ranging speculation. Did dinosaurs have penises, for instance? A good question. Their descendants the birds have cloadal openings, whereas some snakes have not only one penis but two. Did the male dinosaur hold the female dinosaur by the scruff of the neck, like a rooster? Did dinosaurs herd, did they mate for life like geese, did they have harems, did male dinosaurs fight each other at mating season? Perhaps that would help to explain the modified third claw on deinonychus. Lesje decides not to raise these questions. Dinosaurs laid eggs, like turtles, and that will be that.

William says he's still hungry and is going into the kitchen to make himself a sandwich. This is an expression of dissatisfaction with Lesje's ability to meet his requirements: Lesje knows it but doesn't care. Ordinarily she would make the sandwich for him, since William has always claimed to be one big thumb in the kitchen. He will manage to break something out there or cut his finger on a sardine can (William, foe of cans, nevertheless has a periodic hankering for sardines that must be catered to). There will be wreckage and carnage, wounds, mutterings and curses; William will emerge with a tatty sandwich, blood-smeared uneven bread, sardine oil on his shirt. He will display himself, he'll wish to be appeased, and Lesje, she knows, will do this. In the absence of Nate, who has offered, when she comes to think of it, nothing at all. A wide plain. A risk.

The phone rings and William gets to it before Lesje is even out of her chair. "It's for you," he says.

Lesje, chest gripped by a fit of shallow breathing, seizes the phone.

"Hello," says a woman's voice. "This is Elizabeth Schoenhof."

Lesje's throat closes. She's been found out. Grandmothers converge on her, holding out her guilt, their grief.

But far from it. Elizabeth is merely inviting her to dinner. Her and William, of course. Nate and Elizabeth, says Elizabeth, would both be very happy if they could come.

Friday, January 21, 1977

ELIZABETH

Elizabeth is having lunch with Martha in the orange cafeteria of the Museum. They're both eating sparingly: soup, fruit yogurt, tea. Elizabeth has insisted on paying. Martha has not fought her for half of the bill as she once would have. It's a sign of her defeat.

So is the fact that they're eating here at all. The Museum cafeteria is nothing special. Once, in the days of Martha's ascendancy, when Elizabeth thought she might be a real threat, she'd gone to considerable trouble to make sure they met for these lunches in good restaurants, where Elizabeth could demonstrate her own knowledge of the superior menu and get Martha slightly bombed on cocktails and wine. Martha doesn't hold her liquor very well and Elizabeth has found this useful. She would sip delicately at the edge of her own wine glass while Martha downed the carafe, priming herself and finally spewing out a lot more than she should have about Nate's activities and imperfections. Every time Martha said something unflattering about Nate, Elizabeth would nod and murmur agreement, even though these criticisms irritated her, reflecting as they did on her taste in husbands; and Martha's eyes would dampen with gratitude. Not that Martha likes her. Neither of them has any illusions about that. Soon she will not have to take Martha to lunch at all; coffee will be sufficient. After that, she will have dentist's appointments. Lots of them.

Elizabeth has removed the dishes from her tray and set them out on an unfolded napkin, but Martha has no time today for such niceties. She eats from the tray, slurping her soup, her square face bunched into a scowl. Her dark hair is stringy, pulled back and clamped to her scalp with a tortoise-shell plastic clip. She looks brownish, pinched; hardly the confident peasant, hearty and wide-chested, that Elizabeth had first found herself having to deal with. She's here to complain about Nate, as if Nate has broken a window with a baseball and Elizabeth is his mother.

"I hit him," Martha is saying, "right between the eyes. I guess I shouldn't have, but it felt good. He's a prick, you know. Underneath all that *understanding* stuff. I don't know how you can live with him."

Once Elizabeth would have agreed; now, however, she can allow herself a few luxuries. Poor Nate, she thinks. He's such an innocent. "He's a sensational father," she says. "You couldn't ask for a better one. The girls adore him."

"I wouldn't know," says Martha. She bites savagely into her cracker; brittle flakes sprinkle the tray. No class, Elizabeth thinks; she never did have any. Elizabeth has always known that sooner or later Martha would overplay her hand. She herself tries for understatement. She opens her peach yogurt and stirs the contents up from the bottom.

"I never understood at first why you were so nice to me," Martha says, with a little of her old belligerence. "Taking me out to lunch and so forth. I couldn't see it. I mean, if I was you I wouldn't have done that."

"I believe in being civilized about these things," Elizabeth says.

"But then I figured it out. You wanted to *supervise* us. Like some kind of playground organizer. Make sure it didn't go too far. Right? You can admit it now, it's all over."

Elizabeth frowns slightly. She doesn't like this interpretation of her motives, though it may be just slightly accurate. "I hardly think that's fair, Martha," she says. Behind Martha, something of more interest is taking place. Lesje Green has come in with the Curator of Vertebrate Paleontology. Dr. Van Vleet. They're going along the counter now, filling their trays. They often have lunch together; everyone knows there's nothing to it, since Dr. Van Vleet is about ninety and Lesje is known to be living with a young man who works at the Ministry of the Environment. They have lunch together presumably because they can't find anyone else to talk to about the old rocks and bones they're both so stuck on.

Elizabeth has always found Lesje hard to deal with: strange, sometimes pedantic, skittish. Too specialized. Today, however, she follows her with more than usual interest. The tipoff, now that she's thought about it, was that visit to the Museum back in November. The children told her about the dinosaur lady who showed them around, but Nate hadn't mentioned her. He'd asked Elizabeth to go with them, which didn't fit; but Nate is such a bungler it's the kind of thing he would do. Increasingly he has that mooning look, he's rubbing against the furniture. She's almost certain she's right, and tomorrow evening she'll know.

"We were supposed to be having these heart-to-hearts," Martha is saying, "but we never did, really, did we? I mean, we'd both say a lot about *him*, but I never said what I thought about you and you never said what you thought about me. We were never really honest, isn't that right?"

Martha is itching for honesty right now; she'd like a shouting match, right here in the cafeteria. Elizabeth wishes Nate had picked a ladyfriend with more sense of style. But a legal secretary at a two-bit lawyer's office, what could you expect? Elizabeth herself has no time for honesty right now. She doesn't think it would serve any purpose to tell Martha her real opinions, and she already knows what Martha thinks about her.

But in any contest she knows she would win. Martha has only one vocabulary, the one she uses; but Elizabeth has two. The genteel chic she's acquired, which is a veneer but a useful one: insinuating, flexible, accommodating. And another language altogether, older, harder, left over from those streets and schoolyards on the far edge of gentility where she fought it out after each one of her parents' quick decampments.

These fast moves were done at night, to avoid witnesses and landlords. Elizabeth would fall asleep on a pile of her mother's unpacked dresses, beautiful frail dresses left over from some earlier time, and wake up knowing she would have to go out into the strange faces, the ritual tests. If anyone pushed her she pushed back twice as hard, and if anyone pushed Caroline she put her head down and charged, right in the pit of the stomach. She could get big kids that way, even boys. They never expected it from someone that short. Sometimes she lost, but not often. She lost when there were more than two against her.

"You're turning into a hooligan," her mother said in one of her spasms of self-pity, dabbing at blood. In those days Elizabeth was always bleeding. Not that there was anything her mother could do about it; or about much else. Elizabeth's grandfather helped out while he was alive, though he said her father was a rounder, but Auntie Muriel got hold of him in the last months of his life and he changed his will. That's what Elizabeth's mother said, after the funeral.

Then they moved again, to an even smaller apartment, and her mother wandered helplessly around the cramped living room carrying things, a teapot, a stocking, which she didn't know where to set down. "It's not what I'm used to," she said. She went to bed with a headache; this time there was a bed. Elizabeth's father came home with two other men and told her a joke: *What did the chickens say when their mother laid an orange? Look at the orange marmalade.*

No one put Elizabeth to bed, but no one usually did. Sometimes her father pretended to, but it was only an excuse to fall asleep across her bed with all his clothes on. Her mother got up again and they all sat around in the living room drinking. Elizabeth was used to this. In her nightgown she sat on one of the men's laps, his bristly skin against her cheek. He called her "baby." Her mother got up to go to the little girls' room, she said, and tripped over her father's foot. He put it there on purpose: he liked practical jokes. "Most beautiful woman in the world," he said, laughing, picking her up from the linoleum whose pattern of maroon and yellow tapestry flowers Elizabeth can see whenever she wants to. He gave her a loose kiss on the cheek, winking; the other men laughed. Elizabeth's mother started to cry, her thin hands covering the porcelain face.

"You're a turd," Elizabeth said to her father. The other men laughed even more at this.

"You don't mean it, your poor old dad," he said. He tickled her under the armpits. The next morning he was gone. It was after this that space became discontinuous.

Almost no one knows any of this about Elizabeth. They don't know she's a refugee, with a refugee's desperate habits. Nate knows a little of it. Chris knew it, finally. Martha doesn't, neither does Lesje, and this gives Elizabeth a large advantage. She knows there's nothing in her that will compel her to behave decently. She can speak from that other life if she has to. If pushed she'll stop at nothing. Or, put another way: when she reaches nothing she will stop.

Two tables away, Lesje walks towards them, her tray listing badly, that otherworldly expression on her face which probably means she's thinking obscure thoughts but which reminds Elizabeth of someone having a minor epileptic fit. She sits down, almost knocking over her coffee cup with one of those gawky elbows. Elizabeth quickly appraises her clothes: jeans again. Lesje can get away with it, she's skinny enough. Also she's only a curatorial assistant. Elizabeth herself must dress more responsibly.

"Excuse me, Martha," she says. "There's someone I have to speak to." Martha, balked, rips the tinfoil top from her yogurt cup.

Elizabeth walks softly, puts her hand on Lesje's checkered shoulder, says "Lesje."

Lesje shrieks and drops her spoon on the table. "Oh," she says, turning.

"Can't come up behind her," says Dr. Van Vleet. "Learned that a long time ago. Trial and error."

"I'm so sorry," Elizabeth says. "I just wanted to say how pleased we both are that you'll be able to make it tomorrow."

Lesje nods, finally manages to say, "So am I, I mean, we both are." Elizabeth smiles graciously at Dr. Van Vleet and pauses beside Martha just long enough to say how pleasant it has been to see her again and she hopes they can get together soon; she's sorry, but she has to get back to the office now.

She feels very calm. She will manage.

She works in her office all afternoon, dictating memos and filling out request forms and typing a few special letters that need more thought. They've given a definite yes to the Chinese Peasant Art exhibit, which will now need some groundwork; but China is good copy these days and the show should be easy to promote.

Just before closing time she covers her typewriter and gathers her purse and coat. There's one more project she's promised herself she will take care of today.

She goes up the stairs, through the wooden door that keeps out the public, along the corridor with the metal drawers on either side. Chris's workroom. Another man works here now. He looks up from the table as Elizabeth comes towards him. Small, balding, not at all like Chris.

"Can I help you?" he says.

"I'm Elizabeth Schoenhof," Elizabeth says. "I work in Special Projects. I was wondering if you had a few spare scraps of fur. Any kind will do. My children use them for dolls' dresses."

The man smiles and gets up to look. Elizabeth has been told his name but she's forgotten it: Nagle? She will look it up. It's part of her job to know the technicians in every department, in case she needs to use them for anything.

As he rummages among the clutter on the shelves behind his table, Elizabeth looks around. The room has changed, been rearranged. Time has not stood still, nothing here is frozen. Chris is definitely gone. She cannot bring him back, and for the first time she no longer wants to. He'll punish her for that thought later, no doubt, but at the moment she's clear of him.

She walks slowly down the marble stairs, fingering a handful of fur. Scraps. All that's left of Chris, whom she can no longer remember whole. At the door she stuffs the bundle into her purse, then takes the subway up to St. George and along to Castle Frank. She walks along the viaduct till she's roughly in the middle, over the snow-filled ravine and the rushing cars below. Like Auntie Muriel, she needs her burial rituals. She opens her purse and throws the fur scraps one by one into space.

LESJE

Lesje is sitting in Elizabeth's living room, balancing a small cup of what she supposes is excellent coffee on her left knee. In her right hand she's holding a liqueur glass half-full of Benedictine and brandy. She doesn't know how she's ended up with two containers of liquid and no place to put them. She's positive she will very soon spill at least one and probably both of them onto Elizabeth's mushroom-colored carpet. She's desperate to get away.

But the others are all playing a game that substitutes the word "moose" for any other word in the title of a Canadian novel. It has to be Canadian. This apparently is part of the joke.

"As for Me and My Moose," Elizabeth says, and everyone else in the room chuckles.

"A Jest of Moose," says the wife of the man from Greek and Roman who works at the CBC.

"A Moose of God," replies the man, whose name is Philip. Nobody calls him Phil. Elizabeth laughs and asks Lesje if she'll have some more B & B.

"I'm fine," Lesje says, hoping she has murmured, fearing she's blurted. She needs a cigarette but has no free hand. She doesn't read novels and she hasn't recognized a single one of the titles the others, even Nate, even, sometimes, William, have been batting around so easily. *The Lost Moose*, she could say. But that isn't Canadian.

The whole dinner has been like that. Just a couple ·of friends, Elizabeth said. Casual. So Lesje wore pants with a long sweater-coat, and the two other women are in dresses. Elizabeth for once is not in black; she's wearing a loose grey chiffon number that makes her look younger and thinner than she does at work. She even has a necklace on, a chain with a silver fish. The other woman is in flowing mauve. Lesje, in her perky, clean-cut stripes, feels about twelve years old.

She's only been able to see Nate once before this evening. In desperation she called his house; one of the children answered.

"Just a minute." Abruptly; the slam of the phone hitting the floor. It must have tumbled from the table. A shout. "Dad, it's for you!"

They'd arranged to meet at the coffee shop in the indoor mall at the bottom of Lesje's building. Reckless: what if William?

"Why is she asking us to dinner?" Lesje wanted to know, by this time frantic. She couldn't back out now, it would look funny. To William as well. And if she'd said no at first it would have looked funny too.

Nate was cautiously holding her hand. "I don't know," he said. "I've given up wondering about her motives. I never know why she does anything."

"We aren't that friendly at work," Lesje said. "Does she know?"

"Probably," Nate said. "She didn't tell me beforehand she was asking you to dinner. I couldn't tell her not to. She often asks people to dinner; or anyway she used to."

"Did you tell her?" It was suddenly the kind of thing he would do.

"Not exactly," Nate said. "I guess I've mentioned you a few times. I'm thinking about you a lot. Maybe she picked up on that. She's pretty sharp."

"But even if she does know, why would she ask me to dinner?" This would be the last thing she herself would do. One of William's old girlfriends, a dental technician, is in the habit of suggesting they all three of them have lunch sometime. Lesje has consistently vetoed this.

"I guess she just wants to take a look at you," Nate said, "up close. Don't worry, it'll be all right. She won't *do* anything. You'll enjoy the dinner, she's a great cook when she feels like it."

Not that Lesje could tell. She was so paralyzed by apprehension that she could barely chew. The *boeuf bourguignon* could have been sand as far as she was concerned. Elizabeth graciously ignored the large amount left on Lesje's plate. During the first course she asked Lesje three well-informed questions about power-structures in Vertebrate Paleontology, a truthful answer to any of which might have cost Lesje her job if repeated in the right quarters. Lesje hedged awkwardly, and Elizabeth switched the talk to CBC gossip, with the wife of the man from Greek and Roman supplying.

Elizabeth concentrated on William during dessert. She found his work with the Ministry of the Environment fascinating, and so worthwhile. She supposed she really should make the effort to cart all her old bottles and newspapers to those things, those bins. William, gratified, lectured her on the doom awaiting the world if she should fail to do this, and Elizabeth agreed meekly.

Nate, meanwhile, moved in the background, chain-smoking, drinking steadily but without visible effect, avoiding Lesje's eyes, helping with the plate-clearing and pouring out the wine. Elizabeth directed him unobtrusively: "Love, would you get me a slotted serving spoon?" "Love, could you just turn on the coffee while you're out there?" Lesje sat, nibbling the edges of her meringue, wishing the children were there. At least she would have someone she could talk to without blushing and mumbling and the certainty that at any minute she would open her mouth and some tactless clinker would roll out onto the linen tablecloth. Something about suicides or hotel rooms. But the children had been sent to spend the night with friends. Sometimes, Elizabeth said, much as one loved one's children, one wanted to spend a little free adult time. Nate didn't always agree, she said, directly to Lesje. He was such a doting father. He'd like to be with his children twenty-four hours a day. "Isn't that true, love?"

Don't call him *love*, Lesje felt like saying. You can't fool me. But she supposed it was a habit. After all, they've been married for ten years.

Which Elizabeth has taken care to emphasize. There have been references all evening to Nate's favorite foods and Nate's favorite wines and Nate's peculiarities of dress. Elizabeth wishes he would get the back of his hair trimmed more often; she used to do it herself with the nail scissors, but she can't get him to hold still long enough any more. Nate's behavior on their wedding day has been mentioned, though not explained; everyone in the room, including the Greek and Roman couple, seems to know this story. Except Lesje and, of course, William, who was in the bathroom at the time. Where Lesje herself at this moment fervently wishes she could be.

William has produced his pipe, an affectation he by and large reserves for company. "I know a better one," he says. "Ever played Star Trek?" But nobody has, and the rules, as

William starts to expound them, are pronounced too complicated.

"Lifeboat," says the Greek and Roman woman.

Nate asks if anyone would like more B & B. He himself is
going to pour himself a Scotch. Would anyone care to join
him?

"Sensational," says Elizabeth. She explains that this game is
very simple. "We are all in a lifeboat," she says, "and the food
is running out. What you have to do is convince everyone else
why you should be allowed to remain in the lifeboat instead of
being thrown overboard." She says that this game is often
very revealing psychologically.

"I sacrifice myself for the good of the group," Nate says
promptly.

"Oh," Elizabeth says, giving a mock frown. "He always
does that. It's his Quaker upbringing. Really it means he can't
be bothered."

"Unitarian," says Nate. "I just think it's an unduly vicious
game."

"That's why it's called Lifeboat," Elizabeth says lightly.
"All right, Nate's overboard. The sharks have him. Who
wants to begin?"

No one does, so Elizabeth tears up a paper napkin and they
draw lots.

"Well," says the Greek and Roman man. "I know Morse
code. I can help us get rescued. And I'm good with my hands.
When we land on the desert island, I can build the shelter and
so forth. I'm a pretty good plumber, too. A tool man." He
smiles. "It's nice to have a man around the house."

Elizabeth and the CBC woman, laughing, agree that he
should be allowed to stay on the boat.

Elizabeth is next. "I'm a sensational cook," she says. "But
more than that, I have a very strong survival instinct. If you
try to push me overboard, I'll take at least one of you down
with me. How's that? I don't think we should be kicking people out of this boat anyway," she adds. "We should be saving
them and eating them. Let's drag Nate back in."

"I'm already miles away," Nate says.

"Elizabeth's using threats," the CBC woman says. "Any of
us could use the same ploy; I don't think it should count. But
if we're thinking of a long-term plan, I propose that I should
be saved instead of Elizabeth. She's almost past child-bearing
age and if we want to establish a colony, we'll need babies."

Elizabeth goes white. "I'm sure I could still squeeze a few out," she says.

"Not many," the CBC woman says brightly. "Come on, Liz, it's only a game."

"Lesje?" Elizabeth says. "You walk the plank next."

Lesje opens her mouth, then closes it. She can feel herself blushing. She knows this is not just a game, it's a challenge of some sort. But still, she can't think of a single reason why she should be permitted to remain alive. She isn't a good cook, and besides there's nothing much to cook. She can't build shelters. The CBC woman has used up the babies, and anyway Lesje has a narrow pelvis. What is she good for? None of the things she knows, knows well, is in any way necessary for survival.

They are all looking at her, embarrassed now by the length of time it's taking her, her obvious confusion. "If we find any bones," she says at last, "I'll be able to tell you whose they are." As if the history of bones matters, to anyone but her and a few other addicts. She's attempted a sort of joke, but it's hardly witty repartee. "Excuse me," she says, her voice a whisper. Carefully she sets down her cup, then her glass, on the beige rug. She stands up and turns, catching the cup with the side of her foot, and bolts from the room.

"I'll get a cloth," she hears Nate saying.

She locks herself into Elizabeth's bathroom and washes her hands with Elizabeth's peculiar brown soap. Then she sits, closes her eyes, elbows on her crossed knees, hands covering her mouth. The B & B must be getting to her. Is she really this graceless, this worthless? From her treetop she watches an ornithomimus, large-eyed, birdlike, run through the scrub, chasing a small protomammal. How many years to learn to grow hair, to bear young alive, to nurture them? How many for the four-chambered heart? Surely these things are important, surely her knowledge should not perish with her. She must be allowed to continue her investigations, here in this forest of early conifers and pineapple-trunked cycad trees.

Everyone has a certain number of bones, she thinks, clutching for lucidity. Not their own but someone else's and the bones have to be named, you have to know what to call them, otherwise what are they, they're lost, cut adrift from their own meanings, they may as well not have been saved for you. You can't name them all, there are too many, the world is full of them, it's made of them, so you have to choose which ones.

Everything that's gone before has left its bones for you and you'll leave yours in turn.

This is her knowledge, her field they call it. And it is like a field, you can walk through it and around it and say: These are the boundaries. She knows why the dinosaurs do many of the things they do, and about the rest she can deduce, make educated guesses. But north of the field history begins and the fog takes over. It's like being farsighted, the distant lake and its beaches and smooth-backed basking sauropods clear-edged in the moonlight, her own hand a blur. She does not know, for instance, why she is crying.

Elizabeth

Elizabeth is lying in bed, arms at her sides, feet together. The weak light from the street lamps comes in stripes through the bamboo blind, falls in bars on the walls, broken by the shadow of the spider plants, curved fingers which do not hold or reach for anything. The window is open a little at the bottom, the wooden slat covering the three holes in the sash of the storm window is lifted, cold air sifts through. Elizabeth opened it before she went to bed, she needed air.

Elizabeth lies with her eyes open. In the kitchen below her, Nate moves dishes. She notes him, pushes him back. She can see up through the dark ceiling, through the joists and layers of plaster and the worn linoleum, blue squares, which she, slovenly landlady, should have replaced long ago, past the beds where the tenants lie asleep, a mother, a father, a child, a family, up through the pink ceiling of their room and out through the rafters and the patched and leaking roof to the air, the sky, the place where there is nothing between her and nothing. The stars in their envelopes of bright gas burn on. Space no longer frightens her. She knows it is uninhabited.

Where did you go? I know you aren't in that box. The Greeks collected all the pieces of the body; otherwise the soul could not get away from the upper earth. To the happy islands. Philip said that tonight, between the *boeuf bourguignon* and the meringue with chocolate ginger sauce. Then he changed the subject, he remembered and was embarrassed, he knew he shouldn't be talking about funerary customs. I smiled, I smiled. It was a closed coffin, naturally. They shipped him north in dry ice, rigid among the cold crystals, fog coming off him like a Dracula movie. Tonight I thought, they forgot something. Part of him has been left behind.

142

She could not move; nevertheless she had Nate take her to the train in a taxi, where she sat like a slab of rock all the way to Thunder Bay and then on the unspeakable bus. English River. Upsala on one side, Bonheur on the other, Osaquan up the road. He used to point out those names, and the irony, the indignity of having been born and forced to live in English River. "The English," they still said, Scots, French, Indians, what-have-you. The enemy, the despoilers. She was one of the English.

She sat in the back pew, kneeling when the others knelt, standing when they stood, while Chris, surrounded by meager flowers, underwent the ceremony. Luckily it was in English, she could follow it. They even said the Lord's Prayer, a slightly different version. Forgive us our trepasses. When she was young she used to think that meant walking on other people's property. A thing she never did; therefore she did not need to be forgiven. As we forgive those who trespass against us. Get off the lawn, Auntie Muriel used to shout at the running children, opening the front door, then closing it like a mouth behind her voice. The old priest turned towards the people, raising the cup, mumbling, distaste on his face. The Latin was better, you can tell he thought that.

They didn't bury him at a crossroads with a stake, though. Death by misadventure. The shoulders were bowed, the heads bent, his mother in black in the front pew, with a real veil. The other children—Elizabeth supposed that was who they were—lined up beside her.

Afterwards there was coffee at the house. The neighbors brought cookies. One of those small northern bungalows, on a rock, pink and blue like a cake, dark spruce trees all around. Skidoo parked in the shed, the Eaton's Catalogue furniture, the worn store drapes four inches too short. Everything was the way she'd known it would be. The father's carefully learned English, the mother's dark face, baggy with grief and starch. We wanted him to have a chance. He was doing good. Always a smart boy. An education, finished his Grade Twelve, a steady job. Elizabeth thinking: Bullshit. You drove him out. Hit him when he wouldn't turn into you; right in that shed. We told each other a lot.

The mother: You a friend of his? From the city, eh? Then, as she'd feared, throwing back the veil, the bad teeth showing, pushing her dark face towards Elizabeth, her hair turning to snakes: *You killed him.*

But she could never have made it as far as the train, the

taxi even. Chris disappeared without her help or connivance. As far as she knows, his parents, if they still exist, have never heard of her. And her images are all wrong, too. He let on to her at first, hinted, that he was part Indian and part French, Métis, that mythical hybrid; archaic, indigenous, authentic as she was not, his sense of grievance fully earned. He sneered at her, the whiteness of her skin and presumably her blood, made love as if exacting payment, and she'd let herself be bullied. As she would otherwise have not. Then one afternoon, lying depleted on his smoky bed, they'd gone past that into the land of perilous confidences, her scrounging childhood, hunger and unbrushed hair behind her mother's helpless pretensions. Never envy anyone, she'd said, until you know. Now tell me.

It was twilight, drawn curtains, he rubbed his hand over and over her bare shoulder, for the first time he would give her something, give something away, he could hardly do it. It made her wince, that effort, it was not what she wanted. Don't ever drop your defenses, she should have told him; they're there to defend you.

He was only a quarter French, and no Indian at all. The rest was Finnish and English; his mother's name was Robertson. They weren't even poor enough to be romantic, they ran the cigar store, the good one, not the other. No trapper he. The beatings were real enough, but less frequent than he'd said. Was that when her attention had begun to slip, was she that cruel, that snobbish? Probably.

Despite this, she has not known what to answer to that mother's face looming like a moon, a moon seen close, cold and ravaged. No, she's said, more than once. It was malice, pride, it was his own damn fault. It wasn't me.

Now she finally wonders. What if? What if she'd left him alone. Foregone that jag, energy flowing into her. I wonder if you have some leftover fur scraps; my daughters make doll clothes out of them. To Chris, who had nothing left over, no reserves he could draw on, no free gifts to hand out. She'd known what she was doing. To be loved, to be hated also, to be the center. She had what he wanted, power over a certain part of the world: she knew how to behave, what fork to use, what went with what. He wanted that power. He had two ties, one green, one purple. Neither of them would do. He looked better in a T-shirt, she told him; which she should not have done.

She had that power and she'd let him see it and touch it. She let him see he was deficient and she promised, what? A transformation, a touch on the shoulder, knighthood. Then she'd stepped back, showing him that he was after all only a vacation, a beautiful picture on a brochure, a man in a loincloth whacking the head off some nondescript coconut. A dime a dozen. Leaving him naked.

She thinks: I treated him the way men treat women. A lot of men, a lot of women; but never me, not on your goddamned life. He couldn't take it. Does she feel pity for him at last, or is it contempt?

Downstairs Nate rattles the silverware, rinsing it, she knows, before putting it into the plastic basket in the dishwasher. She's heard this sound often enough. She turns her eyes away from the stars, looks instead down through the floor. Nate shuffles, cigarette stub in his mouth, lost in some melancholy dream. Mooning, yearning. She watched him this evening, through the dinner which she did not in the least enjoy, the parlor games, she could see it all, he's in love with that giraffe. Coffee on the rug, a minor irritation, she'll have to get it steam-cleaned; also a satisfaction. Lesje is a clown. But is, despite her gawkiness and lack of poise, a younger woman, quite a lot younger than Elizabeth. Elizabeth finds this banal. Tedious, predictable. However, Nate has been what everyone would call *in love* before. She'll give him permission, express interest, be helpful, wait it out. She's been through this before, she can do it with one hand tied behind her back.

(But why bother, another voice says. Why not let him go? Why make the effort?)

There's something else, she remembers now, and it's dangerous. Before, he wanted to be protected. He wanted a woman to be a door he could go through and shut behind him. Everything was fine as long as she was willing to pretend she was a cage, Nate a mouse, her heart pure cheese. He is, she knows, a hopeless sentimentalist. Earthmother, Nate her mole, snouting in darkness while she rocked him. I think that I shall never see a poem lovely as a tree. When she gave it up he found Martha, who could not do it nearly as well.

But this time he wants to protect. Looking down at the top of his head, the back of his neck, the way his hands move, deliberately, she knows it, even though he may not know it himself.

Elizabeth sits up in bed. Wires light in her legs and fingers, the walls with their shadows are in place again, the floor is there, the ceiling has healed over. Space is a cube around her, she is the center. There is something to be defended.

Stay in your place, Nate. I will not tolerate that void.

Saturday, January 22, 1977

NATE

Sadly, Nate stacks plates. It's the rule that when Elizabeth cooks, Nate does the dishes. One of the many rules, subrules, codicils, addenda, errata. Living with Elizabeth involves a maze of such legalities, no easier to understand because some of them are unspoken. Like an unwary pedestrian, he only realizes he's violated one of these when the bumper hits him, the whistle blows, the big hand descends. Ignorance of the law is no excuse. He imagines Lesje to be without rules.

He sees himself bending to whisper at the bathroom key-hole: *I love you.* Irrevocable commitment, even though he isn't sure whether Lesje, barricaded behind the bathroom door where she'd been for the past half-hour, could really hear him. He isn't sure why she was upset. He'd seen her face as she headed out the door. The coffee stain spreading on the rug behind her; but it wasn't that.

He wanted to reach through the bathroom door, comfort her, he thought about knocking, decided against it. What if she opened the door? If he said that to her face, no wall between, he would have to take action. Even though he meant it. He would find himself in mid-air, hurtled into a future he could not yet imagine, Elizabeth left on the solid earth behind him, feet on the ground where she always claimed they were, a dark hummock, the children's faces two pale ovals beside her. Receding from him.

He thinks of them (riotously bouncing at this moment on their friend Sarah's spare bed, in the dark, stifling laughter) and sees, not their daily faces, but two little portraits. In silver frames, birthday-party dresses, the dead hues of a black and white photo tinted. He and Elizabeth do not own any such portraits. His children immobilized, stilled. Bronzed. He tries

147

to remember what it was like before they were born, finds he can't. He can only go as far back as Elizabeth, trundling through the days and finally climbing ponderously from the car which he'd bought months before for this occasion, doubling over against the hood; himself solicitous and frightened. They wouldn't let fathers into the delivery room in those days. He walked her to the desk; the nurse looked at him disapprovingly. See what you've done. He installed her in a ward room, sat as she clenched and unclenched, watched as she vanished down the corridor in a wheelchair. It was a long labor. He slouched in a chair covered with green vinyl, reading back copies of *Sports Illustrated* and *Parents*, feeling his mouth fog up. He wanted a drink badly and all they had was coffee from a machine. Behind doors an earthquake was taking place, a flood, a tornado that could rip his life apart in minutes, and he was shut out from it.

Around him machines wheezed; he dozed. He was supposed to feel anxious and happy, he knew. Instead he found himself wondering: What if they both die? The bereaved young father stood at the graveside, clogged with grief, as the woman once so vibrant and sensuous, who'd smelled of crushed ferns, descended forever into the earth, cradling a stillborn baby the color of suet. He walked down a road, any road, thumbing, heading for some legendary steamer, pack on his back. A broken man.

When he'd finally been allowed in, the event was over. There was a baby where no baby had been. Elizabeth, depleted, was lying propped up in a white hospital gown, a plastic name on her wrist. She looked at him dully, as if he were a salesman or a census-taker.

"Is it all right?" he said, noticing immediately that he'd said "it" rather than "you" or "she." He hadn't even said, "Was it all right." It must have been; she was here, in front of him, she wasn't dead. They all overestimated it.

"They didn't give me the needle in time," Elizabeth said.

He looked down at the baby, wrapped like a sausage roll, held by one of Elizabeth's arms. He felt relieved and grateful, and cheated. She told him several times afterwards that he had no idea of what it was like, and she was right, he hadn't. But she acted also as if this was his fault.

He thinks they were closer before the birth of Janet, but he can't remember. He can't remember what *close* means, or rather what it would have meant once with Elizabeth. She

used to make omelettes for him at night after he was finished
studying and they would eat them together, sitting in the double bed. He remembers that time as good. Love food, she
called it.

Nate scrapes leftover *boeuf bourguignon* into a bowl; later
he will put it down the Garb-all. His lapses of memory are
beginning to bother him. It's not only Elizabeth, the way (he
deduces) she must have been, that's slipping away from him.
He loved her, he wanted to marry her, they got married, and
he can recall only fragments. Almost a year of law school is
gone now; his adolescence is hazy. Martha, once so firm and
tangible, is transparent, her face wobbles; soon she will dissolve completely.

And the children. What did they look like, when did they
walk, what did they say, how did he feel? He knows events
have taken place, important events of which he is now ignorant. What will happen to this day, to Elizabeth's disastrous
dinner party, the remains of which are now being ground to
shreds by the metal teeth under the sink?

Nate starts the dishwasher, wipes his hands on his pantlegs.
He goes to the stairs, quietly before remembering: the children are away for the night. Lesje too is gone, fleeing almost
directly from the bathroom, stopping only to snatch her coat,
her young man in tow. The bun-faced young man whose
name Nate can't at the moment recall.

Instead of going to his own cubicle, his cell, he pauses at
the children's door, then walks into their room. He knows
now that he will leave; it feels, instead, as though they have
left him. Here are the dolls, the scattered paint sets, the scissors, the odd socks and rabbit-faced slippers they've forgotten
in their haste to pack. Already they are on a train, a plane,
headed for some unknown destination, being carried away
from him at the speed of light.

He knows they will be back tomorrow morning in time for
Sunday brunch, that tomorrow anyway everything will go on
the same, that he will stand at the kitchen table dishing out
scrambled eggs on toast for himself and the girls and for Elizabeth, who will be wrapped in her blue terry-cloth bathrobe,
hair only half-brushed. He will dish out the scrambled eggs
and Elizabeth will ask him to pour her a second cup of coffee,
and it will seem even to him as though nothing is about to
happen.

Yet he kneels; tears come to his eyes. He should have held

on, he should have held on more tightly. He picks up one of
Nancy's blue rabbit slippers, stroking the fur. It's his own
eventual death he cradles. His lost, his kidnapped children,
gone from him, kept hostage. Who has done this? How has he
allowed it to happen?

Tuesday, February 8, 1977

LESJE

Lesje drifts along the street with the drifting snow. Cars in their chains jingle past her, their tires locked in ruts; slush clogs their fenders. In the night there's been a blizzard. She doesn't care that her feet are cold: she has no feet. The trees she passes are heavy with ice. Each twig glitters in the weak sunlight, lit from within; the world glows. Lesje stretches her arms out, feels the blood flow along them to explode in purple at each hand. She knows the blaze of light she sees is only a mitten. But it is a mitten transfigured, its acrylic fibers shining with their own atomic light. Dazzled, she squints her eyes. She's weightless, all pores, the universe accepts her finally, nothing bad can happen. Has she ever felt like this before?

It's only two o'clock. She left the office early, telling Dr. Van Vleet she felt she was coming down with something. Really it's Nate who is coming down with something: he phoned from his house, nasal, forlorn, he has to see her. Lesje walks to the rescue in her gum-soled snowboots, a nurse hurrying over frozen Siberia, driven on by love. She will put her hand on his forehead and miraculously he will revive. By the time she reaches his front steps and stamps her way up them her nose is running.

Nate opens the door, draws her inside quickly, shuts the door before enfolding her. Lesje is pressed against his brown wool dressing gown, which smells of old smoke and burned toast. His mouth comes down on hers; sniffling, they kiss. He half-lifts her, then thinks better of it and sets her down.

"My boots will drip," she says, and bends to unzip them. She tugs at her boot heels, her eyes at the level of Nate's knees. He's wearing work socks, grey with red stripes around the top and white toes and heels. These socks, for some reason, fill her with tenderness and lust: her body is with her again.

In their stocking feet they tiptoe along the hall and up the stairs. Nate leads her by the hand.

"In here," he says. Although there is no one home, they whisper.

Nate folds back the Indian spread. Lesje can hardly see: the room is a blur around her, vision a shaft of light illuminating tigers, off-red tigers in a purplish jungle. Under the tigers there are flowered sheets. Wordlessly Nate undresses her, lifting her arms, bending her elbows as if he's undressing a doll or a child; Lesje stands still. He eases her sweater over her head, presses his cheek against her stomach while he kneels to slide down her jeans. Lesje raises one foot and then the other, stepping out, obedient. There's cold air, a draft somewhere in the room. Her skin contracts. Gently he pulls her onto the bed. She sinks into a hollow, petals flow over her.

He's on top of her, both of them impelled now by fear, the sun moving across the sky, the feet walking inexorably towards them, the sound of a door which has not yet opened, boots on the stairs.

Lesje is lying semipropped on two pillows. His head rests on her belly. The world is again the world, she can see detail, the luminous blur has faded. Nevertheless she's happy. She does not see this happiness as having any necessary result.

Nate moves, reaches for a Kleenex from the night table. "What time is it?" he says. They talk in normal voices now.

Lesje checks her watch. "I'd better leave," she says. She would rather not have Elizabeth or the children come back to find her naked in Nate's bed.

Nate rolls onto his side, rests on an elbow while she sits up, slides her legs over the side of the bed. With one hand she gropes for her underpants, lost somewhere in the flowers. She bends to look on the floor. Two shoes are there, on the oval braided rug, black ones, side by side.

"Nate," she says. "Whose room is this?"

He looks at her, he doesn't answer.

"This is Elizabeth's room," she says.

She stands up and begins to dress, covering herself as fast as she can. This is horrible, this is a violation. She feels grubby; it's almost like incest. Elizabeth's husband is one thing, Elizabeth's bed quite another.

Nate doesn't understand. He explains that his own bed is too narrow for both of them.

This is not the point. She thinks: The bed had no choice.

He helps her pull the tiger bedspread up and smooth the pillows. How can she tell him? She doesn't know why she is so upset. Perhaps it's the suggestion that it doesn't matter, that she and Elizabeth are interchangeable. Or his feeling that Elizabeth's bed is still in some sense his also, he can do whatever he wants in it. Lesje feels for the first time that she has wronged Elizabeth, that she has trespassed.

Lesje sits in the kitchen, elbows on the kitchen table, chin on her hands; Nate lights her cigarette for her. He's baffled. He offers her a Scotch, then a cup of tea. Smoke screens her face.

On the refrigerator there's a child's painting, held in place by a magnetic plastic tomato and a cob of corn. It's of a girl, hair a yellow blob, eyes fringed with enormous lashes, a manic red grin. The sky is a blue line at the top of the page, the sun a bursting lemon.

All the molecular materials now present in the earth and its atmosphere were present at the creation of the earth itself, whether that creation took place by the explosion of a larger body or by condensation of gaseous debris. These molecular materials have merely combined, disintegrated, recombined. Although a few molecules and atoms have escaped into space, nothing has been added.

Lesje contemplates this fact, which she finds soothing. She is only a pattern. She is not an immutable object. There are no immutable objects. Some day she will dissolve.

Nate strokes her hand. He is dismayed but she cannot comfort him.

"What are you thinking about, love?" he says.

NATE

Nate is down in the cellar. He's cutting out heads on the scroll saw, heads and necks for four-wheeled horses. Each horse will have a string on the front. When the string is pulled, the horse will roll along, head and tail moving in graceful rhythm. Or so he hopes.

As he works, he pauses to wipe sweat from his forehead. His beard is dank; altogether he feels like a mildewed mattress. It's a lot cooler down here than it is upstairs, though just as humid. Outside it must be ninety. In the morning the cicadas began their rasping songs well before eight.

"A scorcher," Nate remarked when he'd encountered Elizabeth in the kitchen. She was wearing a light blue dress with a smudge on the back, at the level of the rib cage. "Did you know you have smudge on your dress?" he asked. She liked to be told about such lapses: undone zippers, unhooked hooks, hairs on the shoulders, labels sticking out of necklines. "Oh, do I?" she said. "I'll change it." But she'd left for work in the same dress. Unlike her to forget.

Nate wants a cold beer. He switches off the saw and turns towards the stairway, and it's then that he sees the head, upside down in the square mud-pocked cellar window, staring in at him. It's Chris Beecham. He must be lying on the gravel outside, his neck twisted at right angles so he can get his head down into the window well. He smiles. Nate motions upstairs, hoping Chris will understand and go to the back door.

When Nate opens the door, Chris is already there. He's still smiling. "I was banging on the window," he says.

"I had the scroll saw on," Nate says. Chris gives no explanation of why he's here. Nate steps back to let him in, offers a beer. Chris accepts and walks behind him to the kitchen.

"I took this afternoon off," he says. "It's too hot to work. It's not like they have air conditioning."

This is only the fourth or fifth time Nate has ever seen Chris. The first time was when Elizabeth invited him to Christmas dinner. "He knows hardly anyone," she'd said. Elizabeth has a habit of doing that, inviting people to dinner who know hardly anyone. Sometimes these stray eggs for which Elizabeth plays hen are women, but more often they are men. Nate doesn't mind. He approves, more or less, even though this is the kind of thing his mother woud do if she thought of it. As it is, she runs more to letters than to dinners. Elizabeth's waifs are usually nice enough, and the children like to have guests, especially around Christmas. Janet says it makes it more like a party.

Chris got a little drunk, Nate remembers. They'd had Christmas crackers, and Nate had found a prize eye in his, a plastic eye with a red iris.

"What is it?" Nancy asked.

"An eye," Nate said. Usually it was whistles or small mono-colored figures. This was the first year anyone had found an eye.

"What's it for?"

"I don't know," Nate said. He put it on the side of his plate. Somewhat later Chris reached across and took it and stuck it in the center of his forehead. He then began singing "The Streets of Laredo" in a lugubrious voice. The children though he was funny.

Since then, Nate has come up from the cellar on several occasions to find Chris in his living room, having a drink with Elizabeth. They've been sitting at opposite sides of the room, not saying much. Nate has always poured himself a drink and joined them. He seldom turns down the chance for a sociable drink. One thing has puzzled Nate: although Elizabeth invites lame ducks for festive dinners, she rarely has people over for a drink unless their position at the Museum is either on a par with hers or higher. There's no way Chris fits either of these categories. As far as Nate can figure out, he's a taxidermist of some sort, a glorified custodian of dead owls. A technician, not an executive. Nate doesn't rule out the possibility that Elizabeth and Chris are lovers—Chris wouldn't be the first— but before this she's always told him. Sooner or later. He'll wait for that before believing. Things aren't particularly good between them, but they're still possible.

Nate opens two Carling's Red Caps and they sit at the kitchen table. He asks Chris if he wants a glass; Chris says no. What he wants, instead, is to have Nate drive over to his place with him for a game of chess. Nate is a little taken aback by this. He explains that he doesn't play chess very well, hasn't played much for years.

"Elizabeth says you're good," Chris says.

"That's because Elizabeth can't play at all," Nate says modestly.

But Chris insists. It will cheer him up, he says. He's been feeling down lately. Nate cannot resist this appeal to his Samaritan instincts. He goes upstairs to their room to put on a clean T-shirt. When he comes down, Chris is spinning one of the beer bottles on the kitchen table.

"Ever play spin the bottle?" he asks. As a matter of fact, Nate hasn't.

They take Chris's car, which is illegally parked across the street. It's an old Chevy convertible, once white, a '67 or '68 model. Nate's grip on car models is slipping. He himself no longer has a car, having sold it to finance his scroll saw, his bench saw, his belt-disc sander and other necessary machines.

Chris's car is missing a muffler. He exploits this aggressively, revving the engine like a thunder gun at each stoplight. They fart their way along Davenport, trailing clouds of noise pollution, gathering dirty looks. The top of the convertible is down and the sun, filtered through layers of spent exhaust, beats on their heads. By the time they reach Winchester and Parliament and Chris parks, again illegally, Nate is dizzy. He asks Chris, to make conversation, if there's much prostitution around here. He already knows there is. Chris gives him a look of undisguised dislike and says yes, there is. "I don't mind it though," he says. "They know I'm not in the market. We pass the time of day."

Nate wants to get out of this. He wants to say he has a headache, a backache, any sort of ache severe enough to spring him. He isn't feeling up to having a chess game in ninety-degree weather with a man he barely knows. But Chris is now brisk, almost businesslike. He marches them across the street and lets them into his apartment building, marches them across the stained mosaic-tile entryway and up the stairs, three flights. Nate, panting, lags behind. In the face of such certainty he hesitates to offer his dim excuses.

Chris unlocks his door and goes in. Nate, plunging, follows. The apartment is cooler; it's wood-paneled, must once have been intended for the semi-rich. Although it has two rooms, a wide arched doorway between them makes it seem like one. It smells of darkness: corners, dry-rot, a chemical smell. The chess table is already set up, in the room that also contains Chris's bed. There are two chairs, placed carefully on opposite sides of the chessboard. Nate realizes that this invitation was not a spur-of-the-moment whim.

"Want a drink?" Chris produces a mickey of Scotch from the glass-doored cupboard, pours some into a small tumbler decorated with tulips. Jelly jar, Nate things; he recognizes it from ten years ago. The Scotch is bad but Nate drinks; he doesn't wish to antagonize. Chris, it seems, will drink from the bottle. He sets it beside the chess table, gives Nate a peanut butter jar lid for his cigarette ashes, takes a white pawn and a black one from the table and shuffles them behind his back. He holds out his fists, huge, thick-knuckled.

"Left," Nate says.

"Tough luck," Chris says. They sit down to play. Chris opens with an insulting attempt at fool's mate, which Nate counters easily. Chris grins and pours Nate another drink. They settle down to play in earnest. Nate knows Chris will win, but out of pride he wants this victory to take a decent amount of time. He plays defensively, grouping his men in tight clumps, taking no chances.

Chris plays like a Cossack, swooping forward, picking at Nate's outposts, retreating to puzzling new positions. He jiggles one foot against the floor impatiently while Nate ponders his moves. They're both sweating. Nate's T-shirt sticks to his skin; he'd like an open window, a draft, but it's hotter outside than in here. Nate knows he's drinking more bad Scotch than he should, but the game is getting to him.

Finally he makes a good move. Chris will either have to take his queen's knight and lose his own knight, or he'll lose a rook. Now it's Nate's turn to sit back and stare intimidatingly while Chris worries his choices. Nate sits back, but instead of staring he tries to keep himself from wondering what he's doing here, which would be bad for his game.

He glances around the room. It's almost bare, yet manages to give the impression of disorder. It isn't the objects in the room that do this, but their relation to each oher. Nothing seems to be in the right place. The table beside the bed, for instance, is about a foot too far away from it.

And on the table, which is otherwise empty, is something he now knows he was meant to see. It's a little fish, silver, with blue enameled scales. He's last noticed it hanging on a chain around Elizabeth's neck.

Or one very like it. He can't be sure. He looks at Chris and Chris is gazing at him, the muscles of his face rigid, his eyes still. Fear shoots through Nate, the hairs on his arms rise, his scrotum contracts, the ends of his fingers tingle. He thinks: Chris is drunk. He finds himself wondering whether Chris really has Indian blood in him as Elizabeth implies, he's never been able to place that slight accent; then he's appalled at himself, falling into a cliché like that. Besides, Chris has hardly been drinking at all, it's he himself who's killed three-quarters of that poisonous mickey.

If he's right, if he's been brought here on (he now sees) the shabby pretext of a chess game, just to witness this object, this hostage which may or may not belong to Elizabeth, his options are limited. Chris knows he knows. Chris is expecting Nate to hit him. Then Chris will hit Nate and they'll have a fight. Smashing the chess table, rolling among the light puffs of dust that colonize Chris's floor.

Nate deplores this solution. The question is: Is Elizabeth a female dog or a human being? It's a matter of human dignity. Why fight over Elizabeth, who presumably can make her own choices? Has made them. Whoever wins, the fight would settle nothing.

Nate could pretend he hasn't seen the silver fish, but it's gone too far for that.

Or he could ignore it. Even to himself this would look like cowardice.

"Made your move?" Nate says.

Chris captures the queen's knight, stares at Nate, his chin out, tensed, ready. Any moment he may spring. Nate thinks: Maybe he's crazy. Maybe he's crazy enough to have bought another fish and planted it there. Maybe he's fucking insane!

Instead of taking the white knight, Nate tips over his own king.

"You win the game," he says. He stands up, scoops the fish off the table.

"I'll return this to Elizabeth for you, shall I?" he says, gently, affably.

He walks to the door, expecting at any moment to feel fists on his back, a boot in his kidneys. He takes a taxi back to the house; the driver waits outside while he gathers enough loose change from the surfaces of their room to pay him.

He places the silver fish carefully on the night table, beside his scattered pennies. She should have told him. It isn't friendly, the fact that she hasn't told him. The first time, she told him and they both cried, holding each other closely, consoling each other for some violation they felt as mutual. Then they discussed their problems, sitting up till four in the morning, whispering across the kitchen table. They promised reforms, repairs, reparations, whole new sequences of events, a new order. And the second and the third time. He isn't a monster, he's always stifled his outrage, he's forgiven her.

The fact that she hasn't told him this time means only one thing: she doesn't want to be forgiven. Or, put another way, she no longer cares whether he forgives her or not. Or, it occurs to him, she may have decided it isn't his right to forgive.

Wednesday, February 16, 1977

ELIZABETH

Elizabeth is sitting at the black-topped table in Fran's. Opposite her is William. In front of her is a waffle with a scoop of vanilla ice cream melting on it, and on top of the ice cream is a tentacled formation of partially congealed cinnamon-colored syrup. She watches the syrup run down and hopes the waitress won't comment on the untouched waffle when she brings the check.

Across the table from her William is eating a club sandwich and drinking draft beer. Elizabeth is only half-listening to the conversation, which consists of an account, by William, of recent research on carcinogenic substances to be found in smoked meats. She's more relaxed now. William doesn't seem to notice that they're in Fran's instead of some récherché little hideaway. The first two récherché little hideaways they tried had been full, and according to William they were the only ones in the area. An area Elizabeth no longer knows well.

Under ordinary circumstances she would have reserved in advance, but she needed to seem impromptu. She happened to be passing by the Ministry of the Environment on her way to do some shopping (false; she never shops at Yonge and St. Clair) and remembered their recent conversation (also false). She thought how fascinating it would be to pop in on William and hear a little more about the work he was doing (totally false), and if William wasn't busy for lunch, she'd love to have him join her (true, but not for the reasons William may have suspected).

William was even more flattered than she intended him to be. Even now he's swelling visibly, expounding with fervor on degenerate hams and the evil secret life of bacon. She prods at her waffle with her fork and wonders whether she should press his knee discreetly under the table, or is it too soon? She hasn't yet decided exactly how she'll go on from here. Either she will seduce William, to create some balance in the universe, a tit for a tat, or she'll tell him about Lesje and Nate; or perhaps both.

She cuts off a piece of waffle with her fork, lifts it. Then she puts it back on her plate. She remembers why this is something she can no longer eat.

It's May; Elizabeth is coming to life again. Two weeks ago her mother finally died, after smoldering in the hospital bed for longer than anyone could have expected. Elizabeth sat through that death, watching clear fluid drip from a bottle into her mother's good arm, holding the good hand, watching the good half of the face for any movement, any sign. For two days she didn't eat or sleep, despite Auntie Muriel and the doctor, who said that her mother would not regain consciousness, which was all for the best, and Elizabeth should save her strength. She walked through the funeral step by step, listened to the service, watched her mother float for the second time into the flames. She allowed her hand to be shaken and pressed by the friends of Auntie Muriel. Auntie Muriel planned the whole funeral down to the last detail as if it were an important tea party. She can't tell whether Auntie Muriel is mourning or gloating; there's a pleased fatalism about her. She has the flowers from the funeral around the house in vases—why waste them?—and the house stinks of death.

Auntie Muriel can't seem to stop talking about it. Elizabeth wants to stop talking about it. She wants to stop hearing about it, thinking about it. She never wants to think about her mother again. In two months, less than that, she'll be finished with high school and then she'll get out. Auntie Muriel wants her to go to Trinity College and continue living in the house; she says it will be better for Caroline, which Elizabeth sees as a ruse to trap her.

Elizabeth herself has no such ambitions. She wants only one thing: escape. She can't yet see what form this will take. She can see herself planning, finding a job through the *Star* want ads, hunting a furnished room, packing; making provisions. She can also see herself running out the front door in her nightgown and vanishing forever into a ravine. Both of these things are equally possible.

She can't bear to be inside Auntie Muriel's house with its greyish chrysanthemums, its festering gladioli. The room she

shares with Caroline is papered with small blue roses, their
stems bunched into doilies, Auntie Muriel's version of girl-
hood; the furniture is painted white. On her bed Caroline
keeps a blue fake-fur pyjama bag-in the shape of a cat.

Elizabeth picks up a boy in a drugstore. It isn't the first time,
but it's the first time since her mother's death; and in a drugstore. Before it's been street corners, the entranceways to
movie houses. This is forbidden: Auntie Muriel allows only
formal dances at private schools with the sons of her acquaintances. Elizabeth has no taste for these dances or for the pink-
cheeked, short-haired boys who attend them. She prefers boys
like this one. He has a ducktail and a red leather jacket with
the collar turned up; his black eyebrows almost meet, his chin
is cut where he's scraped it shaving. His shorter friend gets
out of the car, muttering something to him and laughing, as
Elizabeth gets in.

The car is festooned with plastic dice and feather kewpie
dolls. Elizabeth likes such cars. There's danger in them but
she knows she can control it. She enjoys the latent power of
her own hands; she knows she can always stop in time. It
excites and gratifies her to be able to do this, go to the edge
and almost jump. (There's something else, too. The boys, any
boys, any mouth and pair of arms, contain a possibility; some
quality she can only guess at, some hope.)

They drive around for a while, then go to Fran's for a waffle. Food is always part of it. Elizabeth gobbles her waffle as if
she's never seen one before; the boy smokes, watches her
through narrowed eyes. His name is Fred or something and
he goes to Jarvis. She tells him where she lives and he tries
not to be impressed. Elizabeth feels she knows exactly what
Auntie Muriel and her pretensions are worth. This doesn't
stop her from displaying them. Auntie Muriel has her terrors,
which are real enough to Elizabeth, but increasingly she also
has her uses.

They drive around some more, park on a quiet side street.
The smell of Old Spice shaving lotion fills the car. Elizabeth
waits for the leather arm to arrive, across, over, down. She
has no time right now for preliminaries, fumbling with hooks,
inching around the rib cage; she does not want to dole herself
out. She's filled with energy, she can't tell what it is, anger,
fury, denial. What she has in mind is more like a car crash,
time squeezed together. Violence, metal on metal.

He's tangled in the steering wheel. Impatient, more reckless

than he is, she opens the car door, pulls him down onto the
wet grass. Somebody's front lawn. "Hey," he says. He's nervous, he glances up at the curtained windows.

She wants to shout, a huge raucous shout that will startle
the darkness, bring the cold crab eyes in these stone houses
hurrying to their windows; something that will unlock her
throat. She wants to let go of the dead hand she's still holding.

She kisses this mouth that exists only now, does not stop or
pull away when the hands move over her, twists to allow him.
He groans, hesitates. Then for a minute she almost does
scream: she expected pain, but not this kind or this much.
Nevertheless she is grinning, teeth set; she exults. She hopes
she's bleeding, a little anyway; blood would make this an
event. When he goes limp she reaches down to see.

He doesn't understand, he's on his knees beside her, doing
himself up, pulling down her skirt, apologizing! Awkwardly;
he's really sorry, he couldn't help it, he didn't mean to. As if
she's a foot he's stepped on, as if he's merely sneezed.

She gets out of the car a block from the house. It's later
than she thought. The back of her coat is wet and she brushes
at it ineffectually before getting out her key. She's convinced
Auntie Muriel will be standing on the bottom step of the staircase in her powder blue dressing gown, accusing, malignant,
triumphant. Elizabeth has fed her a story about evening choir
practice, which, unbelievably, has worked several times before.
But she's never stayed out so late. If Auntie Muriel is there, if
she knows, Elizabeth can't imagine what she'll do. She can't
imagine any actual punishment—rage, banishment, disinheri-
tance—equal to her dread. When she's at a distance from Auntie Muriel she can think of derisive and vulgar things to say to
her, but in her presence she knows she would be mute. If
Auntie Muriel were roped to the stake she'd be the first to
jeer; but who has the power to put her there? Auntie Muriel
terrifies her because she doesn't know where to stop. Other
people have lines they won't step over, but for Auntie Muriel
such lines do not exist. Elizabeth's other fear is that these lines
do not exist in herself, either.

But when she unlocks the door the hall is vacant. She walks
along the carpet and up the stairs, making it past the inlaid
grandfather clock on the landing, past the Chinese vases on
their spindly stands at the top of the stairs, pressing her thighs
together, blood seeping gently in her clothes. She'll have to
wash these clothes herself, privately, dry them in secret. She
wants Auntie Muriel to know, wants her to see the evidence

of this violation; at the same time she'll do everything to keep
her from finding out.

She opens the door of the room she shares with Caroline.
The overhead light is on. Caroline is lying on the floor between their beds. She's spread out the plaid mohair blanket
from the foot of her bed and is lying on it, arms folded across
her breasts, eyes open and fixed on the ceiling. Above her
head and at her feet are the silver candelabra from the ma-
hogany buffet downstairs. Beside her there's a bottle of lemon
furniture polish. The candles in the candelabra have burned
to stubs, gone out. She must have been like this for hours.

Elizabeth knows as soon as she sees her that she's been
expecting this, or something like it. Caroline would not go to
the hospital; she said she didn't want to see their mother. She
refused to attend the funeral, and Auntie Muriel, strangely,
did not force her. Elizabeth noticed all this, but only from the
corner of her eye. Caroline had been so silent lately it was
easy not to notice her.

Once, a long time ago, Elizabeth strode through the girl's half
of a schoolyard at recess, her arms linked in a chain of other
girls. *We don't stop for anybody.* That was the game: you
couldn't stop for anybody. Elizabeth kept Caroline's arm
gripped firmly under her own; she had to have Caroline with
her in the chain so she wouldn't get run down. Caroline was
younger, she had trouble keeping up. She was Elizabeth's responsibility. But Elizabeth has been concentrating all her energy, for years now, on saving herself. She hasn't had any left
over for saving Caroline.

She drops to her knees, smooths Caroline's hair back from
her forehead above the unblinking eyes. Then she moves one
folded arm and puts her head on Caroline's chest. Caroline is
still alive.

Once the ambulance and the stretcher had come and gone,
but not until then, Elizabeth had knelt on the mosaic tiles of
the second-floor bathroom beside the claw-footed tub and
thrown up her Fran's Special, ice cream, cinnamon syrup and
all. Her penance. About the only one she'd ever been able to
make. If she'd been religious, one of the Catholics so detested
by Auntie Muriel, she could have lit a candle for the repose of
Caroline's soul. But Caroline seemed to have already taken
care of that herself.

At the hospital they said she hadn't drunk any of the furniture polish. The open bottle was a sign, Caroline's last message; an indication of where she'd gone, since for all practical purposes she was no longer in her body.

Elizabeth watches while William finishes off his club sandwich and orders apple pie with cheese and a cup of coffee. She dislikes his tie. Someone with William's choirboy complexion should not wear beige and maroon. If Lesje lives with a man who has such poor taste in ties, she's hardly worth defeating.

William doesn't seem to have noticed that Elizabeth isn't eating; he's explaining why colored toilet paper is so much worse than white. Elizabeth knows she will take scant pleasure in sleeping with him or even in making the revelation she's come here to make. Perhaps she won't bother. She's amazed sometimes at the lengths to which people will go to distract themselves. She amazes herself.

Wednesday, February 16, 1977

LESJE

Lesje is cataloguing giant tortoises from the Upper Cretaceous. REPTILIA, she writes. *Chelonia, Neurankylidae.* GENUS & SPECIES, *Neurankylus baueri, Gilmore.* LOCALITY: Fruitland, New Mexico, U.S.A. GEOLOGY: Upper Cretaceous, Fruitland shale. MATERIAL: Carapace & plastron.

How ignominious to be dug up in Fruitland, Lesje thinks, after so many million years of peace. She's never been to Fruitland but she pictures little souvenir stands where plastic fruits are sold: grape lapel pins, magnetic tomatoes. Or probably, since it's the United States, college students dressed up as giant peaches and apples strolling among the crowds. Like Disneyland.

There's a number in black-ink figures on the slip of paper attached to the carapace, and she adds this number to the filing card. When she's finished with the larger specimens, she knows there's a whole tray of carapace fragments awaiting her. She'll cart it from the storage shelves up to her office, past the sandblasters and dentist's drills they use for cleaning fossils; when she's finished with it she'll cart it down again and slide it into the storage rack. After that she'll start on the fish earbones from the Miocene. There are hundreds of fish earbones, hundreds of tortoise fragments, hundreds of assorted vertebrae, knuckles, claws, hundreds of teeth. Thousands of pounds of rock, locked into the patterns of the once-living. Sometimes she wonders whether the world really needs more fish earbones from the Miocene. On days like this she wonders whether her job isn't, really, just glorified filing.

When she's settled in her cubbyhole of an office with the shell fragments and her clean cards, the phone rings. It's another school group, wanting a tour. Lesje slots them into her calendar. She no longer anticipates school tours with much pleasure. Once she thought she could teach them something. Now she knows there will be at least one child who will want to throw something at the dinosaurs—a bubble-gum wrapper, a pop-bottle top, a pebble—to show he isn't afraid. Mammal cubs, jeering their old enemies. Don't walk on the ledge, she will say. If you push all the buttons at once you won't be able to hear.

Should she make a cup of instant coffee in the wet lab, bring it back to her windowless cubicle, and stay late to finish the tray? Or should she, for once, leave on time?

She peers through the door of the large office adjoining the wet lab. Dr. Van Vleet has already gone, shoehorning his damp rubbers on over his scuffed black shoes and paddling off like a stooped tweed duck into the February slush. Lesje has always been compulsive about her job—whe wants very much to do it well—but she's become irritable with it lately. No one, probably, will ever look at the Miocene fish earbones again, once she slots the tray into place. Except her, surreptitiously easing it back out some day to admire their symmetry and size and to imagine the gigantic fish with their bony sheathing, sliding like huge knees through the ancient oceans.

She completes one more card, then closes the filing-card box and goes for her coat. She slips her arms into it, bundles her head, checks her shoulder-bag for money. She'll stop at Ziggy's on the way back to the apartment and pick up something nice for dinner, something nice for William. Ever since she's come to suspect that she may eventually leave him, she's been very solicitous about William. She buys him surprises, tinned sardines, clams, things he likes. When he sniffles she gets him pills, lemons and boxes of Kleenex. It's as if she wants to make sure he's in good condition when she passes him on, trades him in. See, she'll say to him. Look how healthy you are. You don't need me.

She doesn't know how she'll tell him, though; or even when. Nate doesn't want to make any sudden moves, because of the children. He thinks he will rent an apartment or, better still, part of a house, so there will be room for his machines, and move into it a little at a time. He'll tell the children it's a workshop. He hasn't yet indicated when he would like Lesje to join him, just that he would. Eventually. When the children get adjusted. Sometimes they look at the want ads, trying to decide where he, or possibly they, will finally live.

Lesje looks forward to this time—it would be good to be

with him in a neutral bed with no fear of opening doors—but doesn't exactly believe in it. She can't picture, for instance, actually moving. Folding sheets and towels, taking down her posters (from the Museum, mostly, stuck to the walls with masking tape), putting her few dishes and the frying pan her mother gave her when she left home into cardboard cartons. If she really is going to move, she ought to be able to picture it. (And where will William be? At the office? Standing by with arms folded to see that she doesn't take any of his books, or the shower curtains, which were his own purchases, or the *Organic Eating* cookbook they never use?)

Nate hasn't discussed this future move with Elizabeth, though he's discussed other things. Elizabeth knows about them. He and Elizabeth had quite a good talk about it one night while he was having a bath. It's a long-standing habit of Elizabeth's to talk to him while he's in the bathtub, Nate tells her. Though it bothers Lesje slightly to think of them having habits together she asked, "Was she angry?"

"Not at all," Nate said. "She was very good about it. She's glad I've found someone congenial."

For some reason Elizabeth's approval annoys Lesje more than her anger would have.

"She does think, though," Nate said, "that you should tell William. She feels it's a little dishonest not to. She thinks it's only fair to her. She . . ."

"It's none of her business," Lesje said, surprising herself by her own abruptness. "Why should she care what I tell William?"

"They've become quite friendly," Nate said mildly. "They seem to have lunch together quite a lot. She says it puts her in a false position with William, that she knows and he doesn't."

Lesje hadn't heard about this friendship, these lunches. She felt left out. Why hadn't William mentioned anything about it? Though he rarely tells her who he has lunch with. But this may mean only what she thinks it means: that, like her, he seldom has lunch at all. She sees, too, the threat behind the message; for it was a message, Elizabeth the sender, Nate merely the unwitting deliverer. If she doesn't tell William soon, Elizabeth will tell him herself.

Yet she's been unable to say anything. There hasn't been an opportunity, she tells herself. What's she supposed to do? Interrupt a cribbage game to say, "William, I'm having an affair"?

She swings along the street, head down, carrying the bag of

potato salad and fried chicken she's bought at Ziggy's. William once told her she walks like an adolescent boy. But so does he, so they're even.

When she reaches the apartment, William is sitting at the card table. He has a solitaire game spread in front of him, but he's looking out the window.

"I got some stuff from Ziggy's," Lesje says cheerfully. William doesn't answer, which is nothing new. She walks through the kitchenette, leaving the bag on the counter, and goes into the bedroom.

She's sitting on the bed, pulling off her leather boots, when William appears in the doorway. He has a strange look on his face, as if his muscles are in spasm. He comes towards her, hulking.

"William, what's wrong?" she says; but he pushes her down on the bed, one arm across both shoulders, his elbow digging in beside her collarbone. His other hand rips at the zipper on her jeans.

William has always liked to tumble around a little. She starts to laugh, then stops. This is different. His arm is against her throat, cutting off her wind.

"William, that hurts," she says; then, "William, cut it *out!*" He's got her jeans worked halfway down her thighs before it occurs to her that William is trying to rape her.

She's always thought of rape as something the Russians did to the Ukrainians, something the Germans did, more furtively, to the Jews; something blacks did in Detroit, in dark alleys. But not something William Wasp, from a good family in London, Ontario, would ever do to her. They're friends, they discuss extinction and pollution, they've known each other for years. They live together!

What can she do now? If she fights him off, kicks him in the nuts, he'll never speak to her again. She's almost certain she could: her knee's in the right position, he's crouching over her, fumbling at her nylon crotch. But if she lets him go ahead, there's a good chance she'll never speak to him again. It's absurd, and William, huffing and puffing and grinding his teeth, is absurd too. But she knows if she laughs he'll hit her.

This is frightening; he's hurting her on purpose. Maybe he's always wanted to do this but never had the excuse. What is the excuse?

"William, stop," she says; but William tugs and rips, silently, relentlessly, forcing his torso between her knees. Finally she is angry herself. The least he could do is answer her. She

clamps her legs together, tightens the muscles of her neck
and shoulders, and lets William batter himself against her.
He's pulling her hair now, digging his fingers into her arms.
Finally he groans, oozes, unclenches.

"Finished?" she says coldly. He's a dead weight. She pries
herself out from beneath him, buttons her shirt. She pulls off
her jeans and underpants and mops her thighs with them.
William, pink-eyed, watches her from the bed.

"I'm sorry," he says.

Lesje is afraid he's going to cry. Then she will have to forgive him. Without answering, she goes to the bathroom and
stuffs her clothes into the laundry hamper. She wraps a towel
around her waist. All she wants to do is have a shower.

She leans her forehead against the cool glass of the mirror.
She can't stay here. Where will she go, what did she do? Her
heart is racing, there are scratches on her arms and breasts,
she's gasping for air. It's the sight of William turning into
someone else that has shocked her. She doesn't know whose
fault it is.

Wednesday, February 16, 1977

ELIZABETH

Elizabeth is having a bad dream. The children are lost. They are only babies, both of them, and through carelessness, a moment of inattention, she's misplaced them. Or they've been stolen. Their cribs are empty, she's hurrying through unfamiliar streets looking for them. The streets are deserted, the windows dark; there's no snow on the ground, no leaves on the hedges, the sky overhead would be full of stars if she could only look up. She would call, but she knows the children will not be able to answer her, even if they can hear her. They're inside one of the houses, wrapped up; even their mouths are covered by blankets.

She turns over, forces herself awake. She looks around the room, the looming bureau, the spider plants, the stripes of light through the blinds, making sure she is here. Her heart quiets, her eyes are dry. The dream is an old one, an old familiar. She began having it after Nancy was born. At that time she would wake crying convulsively, and Nate would comfort her. He would take her to the children's room so she could listen and see that they were all right. He'd thought she was dreaming about their own children, but even then she had known, though she hadn't told him, that the lost babies were her mother and Caroline. She's shut them out, both of them, as well as she could, but they come back anyway, using the forms that will most torment her.

She doesn't want to go back to sleep; she knows that if she does she'll probably have the same dream again. She gets out of bed, finds her slippers and dressing gown, and goes downstairs to make herself a warm milk and honey. As she passes the children's room she listens, then pushes open the door just to make sure. Pure habit. She will probably go on doing this for the rest of her life, even after they are really gone. She will go on having the dream. Nothing ever finishes.

Part Four

LESJE

Lesje's knife squeaks on china. They're having roast beef, which is a little tough. Her mother has never known how to cope with roast beef. Lesje cuts and chews; nobody says anything, which is not unusual. Around her is the sound she remembers from childhood, a hollow sound, like a cave where there might be an echo.

They didn't know she was coming until the last minute. Nevertheless her mother has set out the good plates, the ones with pink roses and gold rims that belonged to Lesje's grandmother. The other good plates have blue borders with silver rims and scenes of Scottish castles; they belonged to the other grandmother. The meat plates. Lesje's parents got them because, despite his transgressions, her father was the only son. Her aunt got the milk plates and has never ceased to resent it. There's a third set of dishes for everyday, which her parents bought themselves: oven-to-table stoneware. Lesje feels more comfortable with these, which are a neutral shade of brown.

Her mother offers her more Yorkshire pudding. Lesje accepts, which makes her mother smile; a placid, mournful smile. She has braids wound around her head only in old photographs, Lesje can't remember her with them, but she looks as though the braids are still there, shining through the matronly permanent she renews every two months. A rounded face, tidy features. Lesje's father too is round, which makes Lesje's height and stringiness a family mystery. When she was in her teens her mother kept telling her she would fill out when she got older, to console her for the lack of breasts. But she has not filled out.

Lesje's mother is pleased she's suddenly come to dinner; Lesje hasn't come to dinner that often lately. But she's also puzzled: she throws swift inquiring glances across the table at

Lesje while Lesje wolfs her Yorkshire pudding, hoping for explanations, later, in the kitchen. But Lesje can't explain anything. Since she's never told her parents in so many words that she was living with William (though her mother guessed), she can hardly say she's moved out and is now living with someone else. Marriage is an event, a fact, it can be discussed at the dinner table. So is divorce. They create a framework, a beginning, an ending. Without them everything is amorphous, an endless middle ground, stretching like a prairie on either side of each day. Though she's moved herself physically from one place to another Lesje has no clear sense of anything having ended or of anything else having begun.

She told her mother she'd moved. She also said she hadn't unpacked her own dishes, which is true and was her excuse for inviting herself so suddenly to dinner. But she gave the impression that the move had taken place that very day, whereas in fact it's been three weeks since she hired the U-Haul and bundled her possessions into cardboard boxes. She did it during the day, when William wasn't there, and with no prior announcement. To say she was moving would have demanded an explanation, and she was reluctant to get into that.

It's amazing how quickly her life with William was expelled from the drawers and torn from the walls and how little space it took up. She carried the boxes to the elevator herself, nothing was very heavy, and packed them into the U-Haul, which wasn't necessary at all, a station wagon would have done. Then she lifted them out and carted them up the rickety steps of the house she'd rented. It's a decaying row house on Beverly Street, not a very good one, but she'd only spent a day looking and she'd taken the first space available that was both cheap enough and big enough for Nate's machines. A developer owned it; he was going to turn it into a townhouse, so he was willing to give her a low rate as long as she didn't demand a lease.

She felt she had to get out before William apologized. If he'd apologized—as she'd been sure he would sooner or later—she would have been trapped.

The day after that thing happened—she doesn't know what to call it and has finally decided to think of it as *the incident*—William left early in the morning. Lesje had spent the night in the bathroom with the door locked, lying curled up on the bathmat covered with towels, but this had been overkill as he hadn't tried to get in.

It had pleased her slightly to think of him arriving at work unshowered, unshaven; squeaky cleanliness was one of his fetishes. When she heard the apartment door close she ventured out, changed into fresh clothes and went to work herself. She didn't know what to do or think. Was he violent, would he try it again? She resisted the desire to phone Nate and describe *the incident*. After all it wasn't that bad, she hadn't been hurt, she hadn't really been raped, not technically. Also, if she told Nate she would be putting pressure on him to do something; to move in with her immediately, for instance. She didn't want to do this. She wanted Nate to move in when he was ready, when he wanted to be with her, not because of something William had almost done.

After work she wandered around for a while, sitting in Murray's with a cup of coffee and a cigarette, walking along Bloor Street and looking at the store windows. In the end she went home, and William was sitting in the living room, pink-cheeked, cheerful, as if nothing at all had happened. He greeted her pleasantly and launched into a discussion of the caloric values produced by the controlled fermentation of liquid effluents.

This behavior of William's was more frightening than surliness or rage would have been. Had William forgotten all about the incident? Where had it come from, that burst of pure hate? She couldn't ask him, for fear of provoking it again. She stayed up late, reading a book on ichthyosaurs until after William had gone to bed. Then she slept on the living-room rug.

"More mashed potatoes, Lesje?" her mother says. Lesje nods. She's eating ravenously. This is the first real meal she's had in three weeks. She's been camping out in the almost empty house, sleeping on blankets unrolled on the bedroom floor, eating take-out food, bran muffins, hamburgers, fried chicken. She puts the bones and crusts in a green garbage bag; she has no garbage can yet. She has no stove and no fridge either and she hasn't got around to buying them, partly because she left a month's rent in an envelope for William, which has lowered her bank balance. But also she feels that major domestic appliances like these, even secondhand ones, should be shared by Nate. A stove is a serious commitment.

Lesje eats apple pie and wonders what Nate is doing. When her father says, "How's the bone business?" she smiles wanly at him. If you discovered a new kind of dinosaur, you could name it after yourself. *Aliceosaurus*, she used to write, practicing, Anglicizing her name. When she was fourteen this was her ambition, to discover a new kind of dinosaur and name it *Aliceosaurus*. She made the mistake of telling her father this; he thought it was very funny and teased her about it for months afterwards. She isn't sure what her ambition is now.

Lesje helps her mother stack the dishes and carry them out to the kitchen. "Is everything all right, Lesje?" her mother says, once they're out of her father's earshot. "You're looking thin."

"Yes," Lesje says. "I'm tired from moving, that's all."

Her mother seems satisfied with this. But everything is not all right. Nate comes to her new house in the evenings and they make love on her unrolled blankets, the hard boards jammed against her back. That's fine, but he hasn't yet said when he'll move in. She's beginning to wonder whether he ever will. Why should he? Why should he disarrange his life? He says he has to explain it gradually to the children; otherwise they might become disturbed. Lesje feels that she herself is disturbed already, but she can't tell this to Nate.

She doesn't seem able to tell it to anyone else either. Certainly not Trish or Marianne. She sits with them in the Museum coffee shop, smoking, tensed, always on the verge of blurting. But she can't. She's aware that from the outside William's behavior, the incident (which could be seen as an ignominious failure), her own flight and unconditional arrangement with Nate, might look naïve, gawky, laughable perhaps. *Gauche*, Marianne would think, though she wouldn't say it; or, a new English expression she's taken to lately: *thick*. She would give Lesje good counsel, as if she were planning a wardrobe for her. She'd advise bargaining, pressure, ruses, all things Lesje is not good at. You want him to live with you? Try locking him out. Why get a cow when milk's free? Lesje doesn't want to be the object of such amused, momentary concern. It occurs to her that she has no close friends.

She wonders whether she could talk to her mother, confide in her. She doubts it. Her mother has cultivated serenity; she's had to. Juliet at fifty-five, Lesje thinks, though her mother was never Juliet; she'd been no spring chicken, as the aunts said. No balconies for her father, no elopements; they'd taken the streetcar to the City Hall. Lesje studied *Romeo and Juliet* in high school; the teacher thought it would appeal to them because it was about teenagers and they were supposed to be teenagers. Lesje hadn't felt like a teenager. She wanted to study alluvial plains and marl deposits and vertebrate anatomy, and hadn't paid much attention to the play except to fill its margins with drawings of giant ferns. But how would the Montagues and the Capulets have behaved if Romeo and Juliet had lived? A lot like her relatives, she suspects. Snubs at family gatherings, resentments, subjects that were not discussed, this or that grandmother weeping or raving in a corner. Juliet, like her mother, would have become impenetrable, compact, plump, would have drawn herself together into a sphere.

Lesje's mother wants Lesje to be happy, and if Lesje isn't happy she wants her to appear to be happy. Lesje's happiness is her mother's justification. Lesje has known this forever and is well practiced at appearing, if not happy, at least stolidly content. Busy, gainfully employed. But standing beside her mother, drying the dishes on the ageless dishtowel that says GLASS in blue down one side, she doesn't feel she has the strength to keep up this particular appearance. She wants instead to cry, and she wants her mother to put her arms around her and console her.

It's for William she wants to be consoled. The loss of William, familiar William, does hurt after all. Not because of William himself, but because she trusted him simply, uncaring, unthinking. She trusted him like a sidewalk, she trusted him to be what he seemed to be, and she will never be able to do that with anyone again. It isn't the violence but the betrayal of this innocent surface that is so painful; though possibly there was no innocence, possibly she made it up.

But her mother, encased as she is, would never be able to mourn with Lesje. She'd merely wait until Lesje had stopped crying and wiped her eyes on the dishtowel, and then she would point out all the things Lesje has pointed out to herself already: *No real harm done. You're better out of it. It was the only way. Everything turns out for the best.*

Her grandmothers would not have done this. They would have mourned with her, both of them; they had the talent for it. They would have wept, keened, wailed. They would have put their arms around her and rocked her, stroking her hair, crying extravagantly, ridiculously, as if she'd been damaged beyond repair. Perhaps she is.

Wednesday, March 9, 1977

NATE

In the cellar Nate, leaning against his workbench, fingers the handles of the brushes soaking in their coffee tin of Varsol. He's always meant to put in better lighting down here. Now there would be no point. In the dim yellowish light he feels like some huge insect, white and semi-sighted, groping its way by a touch that is also smell. Paint fumes and damp cement, his familiar atmosphere. He twists the screw on the small red vise, tightening it on a glued and drying sheep's head, part of a Mary-Had-a-Little-Lamb pull toy. He had no difficulty designing the sheep, but the Mary is causing trouble. He can never do faces. A sunbonnet, he thinks.

He's supposed to be packing. He meant to pack, he's been meaning to pack. He has pedaled a stack of cardboard boxes home from the supermarket and bought a roll of strong twine. He's collected newspapers for wrapping; they've been in a neat pile at the foot of the cellar stairs for two weeks. He's even taken some sandpaper and a box of mixed nails and screws to Lesje's and left it in the front room as a pledge of his good intentions. He's explained to her that he wants to proceed gradually. First he'll tell Elizabeth he's decided to move his workshop to a larger, brighter space. She'll be surprised he can afford it, but he can get through that. Then he'll tell the children the same thing. After they're no longer used to having him around all the time he will, by slow degrees, stop sleeping at one house and start sleeping at the other. He wants to make the actual break imperceptible to them, he's said.

He fully intends to implement this plan, but with a crucial difference he doesn't think he needs to discuss with Lesje: he wants to wait until Elizabeth asks him or even orders him to leave. It will save a lot of trouble later if he can give her the impression she's making the decision herself. He isn't yet sure how he is going to arrange this.

Meanwhile he has to cope with Lesje's obvious and growing depression. She hasn't been putting any pressure on him, any spoken pressure. Nevertheless he can scarcely breathe. For three weeks now he's been running up the cellar stairs when he hears the children come home from school so he can act cheerful and unconcerned and make them warm milk and peanut butter sandwiches. He tells them jokes, cooks them dinner, reads them longer and longer bedtime stories. Last night they said they were tired and would he please turn out the light. Wounded, Nate wanted to fling his arms wide, cry out: *I won't be with you much longer!* But surely the point is to avoid such histrionics. He darkened the room, kissed them good night, went to the bathroom to put a hot washcloth over his eyes. Already his reflection in the mirror was fading, the house was forgetting him, he was negligible. He blotted his eyes and went to hunt down Elizabeth.

This also is part of his scheme. He makes a point of trying to have an inconsequential chat with her at least every two days, giving her openings, chances. Perhaps during one of these chats she will dismiss him. They sit in the kitchen and talk about this and that while she drinks tea and he drinks Scotch. Once, not long ago, she would have avoided him in the evenings; she would have gone out or read in her room. It's been her contention that they have nothing of value left to say to each other. Now, for purposes of her own, she seems to welcome the chance to consult him on supplies, repairs, the children's progress at school. This fact alone makes him sweat. She's asked him a couple of times, with no particular emphasis, how things are going with his ladyfriend, and he's been noncommittal.

After these chats, during which he has to clench his teeth to avoid glancing at his watch, he leaps onto his bicycle and pedals feverishly down Ossington and along Dundas to catch Lesje before she goes to bed. Twice he's almost been hit by cars; once he ran into a hydro pole and arrived torn and bleeding. Lesje scrabbled through half-unpacked boxes, looking for Band-Aids, while he dripped onto the grimy linoleum. He knows these rides are dangerous but he also knows that if he doesn't get there in time Lesje will feel rejected and miserable. On several nights, too exhausted to make the trip, he's phoned instead. Her voice has been small, remote. He can't stand to hear her dwindle like that.

No matter how drained he is, he has to make love to her, or at least try to; otherwise she'll feel he's backing off. His knees are bruised from the floor, his bad disk is acting up. He wants to ask her to get a bed or at least a mattress, but he can hardly do that without paying half, and at the moment he doesn't have enough money.

After soothing Lesje he pedals home again. There he clatters dishes in the kitchen while frying a late-night snack of liver and onions. He sings sea chanties or puts on a record, an old Travelers or Harry Belafonte from the early sixties. He's kept these records, not because he's especially fond of the music as such, but because they recall for him a time when he was fond of it. Before his marriage, before everything; when all directions still seemed possible.

Elizabeth, he knows, can hear what goes on in the kitchen. She can't stand the Travelers or Harry Belafonte or noise at night in general, and the smell of liver makes her sick. He found this out early in their marriage and abstained, a compromise. She's big on the value of compromises. He's hoping now that his blatant failure to compromise will convince her she's had enough of him.

He doesn't really feel like singing, or eating either. By midnight he usually has a grinding headache. But he forces himself, tapping his knife against his plate and yelling along with Harry, his mouth full of partly chewed meat. "I see great big black TARANTULA," he bellows. Then, crooning, "Come back, Liza, come back, girl, Wipe de tear from yo' eye . . ." Once, during the era of Chris, he'd sung this song with ridiculous sentimentality. *Liza* was Elizabeth and he wanted her to come back.

He leaves his dishes in the sink, or if he's feeling especially daring, on the kitchen table itself, defying Elizabeth's hand-printed sign:

CLEAN UP YOUR OWN MESS!

Then he staggers up the stairs, gulps four aspirins with codeine, and crashes into bed.

Ordinarily this behavior would produce quick results. A cold request, which, if not obeyed, would lead to a frontal attack, during which he would be accused in a chillingly level voice of everything from chauvinism to arrogant selfishness to sadism. In the first years these arguments convinced him. His inability to complain, to complain skillfully and with feeling, put him at a disadvantage: when she challenged him to produce some habit of hers equally offensive to him, which she was of course prepared to give up on the spot, he couldn't come up with anything. He was used to thinking that everyone's rage and sense of oppression was justified; everyone's but his own. Anyway, he wasn't oppressed. At parties during the raucous sixties he'd been called a white pig, a male pig, even, because of his last name, a Fascist German pig. Instead of invoking his Unitarian past, his long-gone lapsed-Mennonite grandfather whose cheese-factory windows were smashed in 1914 because of his name, his father who'd died in the war, he found it less complicated to turn away and go out to the kitchen for another beer. Nor had he ever told Elizabeth the house was as much his as hers; he didn't really believe it. He stopped eating liver except in restaurants and played his Harry Belafonte records only when Elizabeth wasn't home. The children liked them.

This time Elizabeth hasn't responded to his transgressions. If he happens to see her the next morning, she's calm and smiling. She even asks him if he's slept well.

Nate knows he can't keep up his divided life much longer. He'll get an ulcer, he'll implode. An incoherent anger is growing in him, not only with Elizabeth but with the children: what right do they have to hook him, hold him back? Also with Lesje, who is forcing him to make painful decisions. His anger isn't fair, he knows it. He dislikes being unfair. He will take the first step today, now.

He kneels beside the pile of old newspapers. He'll wrap and box the small hand tools first and transport the boxes, one by one, roped onto the carrying rack of his bicycle. For the larger machines and unfinished toys he'll have to rent a truck. He shoves to the back of his mind the question of how he's going to pay for it.

He picks up a gouge, sliding his hand around the handle. In the early days of euphoria, after he quit his job, when he still believed he was returning somehow to dignity, the wisdom and simplicity of the craftsman, he spent a lot of time carving special handles for his hand tools. On some he incised his initials; on others he made decorative bands, flowers and leaves or geometrical motifs, vaguely Indian. On this particular gouge he made a hand, carved as if the wooden fingers were holding the handle, so that every time he picked up the gouge there was another hand close within his own. It pleased him to use these tools of his, he felt secure, rooted, as if by carving them himself he'd made them already old. He kneels, holding the small wooden hand, trying to recall that pleasure. Holding, holding on. But the tools are floating away from him, diminished, like toys he once played with. The plastic machine gun, the man's hat he wore with the brim turned down, pretending it was a pith helmet.

He places the gouge on a sheet of newspaper, and rolls, starting at the bottom corner. Then, methodically, reading headlines as he goes, he rolls the chisels, the screwdrivers, the rasps, placing the wrapped tools side by side in the bottom of the first box. Old events flash past him, blacken his fingers: the Pakistani pushed onto the subway tracks, he remembers that. A broken leg. The child who strangled while being forced by her mother to stand on one foot with a rope around her neck as punishment. Gossip about Margaret Trudeau, for weeks. An exploding butcher's shop in Northern Ireland. Widening rift between English and French Canada. Murdered Portuguese shoeshine boy; cleanup of Toronto's Sin Strip. Québec language laws: Greek grocers in all-Greek districts forbidden to put up Coca-Cola signs in Greek. He flips through the papers, recalling his own reactions when he first read them.

Nate stops wrapping. He's crouching now on the cellar floor, absorbed in old stories, which come to him across time as one long blurred howl of rage and pain. And his own recognition: What else can be expected? Newspapers are distilled futility. Whenever his mother is being too irritating, too optimistic, he wants to say to her merely, Read the papers. Sheer delusion, the belief that anything can be done, ever. She does read the papers, of course. She even keeps a clipping file.

He's deep in an editorial warning against the creeping Balkanization of Canada when the cellar door swings open. He looks up: Elizabeth is standing at the top of the stairs, her face shadowed by the light behind her head. Nate scrambles to his feet. The chisel he's been holding, intending to wrap it, clanks against the floor.

"You're home early," he says. He feels as if he's been caught burying someone in the cellar.

Elizabeth has a cardigan over her shoulders. She draws it further around her; slowly and without speaking she descends the stairs. Nate backs against the workbench.

"You look as if you're packing," Elizabeth says. He can see now that she's smiling.

"Well, I was just sorting out some tools," Nate says. Now

that it's time, he wants, wildly, irrationally, to deny everything. "To store them," he says.

Elizabeth stands at the bottom of the stairs and surveys the room, the dingy windows, the rags, the piles of sawdust and shavings he hasn't bothered to sweep up.

"How's business?" she asks. She stopped asking that a long time ago. She has no interest in it; she almost never comes down here. All she wants from it is his half of the rent.

"Great," he lies. "Just fine."

Elizabeth gazes back at him. "Isn't it time we stopped this?" she says.

ELIZABETH

Elizabeth tightens the cardigan, around her shoulders, across her back. Her arms are crossed, the wool she's holding bunched into fists. Straitjacket. She stands in the hall, watching the front door as if she expects someone to come through it. But she doesn't expect anyone to come through it. Doors are what people go out by, in their own ways. The doors close behind them and she's left looking at the place where they've just been. Conscious, semiconscious, semiconscience. Piss on them all.

Nate has just gone through the door, carrying a cardboard box. He set the box down on the porch so he could turn to close the door carefully, ever so carefully behind him. He's pedaling off to screw his stringy ladyfriend, as he's been doing for weeks, pretending otherwise. This time he's taking some rasps and chisels with him. Elizabeth hopes he will put them to good use.

In the ordinary course of things she wouldn't have minded this liaison. She doesn't feel she's a dog in the manger: if she doesn't want a particular bone, anyone else is welcome to it. As long as Nate does his share with the house and children, or what they've wearily agreed is his share, he can help himself to any diversions he chooses. Bowling, building model airplanes, fornication, it's all the same to her. But she resents being taken for a fool. Any ninny could have told he was packing; why did he bother to deny it? As for his moronic performance with the midnight fried liver and Harry Belafonte records, a two-year-old could see through it.

She turns away from the door and heads for the kitchen, her body dragging, suddenly heavy. She was calm, she's pleased with how calm she was, but now she feels as if she's swallowed a bottle of aspirin. Small holes glow red in her stomach, eating their way into her flesh. A bottle of stars. All she wanted was a straight confession, and she's accomplished that. He admitted he plans to move his workshop from their cellar to some unspecified place. They both know where this is, but for the moment she's resisted the urge to press further.

She decides to make herself a cup of coffee, then changes her mind. She will eat no more acid this evening. Instead she pours boiling water on a chicken Oxo cube, and sits stirring methodically, waiting for it to dissolve.

She walks through the future, step by step. From this point it can go two ways. He will leave, gradually, without further prompting. Or she can speed up the process by telling him to go. There is no third way. He will not stay now, even if she begs him to.

So she will have to ask him, tell him to go. If she can't save anything else from the wreckage she will save face. They'll have a civilized discussion and they will both agree they are doing the best thing for the children. She will then be able to repeat this conversation to her friends, communicating her joy at this solution to all their problems, radiating quiet confidence and control.

Of course there are the children, the real ones, not the fantasy ones they will drag out as counters in the bargaining process. The real children will not think this is best for them. They will hate it, and Nate will have the advantage of being able to say, *Your mother asked me to leave.* But she will not be deserted, she refuses to be deserted against her will. She refuses to be pathetic. Her martyr mother, sniveling in a chair. She knows she's being manipulated into this position, by Nate—by Nate!—and she dislikes the thought intensely. It's like being beaten at an intricate and subtle game of chess by the world tiddlywinks champion. But she had no other choice.

She'll go on a diet, later, after he's actually gone. That's part of the ritual. She'll tart herself up, maybe get her hair done, and everyone will say how much better she's looking than she did before Nate left. She finds these tactics squalid and disapproves of them when she witnesses them in others. But what else is there? Trips to Europe she can't afford, religious conversion? She's already had a younger lover; she isn't in any hurry to do that again.

She rocks slightly in her chair, hugging her elbows. She's shivering. She wants Chris to come back. She wants anyone, just some arms that aren't hollow and knitted. The cracks be-

tween the boards of the table are widening; grey light wells
from them, cold. Dry ice, gas, she can hear it, a hushing
sound, moving towards her face. It eats color. She pulls her
hands back from the table, clamps them together in her lap.
There's the grip of veins in her neck. Fingers twisting hair
across her throat.

She's staked to this chair, she can't move, a chill moves up
her back. Her eyes flicker, sweep the room for something that
will save her. Familiar. The stove, pot on it, frying pan unwashed, the cutting board by the sink. The frayed and blackened oven glove, not that. CLEAN UP. The refrigerator. Nancy's drawing from Grade One stuck to it, a girl smiling, the
sky, the sun. Joy, she thought when she placed it.

She stares at the picture, pressing her hands together, and
for an instant the sun shines. But there's no friendly smile,
malice is there in the yellow, in the hair. The blue of the sky
too is an illusion, the sun is blackening, its tentacles curl like
burning paper. Behind the blue sky is not white enamel but
the dark of outer space, blackness shot with fiery bubbles.
Somewhere out there the collapsed body floats, no bigger than
a fist, tugging at her with immense gravity. Irresistible. She
falls towards it, space filling her ears.

After a while she's in the kitchen. The house is ticking around
her once more, the furnace hums, warm air sighs through the
registers. From upstairs comes the chuckle of television; she
can hear water singing in the pipes, one child or another running carelessly from the bathroom along the hall. So far she
can always get back. Self-indulgence, Auntie Muriel would
say. Make yourself useful. She concentrates on the yellow circle made by the top of the cup, willing her fingers to un-
clamp, move forward. She lifts the cup and warms her cold
hands with it. Liquid slops onto her lap. She sips, filling time.
When her hands are steady she makes a piece of toast and
spreads it with peanut butter. She will take one step at a time.
Down to earth.

She rummages for the felt pen she makes the grocery lists
with and begins to jot down figures. In one column, the mortgage, the insurance, the electricity and heat, the monthly food
bill. Children's clothes and school supplies. Dentists' bills: Janet will reed an orthodontist. Cat food. They don't have a cat,
but she's bloody well going to get one and charge it to Nate.
His replacement. Repairs. She'll have the roof fixed, finally,
and the porch step.

In the other column she puts the rent from the tenants. She doesn't want to be unfair, just accurate, and she's willing to offset the tenants' rent against the mortgage.

Already she feels better. This is what she needs: small goals, projects, something to keep her busy. Other women knit. She can even sense a hint of that lightness of spirit she hopes to be able to describe, later, to her acquaintances. And really it may not be so bad. Freedom from that other set of rules, that constant pained look which is worse than nagging. Living with Nate has been like living with a huge mirror in which her flaws are magnified and distorted. Fly-eyes. She's been forced to see herself measured constantly beside his set of East York domestic standards, his pious nun-faced mother with her awful Melmac dishes and her faint smell of old wool and cod liver oil. She'll be free of that. It will mean she'll have to carry out the garbage bags herself on garbage day, but she thinks she can live with that.

LESJE

Lesje is having dificulty getting up in the mornings. In that prehistoric era during which she lived with William, she was able to depend on him. He liked being on time for work. He also liked getting up. He'd take a brisk shower, scrubbing himself with some kind of medieval flagellation instrument, and emerge pink as a rubber duck to ferret in the kitchen for Shreddies and milk, rubbing his head with a towel, making forays into the bedroom to prod Lesje and pull the covers off her legs.

But now, alone in the small chilly house, she has to force herself into the air, sticking her feet out one at a time from beneath the blankets, a lungfish ousted from its stagnant puddle. The house, with no furniture, nothing radiating back to her from the bare walls, absorbs what little energy she has. She feels she's losing weight and that the house is gaining it.

Sometimes, gulping instant coffee with artificial whitener, chewing a stale bran muffin, she goes to the living-room door to contemplate the small piles of sawdust Nate is now making. The living room, he says, is the only room in the house big enough for his machines. Though none of these machines has actually appeared yet, he's brought over some hand tools and a few unfinished hobby horses and has even spent a couple of hours in there, rasping and sanding. The piles of sawdust comfort her. They mean Nate is at least in theory moving into the house. Taking possession.

He has explained very carefully why he's still sleeping at what she thinks of as Elizabeth's house. Lesje listened, she tried to listen, but she does not understand. She feels she's blundered into something tangled and complex, tenuous, hopelessly snarled. She's out of her element. If she were in control of this, the moves would be concrete, straightforward. She herself has been straightforward. She loves Nate; therefore she's left William and gone to live with Nate. Why then has Nate not yet come to live with her?

He claims he has. He's even slept over a couple of nights, and after the second of these, watching him hobble around the kitchen in the morning, wincing every time he straightened up, she'd given in, squeezed her budget and bought a second-hand mattress. Which was a little like putting up a birdhouse: you couldn't make the bird move in.

"This is my real home," Nate says. And once, his head resting on her belly, "I want to have a child by you." He rapidly changed it to "with you," then said, "I want us to have a child together," but Lesje was so struck by the content she didn't notice the phrasing. She doesn't especially want to have a baby, not right at the moment; she doesn't know whether she's up to it; but she was touched by Nate's wish. He considered her not only desirable but acceptable. She sat up and lifted his head, hugging him gratefully.

What she can't explain is the gap between what he says he feels and what he actually does. She can't reconcile his procla-mations of love—which she believes!—with the simple fact of his absence. His absence is evidence, it's empirical. It has hardened now to stone, a small tight lump she carries every-where with her in the pit of her stomach.

She climbs the grey steps of the Museum, walks past the ticket-takers, hurries up the stairs to the Hall of Vertebrate Evolution, tracing again her daily path: the human skull, the saber-toothed cat in its tar pit, the illuminated scenes of undersea life, with their hungry mosasaurs and doomed ammonites. The door that leads to her office is reached through this portion of the ancient sea floor. Most of the other offices in the Museum have ordinary doors; she's glad this one is camouflaged to look like rock. If she can't live in a cave, which is what she would prefer at the moment (meditation, bread and water, no complications), this is the next best thing.

Though she's been arriving late, she's also been staying lat-er, sometimes till seven-thirty or eight, cataloguing steadily, squinting hunched over labels and cards, fixing her mind on tibiae, metatarsals, shards of the real world. She finds it rest-ful, this contemplation of details; it stops that small noise in her mind, the worrying of something trapped behind the woodwork. Also she's putting off the return to her empty house.

If she's there alone in the evenings she prowls. She opens the cupboard in the tiny extra bedroom and stares at the four abandoned wire coat hangers, thinking she should do something about the chewed shreds of wallpaper and the mouse droppings on the floor. She tries to make herself do useful things, such as scraping the yellow mineral deposit off the back of the toilet bowl with a paring knife; but she's likely to find herself sitting half an hour later in the same place with nothing accomplished, gazing into space. She realizes now that her life with William, haphazard as it seemed, had at least its daily routines. Routines hold you in place. Without them she floats, weightless. She can never expect Nate till after ten.

She nods through the open door to Dr. Van Vleet, who nods back. He hasn't yet said a word about her lateness. She hopes that when he retires his replacement will be someone equally tolerant, in other ways as well.

When she steps through the doorway of her cubbyhole, Elizabeth Schoenhof is there.

Lesje isn't ready for this. She's been avoiding the cafeteria, the ladies' rooms Elizabeth is likely to use, any corner in which this encounter might take place, and she's assumed Elizabeth was also avoiding her. She doesn't feel guilty and she has nothing to hide. She just doesn't think they could possibly have anything to say to each other.

Now here is Elizabeth, sitting in Lesje's chair and smiling graciously, as if this is her office and Lesje is visiting it. Her purse is on the desk, resting on a tray of eel fragments, her sweater is draped across the chair back. She looks as if she's about to say, "Is there anything I can do for you?"

Instead she says, "I brought these requisition slips myself. The internal mail is so slow."

There's no other chair in the office; there's no room for one. Elizabeth seems to fill all the available space. Lesje backs against a wall chart, the geological ages marked in color blocks. Dinosaurs, a hundred and twenty million years of tawny yellow; man, a speck of red. She's a fleck, a molecule, an ion lost in time. But so is Elizabeth.

She glances over the sheet of paper Elizabeth has handed to her. They want something for the subway display case, preferably a leg and a foot. She'll have to discuss it with Dr. Van Vleet, choose the specimen, sign it out.

"Right," she says. Elizabeth must have turned up the heat Lesje is broiling; she wants desperately to take off her coat, but feels that to turn away at this moment would lose her something. Besides, she needs the covering, the insulation between herself and Elizabeth.

"I felt we should discuss things," Elizabeth says, still smiling. "I think we should work together. It's in everyone's best interests, don't you think?"

Lesje knows she's talking about Nate, not about fossilized feet. But her tone of voice suggests a charitable project of some kind, a benefit concert, a rummage sale. Lesje doesn't think of Nate as a charitable project and she has no wish to discuss him. "Of course," she says.

"Nate and I have always tried to work together," Elizabeth says. "We've managed to stay good friends. I think it's always better that way, don't you? We often talk things over when he's in the bathtub." She gives a cosy laugh. She obviously wants Lesje to think that she herself is one of the chief topics of bathtub discussion.

Lesje knows for a fact that Elizabeth and Nate haven't talked about anything in such intimacy for months and months. Unless he's been lying. Would he lie? She realizes that she doesn't know him well enough to know.

When Elizabeth walks away fifteen minutes later, still smiling, Lesje cannot remember anything that has actually been said. She takes off her coat and hangs it up, then goes to the wet lab to make herself a cup of instant coffee. She isn't sure Elizabeth said anything at all, not clearly, not directly. But she's been left with two impressions. One is that Nate has been, or is about to be, fired for incompetence, and that she herself is therefore free to take him on. That is, if she wants to. The other is that she's just been hired for a job she hasn't applied for. Apparently she is going to be tried out as a kind of governess. Elizabeth, it seems, feels she deserves some time to herself. "It will be so good for the children," Elizabeth said, "to learn to relate to someone with unusual interests."

Lesje thinks she intended something more complicated, less neutral. Something like *foreigner*. Not dirty foreigner, exactly, as when in Grade Four the Irish-headed older girls gathered around her as she walked across the schoolyard. Pee-ew, they said, holding their noses, while Lesje smiled weakly, appeasingly. Wipe that smirk off your face or we'll wipe it for you. She could use a wash.

Elizabeth is too haute Wasp for that. More like *outlandish*, someone from out of the land. Interesting, mind you; as if she'll play the violin and do charming ethnic dances, like something from *Fiddler on the Roof*. To amuse the children.

Lesje sees she has been studying the wrong thing. Modern mammals, that would be of some use. Primate behavior. She recalls once having read something about apes' eyelids. The dominant ape stares, the others lower their eyes, flashing their colored lids. It avoids murders.

Tomorrow, when she's less depressed, she'll ask Marianne about this; Marianne is well up on primate behavior. Or Dr. Van Vleet, or anyone. Surely anyone at all will know more about such things than she does.

ELIZABETH

Elizabeth is lying in bed, the Indian bedspread pulled up to her chin. The window is open a little at the bottom, she left it that way when she set off for work this morning, and the room is chilly and damp. She's looking at the bedside clock, wondering whether it's worth the effort to get up, get dressed and go back to the office for an hour or so. Probably not.

Resting on her left arm is a head. William's head. William's head is on her arm because they've just made love. Before that they had lunch, a lingering, expensive lunch at the Courtyard Café, with cucumber soup and sweetbreads and undertones. And two bottles of white wine, which may have accounted for the undertones. William sighed a lot and shrugged several times, as if practicing subdued melancholy. He told her about a recent study on the effects of an uncooked all-meat diet as practiced by the Innuit, but his heart wasn't in it. Though they alluded to their shared problem, they didn't discuss it directly. Defection is painful.

Elizabeth said (but only once) that she was glad Nate finally seemed to be working out some of his conflicts and that she herself was finding it less of a strain to have him not so much, well, underfoot. This did not perk William up. During the chocolate mousse with Armagnac Elizabeth stroked his hand. They looked into each other's eyes, wryly: each was the other's consolation prize. It was logical; besides, Elizabeth felt she owed him one good fuck. It was partly because of her that Lesje walked out on him so suddenly. She didn't foresee the walkout. What she intended was a confrontation, then a reconciliation, and after the reconciliation Lesje would of course have been honor bound to renounce Nate. Elizabeth could then have been spending her time consoling Nate instead of William.

In the early days, this was how it had worked with Nate and herself, and she'd taken care never to divulge her lovers until she was ready to give them up. In theory at least. But neither William nor Lesje had behaved according to plan. She isn't exactly sure what happened. She went to lunch with William partly to find out, but William didn't want to discuss it.

Copulating with William was not unpleasant, she thinks, but neither was it memorable. It was like sleeping with a large and fairly active slab of Philadelphia cream cheese. Emulsified. It isn't that William is without mystery. He's probably as mysterious as any other object in the universe: a bottle, an apple. It's just that his mystery is not of the kind that usually intrigues Elizabeth. On second thought he isn't totally bland. Remembering the way he wielded his teeth, she's sure he has pockets of energy, even violence, hidden in him, like Mexican jumping beans in a box of cotton wool.

But she doesn't like boxes whose contents she can guess. Why open William? For her he contains no surprises. Chris had been a dangerous country, swarming with ambushes and guerrillas, the center of a whirlpool, a demon lover. Maybe for someone else William would be that: Elizabeth is old enough to know that one woman's demon lover is another's worn-out shoe. She doesn't begrudge Lesje the fascination Nate evidently holds for her, since she's never experienced it herself. What she envies is not the people involved but the fact. She wishes she could feel that again, for anyone at all.

William stirs, and Elizabeth worms her arm out from beneath his head.

"That was terrific," he says.

Elizabeth winces slightly. *Terrific*.

"Was it for you?" he asks anxiously.

"Of course," she says. "Couldn't you tell?"

William grins, reassured. "Hell," he says, "Lesje's not in the same class with you."

Elizabeth finds this remark in extremely bad taste. One does not compare one's lovers, not to their faces. Nevertheless she smiles. "I'd better hurry," she says. "I should put in an appearance at the office, I guess you should, too." Also: the children will be home from school in an hour. But she doesn't mention that.

She doesn't especially want William looking at her from behind, but there's nothing she can do to stop him. She gets out of bed, hooks her brassiere, and pulls her magenta slip on over her head. She chose it in the morning thinking something like this might happen.

"You're damned sexy," William says a little too heartily; that tone might preface a slap on the rump. "Full-bodied."

Elizabeth shivers with irritation. Stupid; sometimes she's very stupid. *Get your goddamn jockey shorts on and get out of my bed.* She smiles at him graciously over her shoulder, and the doorbell rings.

Ordinarily Elizabeth wouldn't appear at the door half-dressed in the middle of the day. Neighbors talk, they talk to their children; someone may have seen William going in with her. But right now she wants to be out of the room.

"It's probably the meter reader," she says. She doesn't know whether this is likely to be true. Since he started working at home, Nate has always coped with such details. "I'll just be a second." She pulls on her blue dressing gown, ties the sash and heads down the stairs in her uncomfortably bare feet. The doorbell rings again as she unchains the door.

Auntie Muriel is standing on the front porch, looking with distaste at the peeling white rocker, the broken step, the neighbors' tiny front lawns with their withered remnants of last summer's gardens. She's wearing a white velour hat shaped like an inverted potty and white gloves, as if on her way to Easter church, and a mink stole Elizabeth remembers from twenty-five years ago. Auntie Muriel does not throw things out or give them away.

Auntie Muriel has never before come to visit Elizabeth. She's chosen to ignore the existence of Elizabeth's disreputable address, as if Elizabeth doesn't live in a house at all, but materializes in Auntie Muriel's front hall at every visit and dematerializes again when leaving. But just because Auntie Muriel has never before done something is no reason to expect she will never do it. Elizabeth knows she shouldn't be surprised—*who else?*—but she is. She feels her wind go, as if someone has rammed her in the solar plexus, and clutches the stomach of her dressing gown.

"I've come here," Auntie Muriel says, with a slight pause before *here*, "becuase I felt I ought to tell you what I think about what you've done. Not that it will make any difference to you." She walks forward and Elizabeth of necessity has to step back. Auntie Muriel, breathing mothballs and Bluegrass dusting powder, marches into her living room.

"You're sick," Auntie Muriel says, looking not at Elizabeth

but at her perfectly arranged room, which shrinks, which fades, which exudes dust under her glance. Illness would be the only excuse for having your dressing gown on in the middle of the day, and a poor one at that. "You don't look well. I'm not surprised." Auntie Muriel herself does not look particularly radiant. Elizabeth wonders briefly if there's something wrong with her, then dismisses the thought. Nothing is ever wrong with Auntie Muriel. She clumps around the room, inspecting the chairs and the sofa.

"Won't you sit down?" Elizabeth says. She's decided how she will handle this. Sweetness and light, reveal nothing. *Don't let yourself be needled.* Auntie Muriel would like nothing better than to provoke her.

Auntie Muriel settles herself on the sofa but doesn't take off her stole or gloves. She wheezes, or perhaps it's a sigh, as if merely being in Elizabeth's house is too much for her. Elizabeth remains standing. *Dominate her through height.* Not a hope.

"In my opinion," Auntie Muriel says, "mothers of young children do not break up families for their own selfish gratification. I know a lot of people do it these days. But there is such a thing as immoral behavior and such a thing as common decency."

Elizabeth cannot and will not admit to Auntie Muriel that Nate's departure was not entirely her choice. Besides, if she says, "Nate left me," she'll hear that it was her fault. Husbands do not leave wives who behave properly. No doubt. "How did you hear about it?" she says.

"Janie Burroughs' nephew Philip works at the Museum," Auntie Muriel says. "Janie is an old friend of mine. We went to school together. I have my grandchildren to consider; I want them to have a decent home."

Philip's relationship to Janie Burroughs was something Elizabeth had forgotten during her witty, lighthearted resumé of her domestic situation at the lunch table last week. An incestuous city.

"Nate sees them on weekends," she says weakly, and knows at once that she's made a serious tactical blunder: she's admitted there is something, if not wrong, at least deficient, about fathers not living at home. "They do have a decent home," she says quickly.

"I doubt that," says Auntie Muriel. "I doubt that very much."

Elizabeth feels the ground sliding from beneath her feet. If she were only dressed, with no man in the bedroom, she'd be in a much better strategic position. She hopes William has the sense to stay put, but considering his general gormlessness she has no right to expect it. She thinks she can hear him splashing in the bathroom.

"I really feel," says Elizabeth with dignity, "that Nate's and my decisions are our own concern."

Auntie Muriel ignores this. "I never approved of him," she says. "You know that. But any father at all is better than none. You should understand that better than anyone."

"Nate isn't dead, you know," Elizabeth says. A fist of heat rises, hovers in her chest. "He's still very much alive and he adores the girls. But he happens to be living with another woman."

"People of your generation do not understand the meaning of sacrifice," Auntie Muriel says, but without vigor, as if the repetition of the thought has finally tired her. "I sacrificed myself for years." She doesn't say what for. It's obvious she hasn't heard a word Elizabeth has just said.

Elizabeth puts her hand against the pine sideboard to steady herself. She closes her eyes briefly; behind them is a network of elastic bands. With everyone else she can depend on some difference between surface and interior. Most people do imitations; she herself has been doing imitations for years. If there is some reason for it she can imitate a wife, a mother, an employee, a dutiful relative. The secret is to discover what the others are trying to imitate and then support them in their belief that they've done it well. Or the opposite: *I can see through you*. But Auntie Muriel doesn't do imitations; either that or she is so completely an imitation that she has become genuine. She is her surface. Elizabeth can't see through her because there is nothing and nowhere to see. She is opaque as a rock.

"I shall go to see Nathanael," Auntie Muriel says. She and Nate's mother are the only people who ever call him Nathanael.

Suddenly Elizabeth knows what Auntie Muriel has in mind. She's going to go to Nate and offer to pay him. She's willing to pay for an appearance of standard family life; even if it means misery. Which to her is standard family life; she's never pretended to be happy. She's going to pay him to come back, and Nate will think that Elizabeth has sent her.

Auntie Muriel wearing a grey wool dress, is standing in the parlor beside the baby grand piano. Elizabeth, who is twelve, has just finished her piano lesson. The piano teacher, hopeless, pigeon-chested Miss MacTavish, is in the front hall struggling into her navy blue trenchcoat, as she's done every Tuesday for four years. Miss MacTavish is one of the advantages Auntie Muriel is always telling Elizabeth she's being given. Auntie Muriel listens for the front door to close, smiling at Elizabeth, a disquieting smile.

"Uncle Teddy and I," she says, "think that under the circumstances you and Caroline should call us something other than Auntie Muriel and Uncle Teddy." She leans over, fingering Elizabeth's sheet music. *Pictures at an Exhibition.*

Elizabeth is still sitting on the piano bench. She's supposed to practice for half an hour after each lesson. She folds her hands in her lap and stares up at Auntie Muriel, keeping her face expressionless. She doesn't know what's coming, but she's already learned that the best defense against Auntie Muriel is silence. She wears silence around her neck like garlic against vampires. *Sullen*, Auntie Muriel calls her.

"We have legally adopted you," Auntie Muriel goes on, "and we feel you should call us Mother and Father."

Elizabeth has no objection to calling Uncle Teddy Father. She can hardly remember her own father, and doesn't much like what she can remember. He sometimes told jokes, she can remember that. Caroline hoards his sporadic Christmas cards; Elizabeth throws hers out, no longer even bothering to check the postmarks to see where he's drifted to now. But Auntie Muriel? *Mother?* Her flesh recoils.

"I already have a mother," Elizabeth says politely.

"She signed the adoption papers," Auntie Muriel says, with unconcealed triumph. "She seemed glad of the chance to get rid of the responsibility. Of course we paid her something."

Elizabeth can't remember how she responded to the news that her real mother had sold her to Auntie Muriel. She thinks she tried to shut the piano on Auntie Muriel's hand; she's forgotten whether or not she succeeded. It was the last time she ever let herself be goaded that far.

"Get out of my house," Elizabeth finds herself saying, screaming. "Don't come back, don't come back!" With the release of her voice, blood surges through her head. "You moldly old bitch!" She longs to say *cunt*, she's thought it often enough, but superstition holds her back. If she pronounces that ultimate magic word, surely Auntie Muriel will change into something else; will swell, blacken, bubble like burned sugar, giving off deadly fumes.

Auntie Muriel, face set, heaves herself erect, and Elizabeth picks up the object nearest to her and throws it at the repulsive white hat. She misses, and one of her beautiful porcelian bowls shatters against the wall. But at last, at last, she has frightened Auntie Muriel, who is scuttling down the hall. The door opens, closes: a bang, satisfying, final as gunshot.

Elizabeth stamps her bare feet, exultant. Revolution! Auntie Muriel is as good as dead; she will never have to see her again. She does a small victorious dance around her pressback pine chair, hugging herself. She feels savage, she could eat a heart.

But when William comes downstairs, fully dressed and with his hair brushed, he finds her curled unmoving on the sofa.

"Who was that?" he says. "I figured I'd better stay upstairs."

"Nobody really," Elizabeth says. "My aunt."

Nate would have comforted her, even now. William laughs, as if aunts are intrinsically funny. "It sounded like a bit of a fight," he says.

"I threw a bowl at her," Elizabeth says. "It was a good bowl."

"You could try Crazy Glue," William says practically. Elizabeth doesn't consider this worth answering. Kayo's bowl, which can never be duplicated. A bowlful of nothing.

Friday, April 29, 1977

LESJE

Lesje, in a grubbier than usual lab coat, sits in the downstairs lab beside the corridor of wooden storage racks. She's drinking a mug of instant coffee, which is all she intends to have for lunch. Ostensibly she's sorting and labeling a tray of teeth, small protomammal teeth from the Upper Cretaceous. She's using a magnifying glass and a chart, though she knows these particular teeth backwards and forwards: the Museum has published a monograph on them which she helped to edit. But she's having trouble concentrating. She's sitting here instead of in her office because she wants someone to talk to her.

There are two technicians in the room. Theo is over by the sandblasting machine, digging away with a dental pick at a semi-embedded jawbone. In Mammalogy, where the bones are real, they don't use dental picks. They have a freezer full of dead carcasses, camels, moose, bats, and when they're ready to assemble the skeleton they strip most of the meat off and put the bones into the Bug Room, where carnivorous insects eat the shreds of flesh remaining. The Bug Room smells of rotting meat. Outside the door, several pictures of naked women are Scotch-taped to filing cabinets. The technicians in that department work to rock and country music from the radio. Lesje wonders if solitary Theo would rather be there.

Gregor, the department's artist, is applying daubs of clay to a bone, some sort of ornithopod femur, it looks like. Though Gregor probably doesn't care that much what it is. His job is to make a mold of it, then take a plaster cast from the mold. Thus slowly and part by part, whole skeletons reproduce themselves. In the nineteenth century, Lesje knows, Andrew Carnegie cast and recast his own personal dinosaur, *Diplodocus carnegiei,* and presented the replicas to the crowned heads of Europe. No one can afford to do that any more; even if there were any crowned heads left.

Lesje tries to think of something to say to the technicians, not about *Diplodocus carnegiei*, that wouldn't do it; some way of opening a conversation. But she doesn't know what might interest them. They do their jobs and leave at five every night for their other lives, lives which she finds unfathomable. She knows though that the Museum is not essential to them the way it is to her. Gregor could just as easily be working in an art store, Theo could be cleaning cement from bricks or paint from old brass drawer handles. Perhaps they want to Scotch-tape pictures of naked women up in here, too.

Nevertheless, she very much wants one of them, either of them, to say, "Come out for a beer." She would watch base-ball games on television with them, eating potato chips and drinking from the bottle. She would hold their hands, roll on the carpet with them, make love as an afterthought, attaching no more meaning to that than to any other healthy exercise, a swim, a jog around the block. It would all be friendly and without any future. She wants actions, activities, with no significance and no hidden penalties.

She thinks with nostalgia of her life with William, which she sees now as having been simple-minded and joyously ado-lescent. The beauty of William was that she hadn't seriously cared what he thought about her. Once she wanted something less two-dimensional. Now she has it. It's true that she didn't love William, though she had no way of knowing this at the time. She loves Nate. She's no longer sure she's cut out for love.

Perhaps it wasn't even Nate himself that attracted her at first, but Elizabeth. Elizabeth and Chris. She'd looked at Elizabeth and seen an adult world where choices had consequences, significant, irreversible.

William never represented such a choice, William was open-ended. She must have thought she could live with William for a million years and nothing in her would really be changed. Obviously William hadn't felt like this. William, like a miser with a sock, had invested things when she wasn't looking, so that his outburst of violence had taken her by surprise. But she's beyond William now, even his rage. William was only momentarily painful.

Nate, on the other hand, is painful almost all the time. Holding her two hands he says, "You know how important you are to me." When she wants him to say he would kill for her, die for her. If he would only say that, she would do any-thing for him. But *how important* invites measurement, the question: *How* important? For her Nate is absolute, but for him she exists on a scale of relatively important things. She can't tell exactly where on the scale she is; it fluctuates.

In the evenings she sits at their newly acquired table, be-side the stove and the wheezy fridge she paid far too much for at the Goodwill store, and broods. When she lived with Wil-liam he did most of the brooding.

"What is it, love?" Nate says. She does not know how to answer.

She prolongs her cup of coffee for as long as possible, but the technicians say nothing. Gregor whistles under his breath, Theo merely picks. Defeated, she carries her tray of teeth up-stairs to the office. She has a school tour at four, once more into the dusky push-button Cretaceous, round and round the cycad trees with a thousand children, her voice unreeling. Then she will go back to the house.

She has to be there early, since this is the first weekend Nate's children are going to spend with them. She's been dreading it all week.

"But there's nowhere for them to sleep," she said.

"They can borrow sleeping bags from their friends," Nate said.

Lesje said they didn't have enough plates. Nate said the children would hardly expect a formal dinner. He would do all the cooking, he said, and the children would wash the dishes. She wouldn't have to do anything extra at all. Lesje then felt she was being excluded, but did not say so. Instead she counted the silverware and agonized over the baked-in grime on the floors. When she lived with William she would have hooted with scorn over such scruples. The truth was that she didn't want the children to go home and report to Eliza-beth that she had no silverware and the floors were dirty. She hadn't cared what William thought of her, but she cares des-perately how she will appear to two young children she doesn't even know and has no special reason to like. They have no special reason to like her, either. They probably think she's stolen Nate. They probably hate her. She feels con-demned in advance, not for anything she's actually done, but for her ambiguous position in the universe.

On Thursday she went to Ziggy's and bought a bagful of delicacies: English shortbread in a tin, two kinds of cheese, chopped liver, fruit buns, chocolates. She almost never eats fruit buns or chocolates, but she'd snatched them off the shelves in desperation: surely this was what children liked. She realized she didn't have any idea of what children liked. Most of them liked dinosaurs, which was all she knew.

"That's not necessary, love," Nate said when she was disgorging the contents of her Ziggy's bag onto the kitchen table. "They'll be just as happy with peanut butter sandwiches."

Lesje ran upstairs, threw herself onto their mattress and cried silently, breathing in the smell of old cloth, old stuffing, mice. That was another thing: the children would see this mattress.

After a while Nate came in. He sat down and rubbed her back. "You know how important it is to me that you should all get along," he said. "If you had kids, you'd understand."

Lesje's belly clenched: she could feel it, a wall of muscle around a central hollow. He'd placed himself and the children, and Elizabeth too, in a tight verdant little oasis where such things as understanding were possible. In the desert without, isolated, single, childless and culpably young, she was made to stand in penance, watching a pantomime she could not decipher.

Nate had no idea he was being cruel. He thought he was being helpful. He stroked her back; she could imagine him looking at his watch to see if he'd done it for the required length of time.

Multituberculata, Lesje murmurs to herself. A soothing word. She wants to be soothed; she is not soothed. She dreads this evening. She dreads the thought of sitting at her own rickety table with its inadequate silverware and cheap plates, feeling her jaws move, making awkward conversation or staring at her hands while two pairs of eyes watch her in judgment. Three pairs.

Elizabeth

Elizabeth sits in the underground gloom of the Pilot Tavern, breathing in the smell of slightly stale French fries, watching the shadows. She spent several evenings with Chris here, once upon a time. It was a good place for them to go because they were unlikely to see anyone Elizabeth knew. She's chosen it now for the same reason.

The waiter has come for her order, but she said she was waiting for someone. Which is true. She has kissed her children good night, left out doughnuts and Coke for the baby-sitter, called a taxi and climbed into it, all so she can sit here in the Pilot Tavern and wait. Already she's regretting it. But she'd kept the card, that business card, tucked into the compartment of her purse where she stores her change and the folder for her identity cards. She knows she doesn't keep things like this unless she intends, sometime, to use them. An available body, stuck in the back of her mind.

She can still leave, but what then? She'd have to go back, pay off the baby-sitter, and lie down alone in the house that is empty but not empty, listening to the barely audible breathing of her children. When they're awake she can stand it. Though they're hardly great company. Nancy lies inert on her bed, listening to records or reading the same books over and over again: *The Hobbit, Prince Caspian.* Janet hangs around Elizabeth with offers of help: she will peel the carrots, she'll clear the table. She complains of stomach aches and isn't satisfied unless Elizabeth gives her some Gelusil or Phillips' Milk of Magnesia, from Nate's abandoned bottles. Nancy, on the other hand, slips from Elizabeth's arms, avoiding hugs and good-night kisses. Sometimes Elizabeth thinks the children are acting guilty rather than sad.

What's she supposed to say? Daddy hasn't exactly left, he's

just left. Mummy and Daddy both love you. Nothing is your
fault. You know he phones you every night, when he remembers. And you've seen him on weekends, several times. But
she and Nate have agreed she won't discuss the separation
with the children until he himself has a chance to have a talk
with them, a talk he's so far postponed. Which hardly matters.
The children aren't fools, they know what's going on. They
know it so well they aren't even asking questions.

The man in the brown suit is hanging over the table; he's
bigger than she remembers, and he's no longer wearing a
brown suit. His suit is light grey and he has on a tie with large
white lozenges on it that seem to glow in the dark. He's become more prosperous.

"See you got here," he says. He lowers himself into the
chair opposite her, sighs, turns his head for the waiter.

When she called, he hadn't remembered who she was. She
had to remind him about their meeting in the subway station,
their conversation about real estate. Then he'd been too effu-
sive: "Of course! Of course!" She found this lapse of his hu-
miliating. And then his laugh, thick as gravy, as if he knew
what she wanted.

He cannot really know. All she wants is oblivion. Temporary but complete: a night with no stars, a road running
straight to a cliff edge. A termination. *Terminal.* Before calling him, she was sure he could offer this. Perhaps he can. His
hands are on the table, blunt, dark-haired, practical.

"I've been on the trail," he says. "Just got back the day
before yesterday." The waiter comes and he orders himself a
rum and Coke, then asks Elizabeth what she'll have. "A Scotch
and soda for the lady." He explains how exhausted he
is. The only thing that breaks the monotony of the long drives
he has to make is his CB radio. You can get quite a few good
conversations going on that. Playfully, he asks Elizabeth to
guess what his handle is. Elizabeth demurs. "The Hulk," he
says, smiling a little shyly.

Elizabeth seems to remember that, earlier, he had flown
rather than driven. Either way, a traveling salesman. Someone
has to sell things, she supposes; nevertheless she's well on her
way to becoming part of an outworn joke. Surely she can do
better than this. But she doesn't want to. Better than this is
Philip Burroughs, the friends of friends, the husbands of
friends, well tailored, predictable. This man has a suitcase full
of crotchless underpants, a halo of sleazy joy. *Carnival.* No

circumspection for him, he won't take off his watch first and
prop it on the night table, fold his undershirt, smell of pepper-
mint, the tablets he's chewed for his ulcer. He's confident, he
leans back, he breathes unspoken promises. For someone else
he would be predictable, but not for her; not yet.

The drinks come and Elizabeth gulps hers like medicine,
hoping to feel lust bloom like a desert flower between her
thighs. The man in the grey suit leans across the table and tells
her in a confidential voice that he's thinking of selling his
house. His wife has a new one in mind, something farther
north, a little larger. Maybe she knows someone who might
be interested? The house he's selling has all-new copper wiring and he's had the floors wall-to-walled. He feels he can
afford the move; he's added a new line. Notions.

"Notions?" Elizabeth says. Her body sits on the plastic-
cushioned bench like a sandbag; heavy, dry, inanimate.

"For birthday parties," he says. Miniature helicopters,
whistles, soft plastic skulls, monsters, toy wristwatches. That
sort of thing. He asks her how her children are.

"Actually my husband and I have separated," she says. Perhaps this news will arouse in him the predatory responses that
the words *separated* and *divorced* are supposed to bring out in
married men. But it seems only to make him nervous. He
glances around, ostensibly to look for the waiter. It strikes
Elizabeth that he's no more eager to be seen with her than she
is to be seen with him. Could he possibly think she's after
him, wants him for domestic use? Preposterous. But it would
be insulting to tell him so.

She wonders if she could try being honest with him. *All I'm
interested in is a one-night stand. One hour if possible, and
you don't have to talk to me. No strings, no lines, no hooks, I
don't want to add to the clutter. I don't want you in my life;
that's why I called you.*

But he begins telling her about an operation he had two
months ago, for plantar warts. A lot more painful than you
might think. It's no use, she might as well cut her losses. The
time for this is over: pickups in the park, fumbling in the mov-
ies. She's forgotten the knack, the trick. How to want.

"I think it's time for me to go," she says politely. "Thank
you so much for the drink. It's been a pleasure seeing you
again." She slides her sweater-coat around her shoulders and
stands up, easing herself out from behind the table.

He looks dismayed. "The night's young," he says. "Have
another."

When Elizabeth declines, he scrambles to his feet. "I'll give you a lift home, anyhow."

Elizabeth hesitates, then accepts. Why pay a taxi? They walk to the parking lot through the warm air. He puts his hand on her elbow, a strangely old-fashioned gesture. Perhaps they could fox-trot, under the parking-lot lights. Her night on the town.

In his car, Elizabeth doesn't strain herself to make conversation. She tells him where she lives and gives semi-attentive murmurs while he complains about the poor quality of hotel food, especially in Thunder Bay. She's stone cold sober. Stone cold. There's some compensation: she's out of it cleanly, no harm done. He must realize she isn't interested. He stops talking and switches on his CB radio, twiddling the dial. Staccato voices crackle and fade.

But before he reaches her street, he turns the car into a dead end and stops it abruptly. The headlights rest on a checkerboard, a black arrow; beyond, a high wire fence. A factory of some sort.

"This isn't my street," Elizabeth says. At the beginning of the evening she would have welcomed this move.

"Don't play dumb," he says. "We both know what you're here for." He reaches down and unhooks the microphone from his radio. "We'll give them a thrill," he says. "Ten-four, ten-four, gimmie a break."

Elizabeth fumbles for the push button on the seat belt, but before she can unlatch it he falls on her. Elizabeth, head forced back by the weight of his mouth gasps for air. One knee is between her thighs, shoving her skirt up; his rump is squeezed against the glove compartment. There's something cold and metallic pressing against her throat and she realizes it's the microphone.

He thrashes, moans; his elbow flails the window. Elizabeth fights suffocation. *He's having a heart attack.* She'll be stuck here, under the body, until they hear her screams over the microphone and come to dig her out.

But in less than a minute his face collapses against her neck and he lies inert. Elizabeth works her left arm up, forcing an air hole.

"Wow," he says, pushing himself off her. "Great stuff."

Elizabeth pulls her skirt down over her knees. "I'll walk home," she says. She can hear her voice shaking, though she doesn't think she's frightened. Idiot, to have expected more.

"Hey, don't you want your turn?" the man says. His hand

scampers like a spider up her thigh. "I'm good," he says. "Take a break and enjoy yourself." His left hand holds the microphone, as if he's expecting her to sing.

"Get your hand off my crotch," Elizabeth says. She feels as if she's opened a serious-looking package and a wind-up snake has jumped out. She's never appreciated practical jokes.

"Hell, I was just trying to be friendly," he says, withdrawing. He hooks his microphone back on the set. "Everyone likes a bit of fun."

"Get off the channel, Mac," says the voice on the radio. "Piss or get off the pot."

"I'll walk home," Elizabeth says again.

"I can't let you do that," the man says. "Not around here." He sits with his hands on his knees, his head bowed; he's looking at the steering wheel. "I've got a nip in the glove compartment," he says. "Live a little, have one on me. Let's both have one." His voice is listless.

"No thanks, really," Elizabeth says, forced back into politeness. She unlatches the seat belt; this time he makes no move to stop her. Sadness radiates from him like heat, she can see that now, it always has. When she leaves he will probably cry. In some odd, shrunken way he wanted to please her. Whose failure is it that she is not pleased?

Outside there are trees, the wind, then houses. She walks to the first intersection, looking for street names. Behind her she can hear the motor running, but he doesn't turn, doesn't pass her. Who is laughing? Something stuck in her throat. Nobody really.

Thursday, October 7, 1976

NATE

Nate is out on the front porch, rocking gently in the rocking chair Elizabeth bought for fifteen dollars five years ago at a farm auction near Lloydtown. Before he sold the car. She'd had him paint it white to cover up the split back, wired together through small holes drilled inexpertly in each half. It would do for the front porch, she said. The same rocker, undamaged and stripped, would have been at least fifty dollars, she told him. Now after five years of weather the chair needs sanding and a fresh coat of paint. But if he does it, Elizabeth will ignore it. She's no longer interested in the furniture.

He holds his mind still and avoids looking along the street to where Elizabeth will soon appear in the late afternoon sunlight, walking through the fallen leaves on her way home from the bus stop. He's waiting for her, he actually wants to see her. This is a sensation so long forgotten that it's almost like a new one. His body in the chair feels angular as the chair, his spine tight. Something is about to happen, some beginning, things are about to change, and he isn't sure he's ready.

Six days ago she said she wanted to have a little chat with him. He expected a lecture on some procedure: the dishes, the laundry, who washed what of whose, who folded what, how objects on the floor were supposed to transfer themselves to the proper shelf. That's what her little chats usually amount to. *Pulling his weight*. He had his defense already prepared: when he does do things she doesn't notice he's done them, so how does she know whether he's pulling his weight or not? He'd delayed, pouring himself a drink, searching for his cigarettes, before sitting down reluctantly opposite her at the kitchen table.

But instead she told him bluntly that she'd stopped seeing Chris. Under the rules they'd agreed on, it was no longer any of his business who she saw. He wanted to remind her of this, of her side of the agreement. "Do what you like," he'd say. Why was she bothering him about it?

"I want you to do me a favor," she said before he could speak. Though she demanded justice Elizabeth did not often request favors, not from him, not lately. "If Chris should come around, I don't want you to let him into the house."

Nate stared at her. She'd never said anything like this before, presumably because she hadn't needed to. Her way of disposing of her lovers was usually terminal. He didn't know what she told them, but when she'd had enough of them they dropped from sight as rapidly, as completely, as if she'd roped a cement block to their legs and heaved them into the harbor. He suspected her of wanting to do the same thing with him—certainly she was fed up with him—but the children prevented her.

He wanted to ask what was wrong: Was Chris likely to come to the house? Why? But she would only say again that her life was her life. Once it had been theirs.

This is what he wants, wants back. This image, of a shared harmonious life, left over from some Christmas card of the forties, a log fire, knitting in a basket, glued-on snow, had been discarded so long ago by both of them that he'd forgotten about it. Now it was here again, a possibility in the present tense. Perhaps Elizabeth wanted it too, perhaps she was willing to try again. He felt he had to act decisively. She'd often accused him of being unable to act decisively. So he asked Martha out to lunch.

Martha was delighted. At a corner table in the Café Jurgens, her choice, she held his hand and told him how wonderful it was to be able to see him like this, spontaneously, outside the allotted hours. He watched her unhappily while she ate a grilled lobster sandwich and drank two whiskey sours. Behind her was a blown-up photograph of, was it Venice?

"You're silent today," Martha said. "Cat got your tongue?"

Nate managed a smile. He was about to tell her he couldn't see her any more, and he wanted to do it gracefully and calmly. He didn't even want to do it, exactly, although things had reached an impasse with them lately. But the fact was that with Chris gone there was an imbalance. Martha, too, would have to be jettisoned; otherwise he might end up living with her. Which he didn't want. It would be much better for everyone if he could fix it up with Elizabeth; better for the children. He felt dismal about this but it was in a good cause. He would try for a clean break. He hoped she wouldn't scream at him. Vitality, he'd once called it.

But she didn't scream. She let go of his hand and lowered her head, staring at the crusts of her sandwich. He thought he saw a tear fall into the mayonnaise.

"You need something more," Nate said, hurriedly debasing himself. "Someone who can . . ."

"That bitch," Martha said. "She finally did it, didn't she? She's been working at it long enough."

"What do you mean?" Nate said. "Really, this has nothing to do with Elizabeth, I just think . . ."

"When are you going to get your own bellybutton back, Nate?" Martha said, almost in a whisper. She raised her eyes, looking him straight in the face. "I bet she even ties your goddamned shoelaces for you."

To the left there's a sudden roar, almost like an explosion. Nate's eyes jerk up. There in front of him, where he hasn't seen it for over a year ("Do what you like," he'd told her, "just don't make me watch") is Chris's old white convertible, this time with the top up. Nate expects to see Elizabeth get out of it and come breezing up the walk, over-affable as she always is when she's got something she wants but he doesn't. He doesn't really believe Chris has been banished, not permanently; he's gone on too long, she's been too intent on him for that. They'll be back to square one, where they've probably been all the time.

But Chris gets out alone. He comes up the front steps, stumbling a little on the one Nate has been meaning to fix, and Nate is dismayed to see how bludgeoned he looks. He has dark horizontal welts under his eyes, as if he's been slugged across the face with a belt. His hair straggles, his hands dangle heavily from the sleeves of his crumpled corduroy jacket. He stares down at Nate, the hopeless challenging stare of a drunk about to ask for a handout.

"Hi," Nate says weakly. He moves to stand up, so they'll be on the same level, but Chris squats, resting on his heels. He smells of whiskey bottles, used socks, faintly rotting meat.

"You've got to help me," he says.

"Did you lose your job?" Nate asks. A fatuous question perhaps, but what is he supposed to say to his wife's castoff lover? He certainly can't order him self-righteously from the porch, now that he's actually here. He looks so beaten; surely Elizabeth alone could not account for such wreckage.

Chris laughs a little. "I quit," he says. "I couldn't stand it, being in the same building with her. I haven't slept. She won't even see me."

"What can I do?" Nate says. Meaning: *What do you expect me to do?* But he genuinely wants to help, anyone witnessing such misery would want to help, though his own knee-jerk sympathy dismays him. The bloody Unitarians again. He should hand Chris over to his mother; she would lecture him on how he should think about the positive things in life instead of dwelling on the gloomy ones. Then she'd put his name on a list, and several weeks later he'd get a parcel in the mail—soap ends extracted from motels, a dozen pairs of children's socks, a knitted chest protector.

"Make her listen," Chris says. "She hangs up on me. She won't even listen."

Nate remembers now the distant ringing of the phone in the middle of the night, two or three A.M., Elizabeth's half-moon eyes in the mornings. A month at least it's been going on.

"I can't make Elizabeth do anything," Nate says.

"She respects you," Chris says. "She'll listen to you." He looks down at the porch floor, then up at Nate with sudden hatred. "She doesn't respect me."

It's a revelation to Nate that Elizabeth respects him. He doesn't believe it anyway; it's a ploy used by Elizabeth against Chris, who is too dim to see through it.

"Tell her," Chris says belligerently. "She's got to live with me. I want to marry her. Tell her she has to."

Warped, Nate thinks. This is very warped. Does Chris really expect him to order his own wife to run off with another man? "You look as though you need a drink," he says. He wants one himself. "Come on in."

Halfway down the hall, Chris following him, he remembers Elizabeth's plea. Don't let him into the house. It was a plea, he sees now, not a cool request. She hasn't renounced Chris; she's fled because she's afraid of him. It would take quite a lot to make Elizabeth afraid for her own safety. She must think he'll attack her, beat her up. The image of Elizabeth in that grip, white flesh buckling under those fists, powerless, whimpering, is only momentarily erotic.

The back of Nate's neck tingles. He's been heading for the

kitchen, with its knives and skewers, but turns instead into the living room, wheeling too abruptly.

"Scotch?" he says.

Chris says nothing. He's leaning in the doorway, smiling: a rat smile, lip lifted back over yellowed teeth. Nate doesn't feel like turning his back on him to go to the kitchen for glasses, but he can hardly walk backwards. Late-movie scenarios unreel: himself conked with a brass candlestick or one of Elizabeth's heavy bowls, left unconscious in the hallway; the children kidnapped, held hostage, barricaded and terrified in Chris's two-roomed hideaway while Chris hunches over his chessboard like the Phantom of the Opera and the police megaphone from doorways; Elizabeth dumped bruised and naked in a culvert, bedsheet knotted around her neck. Preventable, all of it, and his fault; if only he hadn't . . .

Even as his own guilt flashes before him, Nate wants to give Chris something, some food, what? A bus ticket somewhere, Mexico, Venezuela, that's what he himself has often wanted. He wants to reach out, touch Chris on the arm; he searches for some maxim, trite but magical, some parable of hope that will restore Chris in an instant, send him out square-shouldered to face life. At the same time he knows that if Chris makes a move, just one move toward the staircase that leads to the closed door behind which the children were playing, half an hour earlier, an intense game of Admirals, he'll jump him and pound his head against the banister. He'll kill him. He'll kill him with no regrets.

There are footsteps on the porch, resolute, even; the click of the front door. Elizabeth. Now it will explode, Chris will charge her like a moose in heat, Nate will have to protect her. Otherwise she'll disappear down the front walk, ass first, slung over Chris's shoulder, pencils and keys tumbling from her purse. Maybe she would like that, Nate thinks. She used to imply that he himself was not forceful enough.

But "Get out" is all she says. She's behind Chris, in the hall; from the living room Nate can't see her. Chris has turned, his face folding, pleating itself like water hit by a rock. When Nate reaches the hall he's gone. There is only Elizabeth, her mouth set in that tight line of displeasure, pulling her leather gloves off finger by finger.

Watching her, thinking of Chris slinking across the street like a straggler from a defeated army, he knows that at some vague place in the future he himself will need to leave her.

Wednesday, June 22, 1977

LESJE

Lesje, balancing her tray, steers towards an empty table surrounded by other empty tables. She no longer finds it easy to come down for coffee with Marianne and Trish or to join them for lunch. They're still friendly enough, but they're careful. She can remember this feeling and sympathize with it: those in the midst of crisis are bad luck. They're curiosities and you talk about them when they aren't there, but when they are there they silence you. For Marianne and Trish, she's like static electricity.

Dr. Van Vleet is away; he gets rose fever every year, for which he takes herbal remedies prepared by his wife. Lesje wonders whether she will live long enough with Nate to learn herbal remedies and dose him with them. Or with anyone else. She tries to visualize Nate in an old man's V-necked cardigan, dozing in the sun, and fails. Dr. Van Vleet often says "in my day." Lesje wonders if he knew it was his day at the time. She herself does not feel that the time through which she's presently living is particularly hers.

She wants Dr. Van Vleet to be here. He never listens to gossip, he's heard nothing about her so-called private life. He's the only person she knows who is willing to treat her with amused paternal indulgence, which at the moment she feels very much in need of. He corrects her pronunciation, she laughs at his epigrams. If he were here now, opposite her at the table, she could ask him about something, some technical point, and then she wouldn't have to think about anything else. The feeding and breeding habits of the pteranodon, for instance. If a glider rather than a flapper, how did it become airborne? Did it simply wait for a slight breeze to lift it by its twelve-foot wings? Some speculate that because of its incredibly delicate bone structure it would have been unable to touch down anywhere, on water or on land. If so, how did it reproduce? For a moment Lesje glimpses warm tranquil seas, gentle winds, the immense fur-covered pteranodons soaring like wisps of white cotton high overhead. Such visions are still possible, but they don't last long. Inevitably she sees a later phase: the stench of dying seas, dead fish on the mud-covered shores, the huge flocks dwindling, stranded, their time done. All of a sudden, Utah.

She sits down, facing away from the room. Elizabeth is there; Lesje spotted her as soon as she came in. A few months ago she would have gone out again, but there's no longer any point to that. Elizabeth, like gamma rays, will continue to exist whether Lesje can see her or not. There's a dark, somewhat hefty woman with her. They both look at Lesje as she walks by, not smiling but not hostile either. As if they are sightseers and she is a sight.

Lesje knows that when Nate moved completely in, or as completely as he's going to, Elizabeth should have felt deserted and betrayed and she herself should have felt, if not victorious, at least conventionally smug. Instead it seems to be the other way around. Lesje wishes that Elizabeth would vanish into some remote corner of the past and stay there forever, but she knows her wishes are not likely to have much effect on Elizabeth.

She peels the foil top from her her yogurt and sticks the straw into her carton of milk. At least she's been eating better since Nate moved in. Nate is making her eat better. He brought some cooking pots with him and he usually cooks dinner; then he supervises while she eats. It disturbs him if she doesn't finish. The food he cooks is probably quite good, certainly better than she could do, and she's ashamed to admit that she lusts at least once in a while for a package of Betty Crocker Noodles Romanoff. She's been living for so long on convenience food, take-outs, heat 'n serve, she's sure her capacities for appreciaton have been blunted. In this way, as in many others, she cannot seem to avoid being inappropriate.

Her reactions, for instance. *Reactions* is Nate's word. He finds these reactions of hers, not disappointing exactly, but surprising, as if only a barbarian or an illiterate could have the reactions she does. He doesn't even get angry. He merely explains, again and again; he assumes that if she can understand what he's saying she will of necessity agree with it.

For instance. Elizabeth, when she telephones, as she does fairly often, to ask if the children have left their socks or their rubber boots or their toothbrushes or their underpants behind at Lesje's house, is always polite. Of what then can Lesje complain? The truth is that she doesn't want Elizabeth to phone her at all. Especially not at the office. She doesn't want to be disturbed in the middle of the Cretaceous by Elizabeth, wondering if Lesje has happened to see a red and white mitten. It upsets her, and finally, awkwardly, she has managed to blurt this out.

But the children forgot things, Nate said. Elizabeth had to know where these things were. There were not unlimited supplies of such items.

Perhaps, Lesje ventured, the children could stop forgetting things.

Nate said they were children.

"Maybe you could phone her," Lesje said, "or she could phone you. Instead of me."

Nate pointed out that he had never been very good at keeping track of toothbrushes and rubber boots, even his own. It just wasn't one of his talents.

"Mine either," said Lesje. Or hadn't he noticed? On Sunday evenings, when the children were packing for their return, the house looked like a train station after a bomb attack. She did try, but since she didn't know what the children had brought with them, how could she be sure they'd taken the right numbers of things away again?

Nate said that since neither of them was proficient at this and Elizabeth was, having had long practice, it made good sense for Elizabeth to phone when any of the said items disappeared. Lesje could only agree.

Sometimes the children would be there for Friday dinner when Lesje was expecting to come home from the Museum and find nobody there but Nate. "Could you ask her not to spring them on us?" she said after the fourth time.

"What do you mean?" Nate asked sadly.

"I mean, isn't Friday a little late to tell you?"

"She told me on Tuesday."

"No one told *me*," Lesje said.

Nate admitted it had slipped his mind; even so there were better ways of phrasing things. *Spring them* he found rather blunt, even abrasive. "And I cooked dinner," he concluded reasonably. "It didn't inconvenience you, did it?"

"No," Lesje said. She felt at a disadvantage: she'd had no practice at this sort of dialogue. Her parents, at least in her hearing, had never discussed each others' behavior and motives, and her grandmothers had never discussed anything. They'd limited themselves to monologues, wistful reveries from her Ukrainian grandmother, raucous commentaries from her Jewish one. Her conversations with William had centered on an exchange of facts, and even their rare disputes had been more like the squabblings of children: *I want. You did so.* She wasn't used to saying what she felt, or why, or why someone else ought to behave differently. She knew she was not subtle, that she often sounded rude when she meant only to be accurate. Invariably she came out of these conversations feeling like a mean-minded ogre. It wasn't that she resented or disliked the children as such, she wanted to say. She just wanted to be consulted.

But she couldn't say that; if she did, he might bring up that other conversation.

"I want to feel I'm living with you," she said. "Not with you and your wife and children."

"I'll try to keep them out of your way as much as possible," Nate said, with such dejection that she'd retracted immediately.

"I don't mean they can't come *over*," she said generously.

"I want them to feel that this is their house, too," Nate said.

Lesje isn't sure any longer whose house it is. She wouldn't be surprised to get a gracious phone call from Elizabeth saying that she and the children would be moving in the next day and could she please get the spare room ready and make sure all the stray socks and boots had been gathered together? Nate wouldn't protest. He feels they should both try to make things easier for Elizabeth, which as far as Lesje can see means doing everything she wants. He often says he thinks Elizabeth is being very civilized. He also feels he is being civilized. He didn't seem to think that Lesje should have to make any special effort to be civilized as well. She isn't directly involved.

"We have each other," he says. Lesje has to agree that this is true. They do have each other, whatever *have* means.

Lesje sucks up the last of her milk and puts the empty carton on the tray. She stubs out her cigarette and is bending to gather up her shoulder bag when a penetrating voice says, "Excuse me."

Lesje looks up. The dark-haired woman who's been having lunch with Elizabeth is standing beside her.

"You're living with Nate Schoenhof, aren't you?" she says.

Lesje is too startled to say anything. "Mind if I sit down?" the woman says. She's wearing a red wool suit with lipstick to match.

"I almost did, myself," she says neutrally, as if discussing a job she didn't get. "I'm the one before you. But he kept saying he could never leave his family." She laughs as if enjoying a slightly witless joke.

Lesje can't think of anything at all to say. This must be Martha, whom Nate has mentioned in passing. She sounded ineffectual. Lesje expected her to be about five feet tall and mousy. The real Martha does not seem ineffectual, and Lesje now wonders if she herself may at some future date be reduced to an equally pallid shadow. Of course Nate would not have mentioned Martha's large breasts and striking mouth, not to her.

"Having any trouble with *her*?" Martha says, jerking her head.

"Who?" Lesje says.

"Don't worry, she just went out. Queen Elizabeth."

Lesje wishes to avoid being drawn into a conspiracy. To say anything against Elizabeth to this particular person would be disloyal to Nate. "She's being very civilized," she says. No one could object to that.

"I can see he's brainwashed *you*," Martha says with another laugh. "God, the two of them love that word." She grins at Lesje, a red gypsy grin. Suddenly Lesje likes her enormously. She smiles faintly back.

"Don't let them do a job on you," Martha says. "Let them start and they'll turn your head to mush. Fight back. Give 'em hell." She stands up.

"Thank you," Lesje says. She's grateful that anyone, anyone at all, has given her this much sympathetic thought.

"Any time," Martha says. "There's not much I'm an expert on but believe you me, I'm the world's living authority on *them*."

For at least fifteen minutes Lesje is elated. She's been vindicated; her own perceptions, which she has increasingly begun to distrust and even to disown, are possibly valid. Back in her office though, replaying the conversation, it occurs to her that Martha may have had one or two ulterior motives.

Also: Martha didn't say what she's supposed to fight back against, or how. Martha obviously fought back herself. But it's to be noted—a hard fact—that Martha is not currently living with Nate.

Friday, July 8, 1977

NATE

Nate is going to his house; his former house. He can't believe he no longer lives there. Up Shaw Street, past Yarmouth, past Dupont, the railway tracks, the factory where they make some product he's never bothered to identify. Steel girders, something like that, something for which he has no use. It's a hot day, muggy, as they say; the air warm porridge.

He's spent the morning going from shop to shop where his toys are placed, Yorkville, Cumberland, lower Bayview Avenue, the boutique districts, hoping something had sold and he could collect, at least enough to keep him going. One Mary Had a Little Lamb. His share, ten bucks. He wonders if any of the owners was holding out on him; they must be able to tell he's desperate, and desperation, he knows, induces contempt. Waiting in the cute stores with their gingham aprons and patchwork chair covers, their tea cosies in the shape of hens, egg cosies in the shape of chickens, the bayberry soap from the States, all the country pretenses, he felt a little of his mother's dismay. People spent money on this stuff, a lot of money. People spent money on his toys. Wasn't there anything better? It's a living, he thought. Wrong again, it isn't. He threw away a promising career, everyone said it was promising though they didn't say what it promised. He wanted to make honest things, he wanted his life to be honest, and all he has now is the taste of sawdust in his mouth.

But he's glad enough to have the ten. He's supposed to meet the kids at his old house. They'll walk the three long blocks up to St. Clair, Nancy walking ahead of them as if she does not belong with them, Janet keeping close but not deigning to hold his hand; lately she's decided she's too old for hand-holding. These are the ways they demonstrate their anger with him, which otherwise they conceal. Atoning, he'll buy them each an ice-cream bar, and then they'll go to the Italian baker's to pick up the cake for Elizabeth. He'll pay for it and that will be the ten. Though he'll still have change from the five he borrowed from Lesje.

He can't connect the acts of carving the lamb, of painting and varnishing, with their consequence: Elizabeth's birthday cake. He can't connect any act he can think of with any consequence he can imagine. The trees he's passing, leaves limp in the heat, the houses with their patchy lawns or gardens crammed with tomato plants, look segmented, a collection of units, not really attached. The leaves aren't attached to the trees, the roofs aren't attached to the houses; blow and it would all fall down, a Lego town. His body feels the same. There's a toy he once made, a favorite several years back, lathe work, a wooden man built of rings which slipped over a central post. The head screwed on, holding the man together. A clown's smile he used. This is his body, stiff fragments held together by his spine and his screwtop head. Segmented man. Maybe he needs a salt tablet.

He thought that by moving to Lesje's he could rid himself of the need to be in two places at once. But he's still spending almost as much time at his old house as at the new one. Lesje isn't supposed to know this, but she behaves as if she does anyway. He should have two sets of clothes, two identities, one for each house; it's the lack of this extra costume or body that is cracking him apart. He knew in advance, in theory, that separation is painful; he did not know it would also be literal. He has been separated; he is separate. Dismembered. He is no longer a member. His own house rebukes him, fills with ravens: *Nevermore*. It's this pain of his, sentimental, unbearable, that Lesje resents and Elizabeth ignores.

Elizabeth is being very civilized, up to a point. Deliberately, ponderously polite. Whenever he comes to pick up the kids she invites him in and offers him some tea or, depending on the time of day, an *apéritif*: Cinzano, Dubonnet. She knows he never drinks these things but she's rubbing his nose in it, treating him like a guest in his own house. Which is not his own house. He's willing to bet there are some bottles or ends of bottles left in his kitchen cupboard or in the bottom of the pine sideboard—Elizabeth isn't much of a drinker, she won't have finished them—but he can't violate this game by asking. So he perches on the edge of one of his former chairs, sipping a drink he doesn't like but can't refuse, while Elizabeth fills him in on the children—their marks, their latest interests—as if he hasn't talked to them for a year. As if he's an uncle, a new school principal. *I'm their father!* he wants to shout. *I haven't forgotten that*, she'd say. *But sometimes you do.* It's one of her assumptions, so deeply rooted she never bothers to discuss it, that he neglects his children.

He knows he should be getting a birthday present for Elizabeth, he always has before. Even if she herself doesn't expect it the children will. But Lesje would guess, partly because he'd have to borrow the money from her, and then there would be trouble. He doesn't want trouble, he doesn't need any more trouble of that sort. Lesje can't manage to see Elizabeth as a factor, a condition, something to be endured, like a snow-storm; morally neutral. Which is how Nate feels Elizabeth ought to be viewed. Instead she insists on regarding her as—what? her own private troll, a combination of the Dragon Lady and a vacuum cleaner. Nate himself tries to be objective. There's more excuse for his own failure in this respect than for Lesje's.

He wants to tell her she's taking everything too seriously; but how can he do this when among the things she takes so seriously is himself? Elizabeth ceased to do this some time ago, and he isn't even sure he can still do it. But Lesje can, she can do nothing else. He can't remember ever having been listened to so attentively; even his banalities, his random comments. Almost as if he's speaking a foreign language, one with which she is only slightly familiar. She thinks he knows things it would benefit her to learn; she thinks of him as older. Which flatters but alarms him: he can't risk total exposure, bare his confusion or his carefully guarded despair. He's never told her how he jittered in phone booths night after night, dialing her number, hanging up when she answered. Cowardice, failure of nerve.

In the bedroom he's beginning to think of as theirs, she glimmers like a thin white moon for him alone. By seeing how beautiful she is he's made her beautiful. But what if she discovers the truth? What he suspects is the truth. That he's patchwork, a tin man, his heart stuffed with sawdust.

He thinks of her waiting for him, somewhere else, an island, subtropical, not muggy, her long hair waving in the sea breeze, a red hibiscus tucked behind one ear. If he's lucky she'll wait till that happens, till he can get there to be with her.

(Though on the shore, at a discreet distance and despite his best efforts, there's always another hut. He tries to shut it out but it too is indigenous. For the children and, of course, for Elizabeth. Who else would take care of them?)

Saturday, July 9, 1977

Elizabeth

Elizabeth has taken off her shoes and is brushing her hair, standing in front of the bureau with its oak-framed mirror. The air is humid and unmoving, though the window is wide open. The soles of her feet feel tender and swollen. She hopes she will never get varicose veins.

In the glass oval, behind her own face, rigid and it seems to her puffy in the muted light, she can trace the shadow of her face as it will be in twenty years. Twenty years ago she was nineteen. In another twenty years she will be fifty-nine.

Today is her birthday. Cancer. In the Scorpio decanate, as some pretentious little fraud at the last Museum Christmas party told her. Someone from Textiles, floral prints and herbal teas. Since yesterday the earth has turned once on its axis, and now she is thirty-nine. Jack Benny's age, the joke age. If someone asks her her age and she tells it, they'll automatically assume she's being funny as well as lying. Jack Benny, of course, is dead. Not only that, her children don't even know who he was. Before this birthday her age has never bothered her.

She half-empties her glass. She's drinking sherry, has been drinking it for some time. A stupid thing to be doing, a stupid thing to be drinking; but since Nate left, the liquor cabinet is never very well stocked. She doesn't drink steadily the way Nate does and she forgets to replace things. She finished off a heel of Scotch earlier in the day. Another of his leavings.

The children insisted on throwing a birthday party for her, though she tried to head them off. When Nate lived here they'd celebrated her birthday in the morning, simply, with presents only. Parties were for children, she'd told them, and Nate had backed her up. But this year they went the whole hog. They seemed to think it would cheer her up. It was sup-

posed to be a surprise, but she knew what was coming as soon
as Nancy, elaborately and casually, suggested after lunch that
she take an afternoon nap.

"But I'm not tired, darling," she said.

"Yes, you are. You've got big bags under your eyes."

"Please, Mother," Janet said. Janet has lately begun to call
her "Mother," instead of "Mum." Elizabeth wonders if that
tone of weary, superior exasperation has been copied from her.

She climbed the stairs to her room, where she lay on the
bed drinking Scotch and reading *English Tapestry Through
the Ages*. If they were preparing a surprise, she would have to
be surprised.

At five Janet brought her a cup of undrinkably bitter tea
and ordered her to come downstairs when she heard three
whistles. She tiptoed to the bathroom to pour out the tea;
returning, she could hear them arguing in the kitchen. She
creamed her face and put on a black cotton blouse and the
pearl pin she knew Janet considered elegant. When she heard
Nancy's feeble whistles, she tightened the corners of her
mouth, widened her eyes, and negotiated the stairs, holding
on to the banister. Nude descending the staircase, in cunning
fragments. Stewed, descending the staircase. But she wasn't
really drunk. Tiddly, said Uncle Teddy.

They'd lit candles in the kitchen and looped pink and blue
streamers with teddybears on them around the walls. "Happy
Birthday, Mum," Nancy shrieked. "This is a surprise!"

Janet stood beside the cake, hands decorously folded. The
cake was on the table. It had three candles on one corner and
nine on the opposite one. "Because if we put thirty-nine on we
couldn't get them all on," said Nancy. The writing, in impec-
cable baker's script surrounded with bridal wreaths of pink
sugar roses, said "Happy Birthday Mother."

Elizabeth, who hadn't expected to be moved, sat down on
one of the kitchen chairs and locked her smile into place.
Lockjaw. This was the shadow of all the birthday parties she'd
never been given. Her own mother had either forgotten or
found her birth no cause for celebration, though there would
be presents, remorsefully, days after the event. Auntie Muriel,
on the other hand, had always remembered, but had made it
the occasion for a solemn presentation of some large or costly
item, something that radiated guilt in advance, that cried out
to be scratched, lost, stolen. A bicycle, a watch. Not wrapped.

"Thank you, love," she said, hugging each of the children
in turn. "This is the most wonderful birthday I've ever had."

She blew out the candles and opened her presents, exclaiming over the lily-of-the-valley talcum powder from Janet and the puzzle from Nancy that required to have its three white balls and three black balls jiggled into their respective holes. Nancy is good at such puzzles.

"Where's your present from Dad?" Nancy asked. "He said he was giving you one."

"I guess he just forgot this year, darling," Elizabeth said. "I'm sure he'll remember it later."

"I don't understand that," Janet said reflectively. "He gave us the money for the cake."

Nancy burst into tears. "We weren't supposed to tell!" She ran from the room; Elizabeth heard her wailing up the stairs.

"She's been under a strain lately," Janet said in that adult voice Elizabeth finds so hard to bear. She followed sedately, leaving Elizabeth alone with an uneaten cake and a small pile of crumpled wrapping paper.

She cut the cake and filled two plates, then carried them upstairs, prepared to stroke and comfort. She entered the children's room and sat, rubbing Nancy's damp back as she lay face down on her bed. It was far too hot. She could feel sweat condensing on her upper lip, in the hollows at the backs of her knees.

"She's just showing off," Janet said. She was sitting on the other twin bed, nibbling a sugar rose. "There's nothing wrong with her really."

Elizabeth put her head down to Nancy's when the choking noises had subsided.

"What is it, love?"

"You and Dad don't love each other any more."

Oh, hell, Elizabeth thought. He set this up. I should let him cope with it. Just stick them in a taxi and send them over. "I know it makes you unhappy that your father doesn't live here with us any more," she said carefully, correctly. "We felt it would be better for all of us if we lived apart for a while. Your father loves you both very much. Your father and I will always love each other too, because both of us are your parents and we both love you. Now sit up and eat your lovely cake, like a good girl."

Nancy sat up. "Mummy," she said, "are you going to die?"

"Sometime, darling," Elizabeth said. "But not right now."

Janet came to sit on the other side of Elizabeth. She wanted to be hugged, so Elizabeth hugged her.

Mummy. A dried corpse in a gilded case. *Mum,* silent. *Mama,* short for mammary gland. A tree whose hungry mouth is pressed. If you didn't want trees sucking at your sweet flowing breast why did you have children? Already they're preparing for flight, betrayal, they will leave her, she will become their background. They will discuss her as they lie in bed with their lovers, they will use her as an explanation for everything they find idiosyncratic or painful about themselves. If she makes them feel guilty enough they'll come and visit her on weekends. Her shoulders will sag, she will have difficulty with shopping bags, she will become *My Mother,* pronounced with a sigh. She will make them cups of tea and without meaning to but unable to stop will pry, pry like a small knife into their lives.

She doesn't mean to now; she does now. Those careful questions about the other house: What were they given for dinner? How late did they stay up? Did they have a good time? And the equally careful answers. They can sense it's a trap. If they say they like the other house, household, she'll be hurt; if not, she will be angry. "It was all right," they say, avoiding her eyes, and she despises herself for placing them there, making them shift and evade. She wants them to be happy. At the same time she wants to hear of injuries, atrocities, so she can virtuously rage.

She brushed her hair, her face in the mirror a flat plaque. Leaden. She's making it too easy for him, he has it too easy. He isn't the one who has to wipe the noses and wake up in the middle of the night because his children are screaming in their sleep. If she even told him about that, he'd think she was using emotional blackmail. She tips back her glass; reddish brown slides down her throat.

It isn't Lesje she resents. Let him screw whatever he likes, why should she care? It's his freedom she can't take. Free as a goddamned bird, while she's locked in this house, locked into this house while the roof leaks and the foundation crumbles and the earth revolves and leaves fall from the calendars like snow. In the centers of her bones dark metal smolders.

She sits down on the edge of her bed, staring at her crossed wrists, the blue veins where they branch and river. Every second a pulsebeat, countdown. She could lie down with candles at her head and feet. Thirty-nine of them. She could stop time. *Wristwatch.*

With an effort she turns her hand over. It's eleven-thirty.

She checks the children's room. They're both asleep, breathing evenly. She goes back along the hall, intending to go to bed; but instead she finds herself putting on her shoes. She doesn't know what she is going to do.

Elizabeth stands in the hot night outside Nate's new house, Nate's old house, which she's never seen before. Although of course she's had the address and the telephone number. In case of emergencies. Perhaps this is an emergency. The house is dark except for a dim light in the upper window. The bedroom.

She'd wanted to see it, that's all. Make it enter her head so she can believe in its existence. (A dump, a slum; probably cockroaches. This tattiness pleases her; the house is much worse than her own.) But she goes quietly up the front steps and tries the door. She isn't sure what she'll do if it's open. Creep up the stairs, fling open the bedroom door as in some antique melodrama? But the front door is securely locked.

They've locked her out. They're ignoring her, giggling in the bedroom while she stands down here in the night, discarded, invisible. She will make a mark: a brick through the window, her initials on the door? She has nothing to write with. Should she kick over the garbage can, litter trash on the porch, scream? Look at me, I'm here, you can't get rid of me that easily.

But she can't scream; her voice has been stolen. The only power she has left is negative.

Suddenly she thinks: What if they look out the window and see me standing down here? Her face is flushed, the skin under her blouse is wet and prickling; her hair sticks to her neck. Disheveled, a disheveled cliché. They will laugh. She turns quickly away from the house and begins to walk north, sober now, annoyed with herself for having allowed herself to be led to this ignominious, this vacant street.

And worse: where are the children? Locked in the house, alone. *Ladybird, ladybird.* She's never left them alone like this before. She thinks of fires, of murderous climbers, silhouetted against their open window. Gross negligence. But if the children die it will be in a way Nate's fault. On her birthday; an obscure revenge.

Even to think this terrifies her. She thinks instead of the cake, the candles. *Little Nancy Etticoat, in a white petticoat and a red nose.* And Nancy, looking at the picture of the melting woman in the *Little Riddle Book,* said, *Is that me?*

Pleased to be in a book. She was much younger then.

"If you blow out all the candles at once," Nancy said, "you'll get your wish." Nancy doesn't yet know about wishes, their danger. *The longer she lives, the shorter she grows.*

Part Five

NATE

This is it. Nate has spent several months avoiding this. He would rather be doing anything else at all. He has a brief vision of himself on a balsa raft, floating down the Amazon with malarial steam rising around him. A crocodile, or would it be an alligator, raises its head from the murky green water, stinking like a dead snake, hissing, lunging for him. Deftly he inserts a stick between its open jaws, twists and its helpless, it falls astern and he floats serenely on, sunburned and emaciated but not done yet, not by a long shot. He wishes he hadn't lost his pith helmet in that skirmish. He's on his way to discover something, or perhaps he's already discovered it. A lost civilization. In his back pocket is a creased and water-stained map, which will be the only clue if the poisoned arrows get him. Delirious, he'll be. If he can only reach Lima. He tries vainly to remember which side of South America Lima is really on. A miracle of endurance, they will say.

But the pressure, the unavoidable vortex has him at last and he's being swept along, out of control, toward some chasm he can dimly perceive. He tries not to panic, though he can feel his eyes jerking, making the room flicker like an old film. He concentrates on his Adam's apple. He refuses to gulp, she'd spot that in a flash. He uncrosses his legs and crosses them again, left over right, the first step in a Boy Scout reef knot. There's nothing to drink but bloody tea, there isn't even a beer, and he knows for absolute goddamn certain that this is deliberate on Elizabeth's part. She thought it would unsettle him and she's right, right, right.

It's the mention of lawyers that's confused him. At the first words, "my lawyer," she said, and "your lawyer," he started shallow breathing. He knows he used to be a lawyer himself. Who should know better than he does that there's no mystery, no occult power? It's all paper and verbiage. But fake though the structure is, it could wreck his life.

"Couldn't we do it without lawyers?" he asks, and Elizabeth smiles.

She's placed herself on the sofa, where she's curled with every show of comfort. He, on the other hand, is sitting on a pine pressback chair, from which, he notes, the cushion has been removed since the last time he was here. His ass hurts, bone against wood, his spine hurts, this chair was always too low for him.

"You can't have a divorce without lawyers," she says.

Nate begins to explain that there is in fact a way of doing it, but she stops him. "That would hardly be fair," she says. "You know the law, I don't. I feel I need protection."

Nate is hurt. Protection from him? It's a question of support for the children. She ought to know he will do anything he can.

She has a piece of paper, which she passes over to him. She hopes he will realize she's tried to be more than fair. She talks about dentists' bills while Nate focuses with an effort on the black marks in front of him. The children are upstairs watching television in their room, where Elizabeth has sent them. For several weeks she hasn't let him come into the house when he's arrived to pick them up for the weekend. He's had to lurk outside, once in the rain, like some pervert or magazine salesman, waiting for them to emerge from the front door with their pathetic little overnight cases. It was part of her campaign, part of the squeeze to get him into this corner where he now crouches. When he walked through the door today, Nancy thought at first that he was moving in again. *Home.*

He must make it clear to Elizabeth that he will not tolerate having the children used as weapons against him. (*Make it clear,* a joke. What power does he have, how does he know what she says to them when he isn't there?)

"Mummy says single-parent families have to work harder and pull together," Nancy told him last week.

"You aren't a single-parent family," Nate said. Elizabeth was behaving as if he were dead. But he wasn't dead yet and he wasn't going to die to oblige her. Unlike Chris. In the past few weeks he's felt a growing kinship with Chris, with that fatal desperation. "You have two parents and you always will have."

"Not if Mummy dies," Nancy said. Nate wants to talk to

Elizabeth about this, this theme which has come up more than once. Has she been taking pills, has she been slashing her wrists where the children can see? Nate doesn't think so, doesn't think she'd go that far to spite him. She isn't looking well, she's puffy and white but she's neatly dressed and, though he looks, he can see no bandages or scars.

He knows what will happen if he tries to discuss the children's state of mind. He can foresee the scorn: What right does he have to comment? He's opted out. She acts as if he's gone off to loll in flowers and roll around on carpets of naked women, when the fact is he spends most of his life scrabbling for money. The recession hasn't ended. Maybe, he thinks, peering at Elizabeth's neatly typed list, he should point this out. For the first few years of it people believed it would, but now they've buckled themselves in for the long siege. They're no longer willing to pay eighty dollars for Jerome Giraffe and Horace Horse, no matter how lovingly hand-crafted. As for naked women, Lesje is hardly speaking to him. She claims he's deliberately trying to postpone the divorce.

"It's just a formality," he told her. "It doesn't mean anything."

"It may not mean anything to you," she said, "but Elizabeth thinks she's still married to you. Which she is."

"Only on paper," Nate said.

"If it doesn't mean anything to you, why not do it and get it over with?" Lesje said. Nate feels she is unhealthily obsessed with this question. A minor question, he tells her. He's tried to explain to her several times that relationships of ten years' standing (eleven? twelve?) don't just come to a dead stop. Elizabeth is the mother of his children. It's true she asked him to come over and help hang the new curtains in the children's room and it's also true he went; perhaps he shouldn't have. But that was a month and a half ago; he doesn't see why Lesje keeps bringing it up. They love each other, he tells her; who cares what's on file in the Registry Office? But Lesje turns away from him in bed, curling in on herself. Or she stays late at the Museum, or she brings home thick books filled with diagrams of fossil teeth and reads them at the kitchen table until she thinks he'll be asleep.

"Dinosaurs are dead," he said to her one day, trying to lighten things up. "But I'm still alive."

"Are you sure?" she said, with one of those ball-shriveling looks. As if he was a teeny little dog turd.

It's this, this desert, this growing fiasco, that has driven him finally into Elizabeth's mushroom-colored parlor. Her net.

He has a swift desire to stand up, lean over her, put his hands around her neck and squeeze. There would be some satisfaction in that. His mother has taken to saying that men should be protective of the rights of women; Nate can see this in the abstract. He knows about seamstresses, cookie workers, female university teachers, rape. But in concrete cases like his he sees no need for it. He is the one, surely it's obvious, who needs protection.

He resorts to an amusement of his high-school days, when he would practice silent metamorphoses on his teachers. *Hocus pocus*, and Elizabeth is a giant white sponge. *Presto change-o*, she's a big vanilla pudding. *Abracadabra,* a set of mammoth false teeth. *Kapow,* and she has bubonic plague. The mother of his children gasps, turns mottled and purpled, swells and bursts. He'll have the carpet cleaned, her carpet, and that will be that.

"Don't you agree?" Elizabeth says.

His eyes jerk from the page; he forces himself to look at her. Eye contact with the jury, so they were taught, always a good thing. He knows it will be dangerous to say, "Of course," so he'll have to admit he hasn't been listening.

"About the dentists' bills?" he asks hopefully.

Elizabeth gives him again her tolerant smile. "No," she says. "About the correspondents. I was saying it would be better if I divorce you rather than the other way around, since it wouldn't be very good to use Chris as a correspondent."

Nate wants to ask why not, since Chris is unlikely to be bothered by it. Whereas he can foresee certain difficulties with Lesje. But he knows this would be a tactless question. Also, the point in law is dubious. Though Elizabeth could swear she committed adultery, there's nothing but hearsay to back her up.

She says it would be bad for the children to drag the whole thing up again. She's right, of course she's right; everything these days, it seems, is bad for the children.

"I don't know," Nate says slowly. "Maybe we shouldn't use those grounds at all. Maybe we should go for marriage breakdown. That's a little more accurate, wouldn't you say?"

"Well, if you want to wait three years . . ." Elizabeth shrugs. "It's all the same to me, as long as I get the support payments." She says something about postdated checks and Nate nods vaguely. He's caught in a vise, the handle is turning, slowly, inexorably. What will squirt out of him? Turkey juice, nickels and dimes. No matter what he does he's screwed. Opt for a quick adultery case and Lesje will resent being dragged into it. "I didn't break up your marriage, remember?" she's said at least once too often. But wait three years and she'll resent that, too.

Nate fervently wishes he lived in California, Nevada, anywhere but this tight-assed churchified country. It's all the fault of Québec. Marriage, which ought to be a sieve, is a lobster trap, baited with flesh. How did he get into it? He can't remember. He scrabbles vainly, groping for a way out.

Can he, might he, ask Elizabeth whether she's slept with anyone else recently? Anyone, as it were, still alive? How to phrase it? He can't, he doesn't dare.

Saturday, September 3, 1977

Elizabeth

Elizabeth is sitting with her legs tucked under her, her flow-ered skirt (new, mauve tones, bought on impulse on a day of malaise) spread around her. She felt this position would cre-ate an effect of casual ease. She wishes to appear tranquil, serene, like her favorite stone Buddha in the Oriental collec-tion. It will give her an advantage.

Not only does she wish to appear serene, she wishes to be serene. Sometimes she thinks she has achieved this; at other times she thinks it may only be immobility. Is the statue a Buddha or a chunk of stone? For instance: she does not ap-pear, for the moment, to be interested in men. She still tries, examining strangers in the subway, picturing various members of the Museum staff in exotic postures, but nothing flickers. She's stopped accepting invitations to dinner: she's no longer willing to be that bored simply to eat. If she wants to devour the ground-up livers of deceased geese, the plucked carcasses of birds, wild or domestic, the pancreases of young cows, she can buy them herself.

She didn't used to get bored. She used to guess what the next move would be and then try to manipulate it. But now she knows the moves and can't be bothered going through the crude flatteries that will get her what, by popular consent, she is supposed to want. It takes two to tango and nobody waltzes anymore. Rather than a parody, knee-squeezing at the Court-yard Café, she'd prefer a greaser, someone with no vocabu-lary at all, a leather shadow, a direct question in a back alley. Yes or no.

(Like Chris. Yes or no. Yes, she said, and then, after a long time, no. It was the pause that got him. The real reason she doesn't want Chris mentioned in the divorce proceedings has nothing to do with the law, with Nate or even with the chil-

dren. She doesn't want him involved. To have his name ut-
tered in that ritual way might cause him to materialize in the
witness box, pale and accusing or—worse—fragmented, his
head watching her with a Cheshire grin, his body still con-
torted in agony. She's got him safely buried, she wants no
resurrection.)

She would like to sit here undisturbed in this quiet room,
nibbling the biscuit that lies so far untouched on her saucer,
thinking peaceful thoughts and letting events arrange themselves. Which isn't so easy. Elizabeth knows, from long expe-
rience, that events need help. Also her effortless pose is cutting off the circulation in her legs. But she doesn't want to
change position, she doesn't want to move. It might suggest to
Nate the idea that he too can move, that he is free to get up
and walk out at any time. She knows—who better?—that
there is always that freedom, that exit. One way or another.
Nate, on the contrary, has never discovered it.

They've begun to talk about money, to discuss the details of
her list. Item by item she leads him down the page. She has
left this till the end, till she's certain he can see quite clearly
that her cards are on the table. Her aces. If he wants a
quickie, she'll dictate the terms. If he wants to wait the three
years, it will give her time to maneuver, and she can always
change her mind about contesting and make him wait five. The
main point for him to grasp is that she doesn't care what he
decides. In a way she really doesn't. It's not as though she's in
any hurry to dash off and marry someone else.

He's telling her that, as she knows, he doesn't have very
much money, hardly any in fact, but that he'll do everything
possible. She indicates that his lack of money is no concern of
hers. Whether he has a million dollars or ten, the children will
continue to eat, wear clothes, go to the dentist, play with toys.
They need allowances and lessons. Janet wishes to take dancing, Nancy has been skating for a year and Elizabeth doesn't
see why she should give it up.

"Of course I could support them entirely on my own salary," she says. "Realistically I could do that, though we would
have to cut down on certain things." She thinks of saying,
We'd have to send the cat to the Humane Society, but decides
this would be going too far. For one thing the cat, although
promised, has not yet been acquired, and a cat in the bush is
no hostage. And if they already had it the children would
never forgive her for disposing of it. Nate or no Nate. She'll

send him the bill, though, when it has to be fixed. "But I thought we'd agreed that you were going to participate as much as possible. The children need to know that both of their parents love them."

Nate is angry. "You really think that because I don't have any goddamned money I don't love my kids?" he says. "That's pretty crass."

"The children will hear you," Elizabeth says softly. "Maybe I'm a crass person. I guess I believe that if you really love someone you're prepared to make certain sacrifices." *Sacrifices.* This is straight out of the doctrine according to Auntie Muriel. She shifts her legs. She doesn't like to hear herself using Auntie Muriel's phrases, even when she believes in them. Though Auntie Muriel would have left out the word *love.*

She realizes the sentence is ambiguous: she could have meant the children or herself. Does she want Nate to love her and make sacrifices for her? Probably she does. It's hard to renounce tribute from those who once willingly paid it; hard not to exact. She lies on a bed, not her own in any real sense then, while Nate srokes his hands over her, shoulders, breasts, belly, the stretch marks from the children, he likes to finger those, any trace of mutilation, thighs, again, again. He's always considerate, he waits for her. Is this what she wants? All she could think of at the time was: Let's get on with it.

She tries to remember whether she ever loved him and concludes that she did, though in ways that were not sufficient. Nate was a good man and she recognized goodness, though she could not withhold a slight contempt. On their wedding day, what had she felt? Safety, relief: at last she was out of danger. She would become a homemaker, she would make a home. This in itself seemed to her improbable, even at the time. What else had happened, besides the usual erosion, attrition, the death of cells? She'd made the home but she could not quite believe in it, make it solid. And safety was not all she wanted. *Slumming,* Auntie Muriel said when she'd married Nate, but that was wrong. Slumming was dangerous and Nate was not that. Or not in the usual way.

She hasn't heard from Auntie Muriel lately; she expects never to hear from her again. This ought to make her feel victorious. *Happy and glorious.* Auntie Muriel either, has to cut her out completely or pretend that last unthinkable scene, hairbreadth escape for her white velour potty hat, never happened. It's quite possible that Elizabeth will receive a call in

December, as usual, setting the date of the New Year's visit. She can't imagine going. She also can't imagine not going. She will sit on the slippery pink chesterfield once more, surrounded by polished surfaces, the baby grand piano, the silver tray, Auntie Muriel squatting across from her with her pebble-colored eyes, and the past will yawn around her, a cavern filled with menacing echoes.

"Exactly what sacrifices do you want me to make?" Nate says, still angry. Meaning: *You can't get blood from a stone.*

"Nate," she says, "I know how difficult this is for you. Believe me, it's difficult for me, too. But let's try to be as calm about it as possible. I'm not trying to torture you," she adds. "You have to take that on faith."

This is more or less true. She isn't trying to torture Nate: torture is a by-product. She's merely trying to win. Looking at him, watching him subside back onto his chair, she knows she will win, there's no way she can help winning. She'll win, and she hopes it will make her feel better.

Saturday, September 3, 1977

LESJE

Lesje is in the living room, in the Upper Jurassic, where she runs along the path worn by the iguanodons. She's wearing her Adidas and a navy-blue sweatshirt that says SMALL IS BEAUTIFUL on it in red. This was once William's idea of a good thing to give her for her birthday; it didn't occur to him that the lettering would run across her chest. She hasn't worn it much. She carries her binoculars in their leather case, slung over her shoulder where they thump unpleasantly against her hip.

There's nothing behind her, nothing in front of her but the muddy path. To either side the undergrowth is unbroken; moisture drips from the fronds, it's hot as a steambath, her flesh simmers. The lake is miles away. She slows to a walk. In the distance ahead, where she knows there will be open space, scrub and hot sunlight, she can hear the raucous cries of the circling pterodactyls, intent on carrion.

There's nowhere else she wants to be, but this time it isn't exploration; she knows the terrain too well. It's merely flight.

She cuts herself off, gets out of her chair, walks back to the kitchen with her empty cup, tracking sawdust. He should sweep up. She turns on the element under the kettle, adds brown powder to her cup.

It's Saturday, and for once she's alone. There's a good reason: Nate is over at Elizabeth's house and at last they're discussing the divorce. She's wanted this to happen for a long time, so it's unfair of her to resent being left out of it. Shut out, like a child whose parents have closed the door on important matters, things they consider too adult for her to hear. She'd like to tiptoe, press her ear to the keyhole. She'd like to spy. She wants to hear what is being said about her. If anything.

But it's none of her business. Now it's started, though, it will continue. Elizabeth has him hooked. She'll demand more and more conferences of this sort, more negotiations. It could go on for years.

She pours boiling water into her cup, adds white from a jar. She doesn't really want to drink this but she has to do something. To pass the time she begins to classify Elizabeth, a familiar exercise by now. If she had Elizabeth on a shelf, nicely ossified, the label would read: CLASS: *Chondrichthyes;* ORDER: *Selachii;* GENUS: *Squalidae;* SPECIES: *Elizabetha.* Today she classifies Elizabeth as a shark; on other days it's a huge Jurassic toad, primitive, squat, venomous; on other days a cephalopod, a giant squid, soft and tentacled, with a hidden beak.

Lesje knows scientific objectivity is a fraud. She's read the stories of plunder and revenge, of evidence stolen from one scientist by another, of the great dinosaur hunters who bribed each other's workmen and attacked each other's reputations. She knows that a passion for science is like any other passion. Nevertheless she wishes scientific objectivity really did exist and that she could have some of it. Then she would be able to apply it to her own life. She would become philosophical and wise, she would be able to cope with Elizabeth in some way more adult, more dignified than this secret game, which is after all little better than juvenile name-calling.

As it is she can't cope. Neither, it seems, can Nate. Although he indulges in private fits of rage, a relief anyway from the earlier phase in which he refused to criticize Elizabeth at all, when he actually has to confront her, haggle over money or the children's visits, he turns to putty. He justifies this by saying he's doing it for Lesje, he doesn't want to jeopardize the divorce. He's perennially short of money, but Elizabeth gets her support check on the dot each month. He's taken to borrowing small sums from Lesje, five dollars, ten dollars. How can she refuse, how can she refuse him cigarettes and the odd case of beer when he's so obviously going quietly mad? She feels sorry for him. She doesn't want to feel sorry for him. He doesn't want it either. So she says nothing and lends him the money.

A week ago Lesje raised again the subject of a child, for herself, for them. She was tentative about it; but maybe, before she gets too old, maybe now is the right time?

Nate was reluctant. He could hardly afford it now, he said.

"But it was your idea in the first place," Lesje said. She felt as if she'd propositioned him and been rejected. Was she unattractive? Genetically deficient?

Nate explained that when he said he wanted to have a child with her he'd been expressing a wish, a desire, not making a practical suggestion that was meant to be acted on right away.

Lesje, who felt she seldom made this distinction, tried to understand it. She supposed he was right. Elizabeth's children were living on Nate's income, what there was of it, and she and Nate were living on hers. She could hardly sabotage this arrangement by having a child. She isn't absolutely positive she wants to have a child, but she resents being denied one by Elizabeth.

Perhaps, Lesje thinks, she should join a discussion group. She's heard about such groups, she reads about them in the family sections of the papers Nate brings home every night. They meet in church basements and offer bandages to those wounded by the shrapnel of exploding families. Maybe she should go and drink cups of tea with such a group and eat cookies and bitch about Elizabeth. But she knows she can't. She's hopeless in groups, she'd be afraid of what she might say. In any gathering of the disabled she will always be the least disabled, or pretend to be. Also, the groups have names like Second Time Round and are aimed at married couples, and she isn't married.

She supposes that if she had independence and strength of character this wouldn't bother her, in fact she would welcome it. Many women no longer use their husbands' names, they object to being called "my this" or "my that," and Nate, when he has to introduce her to anyone, which isn't all that often, doesn't use the possessive. He simply uses her name, without even a Miss, and this pleases him. He's glad, he says, that her name isn't Mrs. Schoenhof. God forbid she should in any way resemble his mother or his wife. But instead of making her feel like an entity in her own right, as Nate claims it's supposed to, this makes her feel like a cipher. Though her own conservatism, unsuspected till now, appalls her, she wants to belong, to be seen to belong; she wants to be classifiable, a member of a group. There is already a group of Mrs. Schoenhofs: one is Nate's mother, the other is the mother of his children. Lesje isn't the mother of anyone; officially she is nothing.

Surely she didn't used to be like this, plugged into this constant inner whine, critical, begrudging. Maybe she's been thinking too much about Elizabeth. *If you make that face too much,* they said at school, *you'll grow up to look like that.* If she isn't careful she'll turn into Elizabeth. Sometimes she thinks Nate is an obscure practical joke being played on her by Elizabeth, for an unfathomable reason of her own. So laugh, she tells herself. But she can't.

It's no good, she should say to him. It's no use. But that isn't true: it is good, it is of use. Some days, some minutes. From time to time.

The fact is that she's addicted to Nate's version of her. Sometimes, when he touches her, she feels not naked but clothed, in some long unspecified garment that spreads around her like a shimmering cloud. She's realized with something close to panic that the picture he's devised of her is untrue. He expects her to be serene, a refuge; he expects her to be kind. He really thinks she is, underneath, and that if he can dig into her far enough this is what he'll unearth. He ought to be able to tell by now that she isn't like this at all. Nevertheless she wants to be; she wants to be this beautiful phantom, this boneless wraith he's conjured up. Sometimes she really does want it.

Lesje paces the kitchen floor, which needs washing. Not that it looks any different clean. White lumps in her coffee, the sink is paved with cups and spoons, similarly lumpy. She should take a bath. Instead she puts her cup into the sink with the other cups and goes out, locking the door.

She walks south on the heated sidewalk, then west along streets of crumbling red insulbrick siding, sagging porches, old houses skewed and crowded. This place is more and more familiar to her; it's almost the land of the grandmothers. Her small grandmother's house was on this street, or possibly not this street but the one next to it; her round grandmother lived a few blocks further west, nearer the gold-domed church, but in the same kind of house.

She hasn't thought much about these streets since the year both grandmothers died and she'd ceased to visit. She could remember the grandmothers themselves, what they looked like, certain rooms in their houses, but not the houses themselves. It was as if this district had been neatly snipped from the map. But now she wants to find the houses again, the actual houses. They will be a kind of evidence, since the grandmothers who are the real evidence are gone.

She stands still. She's in a small street choked with trees, parked cars, with children playing between them and running out onto the pavement. The houses look smaller than she expected; some of them have been painted, bright blue, yellow, the cement between the bricks done carefully in a different color. She doesn't recognize anything; if she wants to find her grandmothers she'll have to look elsewhere. New people are here now, from other countries. They in their turn will make money and shift north. This is not a settled neighborhood, here for eternity as she thought when she was a child, but a way station, a campground. In some distant future archeologists will dig through the rubble and unearth the successive layers. *The black people have it now,* her grandmother said; talking about her store.

If her grandmothers had lived, they too might have moved north. In any case they would have discarded their dark dresses, gone on day excursions to Niagara Falls, had their hair permed as her mother had done, bought crimplene pantsuits. Assimilated. As it is they're fixed, mounted specimens in her head, cut from their own wrecked and shadowy backgrounds and pasted here. Anachronisms, the last of their kind.

A mother's blessing, that's what we had then. That was important. If a young man goes to war he has to get a mother's blessing. I was the first one to work in Eaton's, the rest was all English. They didn't like it. I just didn't say nothing, when they said what kind of a name is that. I kept my mouth shut and I got along good enough that way. What we had back then, we had the flowers on our head, and the dancing. They try to do it now but it's not the same.

At the time Lesje had not been able to think of her grandmother as having ever been thin, much less young. She seemed always to have been what she was, seamy-faced, melancholy, smelling of underarms and furniture polish. The other grandmother had danced too, or so she claimed. She'd mentioned handkerchiefs; Lesje hadn't understood, so finally she'd pulled a crumpled Kleenex from her sleeve and waved it in the air. All Lesje had been able to picture was her grandmother at her present age, hopping about ridiculously in her tiny black boots, waving handfuls of Kleenex.

A man, olive-skinned and short, brushes past and says something Lesje doesn't understand but guesses is not friendly. She doesn't know where she is, she'll have to take bearings. The sun is going down so that must be west, towards the golden church she's seen from the outside but was never allowed to enter. She'd never been in a synagogue either, before the funeral. She turns back, trying to retrace her way.

She didn't listen properly, their stories bored her, she felt them as attempts to convert her, to one side or the other. She was impatient with them and their complaints and bickering, with these stories which were so foreign and which, like their endless stories about wars and suffering and horror, children spitted on swords, had nothing to do with her. The old country, archaic and terrible; not like here. Now she wants these voices back; even the squabbling, even the rage. She wants to dance with flowers on her head, she wants to be endorsed, sanctified, she doesn't care who by. She wants a mother's blessing. Though she can't imagine her own mother doing such a thing.

This is the problem. She knows by now that people do not behave the way she wishes them to. So what should she do, change wishes?

When she was ten she wanted to go to the Museum, not with one grandmother on Saturday mornings as usual, but with both of them. One would hold her right hand, one her left. She didn't expect them to speak to each other, she'd heard them say often enough they would sooner die than do that. But there was no rule against walking. The three of them would walk together, slowly because of her fat grandmother, up the stone steps of the Museum, herself in the middle, and in under the golden dome. Unlike the dinosaurs, this was something that might really happen; when she finally saw it never could, she forgot about it.

As for Nate, it's simple. All she wants is for both of them to be different. Not very different, a little would do it. Same molecules, different arrangement. All she wants is a miracle, because anything else is hopeless.

Friday, November 25, 1977

NATE

Nate, slumped in a horseshoe booth in the bar of the Selby Hotel, drinks draft beer and watches television. It's Friday night and voices babble, it's hard to hear the sound. Over the past few months more driblets of dirt concerning the Mounties have been trickling in, and these are now being relentlessly scrutinized by a trio of pundits. The Mounties, pretending to be Separatist terrorists, sent violent letters somewhere. They burned a barn and stole some mail, and there's some suggestion that an erstwhile head of Intelligence was a double agent for the CIA. The Prime Minister claims he knew nothing about it, and furthermore he doesn't think it's his place to know such things. This is old news which is not being treated with any new wisdom. Nate smokes, watching the ghostly heads frown and smirk, skeptical.

His mother is gathering signatures on a letter of protest, as usual. There will be a lot of talk and nothing will happen. He dislikes the pundits for pretending something will, their earnestness and tired outrage. Right now he'd rather hear about the hockey scores, though the Leafs are fucking up as usual. Around him smoke rises, glasses clank, voices shuffle through their routines, desolation spreads, as far as the eyes can see.

Martha comes in and stands uncertainly at the far end of the bar. Nate lifts his arm to catch her attention. She sees him and strides forward, smiling.

"Long time no see," Martha says. This is heavy irony, as Nate now sees Martha every day at the office. But tonight he's taking her to dinner. He owes her something. As soon as she sits down he realizes he's made a blunder, he shouldn't have suggested the Selby. They used to drink here a lot. He hopes Martha won't become maudlin.

So far she's not showing any signs of it. She plops her elbows onto the table. "Jeez, my feet are sore," she says.

Nate interprets this the way he's always interpreted this bluntness, her insistence on the vernacular: it's a cover-up for other, more delicate things. He thinks she's done something to her hair, though he has trouble remembering what her hair was like before. She's thinner than she used to be. Her breasts rest on her folded arms, she smiles at him, he feels a twitch of desire. Against his will. It can't be the boots, Martha has always had boots.

He orders two more drafts and reminds himself that this dinner is purely routine. Without Martha, or with Martha against him, he would never have been able to get even the menial job he's doing now. Young lawyers, lawyers younger than he is—it suddenly alarms him to see how much younger—are a dime a dozen now, and why should the firm have rehired him after his desertion? He's rusty too, he's forgotten a lot, things he once thought he'd never again have to remember. But he's desperate for money, he didn't know where else to go.

He's grateful to Martha for not laughing, not sneering. She didn't even say, *I knew you'd be back.* She'd listened to him as if she were a nurse or a case worker; then she said she would see what she could do.

What he's got isn't what he would have chosen. He does the legal aid. *Legal Band-Aid.* Because of the firm's radical reputation, it feels it has to take on more than its share of legal aid cases; there's more coming in than Adams and Stein and the juniors can handle. Nate is their Office Overload. He takes part-time pay for what has turned out to be a full-time job, shepherding the unimportant cases, the ones no one else wants to take because they're foredoomed to failure, the thugs, housebreakers and junkies, through the courts, into the pen, through the courts again, into the pen. He knows it's a circular process.

He's resurrected his briefcase and his two suits, wondering as he dug through the trunk at the back of the cupboard in his old room why he had never thrown these things away. He polishes his shoes now and cleans his fingernails; the permanent cuticle of blackened paint has almost vanished. In the mornings, he breathes the antiseptic smell of jails, the smell of coops, caged flesh, sour air breathed in and out too many times; the smell of boredom and hatred. He listens to the lies of his clients, watches their eyes twitch momentarily away from his, knows they're scornful of him and his polished shoes and his belief in them.

They don't know he doesn't believe in them. He goes to court with them, does what he can, plea-bargains, makes shoddy little deals with the Crown prosecutors. He listens to the shoptalk, the jocularity of the other lawyers, which he once found offensive; lately he's been joining in. Sometimes he wins a case and his client goes free, but not often. Even so it's no triumph. The pettiness of petty crime, the absurd particularity grates on him. There seems to be no connection between what happens to these men and what they've done: two radios and a stereo, shooting up in an alley, the contents of some old lady's bureau drawers.

His mother would say his clients are products of their environment, which no doubt is true. Culture shock, they suffer from it; the point at which one set of skewed rules collides blindly with another. His mother manages to combine this view with a belief in human dignity and free will, at least as it applies to herself. Nate doesn't feel capable of this logical contradiction. He doesn't judge these people, nor does he feel he's an instrument of justice. He does a job. He might as well be working for the SPCA. He'd like to be in on the Mountie stuff: the firm is acting for a maniac fringe newspaper vandalized at the time. But Stein is taking that, naturally.

The waiter plunks down their two drafts and Martha sprinkles hers with salt. "So how's it going?" she says. She drinks, leaving a suds moustache on her upper lip. He used to love that, the way she swills her beer. Tenderness floats in him, hovers, is gone.

On the screen, which he can see but she can't, it's now René Lévesque, gesturing, shrugging, explaining, sad eyes peering from his creased mime's face. Something about the economy, from what Nate can catch. These days they're saying they never meant separation, not just like that. Nate is disappointed in him; the whole thing so far has been an anticlimax. Missed chances, compromise and hedging, like the rest of the country. It's a world of unfreedom after all. Only a fool could have believed in anything else, and Lévesque is no fool. (Like Nate: not any more.) He looks less and less like a clown. More like a turtle: wisdom has wrinkled him, encased him in a useful shell.

"Hey, dreamer," Martha says. The first sign she's given

that they were once lovers: it's her old word. Nate lowers his eyes to her.

"Great," he says. "I guess." He'd like to express as much enthusiasm as possible. Martha wants to believe her action, her good turn, has made him happy. He knows she's gone out of her way for him; he doesn't know why.

Martha gives him no clues. "Down the old rat hole," she says, and empties her glass.

In the dining room of the Selby, less than he would have liked, more than he can afford, they eat liver and homefries and Martha talks about the office: who's left, who's come, whose marriage is splitting up, who's having it on with whom. As usual Martha knows all about these things; she reports them jovially. "Better her than me," she says, or "Good luck to him." Nate settles into familiar comfort with her, as if he's listening to the breathing of some large, warm-flanked animal.

He'd like to nuzzle into her, shove his head under her arm and close his eyes; but Martha is treating him like a friend, an old friend, trustworthy and neutral. She acts as if she can't remember ever having cried, ever having hit him or screamed, and Nate reflects once more upon the shamelessness of women. Their lack of shame. They believe whatever they do is justified at the time, so why be guilty? Nate envies this. He himself knows he did not treat Martha as well as he'd intended, but she seems to have forgotten all about that, as well.

With the canned cherry pie Martha describes her latest interests: she does volunteer fund-raising for Nellie's Halfway House, and on Tuesday and Thursday evenings she goes to yoga class. Nate can't quite imagine Martha, ample but hardly graceful, wearing a black leotard and bent into a pretzel, nor can he picture her identifying to any extent with the battered wives sheltered by Nellie's. She was never much at exercise, and theories, *issues* as she called them, left her cold. He knows: he once tried to get her to buy a bicycle, and when he would talk about what was at stake in Québec, in Israel, in Cambodia, she would say she got enough of that on the television news. But here she is now, improbability materialized, sitting across from him, forking in pie crust and talking about the reform of rape laws.

Nate tells himself that it's just like Martha to take up a cause or a hobby after the peak, during the slow descent into that outmoded trough inhabited by people like his mother:

Christadelphians, vegetarians of the autointoxication school, Esperanto-speakers, lecturers on spaceships, Unitarians. This was always Elizabeth's view of her, based, as far as Nate could see, on Martha's wardrobe. According to Elizabeth, women's lib is on the wane; and interest in Eastern cults is not what it was. But none of this seems to bother Martha. She comments on Nate's appearance: he looks oxygen-starved, she says. Very few people breathe properly. He should try a little full breathing and a simple version of the Salute to the Sun. Martha personally guarantees it would do wonders for him.

Then she veers back to the law. She has pronounced views on the family court system; in fact, if she can save enough money she would like to go to law school and become a lawyer herself, so she can do some specialized work in this field. As far as school goes, it will be a cinch, since she knows quite a lot of the stuff already; God knows she's typed enough of it. Nate blinks. He sees now that he thinks of Martha as not exactly stupid, but certainly not ultra-bright. Though quite possibly she knows more law at this point than he does himself. She might be all right, she might even be quite good. For family court.

But Nate feels diminished. He's gone for days, weeks, months of his life without thinking once of Martha. His hands retain only a faint memory of the insides of her thighs, her taste has faded from his tongue, he can't even remember her bedroom: what color are the curtains? Yet he's aggrieved that he himself has been so easily, so quickly forgotten. Was he that unimportant? He tells himself that Martha cannot possibly have a new man up her sleeve, someone who holds for her the same significance that he himself once held; otherwise she would not be so interested in law school.

He pays the bill and they walk towards the door, Martha in front. She's carrying her coat over her arm, and he watches her haunches under the gored tweed of her skirt. Will she perhaps invite him back? They could sit in her living room and have a few drinks. Nothing more than that. He deliberates: of course he shouldn't accept. It's Friday night, the children will be there, Lesje's expecting him. He didn't tell her where he was going; he said he had to do some legal work. Taking Martha to dinner was legal work in a way, but this would have been too difficult to explain.

On the street, however, Martha thanks him, dismisses him. "See you Monday," she says. "Back at the old grind." She walks towards the corner, in her boots, waving for a cab. He watches her stop one, open the door, get in. He would like to know where she's going, but she'll go there whether he knows or not. The world exists apart from him. He's rehearsed this often enough in theory; he's just never known it with certainty. It follows that his body is an object in space and that someday he will die.

Now he can remember having had this perception several times before. He stands where she's left him. He doesn't want to go home.

ELIZABETH

Auntie Muriel is in the hospital. That in itself is incredible enough. First, that anything should ever go wrong with her. Elizabeth has never thought of her aunt as compounded of mortal flesh like other people; rather as being, from neck to knees, built of a warty growth, something like gum rubber, impermeable and indestructible. Second, that if something has gone wrong with her, which Elizabeth still doubts, Auntie Muriel could have brought herself to admit it. Nevertheless she's in the hospital, the Princess Margaret to be precise, and Elizabeth has been summoned. Despite her vow never to see Auntie Muriel again she has not dared to refuse.

She sits in the visitor's chair beside the raised bed, while Auntie Muriel, wearing an ice-blue bed jacket, cranked up and propped up, complains. They put extra chlorine in the water here, she can taste it. She can remember when water was water but she doesn't suppose Elizabeth can tell the difference. At first she could not get a private room. Can Elizabeth imagine? She had to share a room, share one, with a terrible old woman who wheezed at night. Auntie Muriel is convinced the woman was dying. She could hardly get any sleep. And now that she's finally here in her private room, no one pays any attention to her. She has to ring and ring, three times even, before the nurse will come. They all read detective novels, she's seen them. The night nurse is from the West Indies. The food is atrocious. She cannot tolerate beets, she always ticks the other vegetables on the menu but they bring beets. Sometimes Auntie Muriel thinks they do things like this to her on purpose. She will speak to Doctor MacFadden, tomorrow. If she has to stay here for a little rest and some tests, which is what he says, the least he can do is make sure she's comfortable. She's never been sick a day in her life, there's nothing really wrong with her now, she isn't used to hospitals.

Elizabeth thinks this may be true. She connects her own stays in hospitals with the births of her children, but of course Auntie Muriel has never undergone that. Elizabeth can't imagine her giving birth, much less engaged in the preliminaries. It's difficult to picture weak-chinned Uncle Teddy storming those elastic-sheathed barricades, uncovering those thighs the hue of potato sprouts; difficult to picture Auntie Muriel allowing it. Though she might have done it out of a sense of duty.

Auntie Muriel has brought her petit-point cushion cover with her to the hospital, the same piece she's been doing for years: pansies in a basket. In times past it has reposed on various chairs and sofas in Auntie Muriel's house, testimony to the fact that she's not a lazy woman. It looks out of place on the hospital coverlet. Auntie Muriel lifts it as she talks, lets it fall.

Elizabeth sits in the visitor's chair. She's brought some flowers, chrysanthemums, in a pot rather than cut; she thought Auntie Muriel might like something that was still growing, but Auntie Muriel immediately pronounced them too smelly. Doesn't Elizabeth remember that she can't stand the smell of chrysanthemums?

Perhaps she does remember; perhaps she conveniently forgot. She'd felt she should bring something, some offering, for Auntie Muriel is going to die; is dying at this very moment. Elizabeth, as the next of kin, was the first to be notified.

"It's all through her," Doctor MacFadden said in his semi-whisper. "It must've started as cancer of the bowel. The colon. I expect she was in considerable pain for some time before she came to see me. She's always said she was strong as a horse. It was the blood that frightened her."

Considerable pain, naturally. She'd grit her teeth for weeks before forcing herself to acknowledge that she had a colon and that this portion of her had turned traitor. And Auntie Muriel must have been as surprised as Elizabeth to find she could actually bleed. But frightened? A word surely alien to Auntie Muriel's vocabulary. Elizabeth stares at her, pitiless, unbelieving. Such malevolent vitality cannot die. Hitler lived on after the discovery of his smoldering teeth, and Auntie Muriel too is one of the immortals.

But she has shriveled. The flesh once compact and stolid is drooping on the bones; the powder Auntie Muriel has continued to apply is caked in small ravines of collapsing skin. Her throat is a cavity above the virginal bow of the bed jacket, her prowlike bosom has withered. Her color, once a confident beige, has faded to the off-white of a dirty tooth. Her eyes, once slightly protuberant like those of a Pekinese, are being sucked into the depths of her head. She's falling in on herself, she's melting, like the witch in *The Wizard of Oz*, and seeing it Elizabeth remembers: Dorothy was not jubilant when the witch turned into a puddle of brown sugar. She was terrified.

Auntie Muriel has not yet been told. Doctor MacFadden doesn't feel she's one of the kind that can benefit from such an early revelation. Elizabeth, as delicately as she could, has pressed for a possible date. How long can Auntie Muriel be expected to, well, hang on? But he was vague. It would depend on many factors. There were sometimes astonishing reversals. They would keep her on analgesics and, if necessary, sedatives, and of course they were hoping that she'd get a certain amount of moral support from her family.

Meaning Elizabeth, who is now questioning her motives for even being here. She should have told the old bitch to kiss off a long time ago and stuck to it. There's not even a practical excuse for her presence: she knows the terms of Auntie Muriel's will, which are unlikely to change. A few thousand to the children when they turn twenty-one, and the rest to Timothy Eaton's bloated warthog of a church. Elizabeth doesn't care. She's practiced not caring.

Has she come to gloat? Possibly. Revenges sweep through her head. She'll tell Auntie Muriel she's going to die. Auntie Muriel won't believe it, but the mere suggestion will cause outrage. Or she'll threaten to bury her somewhere other than her own cemetery plot. She'll cremate her and sprinkle her over Center Island, where the Italians play soccer. She'll put her in a jam jar and plant her in Regent's Park; dark feet will walk over her. That'll fix her.

Elizabeth does not approve of this, this vengefulness she cradles; nevertheless it exists. She stares at Auntie Muriel's hands, which squeeze themselves against the blue bed jacket; which she cannot bear to touch.

The woman who grabbed her arm that day outside Eaton's College Street, when they'd just come out after seeing the Toronto Children's Players Christmas show, a special concession on Auntie Muriel's part, *Toad of Toad Hall*. Beside them, the Sally Ann sextet sang and jingled. A scruffy brown cloth coat and that smell on her breath, sweet and acid. The woman had only one glove; it was the naked hand on Elizabeth's arm. Elizabeth was eleven. Caroline was with her. They were both wearing the blue tweed coats with velveteen collars and matching velveteen hats that Auntie Muriel considered the proper thing for downtown excursions.

The woman was crying. Elizabeth couldn't understand what she was saying; her voice slurred. On her own blue tweed arm the hand convulsed, slackened, like a dead cat twitching. Elizabeth took Caroline's hand and pulled her away. Then she ran. *That was Mother*, Caroline said. *No it wasn't*. Outside Maple Leaf Gardens, out of breath. *Don't say it was*.

That was Mother, Caroline said. Elizabeth punched her in the stomach and Caroline doubled over, crouching on the sidewalk, screaming. *Get up*, Elizabeth said. *You can walk, we're going home*. Caroline squatted on the sidewalk, howling, faithful.

This is what Elizabeth cannot forgive. She can't forgive her own treachery. Auntie Muriel must not be allowed to get away with it. She must, for Elizabeth's benefit, visibly suffer. At last.

"You never listen to me," Auntie Muriel says.

"Pardon?" says Elizabeth. Even Auntie Muriel's voice is different. It's no longer an accusation, it's a whine.

"You never listen to me," Auntie Muriel says. "I gave you all the advantages."

Not all, Elizabeth thinks, but she can't argue.

"I said you didn't know. You think I was hard on her but I gave her money, all those years. It wasn't your Uncle Teddy."

Elizabeth realizes that Auntie Muriel is talking about her mother. She doesn't want to listen, she doesn't want to listen to another genealogy of her own worthlessness.

"I never missed a week. Nobody gave me any credit for that," says Auntie Muriel. "Of course all she ever spent it on was drink. I gave it to her anyway; I wouldn't have her on my conscience. I don't suppose you understand what that means."

Elizabeth can do without this information. She'd prefer to think of her mother as having been entirely destitute, a wronged party, a saint under the street lights. Even when she was older, when she'd known she could find out where her mother was, she had chosen not to. Her mother, like clouds or angels, lived on air, or possibly—when she thought about the more material aspects—on Uncle Teddy. The image of the two sisters meeting, perhaps touching each other, disturbs her.

"Did you see her?" Elizabeth says. "Did you talk to her?"

"I left instructions at my bank," Auntie Muriel says. "She hated me. She wouldn't see me, she used to call me on the phone when she was drunk and say. . . . But I did my duty. It was what Father would have wanted. Your mother was always the favorite."

To Elizabeth's horror, Auntie Muriel is beginning to cry. Tears seep from her puckered eyes; a reversal of nature, a bleeding statue, a miracle. Elizabeth watches, remote. She ought to be rejoicing. Auntie Muriel is finally tasting the ashes of her life. But Elizabeth does not rejoice.

"You think I don't know," Auntie Muriel says. "I know I'm dying. Everyone here is dying." She picks up her embroidery hoop again, stabs at it with the thick needle, shutting out knowledge of her own tears, which she makes no effort to wipe from her face. "You knew," she says, accusing now. "And you didn't tell me. I'm not a baby."

Elizabeth hates Auntie Muriel. She has always hated her and she always will hate her. She will not forgive her. This is an old vow, an axiom. Nevertheless.

Nevertheless, this is not Auntie Muriel. The Auntie Muriel of Elizabeth's childhood has melted, leaving in her place this husk, this old woman who now drops her blockish embroidery and with eyes closed and weeping gropes with her hands across the hospital covers.

Elizabeth wants to get up out of the visitor's chair and walk, run from the room, leaving her there alone. She deserves it.

Nevertheless, she leans forward and takes Auntie Muriel's blinded hands. Desperately the stubby fingers clutch her. Elizabeth is no priest: she cannot give absolution. What can she offer? Nothing sincerely. Beside her own burning mother she has sat, not saying anything, holding the one good hand. The one good fine-boned hand. The ruined hand, still beautiful, unlike the veined and mottled stumps she now cradles in hers, soothing them with her thumbs as in illness she has soothed the hands of her children.

Sickness grips her. Nevertheless, nevertheless, she whispers: It's all right. It's all right.

Saturday, April 15, 1978

NATE

Nate on the subway hurtles eastward through the familiar tunnel, his face cadaverous in the dark window opposite, topped by a poster depicting a brassiere turning into a bird. He's going to his mother's to collect the children. They've been there overnight; he's spent the morning alone with Lesje, who has intimated more than once since he returned to what everyone else calls *work* that they haven't been seeing much of each other lately. She means alone.

This morning they were alone, but nothing out of the ordinary happened. They ate boiled eggs and then he read the Friday night papers, sitting in the front room in the sunlight, among the idle machines and the unfinished rocking horses. He'd thought he would be able to continue with the toys, in the evenings and on weekends, but he's too tired. It isn't only that. He can't put the two things together in his head, assault and battery back of the warehouse on Front Street East, Jerry the Giraffe with its oblivious smile. Reality is one or the other, and day by day the toys fade, lose blood. Already he sees them as museum pieces, quaint, handmade, a hundred years old. Soon they will vanish and this room will fill with paper.

Lesje had wanted the whole weekend, but he could not refuse Elizabeth, who is adamant these days about needing time to herself. Nate wonders idly what she does with it. He hopes she's seeing a man, which would make life easier. For him. In any case it would not have been Elizabeth he'd be refusing, but the children. Put that way it's impossible, which Lesje cannot quite grasp. Her obtuseness, her refusal to see that their predicament is theirs, not his or hers, infuriates him. It's a simple and obvious fact that he's doing much of what he's doing for her, or, to rephrase it, if it wasn't for her he wouldn't have to do it. He's tried to explain this but she seems to think he's accusing her of something. She stares out the window, at the wall, at any available space except the one between his ears.

Luckily there's his mother. Nate feels his mother is always willing to take the children, always waiting in fact for chances just like these. After all, she's their grandmother.

Nate gets off at Woodbine, climbs the stairs, emerges into weak April sunlight. He walks north to the street of jerry-built boxes that contains his childhood. His mother's house is a box like the others, covered with the dingy beige stucco that never ceases to remind him of certain radio programs: *The Green Hornet, Our Miss Brooks*. The woman in the house next door to it has a statue on her lawn, a black boy dressed as a jockey and holding a coach lamp. This statue is a source of perpetual irritation to Nate's mother. Nate sometimes teases her by equating this statue with the soulful painting of the black boy at the front of the Unitarian church. Lower class Catholics, he says, have plaster Marys and Jesuses on their lawns; maybe the woman next door is a lower class Unitarian. Nate's mother has never found this particularly funny, but Nate would be disappointed if she did.

He rings the doorbell, lights a cigarette while he waits. His mother, wearing the frazzled turquoise bedroom slippers she's had for at least ten years, finally opens the door. The children are downstairs in the basement playing dress-up, she says as he takes off his pea jacket. She keeps a cardboard box down there for them. In it are the few garments she hasn't found suitable for giving away to service organizations: evening gowns of the late thirties, a cut-velvet cloak, a long magenta slip. Every time he sees them, Nate is freshly amazed by the fact that his mother once went to parties, danced, was courted.

His mother has tea made and offers Nate some. He wonders is she might have a beer in the house, but she doesn't. She buys beer only for him, he knows, and this was short notice. He doesn't complain or press the point; she seems a little more tired than usual. He sits at the kitchen table with her, drinking tea and trying to avoid looking at her map of world atrocities, on which the stars are multiplying like mice. Soon the children will finalize their costumes and come upstairs to display themselves, which is the point of the whole game.

"Elizabeth tells me you've gone back to Adams, Prewitt and Stein," his mother says.

Nate feels conspiracy roping him round. How does Elizabeth know? He hasn't told her, he hasn't wanted to admit that defeat. Is it Martha, is that network still in operation? Elizabeth never used to phone his mother; but perhaps— treachery!—it's his mother who phones Elizabeth. It's the kind of thing she would do on principle. Though they've never been close. She's been slow to accept the fact that he and Elizabeth have separated. She hasn't said so, but he can tell she considers this bad for the children. For instance, she never mentions Lesje. He wishes she would protest, criticize, so he could defend himself; tell her what a termite's life Elizabeth led him.

"I'm so glad," his mother says, her china-blue eyes shining as if he's just won something: not a lottery but a prize. "I always felt that was what you were really suited for. You must be happier now."

Nate's throat is gripped by fearful anger. Can't she tell, couldn't any idiot see that he's compelled, forced, he has no choice? The weight of her ideal son presses on his chest, a plaster mannequin threatening to enter and choke him. Angel of the oppressed. She'll absolve anyone of anything, any crime, any responsibility, except herself, except him.

"I'm not," he says. "I am goddamned well not *suited* for it. I'm doing it because I need the money."

Her smile does not fade. "But it's the right thing," she says brightly. "At least you're doing something with your life."

"I was doing something with my life before," Nate says.

"There's no need to raise your voice, dear," his mother says with wounded complacency. He hates it, this tone, which is supposed to make him feel, does make him feel as if he's jumping up and down like an ape, swinging a club and thumping his chest. Years of her moral smugness, burying him like snow, like layers of wool. Intolerable smugness of all of them, Elizabeth, his mother, even Lesje. She complains but her complaints are smug, hedged bets. He knows that silent equation, he's been well schooled: *I suffer, therefore I am right.* But he suffers too, can't they see that? What does he have to do, blow his head off before they'll take him seriously? He thinks of Chris, lying shattered on the bier of his mattress, mourned by two policemen. *Serious.* Not that he would.

"If you want to know," Nate says, nevertheless lowering his

voice, "I hate every minute of it." Wondering if he actually does, he's good at it, as good as you can be at something like that.

"But you're helping people," his mother says, baffled, as if he's failed to grasp an elementary geometrical axiom. "Isn't it legal aid? Aren't they poor?"

"Mother," he says with renewed patience, "anyone who thinks they can really help people, especially doing what I'm doing, is a horse's ass."

His mother sighs. "You've always been so afraid of being a horse's ass," she says. "Even as a child."

Nate is startled. Has he? He tried to remember manifestations of this.

"I suppose you think I'm a horse's ass, too," his mother says. Implacably she smiles on. "I guess I am one. But I guess I think everyone is."

Nate is unprepared for this degree of cynicism, coming from his mother. She's supposed to believe in the infinite perfectability of man; isn't she? "Then why do you do it all?" he says.

"All what, dear?" she asks, a little absentmindedly, as if she's had this conversation with him several times before.

"The Korean poets, the crippled vets, all that." He sweeps his arm, taking in her red-starred map, her mushroom cloud.

"Well," she says, sipping her tea, "I had to do something to keep myself alive. During the war, you know. Right after you were born."

What does she mean? Surely this is metaphorical, she's only talking about housewifely boredom or something like that. But she leaves him no doubt. "I thought of several ways," she continues, "but then I thought, what if it doesn't work? I could have ended up, you know, damaged. And then you start thinking about whoever might find you. It was right after your father, right after I got the cable, but that wasn't the only thing. I guess I simply didn't want to live on this kind of an earth."

Nate is horrified. He can't, he cannot see his mother as a potential suicide. It's incongruous. Not only that, she hasn't once mentioned him. Could she have abandoned him so easily, just left him in a basket and stepped blithely off into the unknown? His father is unforgivable enough, but at least he died by accident. Irresponsible, a bad mother, she couldn't. Potential orphan, he sways at the lip of the abyss which has suddenly gaped in front of him.

"At first I did knitting," his mother says, with a small laugh. "I knitted socks. You know, for the war effort. But it didn't keep me busy enough. Anyway I guess I felt I would rather do something more useful than just knitting. When you were old enough I started with the veterans, and one thing leads to another."

Nate stares at his mother, who however looks just the same as she always looked. It's not only the revelation but the unexpected similarity to himself that appalls him. He has thought her incapable of such despair, and he now sees that he's always depended on it, this incapability of hers. What now, what next?

But his children intervene, clumping up the cellar stairs in toeless high heels, wrapped in cut velvet and satin, their mouths reddened with some long-discarded lipstick of his mother's, their eyebrows penciled black. He applauds boisterously, relieved by their presence, their uncomplicated delight.

Nevertheless he thinks: *Soon they will be women,* and that recognition runs through him like a needle. They will demand brassieres and then reject them, blaming both needs on him. They will criticize his clothes, his job, his turn of phrase. They'll leave home to live with surly, scrofulous young men; or they'll marry dentists and go in for white rugs and hanging sculptures made of wool. Either way they will judge him. Motherless, childless, he sits at the kitchen table, the solitary wanderer, under the cold red stars.

At the front door he kisses his mother as usual, the obligatory peck. She acts as if nothing has happened, as if they've been talking about something he's known all along.

She starts to close the front door and suddenly he can't handle it, this closing of the door. He vaults the low iron railing of the cement porch, hurdles the short hedge onto the neighbors' lawn. He leapfrogs the black jockey and takes the next hedge and the next, landing on grass yellow from winter, mushy with melted snow; his heels sink, mud splatters his legs. Behind him he hears the chorus, the army of tired female voices: *childish.* To hell with them. He soars, over dog dirt, into soggy beds of someone's crocuses, up again. His children race along the sidewalk, laughing, calling: *"Daddy! Wait for me!"*

He knows he will land soon; already his heart is pounding. But he aims again for it, that nonexistent spot where he longs to be. Mid-air.

Tuesday, May 30, 1978

LESJE

Lesje is holding a piece of paper. She's tried to read it four or five times, but she can't seem to get it into focus. Which is stupid, since pieces of paper exactly like it arrive in her mail almost every day. It's a letter, printed with a blue ballpoint pen on lined notebook paper, addressed to *Dinosaurs*, care of the Museum.

Dear Sirs:

I am in Grade Six and our Teacher has made us do a Project on Dinosaurs and I was wondering if you can give full answers with examples.
1) What does Dinosaur mean
2) Why is it called the Mesozoic
3) Trace the geological developments that took place in this Era in North America, please include Maps
4) what is a Fossil
5) Why were no Dinosaur fossils been found in Ontario

Please send the answers very soon as my Project is due on June 15.

Yours truely, Linda Lucas

Everything about this letter is familiar to Lesje. She knows it's been sent by a wily child, bent on shortcuts, who would rather copy out a ready-made answer than condense one from a book. She even recognizes the questions, which have been rephrased slightly, first by the teacher, then, more drastically, by the student, but which are still almost identical to some of those in the Museum pamphlet on dinosaurs which she herself helped to prepare and edit. The teacher takes shortcuts too.

Ordinarily she would simply clip several mimeographed sheets together and attach a form letter. *Thank you for your interest. We hope these fact sheets will help you to find the information you require.* Today though, looking at the round ingenuous printing, she realizes she's angry. She resents the implications of the letter: that dinosaurs are too boring to be worth much time, that she herself exists to be exploited. She resents the absence of a stamp and a return envelope. DO YOUR OWN HOMEWORK, she wants to scrawl, in red crayon across the neat blue printing. But she can't do that. Answering these letters is part of her job.

She reads the letter again, and the words float. Why is it called the Mesozoic? The correct answer, the one the teacher wants, is on the fact sheet. *Meso,* middle, *zoos,* life. After the Paleozoic, before the Cenozoic. But does the Mesozoic exist? When it did it was called nothing. The dinosaurs didn't know they were in the Mesozoic. They didn't know they were only in the middle. They didn't intend to become extinct; as far as they knew they would live forever. Perhaps she should write the truth: *The Mesozoic isn't real. It's only a word for a place you can't go to any more because it isn't there. It's called the Mesozoic because we call it that.* And risk an outraged letter from some beleaguered teacher: What sort of an answer is that?

Her hands are shaking, she needs a cigarette. She can't deal with this letter at all, right now she's devoid of answers, she knows nothing. She would like to crumple the letter and chuck it into the wastebasket, but instead she folds it neatly in two so she can't see the printing and lays it beside her typewriter. She puts on her raincoat and carefully does up the buttons and the belt.

There's some bread and cheese in her desk drawer which she intended to have for lunch but instead she'll walk up to Murray's. She'll find a single table and watch the office workers bolt their food, and the breathless, soup-spotted waitresses. She needs to get out of the Museum, if only for an hour.

Last night she fought with Nate, all-out for the first time, after the children were asleep upstairs, or possibly not asleep. That was another thing: the children were there, and it was a weeknight. They'd agreed that the children wouldn't come on weeknights, but Nate had a last-minute call from Elizabeth. Recently all her calls have been last-minute.

"Her aunt just died," Nate told her when she came in the door and found the children eating macaroni and cheese and playing Scrabble at the kitchen table. "Elizabeth felt it would be better for the children to spend the night here. She doesn't want them to be upset by her own reaction."

The children did not appear unduly traumatized, and Lesje didn't believe Elizabeth was either. This was just another flank attack. She said nothing until after the children had washed the dishes and Nate had read to them and tucked them in. They were old enough to read to themselves, but Nate said it was a tradition.

When he came downstairs, he announced that he felt he should go to the funeral.

"Why?" Lesje said. The aunt was Elizabeth's, not Nate's; the funeral was none of his business.

Nate said he felt he should give Elizabeth some support. She would be brought down by the funeral, he said.

"From everything you've told me," Lesje said, "she hated that aunt."

Nate said that although this was true, the aunt had been important in Elizabeth's life. In his opinion the importance of something to someone had nothing to do with its positive qualities but only with its impact, its force, and the aunt had been a force.

"I've got news for you," Lesje said. "Elizabeth doesn't need any support. Elizabeth needs support like a nun needs tits. I've never seen anyone who needs less support than Elizabeth."

Nate said appearances were deceptive and he felt that after twelve years of marriage to her he was perhaps in a better position than Lesje to judge how much support Elizabeth needed. Elizabeth, he said, had had an unhappy childhood.

"Who didn't?" Lesje said. "Who didn't have an unhappy childhood? What's so special?" If he wanted unhappy childhoods, she'd tell him about hers. On second thought, she probably wouldn't, since the unhappiness in it had been without event. She could not, she knew, match the almost flamboyant melodrama of Elizabeth's, which Nate had conveyed to her fragment by fragment. In any competition for unhappy childhoods she would lose.

Nate said he thought they ought to keep their voices down, since they had to think of the children.

Lesje thought of the children and saw a blur. The fact was that though the children were in her house almost every weekend she could hardly tell one from the other, she so seldom looked directly at them. She did not dislike them; she was afraid of them. On their part, they had their own oblique methods. They borrowed her belts and shirts without asking, which Nate said meant they had accepted her. They mixed themselves drinks of milk and chocolate powder and ice cream and left the unwashed glasses around the house, brown scum hardening in them, for Lesje to find on Mondays or Tuesdays after they had left. Nate said she should speak to them about anything they did which she objected to, but she wasn't such a fool. If she ever really did that he would hate it. Though they were always scrupulously polite to her, as she knew they'd been told to be. By both parents no doubt. The children were not individuals, they were a collective, a word. *The children.* He thought all he had to do was say *the children* and she would shut up, like magic.

"To hell with the children," she said recklessly.

"I know you feel that way," Nate said, with patronizing resignation.

She ought to have backed down, explained that this wasn't what she meant really. She'd done it often enough before. But this time she said nothing. She was too angry. If she tried to say anything at all, it would come out in the form of her grandmother's curses: *Jesus asshole poop! I hope your bum falls off! I hope you die!*

She ran up to the bathroom, her boots crashing on the uncarpeted stairs, not caring if the children heard, and locked herself in. On the spur of the moment she'd decided to kill herself. She was amazed by this decision; she'd never considered anything remotely like it before. People like Chris had merely puzzled her. But at last she could see why Chris did it: it was this anger and the other thing, much worse, the fear of being nothing. People like Elizabeth could do that to you, blot you out; people like Nate, merely by going about their own concerns. Other people's habits could kill you. Chris hadn't died for love. He wanted to be an event, and he'd been one.

She knelt beside the tub, clutching the knife she'd snatched from the counter on her way past. Unfortunately it was a grapefruit knife. She would have to saw rather than slash, which wasn't the effect she'd had in mind. But the end result would be the same. Nate would break down the door, when he got around to it, and find her floating in a sea of pink. Warm water, she knew, made it come out faster. He'd smell the salt, the dead bird smell. What would he do then? With her effigy, waxen and staring.

But this wasn't really what Lesje wanted to do. After a

while of thinking about it she stashed the grapefruit knife in the medicine cabinet. Nate hadn't even seen her take it; otherwise he'd be up there pounding at the door. (Wouldn't he?) She was still angry though. With some deliberation, she flushed the remaining pills in her green plastic dial-a-pill dispenser down the toilet. When Nate came to bed she turned to him and put her arms around him, exactly as if she'd forgiven him. If children were the key, if having them was the only way she could stop being invisible, then she would goddamn well have some herself.

In the morning she was unrepentant. She knew she'd committed a wrong and vengeful act, an act so vengeful she could not have imagined herself doing such a thing a year ago. Surely no child conceived in such rage could come to much good. She would have throwback, a reptile, a mutant of some kind with scales and a little horn on the snout. It's long been her theoretical opinion that Man is a danger to the universe, a mischievous ape, spiteful, destructive, malevolent. But only theoretical. Really she believed that if people could see how they were acting they would act some other way. Now she knows this isn't true.

She would not recant. Nate, ignorant of what was in store for him, ate corn flakes and made conversation. It was raining, he noted. Lesje, gnawing a bran muffin, hair falling over her face, peered out at him like Fate, sullen, gauging. When would her body strike?

"I'd just like you to realize," she said, to let him know she was still at large, had not been caged and propitiated, "that if you die Elizabeth gets your body. I'll have it sent to her in a crate. After all she's still your wife."

Nate treated this as a joke.

Winding down the stairs, hands held quiet in her raincoat pockets, she vacillates. She has a narrow pelvis, she'll die in childbirth, she knows nothing about children, what about her job? Even with Nate working part time they can't afford it. It isn't too late, nothing can have happened so soon. She'll crack open another package, take two pills and a hot bath, and everything will go on as before.

But then she thinks: Not this time. She wants no more encounters, spurious or otherwise, with the grapefruit knife.

Under the golden dome, head down, steering for the door, she feels a touch on her arm. Nate, she hopes, bringing reconciliation, capitulation, a graceful way out. But instead it is William.

"I just happened to be in the Museum," he says, "and I thought I'd look you up."

Lesje knows perfectly well that William never just happens to be anywhere, much less the Museum. Wonderful, transparent William, easy to read as a phone book, everything in alphabetical order. He has something to say to her, therefore he's come to say it. He didn't telephone first because he knew she might refuse to see him. Quite right, she would have. But now she smiles, she grins.

"I was just going up to Murray's for some lunch," she says. She will not alter anything for William.

William, although he thinks Murray's is grubby and the food will give you cancer of the colon, says that in that case does she mind if he joins her? Not at all, Lesje says, and its true, she doesn't mind. William is now safely in the past. She walks beside him, air filling her bones. It's pure joy to be with someone who cannot affect her.

Lesje has a chopped egg sandwich and a cigarette. William has a Western. What he feels, he says, dabbing buttery crumbs, is that enough time has gone by and he would just like her to know that he realizes he didn't behave very well, at the end, if she knows what he means. His blue eyes regard her candidly, his pink cheeks glow.

Lesje does not mistake this verbal construction of William's for true repentance. Rather it's an entry on William's balance sheet, that balance sheet required by London, Ontario, that little page William carries around in his head on which everything must eventually tot up right. One attempted rape, one apology. But Lesje by now is willing to accept a convention of decency. Once she would have demanded sincerity.

"I guess nobody behaved very well," she says.

William is relieved, and glances at his watch. He will stay another ten minutes, she calculates, doing the thing properly. He has not really wanted to see her. Right now he's thinking about something else and she finds, trying to guess, that she does not know what it is.

She cups her hand across her face, watches him through the smoke. It dismays her that she can no longer judge William as easily, as glibly as she once could. What she wants to ask him

is: Have you changed? Have you learned anything? She herself feels she has learned more than she ever intended to,
more than she wants. Does he find her different?

She studies his face: perhaps it is thinner. She can't remember. And those sky-blue eyes, they are not the eyes of a Cau-
casian doll, a hat mannequin, as she'd once thought.

William sits opposite her, drinking water from a Murray's
glass with a trace of lipstick on the rim. His fingers hold the
glass, his other hand lies on the table, his neck comes out of
his shirt collar, which is light green, and on top of that is his
head. His eyes are blue and he has two of them. This is the
sum total of William in the present tense.

ELIZABETH

Elizabeth, hatless but with gloves, is standing in one of the more desirable districts of the Mount Pleasant Cemetery. Near the old family mausoleums, Eaton's Department Stores, Weston's Biscuits; not, heaven forbid, in the newer parts with their adolescent trees or in the strange surburban areas of square flat stones with Chinese markings or ornate monuments with plastic-encased photos beside the names.

Two men are shoveling earth onto Auntie Muriel, who, although she's incinerated all the members of her immediate family she could get her hands on, has chosen to have herself lowered more or less intact into the earth. A roll of green pseudo-sod stands ready to cover the unpleasantly exposed brown earth once Auntie Muriel is safely tamped down.

Elizabeth's hair blows in the warm breeze. It's a fine spring day, which is too bad; Auntie Muriel, she is sure, would have preferred a heavy drizzle. But even Auntie Muriel cannot arrange the weather from beyond the grave.

Though she's managed to arrange almost every other detail of her own funeral and interment. Full instructions were in her will, composed before her death, when she was finally, irrevocably dying. Her coffin and plot had been bought and paid for. Her wardrobe, including the underwear, had been meticulously selected and laid aside, Scotch-taped in tissue paper. ("It's an old dress," Elizabeth can imagine her saying. "No sense burying a good one.") She'd vetoed beautification of her corpse as a waste of money and had opted for a closed coffin. She'd even selected the hymns and Bible readings for the service. They'd been enclosed in a separate sealed envelope, addressed to the church. Elizabeth, knowing this, felt she was hearing Auntie Muriel's own voice, intransigent as ever, projecting itself through the mouths of the gathered mourners.

Timothy Eaton had found itself embarrassed by Auntie Muriel. In death as doubtless in life, Elizabeth thought, listening to the diffident voice of the young man who had phoned her. "It's about the service," he said. "I'm wondering whether you might consider some changes. The selections are a little incongruous."

"Of course," Elizabeth said.

"Good," said the man. "Perhaps we could meet and go over . . ."

"I mean, of course they're incongruous," Elizabeth said. "Didn't you know her? What did you expect? Let the old reptile get what she wants. She always did in life." They were inheriting the loot; the least they could do was go through with it, whatever it was.

She thought the man would be offended—she was intending to be offensive—but she was almost sure she heard a snicker at the other end of the line.

"Very well, Mrs. Schoenhof," the voice said. "We'll charge ahead."

Nevertheless, Elizabeth had been unprepared when the organ burst forth with the opening hymn: "Jesus Christ Is Risen Today." Was it the old beast letting everyone know she considered herself immortal, or was it just something Auntie Muriel had stuck in because she happened to like it? She glanced around at the surprisingly large group of mourners, old fellow-parishioners, distant relatives: they were singing, gamely though uneasily. After the hymn the minister cleared his throat, rotated his shoulders like a diver warming up, then launched into the Bible reading.

"'How much she hath glorified herself, and lived deliciously, so much torment and sorrow give her: for she saith in her heart, I sit a queen, and am no widow, and shall see no sorrow. And the kings of the earth, who have committed fornication and lived deliciously with her, shall bewail her, and lament for her, when they shall see the smoke of her burning.'"

He was doing his best, rolling the r's and acting as if he knew what was going on, but a puzzled whispering rose from the congregation. Auntie Muriel was verging on bad taste. She should have chosen something more conventional, grass withering and passing away, everlasting mercy. But fornication, at a funeral? Elizabeth remembered the young minister they'd sacked, with his hot-coal eyes and his fondness for blood-hued suns and rending veils. Perhaps they suspected Auntie Muriel of being one of the same kind, hidden all these years in their midst. Possibly not entirely sane: look at the sister, the niece.

Elizabeth had little doubt that this was a personal message aimed directly at her: Auntie Muriel's last word on the subject of her mother, fiery death and all, and probably on herself as well. She could imagine Auntie Muriel poring through the Bible, bifocals on the end of her nose, searching for the right verses: scathing, punitive, self-righteous. The joke was that the congregation didn't realize this. Knowing their habits of mind, Elizabeth felt it was likely they thought Auntie Muriel was repenting, even confessing, in some bizarre way. To a secret life of delicious living.

" 'Therefore shall her plagues come in one day, death, and mourning, and famine; and she shall be utterly burned with fire: for strong is the Lord God who judgeth her.' " The minister shut the Bible and looked up apologetically, and everyone relaxed.

Auntie Muriel had not composed her own eulogy, which laid heavy stress on the words *dedication* and *generosity*. Everyone knew what that meant. Elizabeth let her eyes wander, over to the familiar bronze dead of World War One, then to the other wall. READY TO EVERY GOOD WORK. Some female Eaton or other.

But at the final hymn Elizabeth nearly disgraced herself by laughing out loud. Auntie Muriel had chosen "Away in a Manger," and the faces around Elizabeth shifted rapidly from bewilderment to panic. Voices faltered and stopped, and Elizabeth dropped her face into her cupped hands and snorted. She hoped these snorts would be mistaken for grief.

"Mother, stop laughing," Janet hissed. But though she kept her mouth closed, Elizabeth could not stop. When the hymn ended and she could raise her head again, she was astonished to see that a number of people were crying. She wondered what they were mourning: it could not possibly be Auntie Muriel.

The children are attached to her hands, Janet on the right, Nancy on the left. They're wearing their white knee socks and Mary Janes: Janet's idea, since these were what they wore to visit Auntie Muriel. Janet is weeping decorously; she knows this is what you do at funerals. Nancy is looking around, her head swiveling unabashed. "What's that, Mum? Why is he doing that?"

Elizabeth herself is dry-eyed and feels slightly giddy. There is still laughter in her throat. Was the service the result of premature senility, or could it be that Auntie Muriel at last had been making a joke? Perhaps she'd planned it for years, that moment of helpless astonishment; gloated over it, picturing the faces of her old associates as they realized that she might be other than what she seemed. Elizabeth doubts it, but hopes so. Now that Auntie Muriel is actually dead, she is free to restructure her closer to her own requirements; also, she would like to find something in her to approve.

Nate is there, on the other side of the grave. He kept apart from them during the service; perhaps he didn't want to intrude. He looks across at Elizabeth now and she smiles at him. It was sweet of him to think of coming; she didn't ask him to. Sweet but not necessary. It occurs to her that Nate in general is not necessary. He can be there or not. Elizabeth blinks, and Nate vanishes; she blinks again and he reappears. She finds herself able to be grateful for his presence. She knows well enough that her momentary gratitude may not lead to anything and will evaporate the next time he's late picking up the children. Nevertheless, that war is over. *Dismissed.*

"I'm going over to see Dad," Nancy whispers, letting go of Elizabeth's hand. Nancy wants the excuse to walk quite near the grave and get a closer look at the men shoveling; but also she wants to be with her father. Elizabeth smiles and nods.

Hilarity is draining from her, leaving her shaky. She's finding it difficult to believe that Auntie Muriel, now shriveled, boxed, dirted over and done with, actually did all the harmful, even devastating things she remembers her doing. Possibly Elizabeth has exaggerated, invented; but why would she invent Auntie Muriel? Anyway, Auntie Muriel really was like that; Elizabeth should know, she's got the scars.

Why then can she suddenly not bear to see Auntie Muriel being merged, leveled, as if she's a flower plot? Prettied over. "She was awful," Elizabeth wants to say, testify. "She was *awful.*" Auntie Muriel was a phenomenon, like a two-headed calf or Niagara Falls. She would like to bear witness to this fact. She wants it admired; she doesn't want it diminished or glossed over.

Auntie Muriel is out of sight now, and the older mourners are beginnning to shift, fade away toward their cars. Their scarves and the wreaths flutter.

Elizabeth would like to leave now too, but she can't: Auntie Muriel's death is not yet complete for her. She didn't sing at the funeral or join in the prayers. If she opened her mouth, she felt, something disreputable would come out. But she has to say something, some word of dismissal, before the green rug is finally installed. *Rest in peace* seems inappropriate. Auntie Muriel had nothing to do with rest or peace.

"Ancestral voices prophesying war," she hears herself murmuring.

Janet looks up at her, frowning. Elizabeth smiles absently; she's searching her head for the source. *Stately pleasure dome.* They'd had to memorize the whole thing in Grade Eleven. Where Alph the sacred river ran, something about caverns, down to a sunless sea. She remembers the teacher, a Miss Macleod, who had frizzy white hair and talked about fairies, revolving in a circle with her eyes closed. *Those caves of ice.*

Except for the shovels, it's very quiet. The cloudy green of the trees stretches into the distance, spongy, soft as gauze, there's nothing to push against, hold on to. A black vacuum sucks at her, there's a wind, a slow roar. Still clutching Janet's hand, Elizabeth falls through space.

It's Nate who picks her up. "All right now?" he says. He rubs clumsily at the mud on her coat.

"Don't do that," Elizabeth says. "I'll get it dry cleaned."

Now that she's obviously still alive, Nancy decides it's safe to cry. Janet, exasperated, asks Nate if he's got any liquor on him; to revive her, Elizabeth assumes. For once he doesn't, and for Janet this is the last straw. Her parents are graceless, and incompetent as well. She turns her back.

"I'm perfectly all right," Elizabeth says. It maddens her, this need everyone has to be told she's all right. She isn't, she's frightened. She's done other things but she's never blacked out like this before. She foresees a future of sudden power failures, keeling over on the subway, at intersections, with no one to drag her out of the way. Falling down stairs. She decides to have her blood sugar tested. The old ladies, those that are left, regard her with friendly interest. As far as they're concerned this is exactly what she should have done.

The two men are lifting the carpet of green plastic grass, unrolling it. The funeral is over now, she can take the children home.

Instead of riding back in the undertaker's car, to the funeral parlor or the church where coffee and cake will be served, they'll walk to the subway. At home they'll change their clothes and she'll make them something. Peanut butter sandwiches.

It suddenly amazes her that she is able to do this, something this simple. How close has she come, how many times, to doing what Chris did? More important: what stopped her? Was that his power over her, that piece of outer space he'd carried, locked in the pressures of his body until the final explosion? She remembers a high-school game she'd heard about but never played: *chicken*. They would drive to the bluffs, race their cars, heading for the long drop to the lake, trying not to be the first to brake. Standing in the sunlight, she feels the horrified relief of someone who has stopped just in time to watch an opponent topple in slow motion over the edge.

But she's still alive, she wears clothes, she walks around, she holds down a job even. She has two children. Despite the rushing of wind, the summoning voices she can hear from underground, the dissolving trees, the chasms that open at her feet; and will always from time to time open. She has no difficulty seeing the visible world as a transparent veil or a whirlwind. The miracle is to make it solid.

She thinks with anticipation of her house, her quiet living room with its empty bowls, pure grace, her kitchen table. Her house is not perfect; parts of it are in fact crumbling, most noticeably the front porch. But it's a wonder that she has a house at all, that she's managed to accomplish a house. Despite the wreckage. She's built a dwelling over the abyss, but where else was there to build it? So far, it stands.

Friday, August 18, 1978

NATE

Nate sits on a folding wooden chair behind a card table, on the east side of Yonge Street a block south of Shuter Street. The afternoon sun beats down on his head. He shades his eyes with his hand; he should have worn sunglasses. He wishes he could drink beer, just one can anyway of Molson's tucked between his feet, a quick lift to the mouth. But it wouldn't look good.

Across the street the intestinal tubing of the Eaton's Center festoons itself over walls and stairways. Shoppers enter and leave, legs brisk, faces thrust forward, intent on small lusts, small consummations of their own. Those on his side of the street are less hopeful. Old men with the shuffle of the perennially drunk, youths with armless black T-shirts cinched into their jeans by studded belts, their arms tattooed; pasty office workers in summer suits whose pinkish eyes evade his own; disgruntled women with fat ankles and scuffed shoes, their fingers locked on shopping bags. Few smile. Some scowl, but most are blank-faced, keeping their muscular twitches of anger or joy for safer, more private moments.

Nate fixes each approaching pedestrian with what he hopes is a compelling stare: *Your Country Needs* You. Most glance at the sign propped on the table and quicken their pace, trying to get past before he can rope them into anything upsetting, any commitment. RCMP WRONGDOING, the sign says, rapping the Mounties, lightly across the knuckles. CORRUPTION or, even better, SIN, would have brought more money.

Some pause and he hands them leaflets. Occasionally he gets a nibble of interest and goes into his spiel. He's collecting signatures on a petition, he says; surely they are opposed to RCMP Wrongdoing? He mentions mail-opening but leaves out

279

barn-burning and office-wrecking in Québec. Most people have no barns or offices and are indifferent or hostile towards Québec, but they do have mail. To show their seriousness, signers of the petition are being asked to contribute a dollar each to a fund which will be used to further the campaign.

Nate speaks quietly, without undue fervor. Anything like fanaticism must be avoided. He's supposed to represent the average decent-minded citizen. But knows he does not. It gives him a wry satisfaction that most of those who have so far responded with any enthusiasm have come from the ranks of the black-shirted youths, obvious dope-pushers, fences and petty thieves. At any moment he expects to see a client or a former client among them.

"Jail the bastards," one says. "Bust into my place last weekend and went through it like a goddamn chainsaw. Didn't find nothing on me though."

He wonders what his mother would make of this phenomenon, concludes she would not be offended or even surprised. "A signature is a signature," she would say. Will say next weekend, when her capable buttocks will rest squarely on this very chair, her feet in their sensible crepe-soled shoes hold down this sidewalk.

It should have been her today, but she twisted her ankle at the hospital. "A twist, not a sprain," she'd said on the phone. "They're very short of volunteers, otherwise I wouldn't ask you. I've never asked you before."

This isn't true, she has asked him before. Pieces for Peace, rescue the Korean poet, ban the bomb. It's just that he's never agreed to do anything before. He wonders why, this time, he has. Not that this enterprise is any more likely to succeed than her other enterprises. But collecting signatures against RCMP Wrongdoing does not at the moment seem any more futile than most other things in his life.

A middle-aged man scans the leaflet, then thrusts in towards Nate as if it's hot, glancing behind him. "I'll give you a dollar," he whispers, "but I can't sign my name." He has an accent, not French, not Italian. Nate thanks him and stashes the dollar in the cash box. More people than he would have imagined seem to think they'll be in deep shit if they sign their names. The Mounties will get hold of them, whip the bottoms of their feet with dog whips, apply electric hair-curling machines to their genital organs; at the very least, open their mail.

Nate doubts it; he doubts that the Mounties even care. Nothing like that will happen here, not yet. Which is probably why he's never done anything like this before. It's too safe. He's held out for some overwhelming choice, danger, his life on the line; a careless laugh, eyes shining, death one false step away. Instead he broils in the August sun, wheedles strangers, lights another cigarette to combat the exhaust fumes from the street.

When he went upstairs to the office to collect his stack of leaflets, they greeted him like the prodigal son. Three women in wrinkled summer dresses shot from their cubbyholes to shake his hand; his mother was a wonder, they said, so much energy, he must be proud. The director invited him into his brownish office, its desk stacked waist-high with grimy papers: letters, forms, old newspaper clippings. Nate explained about the twisted ankle and made it as clear as he could without being rude that he was merely temporary, a substitute. There seemed no need to add that he finds the petition a kind of joke. It's supposed to go to the Prime Minister, who will doubtless make paper airplanes with it. Why not? He's read the letters to the editor, he knows that most people will allow six million Québeckers, Pakistanis, union leaders and transvestites to have their fingernails pulled out rather than admit that the paint is chipped on the bright red musical Mountie of their dreams.

Possibly the director himself knows it's a joke. He was grinning at something. He'd smiled like a clown penny bank, white teeth slightly open and acquisitive, his blandness deceptive. His eyes above his apple cheeks were shrewd and in that gaze Nate had squirmed. They all acted as if he is in truth what he's spent so much effort to avoid becoming: his mother's son. Which maybe he is.

But not only, not only. He refuses to be defined. He's not shut, time carries him on, other things may happen. By his elbow is this morning's *Globe*, which he hopes to scan later when the stream of prospects thins. Perhaps there will finally be some news. A small part of him still waits, still expects, longs for a message, a messenger; as he sits in his booth proclaiming to others a message he suspects is a joke.

At four o'clock his replacement, a German Catholic theologian, he's been told, will arrive and grip his hand earnestly as if he is indeed a kindred spirit. Nate, embarrassed, will leave the booth and join the walkers, those homeward bound, those merely wandering; he will lose himself among the apathetic, the fatalistic, the uncommitted, the cynical; among whom he would like to feel at home.

LESJE

Uniformed in her lab coat Lesje descends, winding around the totem pole on her way to the basement. She isn't doing lab work today but she wears the lab coat anyway. It makes her feel she belongs here. She does belong here.

She remembers the way she once followed with her eyes those others she used to glimpse on her Saturday excursions, men and women but especially the women, walking purposefully along the corridors or whisking through the doors marked STAFF ONLY. Then she'd seen their lab coats as badges, of nationality, membership of some kind. She'd wanted so much to be able to go through those doors: secrets, wonders even, lay beyond. Now she has keys, she can go almost anywhere, she's familiar with the jumble-sale pieces of rock, the fragments, the dust-covered bundles of unsorted papers. Secrets perhaps but no wonders. Still, this is the only place she wants to work. Once there had been nothing equally important to her, but there is still nothing more important. This is the only membership she values.

She will not give it up. Fists jammed into her lab-coat pockets, she paces the basement floor, among the cases of mannequin Indians in their stolen ceremonial clothes, the carved masks, joyous, fearful. She walks briskly, as if she knows where she's going; but in fact she's soothing herself, running the Museum through her head once more, room by familiar room, a litany of objects. How soon will it be before she will never see it again?

Sometimes she thinks of the Museum as a repository of knowledge, the resort of scholars, a palace built in the pursuit of truth, with inadequate air conditioning but still a palace. At other times it's a bandits' cave: the past has been vandalized and this is where the loot is stored. Whole chunks of time lie here, golden and frozen; she is one of the guardians, the only guardian, without her the whole edifice would melt like a jellyfish on the beach, there would be no past. She knows it's really the other way around, that without the past she would not exist. Still, she must hold on somehow to her own importance. She's threatened, she's greedy. If she has to she'll lock herself into one of these cases, hairy mask on her face, she'll stow away, they'll never get her out.

Will they ask her to leave? Resign. She doesn't know. A pregnant paleontologist is surely a contradiction in terms. Her business is the naming of bones, not the creation of flesh. The fact is that she's missed her period twice in a row. Which could be what they call *strain*. She hasn't yet gone for tests, for confirmation, she hasn't thought past the fact. She will be an unwed mother. Of course that is becoming more common, but what will Dr. Van Vleet, a gentleman of the old school who demonstrably does not live in the year 1978, do then?

And what will Nate do, what will she do? It's hard to believe that such a negligible act of hers can have measurable consequences for other people, even such a small number of them. Though the past is the sediment from such acts, billions, trillions of them.

She's not used to being a cause, of anything at all. On her office wall the tree of evolution branches like coral towards the ceiling: Fishes, Amphibians, Therapsids, Thecodonts, Archosaurs, Pterosaurs, Birds, Mammals and Man, a mere dot. And herself another, and within her another. Which will exfoliate in its turn.

Or not; she's thought about that. She could have an abortion, stop time. She knows it's easier than it used to be. She hasn't yet told Nate, she doesn't need to tell him. Everything could go on as before. Which is not what she wants.

She can't tell whether he will be delighted or angry or despairing; possibly, considering his feelings about his two other children, he will be all three. But whatever his reaction is, she knows her final decision will not be based on it. Nate has been displaced, if only slightly, from the center of the universe.

She climbs the back stairs and walks forward through European Costumes, skirting the Chinese Peasant Art Exhibit, which doesn't much interest her. As she rounds the corner towards the main staircase, she glimpses a square dark figure

on the floor above. It's Elizabeth. Elizabeth doesn't see her.
She's looking over the balustrade, out over the rotunda. Lesje
has almost never seen Elizabeth like this, unconscious. It's as
if she's seeing her on the last day of her life. Lesje isn't used to
this; she's used to thinking of Elizabeth as permanent, like an
icon. But Elizabeth standing by herself, unconnected with anyone, is shorter, worn, ordinary; mortal. The lines of her face
and body slope down. Even though she knows her own preg-
nancy will cut no ice with Elizabeth, may even make her de-
lay the divorce as long as possible, to prove something—
what? That she's first wife?—Lesje can't remember why she
has been afraid of her.

Will they still be doing this in twenty years? Older women,
old women, wearing black and not speaking; ill-wishing; never
seeing each other, but each keeping the other locked in her
head, a secret area of darkness like a tumor or the black vortex at the center of a target. Someday they may be grandmothers. It occurs to her, a new idea, that this tension between the two of them is a difficulty for the children. They
ought to stop.

Still, she doesn't feel like going through the charade of nod-
ding and smiling; not right now. She ducks into the open elevator and is carried up.

She enters the Gallery of Vertebrate Evolution the wrong
way, past the EXIT sign. She's feeling slightly dizzy, probably
because she hasn't eaten all day. Too much coffee. She sits
down on the padded ledge that separates the pedestrians from
the dinosaurs. She longs to smoke a cigarette in the soothing
Cretaceous dusk before walking out into the blast-furnace of
the afternoon, but she knows about the fire hazard. Instead
she'll just rest. It's warm here also, too warm, but at least it's
dark.

Here are her old acquaintances, familiar to her as pet rab-
bits: allosaurus, the carnivore, parrot-beaked chasmosaurus,
parasaurolophus with its deer-antler crest. They're merely
bones, bones and wire in a scenery of dusty plastic, and she's
an adult; why does she continue to think of them as alive?

When she was much younger she used to believe, or try
hard to believe, that at night when the Museum was closed
the things inside it carried on a hidden life of their own; if she
could only find her way inside she would be able to watch. Later
she abandoned this daydream in favor of a less extravagant
one: the things were silent and unmoving, true, but somewhere there existed an implement or force (a secret ray, at-

omic energy) that would bring them back to life. Childish plots, based no doubt on the odd science-fiction comic book or on that Christmas matinée of *The Nutcracker Suite* she'd been dragged to when they'd decided, so disastrously, that she should take ballet.

Now, however, looking up at the immense skulls towering above her in the dim light, the gigantic spines and claws, she almost expects these creatures of hers to reach down their fingers in friendly greeting. Though if they were really alive they'd run away or tear her apart. Bears, however, dance to music; so do snakes. What if she were to press the buttons on the filmstrips and, instead of the usual speeches or the cries of walruses and seals used to simulate the underwater voices of the marine reptiles, some unknown song were to emerge? Indian music, droning, hypnotic. *Try to imagine,* says the brochure she wrote, a guide for parents and teachers, *what it would be like if suddenly the dinosaurs came to life.*

She'd like to; she'd like to sit here for an hour and do nothing else. She'd close her eyes and one after another the fossils would lift their ponderous feet, moving off along the grove of resurrected trees, flesh coalescing like ice or mist around them. They'd dance stumpily down the stairs of the Museum and out the front door. Eight-foot horsetails would sprout in Queen's Park, the sun would turn orange. She'd throw in some giant dragonflies, some white and yellow flowers, a lake. She'd move among the foliage, at home, an expedition of one.

But she can't do it. Either she's lost faith or she's too tired; at any rate she can no longer concentrate. The fragments of new images intrude. She looks down at the pebbles, the bark chips, the dusty cycad trees on the other side of the ledge, a thousand miles away.

In the foreground, pushing in whether she wants it to or not, is what Marianne would call her life. It's possible she's blown it. This is what they mean when they say *maturity:* you get to the point where you think you've blown your life. She should have learned more, in advance, she should have studied more before jumping in; but she isn't sorry.

True, there's a chance she's done a stupid thing. Several, many. Or she may have done a wise thing for a stupid reason. She will tell Nate today, this evening. Will he forgive her?

(Forgiveness is not what she needs; not, anyway, from Nate. She would prefer instead to forgive, someone, somehow, for something; but she isn't sure where to begin.)

NATE

Nate is running. He jogs up University, against the traffic, the sun glinting on the roofs and windshields of the oncoming cars, beating on his head. The blood in his ears is a gong, he heats like metal, the sidewalk thumps relentlessly against the soles of his feet. He tugs at his blue-striped shirt, neat citizen's shirt for the collection of signatures, pulls it loose from the waist of his cords, lets it flap behind him. There's a muggy wind which smells of garages and spilled oil.

At the Parliament Buildings he waits for a gap in traffic, sprints across, continues, under the porte-cochère, along beside the pinkish stone which used to be dingy brown before they sandblasted it. One day he may go into politics, he's thought about it. Provincial, not municipal. Not federal, he has no yen for exile. But not yet, not yet.

His shadow paces him, thin and pinheaded, stretching away to his right, a blackness flickering over the grass. A premonition, always with him; his own eventual death. Which he will think about some other time.

He should pay more attention though, at least try. A regular schedule would do him good. Up at six, run for half an hour in the morning mists before the exhaust fumes get too bad. Then a frugal breakfast, watch the eggs and butter, cut down to a pack a day. With every drink a brain cell dies. Luckily there are billions of them; it will take him a while to go senile. If he could run he'd feel better, he could take hold, he knows it. Same time every day, on and on forever.

Right now he's not going to make it around. Sweat drenches him, his breath rasps in his throat, oxygen sharpens all the edges. There's nothing he will do forever. He heads for the War Memorial, halfway, but throws himself down on the grass before he reaches it, rolling onto his back. Small dots swim in the amniotic blue; rods and cones, black stars in his head. Beneath him grass strains upwards.

He'd like to be able to take Lesje somewhere, out into the country, the country which surely lies all around, though he can't remember the last time he was there. But how would they get there? A bus, a walk along some uncharted and dusty gravel road? Never mind. They could make love, slowly and gently, under some trees or in a field, gold waving over them and the smell of crushed grass. The possible day shimmers ahead of him, an oval of light; in this light Lesje is indistinct, her features shine and blur, her dark hair melts in his hands, her body extended white and lean on the grass shifts itself, glows, fades. It's as if he's too close to her to be able to see her, fix her in his mind. When he's away from her he can barely remember what she looks like.

Though he can see Elizabeth distinctly, every line and shadow. He used to take Elizabeth out into the country, before Janet was born, before he sold the car. But she didn't want to climb fences and crawl under bushes and he'd lacked the trick of persuading her. Instead they went to auctions, farm sales, families giving up or too old who were selling off their belongings. Elizabeth did the bidding, kitchen chairs, bundles of spoons, while he stood at the soft drink and hot-dog stand, hands in his pockets fingering pennies, keys, feeling out of place, a scavenger.

He thinks of Elizabeth, briefly, with detachment. For a moment she's someone he once knew. He wonders what has become of her. It's the walks they never took, the fields he could never convince her to enter he regrets now.

He sits, takes off his damp shirt and wipes his head and chest with it, then spreads it beside him for the sun to dry. He's chilly now despite the heat. In a few minutes, when he gets his breath, he'll light a cigarette and smoke it. Perhaps he'll throw half of it away. Then he'll stand up and put his shirt back on. He'll wait for a gap in the traffic and run across the road, lightly, on the balls of his feet.

He'll walk north, past the Planetarium and its hoarding, which he can see from here. THE PLANETARIUM IS STILL OPEN. They're adding a wing to the Museum; Lesje says it's none too soon. *ROM Wasn't Built In A Day*, says the plywood wall, punning on the Museum's name, pleading for money. Another worthy cause. They'll suck him dry, despite his sawdust heart.

He'll climb the steps and lean in the same spot where he used to do time for Elizabeth, one shoulder against the stone. He'll light another cigarette, watch the museum-goers passing in and out like shoppers, and wait for Lesje. She won't be expecting him. Perhaps she'll be surprised and pleased to see him; once he could count on it. Perhaps she'll only be surprised, and possibly not even that. He anticipates this moment, which he cannot predict, which leaves room for hope and also for disaster. They will either go for a drink or not. In any case, they will go home.

Friday, August 18, 1978

ELIZABETH

Elizabeth stands looking at a picture. The picture is framed
and glassed. Behind the glass, bright green leaves spread with
the harmonious asymmetry of a Chinese floral rug; purple
fruits glow among them. Three women, two with baskets, are
picking. Their teeth shine within their smiles, their cheeks are
plump and rosy as a doll's. *A Fine Crop of Eggplants,* the cap-
tion says, in Chinese, English and French. Elizabeth reminds
herself to pick up some hot dogs on the way home, the children's request, and for herself cooked chicken. They'll sit
on the front porch, Nancy's idea of a picnic. Perhaps by then
it will be cooler.

A man in overalls, pushing a large floor-polishing machine,
reaches Elizabeth's corner and tells her to move. She walks
along the wall. It's just after closing time and most people
have left the Museum. She's been waiting for this comparative
emptiness to take a close look at the exhibit, which opened
four days ago, but which she's been too busy to see. She's
pleased with the press coverage, though. China is news, unlike,
for instance, India, which was news several years ago, during
that war. And the crowds have been good, though of course
not as good as the long lineups they had for *The Art of Ancient China* exhibit a few years ago. People will stand in line
for quite a long time to see gold, especially gold unearthed
from tombs. Elizabeth still remembers the horses, those fierce-
toothed horses from some Emperor's grave. They weren't
gold; she can't remember what they were made of, but keeps
an impression of darkness. An omen, a catastrophe, rearing
up, bearing down.

There is no catastrophe in these paintings, however. *The
New Look of Our Piggery*, Elizabeth reads. She's not much
interested in pigs. These pigs are like toys, like the plastic pigs
from the farm set the children still play with occasionally.

They're discreet and neat and evidently they don't root or shit. Squashes and pumpkins grow like decorative borders between the rows of sties.

The floor polisher is following her. She crosses over, turns the corner into the second aisle. The paintings are hung on movable screens which divide the gallery. They've done a good job setting up the exhibit, she thinks; the life-size black and white photos of the actual artists add a nice touch. She can remember when this whole section was used to display medieval armor and weapons: crossbows, maces, halberds, inlaid blunderbusses, muskets. Only the parquet floor remains the same.

Do Not Allow Lin Piao and Confucius to Slander Women, she reads, and smiles. *Everyone Helps in Building Each Others' Houses.*

Suddenly Elizabeth feels, not lonely, but single, alone. She can't remember the last time anyone other than her children helped her to do something. She knows it rains in China, even though it does not rain in these pictures. She knows the people there do not invariably smile, do not all have such white teeth and rosy cheeks. Underneath the poster-paint colors, primary as a child's painting, there is malice, greed, despair, hatred, death. How could she not know that? China is not paradise; paradise does not exist. Even the Chinese know it, they must know it, they live there. Like cavemen, they paint not what they see but what they want.

Persimmons Are Ripe at the Foot of Mount Chungman, she reads. Orange-yellow globes crowd the page; among the interwoven branches girls climb, happy faces peer, bright and uniformly patterned as birds. Elizabeth blinks back tears: foolishness, to be moved by this. This is propaganda. She does not want to line up and learn to throw grenades, she doesn't want to work a threshing machine, she has no desire to undergo group criticism and have a lot of other people tell her what to think. This isn't what touches her so that she's fumbling in her purse now for a Kleenex, a scrap of paper, anything she can use to blot her face. It's the turnips in their innocent rows, ordinary, lit from within, the praise lavished on mere tomatoes, the bunches of grapes, painted in all their translucent hues. As if they are worth it.

Elizabeth dabs at her nose. If she wants to see grapes she can go to the supermarket. She has to go there anyway, since there's nothing in the house for dinner.

China does not exist. Nevertheless she longs to be there.

ABOUT THE AUTHOR

MARGARET ATWOOD is a writer who, though still in her thirties, has conquered more literary territory than most do in a lifetime. In addition to *Life Before Man*, she is the author of seven books of poetry (the first won the Governor-General's Award in 1966), *Dancing Girls*, *Lady Oracle*, *Surfacing*, and *The Edible Woman*, all of which were widely praised in Canada, the United States and England. *Survival*, a thematic study of Canadian literature, earned her an enduring reputation as a critic of the first order. Her fiction and critical articles have appeared in Canadian and American literary magazines. Ms. Atwood has lived and worked in Canada, the United States, England and Italy. She is currently living on a farm near Allston, Ontario.

NEW FROM POPULAR LIBRARY

CURRENT BESTSELLERS
from POPULAR LIBRARY